The Northwest Maine Pack is settling down now that Diego, the new pack leader, has taken full control. Saoirse presents him with a surprise, making him happier than ever. But making leadership decisions is not always easy.

John struggles with his place in life but knows one thing for sure. Freddie, Saoirse's bestie, is his mate. Sadly, Freddie doesn't know about werewolves. John moves to Boston, leaving a gap in pack security. Diego contacts the family of Canadian hunters to see if anyone is willing to fill the gap.

Grant volunteers for the position, since he is haunted by the memory of the black she-wolf he saw on pack grounds. His wolf says she is their mate, but he doesn't even know what she looks like as a human.

Nathan has been without any real love in his life since his family disowned him years ago. He believes his luck has changed when his wolf meets an unfamiliar she-wolf, and they mate. Unfortunately, the next morning, the woman has no memory of anything they did the night before.

Everyone has waited a long time for what they want most. But the path to true love is rarely an easy one—especially when you are a werewolf.

Worth the Wait
Copyright © 2020 Fiona McGier
ISBN: 978-1-4874-2882-2
Cover art by Martine Jardin

Published by eXtasy Books Inc or
Devine Destinies, an imprint of eXtasy Books Inc

Look for us online at:
www.eXtasybooks.com or www.devinedestinies.com

Worth the Wait
Northwest Maine Academy 2

By

Fiona McGier

DEDICATION

To Paul. Werewolves are not the only ones who mate for life.

AUTHOR'S NOTE

This is the second book in the *Northwest Maine Academy* series. The first book, *When a Wolf Howls,* introduced most of the characters in this book. It was the story of the romance between the Pack Leader, Diego Vargas, and his now-wife, Saoirse McColl Vargas. He is a shifter, carrying a wolf inside of him. She is a scientist who had no idea that werewolves even existed. That is, until she moved into a compound that included many shifters and their families. And she fell in love with the man destined to take over when the old pack leader, on his deathbed, appointed him to the position.

This book continues their story, as well as exploring the romantic lives of three of the supporting characters from Book One. I love happy endings, so all four of the happy couples will achieve their bliss. But for all of them, it will take what seems like forever, to them. Hence the title: *Worth the Wait.*

PART ONE: SECOND CHANCE AT LOVE

CHAPTER ONE

"Why did they ask you?" Grant asked, closely watching his mother, Gertrude, as she sat behind her oak desk.

This office on the first floor of the house he'd grown up in was where she took care of all the family businesses. There were many pictures of him at various ages, along with his siblings. A large portrait sat behind her. It showed her as a young woman on her wedding day, smiling as she held the hand of the young man who was her husband. Grant was always amused by that. Though he was one of the older kids, even *he* couldn't remember their father's hair as blond. It had turned gray at a young age, a silver color that made him look much older than he was until he actually grew older.

Gertrude shrugged. "Who knows? Maybe because we're known to them, since we've done business together? Maybe because we were just there, and that reminded Diego of our special skill set?"

His younger brother, Glen, stroked his heavy beard and snorted. "Or maybe he wants one of us around in case there's any future trouble? Changes in pack leadership can cause lots of unrest until things settle down. And we've got a track record of helping them clean up their messes."

Gertrude pursed her lips in disapproval. "Glen, stop. We've enjoyed their hospitality many times when we've wanted a change of location for a holiday. They've always been glad to host us, either all together, or in smaller groups. Why shouldn't we be called when they have problems that they know we can take care of for them?"

The door was thrown open, and a force of nature entered. Grant's oldest sibling, his sister Griselda, swept into the room. "Hi. Sorry I'm late. Couldn't be helped. What'd I miss?"

Guy, another brother with a beard, snickered. "Take too long kissing goodbye?"

She shot a withering look at their youngest brother. "No, Guy. I was talking with his mother when I got the text from Mom. And I don't generally kiss his mother at all . . . if I can help it."

Smiles traveled around the room. Everyone was used to the bickering that ran through the fabric of their familial relationships.

Gertrude explained. "Seems that the Northern Maine Pack leadership has need of a temporary replacement for one of their ranking members. Remember John, Joe's second child, and only son? He's been their second in command, so the head of their security, ever since he got old enough and strong enough to do the job. But he's taking a leave for a while, and they'll need someone to replace him."

"For how long?" Grant asked.

"I don't know. I don't think they know, either. I got the impression from Diego that this is kind of sudden, and not something he's happy about. Like Glen said, pack leadership change can be very unsettling, especially for a pack that's been under the same leader for damn near sixty years. Having another change so soon is adding another layer of uncertainty. I think he's trying to minimize the number of people who are aware of what's been going on within their ranks. So asking us to send someone to help out is a no-brainer, since we're already known to them."

"But we're not very good at following orders," Griselda pointed out, wearing a grin. "We're all kind of independent. Our family crest says *Doesn't play well with others.*"

Gertrude sighed. "I know. That's what I told him. But I said

2

I'd check with my brood to see if any of you might be interested. He's got a couple of packs he's in contact with that he can ask next. But we were the first ones he called."

"Well, I'm out," Griselda said with a toss of her white-blond hair. "I'm not about to leave town and have my man be prey to other females while I'm not here to fend them off."

Gertrude nodded. "That's what I figured you'd say."

"Can't let up the pressure now, huh, sis? Almost got him ready to propose? Be a shame if all of that work you've done on him, softening him up, made him ready to get married, then some other woman was closer than you when he worked up the nerve to propose."

Guy ducked as the accurately named *throw-pillow* flew his way.

"I'm not interested," said Glen. "I've got more clients than I can deal with already. I don't trust any of my partners enough to let them handle the ins and outs of my business."

Guy added, "And I just got a contract to photograph the effects of climate change on polar bears, so I'm headed up to the great white north in the very near future. Like, in a week or so."

Gertrude turned to him. "Grant?"

He appeared to be considering his words before speaking.

"I might be interested. I was talking with Nathan, their fourth, over dinner when we were there. He said it was too bad that their leader's wife was heading out of town, because she and I would have a lot to talk about. Her degree is in biological research, and she's been trying to isolate and identify possible markers in the blood to see if there's any way to predict which young ones will discover they're shifters when their hormones turn on."

Glen grinned. "I think it's pretty obvious when they fall on the ground and their bones start cracking and shifting around. *Yup, that one's got a wolf inside trying to get out.*"

"But not before that," Grant stressed. "Lots of people send their kids to the Maine Academy for high school because they don't know if their kids will present or not . . . or when. If there was a way to predict it, parents would at least have the peace of mind of knowing their kids were in a safe place for their first time."

"Wouldn't that mean fewer people would send their kids to the academy?" Griselda asked.

"I wondered about that, too. But Nathan said their belief is that they might actually end up with even more applicants. Right now, some are willing to chance that it won't happen, and sometimes it's a disaster when it does. This way, they would know for sure."

"It does tend to run in families, but that's not really dependable. Your father and I were both shifters, and all of you are also. But then there's Joe and Janine's Jennifer. Both her parents were shifters, and she's the oldest. But no wolf inside of her."

Grant nodded, agreeing with his mother. "That's right."

She regarded him closely. "So you're volunteering? What about your job?"

He shrugged. "I've been kind of unhappy at work lately. Running a lab is not what I expected. Having to produce results that the client wants, instead of what actually happens, is totally bogus. I've actually been considering going back to earn my doctorate, but I'm not even sure what I'd want to get it in."

"I always thought you were heading towards being a medical doctor," Glen said with a wink. "All of those pretty nurses to toady to your every whim."

Another pillow thrown by Griselda hit him in the face, and he pretended to be wounded. "Ow! Mom, did you see what she did? Tell her to quit throwing things around."

Gertrude glared sternly at Griselda, her lips twitching in

amusement. "Grisel, stop abusing your brothers."

Griselda stuck her tongue out at Glen. "Sexist!"

He laughed. "You're so easy to bait, sis!"

"Besides," Guy pointed out, "the last time I was in the hospital, when I had my appendix removed, many of the nurses were men."

Grant chuckled. "I'm pretty sure I'll eventually become a doctor — or maybe a nurse. But I got too burned out by years of classes. I needed a break. That's why I've been working these past few years. Maybe I just need another change of scenery. And the chance to work in the lab with Mrs. Vargas, trying to do something useful with the skills that I already have? It's a tempting addition to just being able to live somewhere else for a while."

"Just be sure it's only in the lab that you want to work closely with her," Guy teased. "Diego might be injured, but he's not the kind of man to take kindly to anyone flirting with his wife."

Grant grimaced. "Not my type. That red hair could stop traffic. Besides, I don't like my women to be whiter than my ass. I'm not even sure that's possible, but I'm not interested in finding out."

Griselda snickered. "I keep telling you boys, y'all need to do some nude sunbathing."

She managed to duck all three pillows thrown her way.

Gertrude shook her head at everyone. "Fine. I'll let Diego know that you'll be heading down there. When? After you give two weeks' notice at the lab?"

He tried to look sheepish. "Um, actually I gave notice last week. I only have to work until Friday, then I'm free."

Glen got up, stretching. "So, is this family meeting adjourned? I haven't eaten since early this morning, and I'm not going to make it until dinner unless I grab some kind of snack."

Guy headed toward the door. "Race you to the kitchen! Loser has to cook."

Griselda was already pounding down the hall, yelling behind her. "I call not cleaning up either!"

Gertrude shook her head, turning her attention to him.

"Kids," he said, rolling his eyes.

"You're really serious? You'll go? What if it gets extended into a longer visit?"

"You mean if John decides not to come back?"

She nodded.

"I guess I'll cross that bridge when and if it happens. They'll probably bump everyone else up a notch, so that'll make me the fourth. They can always promote someone from their security ranks if that happens. We'll see. But either way, I'm out of a job and need a change and a new challenge. This is just what I've been waiting for." He got up. "I'm feeling kind of peckish, too. I'm going to see what they're rustling up in the kitchen."

"You do that," Gertrude said. "And I'll call Diego back."

He stopped at the door to blow her a kiss, before heading toward the noise coming from the kitchen.

It wasn't until much later that night, after having eaten dinner and gone home to bed, that Grant listened to his wolf berate him.

Why didn't you let them know that we claim her?

Instantly, he was swept along on the current of lust his wolf had felt the last time he was at the Maine compound. He'd been slammed by a tidal wave of emotions when a large black she-wolf appeared in front of them. She had put her body directly in front of the two renegade wolves, thereby protecting the pack leader and his wife. He smiled, wondering what the female might look like as a human. As a wolf, she was enticing enough.

I can't do that. If my brothers even suspected we were interested in her, their competitive instincts would take over, and they'd want to fight us for her.

His wolf snarled softly in his mind. *You always underestimate our abilities. We are the oldest. We are the strongest. We would win any battle.*

I won't fight my own brothers that fiercely. I won't hurt either of them. It's better this way, you'll see. They'll be miles away, and we can slowly approach the female so as not to scare her off.

Why not let me approach her wolf? It would be quicker. Wolves mate as they will, with no time wasted in what you call courtship.

I want to capture her human self also. As you say, the wolf part of her will be easy to convince. It's the human I have to encourage to see me — us — as her mate.

Temporarily mollified, his wolf quieted down. And Grant took matters into his own hands, relieving the pressure of their yearnings.

CHAPTER TWO

The following Sunday, Grant drove down into Maine from his home in Canada. He'd found someone to take over his apartment completely furnished. Then he'd packed his few remaining belongings into his small truck and headed across the border to a new life.

At the compound's gate, he stopped and waited while the security people checked with their leader to be sure he was allowed to enter. An older woman with gray hair nodded to indicate the gate should be opened. Grant recognized her from his last visit to the compound.

"Welcome to the pack, Mr. Knutsen." She gave him a small nod with a smile.

He grinned back. "Thanks . . . Diya, is it? Never been a part of one before. There's a first time for everything, I guess."

He had no trouble finding the main mansion, despite the many smaller roads that led to the neighborhoods where many of the pack members lived. He'd been the one driving when the family had been asked to come down to hunt and kill the two pack members who had betrayed the leader's trust. That was when he'd seen the large black she-wolf that had so intrigued him. He had no idea who she was, but he'd been close enough to her to realize simultaneously that she was female, and that he wanted to be her mate. The details still needed to be worked on. But he was a researcher, so details were his specialty.

We need to find her, his wolf growled softly in his mind.

I know. We will. We'll be here for some time, so there's no hurry.

We will fight for her if we must. And we will win.

He grinned at his alter ego's confidence. He pulled up to the main stairs that led to a patio in the front of the house. To his left was the field where they'd begun their hunt. The mansion was an imposing edifice, strong and sturdy, to survive the brutal Maine winters, yet now covered with the glow of the early evening summer sun.

He was expected, since he'd texted from the front gate. So he wasn't surprised to see Nathan come down the stairs to greet him.

"Hi, Grant. Do you want me to park your truck for you?"

He shook his head. "Nah. But if you ride with me, you can tell me where a new pack member is supposed to park. I don't plan on needing to go into town for a while, so I'll need to know where vehicles are kept until they're needed."

Nathan opened the passenger door and got into the truck. "It's further away than the visitor lot you parked in the last time. It's behind the garage, and that's quite a ways behind the mansion. So just keep heading the direction you're going, and I'll tell you when to turn."

They chatted about the weather, the current status of their favorite teams in the World Cup standings, and other inconsequential things as he parked the truck, then pulled his two knapsacks out of the back end.

"That's all you have?"

"Why? Will I need more? Mom said I'd have a furnished apartment."

Nathan shook his head. "You won't need furniture. But I'm not sure I could reduce my worldly belongings to just two small packs."

He shrugged. "I've got my laptop, some clothes, and a few books. What else does a man need?"

Nathan grinned. "I guess. We'll supply you with academy polos, which will take care of some of your clothing needs. And you're right, the apartment is furnished. Let's go through the back entrance to the dining room. Are you hungry? I think the buffet is still open."

"I could eat." Grant followed the tall, thin but wiry blond man up the back stairs.

There were few people left in the dining room, and the buffet was in the process of being emptied. Nathan left Grant sitting at a table, saying he was going to the kitchen to tell the chef, Janine Johnson, widow of the late pack leader, that he'd arrived.

Nathan rejoined him after a few minutes. "Janine said she'd be right out."

Ten minutes later, a short but elegant black woman emerged with a covered tray. She had an apron on over her stylish clothing, and her medium-length graying hair was held back by a headband. She smiled at him.

Grant rose to greet her with a bow. "My lady. You're even more beautiful than the last time I saw you."

"That's because this is a happier occasion," she said. "I put some of the food under warming lights when Diego told me you were driving down today." She removed the cover of the tray she'd set down in front of him.

Grant inhaled appreciatively. "Smells great! I stopped along the way a couple of times, but not for an actual meal."

"Dig in, and enjoy," Janine said as she sat down, taking one of the cups of coffee Nathan had brought to their table.

As he ate, Grant glanced around at the people who were finishing up their dinner, but none of them sparked any recognition. Janine asked after his mother before questioning him about his siblings. Janine had known his family since before he was born. She enjoyed hearing about the jobs he and his siblings had, as well as their antics involving family dynamics and romances.

When he had finished eating everything, he pushed himself back with a satisfied sigh. "If this is the kind of food I can look forward to, I'm even more determined to make myself a place here in your pack."

A quick shadow flitted across Janine's face. "Well, John isn't sure how long he's going to be away, so hopefully you aren't on a deadline as to when you need to get back."

He shook his head. "Nope. Footloose and fancy-free, that's me. I'm here for as long as you need me to be. In fact, I'm honored to be welcomed as a part of your pack."

Nathan got a text, which he read. He looked up. "Diego asks that you and I join him in ten minutes, in one of the smaller conference rooms. He wants to formally introduce you to the other ranking members. John will be there, also."

Janine's smile was sad. "He's planning on leaving tomorrow. He's already out of his apartment and sleeping on the sofa in my place. He's anxious to *start the next chapter in his life*, as he says."

Nathan patted her hand, resting on the table. "He'll be fine. He's a grown man."

"I know. It's just that I'm a mother, and Jennifer already lives in Portland. Boston is so far away. And now I'll only have one of my children still living in the compound."

"But Jerene is the one with the grandchildren, right? So you'll still have them to fuss over." Nathan grinned at her, anticipating her reaction.

She responded by lightly punching his shoulder as she rose. "I don't fuss. I take care of. And I feed. Now you better show our new member to his quarters, so he can stash his stuff. Then you need to get to that meeting with Diego."

Grant tried to insist that he be allowed to carry the empty tray into the kitchen, but Janine resisted his offer. "No. It's even lighter now than when it was carrying food. You two run along. You don't want to be late for your first meeting with your new pack leader."

11

Grant was pleasantly surprised at the size of the apartment he was shown to. It had a moderately-sized sitting area, with a dining room table in front of a counter that had a sink, a microwave, and a medium-sized fridge. Beyond that was a spacious bedroom with a queen-sized bed. There was a balcony accessible from the bedroom, with chairs and a small table, for sitting out to enjoy the fresh air. And the bathroom had a large shower stall, with multiple shower heads for maximum water exposure. "This is much nicer than any apartment I've ever been able to afford," he remarked as he tossed his packs onto a table in the bedroom.

Nathan handed him the key. "There are a few people who can get in if they want to. There is a maid—I think Sharon takes care of this area. She will clean as often, or as infrequently, as you choose. Just let her know. And of course, Diego has a master key that gets him into anywhere in the building."

Grant nodded. "I'd expect as much. I don't have anything to hide, so that all sounds fine with me."

Nathan glanced down at his watch. "We'd better get moving. I think we're late already. But Diego knows that we were in the dining room before, and you hadn't seen your place yet. I'm sure it will be fine."

They passed up the elevator for the stairs, taking the steps two at a time to get down to the main floor. Nathan led them briskly along a long hallway until he stopped at a closed door and opened it, waving for Grant to go in first.

John, who was seated close to the door, rose from his chair and held out his hand to Grant.

"Hello, again. And I have to thank you for being willing to help out this way, especially on such short notice."

Grant had clasped John's hand and was smiling, about to reply, when his nostrils flared.

She's here!

The smile froze on his face as a tall, dark-skinned woman

rose from the chair behind where John was standing. She also extended her hand in greeting.

Grant's brain went into overdrive. *She's almost as tall as me. She's gotta be damn close to six feet. Her voluptuous curves don't stop!* He began sweating, so he made himself look at her face instead. Her hair was cut very short, and she wore huge gold hoop earrings that glinted when she moved. But it was her face that transfixed him. Her dark eyes reflected intelligence, her dimples as she smiled suggested good humor, and her full lips made his mouth water. He wanted to take her into his arms, to kiss her, and proclaim his undying love for her immediately. He knew he couldn't, but his wolf was insistent.

It's her! She's ours! Let her know she has met her mate.

He was rooted to the spot, at the mercy of warring factions in his head. He was still smiling but realized that he hadn't stopped shaking John's hand. He forced his body to obey and turned to shake the woman's hand. That was a big mistake. Her skin felt like warm silk. Just touching her hand had rendered him even more speechless. His hormones were racing, his cock had hardened to a rock, his heart was pounding, and he was having trouble breathing.

Take her now!

"No!" he croaked out. He realized, horrified, that he'd spoken aloud when he was met by puzzled stares from everyone in the room.

He spoke sternly to his wolf. *I have to get control . . . now! Be quiet!*

He grinned apologetically and forced himself to let go of the hand he wanted to get onto his knees and beg to hold forever. "Um, you know that uneasy feeling when your wolf is talking to you, and you realize you've just answered out loud?"

That made everyone in the room smile. Everyone except the pack leader's wife nodded in recognition.

"Oh yeah, that happens more than I like to admit," John

said.

Grant's feet finally agreed to do as they were told. He moved farther into the room, collapsing onto an empty chair next to John, and across the table from the beautiful woman.

Nathan had also moved into the room and sat next to the woman.

Grant's wolf snarled a challenge, but he ignored it. He forced himself to look away from her.

"Well, now that we're all here, let's be sure that you remember everyone," Diego said with a smile. "I'm Diego, but then you know that since you were just here recently. Unfortunately, that day was such a drain on me that I don't remember much of what happened. I'm told I was all but carried back upstairs, and I collapsed for a couple of days."

Grant leaned forward, speaking earnestly. "But you did something that I'd never seen done. You partially shifted and were able to control not only your own wolf but the wolves of two others. They were both unwilling to obey you, but the sheer force of your will made them both shift. That took an enormous amount of power. And to think that you did that while still suffering from the injuries of a leader's challenge? I'm honored to be asked to serve such a leader for as long as I'm needed."

Diego inclined his head in acknowledgment. "I'm grateful. A change in pack leadership always creates a period of unrest. Ours was made worse by a second challenge from the same man. Then we had to mete out pack justice, which was unpleasant. We are very thankful for the services your family provided to help us. Very few remember a time when Joe had to do the same thing, and your parents came down to do him that favor. But everyone remembers that his actions led to fifty years of steady leadership, with peace and quiet. We're all hoping for that again."

"You deserve it," Grant said emphatically. "And I'm glad

to do my part to help."

Diego took the hand of the red-haired woman sitting next to him. "You might not remember my wife, since I barely had time to introduce her at your last visit. Grant Knutsen, may I present my wife, and fifth in command, Saoirse McColl Vargas."

Saoirse grinned when he stood up and gave her a small bow. "I'm pleased to officially meet you, Grant. And very grateful that you're willing to join the pack to help us. Your family seems to do that a lot."

"Nathan mentioned your degree in biological research. And that you're trying to isolate any substance in our bodies that might lead to an early indicator that there is a wolf about to present itself . . . before it actually does?"

Saoirse looked surprised. "Yes, I've been working on that for a while. My more senior students have been helping. I'm kind of stuck right now. Is your background in biology?"

He nodded. "Yeah. I've got a master's in research, and I've spent the last few years running a lab up in Montreal. But I had already given them my notice when Mom got the call about you needing someone to be a substitute in security down here. I'm only too happy to help you in your quest to determine how to predict which kids will ultimately find out they're not alone in their head and body, *before* the wolf makes itself known by appearing."

Her smile was genuine and warm. "Thanks." She turned to her husband. "Diego, I approve."

The pack leader grinned. "I'm so relieved, *cara mia*. If you didn't like him, I'd have a lot more phone calls to make."

She stuck her tongue out at him.

He ignored that disrespect and continued his introductions. "John Johnson is my second in command. He's the one who is taking leave for an unspecified length of time."

"We've known each other since we were kids, Diego," John

reminded him, then turned to speak directly to Grant. "See, the thing is, I haven't lived on my own since college. It's been a while, and I'm kind of wondering if I'll be able to handle things away from the pack. Only one way to find out, right?"

"I'm willing to stay as long as the pack needs me to, so it's cool," Grant replied. "I had to move out of my mom's house years ago, before I could feel like a real adult. And moving down here is the furthest I've ever lived away from my family."

Diego continued with his introductions. "My third in command is Monique Martin, who will now be moving up to become my second. She'll take over as head of security and be responsible for working with Diya, the leader of the guards, to maintain pack safety."

Grant looked over to find Monique watching him intently, as if she was studying him and his reactions. Her smile when he nodded at her was only on her lips. Her gaze was steady.

She doesn't miss much. I wonder if she suspects what my problem was.

No matter. She will belong to us, his wolf drawled lazily in his mind, supremely confident in the outcome.

"And you know Nathaniel Taylor, our fourth in command, who will now move up to third. He will be the one to direct the maintenance training for all of those involved with security. That means that you, Grant, will become our fourth. It will be your responsibility to help out as needed whenever those above you have need of an extra body."

"I'm just curious—" Grant began.

Diego waved a hand to cut him off. "Why we didn't just promote someone from within? I thought about it, but ultimately decided not to do it. There have just been too many changes recently. No one wants to cause any more unrest by moving around or changing positions. I think we all just want things to settle down and get back to normal. We have to do that before the students return in a month or so. Parents trust us to provide a stable environment for their kids. We are, first and foremost, a school. Monique is also our principal."

Monique cleared her throat. "We need to talk soon about some of the inquiry letters I've received."

Diego replied, "Tomorrow morning, at nine?"

She nodded.

Diego looked around, smiling. "Then I think we've got everything taken care of—at least for now. This meeting is adjourned."

When he got up, everyone else did, also. He made his way around the table, holding his right arm out to John for a handshake. They shook hands, then moved closer for a hug.

"Take care, old friend," Diego said. "It's scary and exciting out there, all at the same time."

John grinned. "But that's what I'm looking forward to discovering for myself. And to finding out what my place is and where I need to be."

Saoirse had also moved closer to John and grabbed him for a long hug. "Say *hi* to Freddie for me," she whispered, obviously forgetting that everyone else in the room had the enhanced hearing of their wolves.

Nathan shook John's hand, as did Monique. Finally, John turned to Grant for one last handshake.

"Good luck," Grant said. "I hope you find what you're looking for."

John looked startled but quickly recovered his composure with a smile. "I hope so, too."

As everyone filed out into the hall, John addressed everyone in general. "Anyone want to join me for a run in the moonlight?"

There was a general murmur of agreement.

Saoirse cleared her throat. "Um, I'll pass. I can't keep up with you guys when you're running on four paws and all I have is two legs."

Diego pulled her close, kissing her lips. "I'll see you later, *querida.*"

"I'll try to wait up for you. But if not, you can always wake me, in that *special* way you do, when you come back in." She gave him a saucy wink, then turned and strolled down the hall to the stairs.

As they walked down the hall, Grant remarked to Diego, "I noticed you're not wearing a splint on your left arm anymore. Has it healed enough for you to run as a wolf?"

"Not for very long. Each time I shift back and forth, it repairs more damage. Rachel, our doctor, thinks it might be another few weeks before the bone is totally healed. It's still a lame leg, for now. But I don't want to miss the opportunity to bay at the moon in celebration of our newest pack member. And to call out for good fortune for our departing John. I'll go out to the clearing where we usually meet each other before a longer run. Then I'll head back inside while the others show you our favorite spots. I know you've run here before, but this will be your first time as a resident. I hope you enjoy your time here."

Grant glanced at the back of Monique, walking in front of him. "Oh, I'm sure I will."

When they all reached the area just inside the trees, where everyone removed their clothing before they shifted, Grant tried not to be too obvious watching Monique. He'd already stripped when he glanced over and almost swallowed his tongue.

Oh my God! In clothing, Monique's an attractive woman. Naked, she's a goddess! Look at that regal bearing. She stands proud in her nudity, with no self-consciousness at all, and doesn't seem to be aware of the effect she has on me. Being this close to her, with both of us unclothed? It's the biggest strain I've ever had to fight in my life! He moaned softly. *I've never shifted with such a huge hard-on! Hopefully, the twilight makes it, if not invisible, at least harder to see.*

We will take her tonight! His wolf insisted.

No! We will not! We need to be patient. She's a complex woman. Her wolf might agree, but we need her to agree also. You have to give me the time I need to convince her human half that I'm her mate.

Grant's wolf was already preparing to take over their body. He dropped to the ground onto all fours, as everyone else was doing. He grimaced with the pain of his bones remaking themselves into a wolf's skeletal structure. He could feel his organs shifting and his face stretching into an elongated snout as his humanity faded. Once he was shifted, he could feel his wolf-cock pushing its way out of the sheath. He tried to will it back into submission.

If you take too long, I will take her as a wolf, and leave you humans to work things out later.

Agreed.

Then there was no longer any need for words as the sheer pleasure of being an animal out racing in the moonlight took over. He enjoyed feeling the grass under his paws and smelling all the delightful odors of the forest on a warm summer evening. Everyone was obviously enticed to forget anything else, as they howled out their pleasure and began to run.

CHAPTER THREE

In the morning, Grant entered the dining room and breathed in deeply. The smell of bacon was accompanied by a pastry smell, and a quick look at the buffet showed him that waffles were offered, along with numerous kinds of syrups and preserves.

As he was getting himself a cup of coffee, he heard his name. He turned to see Nathan sitting with Monique at a table that had many empty chairs. He took his coffee over and sat down across from Monique. Once again, her smile didn't reach her eyes, and he wondered if he had somehow offended her the previous evening. But he didn't have time to think about it.

"What would you like to do this morning?" Nathan asked. "I can show you the gym building right after breakfast if you like. There's a weight room, with room for sparring, which we all do often, to keep in shape. There's also a full gym with basketball hoops, and an indoor pool with a retractable roof, for those rare Maine days when it's sunny at the same time as it's warm enough to swim. As part of the security detail, we're expected to keep ourselves in top shape. You never know when you'll be called upon to use your body to protect the pack."

Grant nodded. *Don't think about Monique in a bathing suit. Monique in tiny gym shorts and an exercise bra. Monique naked . . .*

He cleared his throat. "Can I get some breakfast first? I usually don't function well until after at least a couple of cups of coffee and some food."

Nathan grinned. "I've been up for hours. I already ran this

morning, and this is my second breakfast."

Grant glanced at his watch. "It's only eight-fifteen!"

Nathan shrugged. "I've always been an early riser."

Monique spoke up. "Me too. The kids woke me up at six, like they do almost every day. We had breakfast together, then we hit the gym."

Grant tried not to let his surprise show on his face, and asked, casually, he hoped, "You work out at the gym with them? How old are they?"

"James is thirteen. He usually just sits and reads a book. He's not much for exercise lately. Selma is ten, and Selena is eight. They can't do any lifting because they're still too young. But they like the treadmills and the elliptical machines. Then we all do some laps in the pool."

"Um, I'm going to get some food," Grant said. "Can I bring anyone anything?"

Monique stood up. "No. I've got that meeting with Diego to get ready for. I'll see you both later."

Grant hoped he wasn't staring, but just watching her walk away from him was an enticing view. He shook himself once she had rounded the corner and was out of sight. Then he walked over to the buffet and piled his plate with waffles, bacon, and a couple of fried eggs for extra protein. He poured syrup over the whole thing and brought it back to the table where Nathan was buttering some toast. Grant sat and began to eat.

"So, like I said, I can show you the gym building, then you can work out anytime you want to," Nathan said while chewing his toast. He took another sip of coffee.

Grant swallowed, then drank some orange juice. "I'd also like to find out where the lab is that Mrs. Vargas does her research."

"She'll freak out if you call her that. She'll insist you call her Saoirse—especially if you're going to be working together in the lab."

Grant acknowledged that with a nod, while he continued to eat.

"The lab is in the academic section of the mansion. It's actually part of her classroom. She teaches all the physical sciences in there, including biology, chemistry, and even some physics, I think. She got to redesign the lab when she was hired last year. It hadn't been updated for a long time, so when our previous teacher retired to travel the world with his wife, Diego offered the chance to redo it as part of the job. Saoirse had worked in a lot of labs before and had definite ideas about what did and didn't belong in there. It's a whole new place now."

Grant pushed his now-empty plate away and took another sip of coffee. He stared in surprise at Nathan. "Wait a minute. Did you say *last year*? So in one year, she was hired as a new teacher by Diego, who was the principal. She redesigned the lab, discovered werewolves really exist, fell in love with Diego, watched him face a challenger, twice, after Joe named him as pack leader. And then they got married?"

Nathan grinned. "Yeah. I guess it does all sound kind of rushed when you put it that way. But he knew from the start that she was his mate. From what I've been told, our wolves always are the first to know, and they're not shy about insisting we listen to them."

Grant made a face. "Don't I know it!"

His wolf snarled softly inside his head.

"Are you married?" he asked.

Nathan shook his head. "No. Haven't met the right female yet. I've sampled a few, but I'm sure you know that it's tricky when you have sex with shifter females. If her wolf decides you're mated, it's very difficult to convince her that your wolf doesn't agree."

"I've never lived in a pack situation before. My parents

decided years ago that being a family unit was enough of a pack for them. Both of them were shifters, and so are all of us kids. We all used to run and hunt together here, when we were younger and on vacation. Dad was older than Mom, and he passed away a year ago, from lung cancer. Even the abilities of a shifting body can't repair the damage from being a smoker forever."

"So you've never had sex with a female shifter?"

"No. Why? Is it that different?"

"Well, it can be complicated, like I said. But the added benefit is you get to have sex as humans *and* as wolves. It adds a whole new dimension. But I'm not sure I believe in that whole *you'll know*, thing. I mean, how can your wolf or you know so quickly?"

Grant shifted around on his chair, his cock pressing against the seam of his jeans as he imagined sex with Monique's black wolf, as well as with the magnificent female he'd seen nude last night.

"Just a word to the wise," Nathan added. "You don't have to be a monk. But be careful around shifter females."

Grant got up to get more coffee and tried to sound casual when he sat back down. "Who is Monique's husband?"

"She's a widow. Only those of us with the highest security clearance know her story, so keep it to yourself. Her husband was the leader of a pack near Detroit. He faced down a lot of challengers since they were so near a big city. But he didn't win the last one. Monique took the kids and left, to avoid having to serve the man who'd killed her husband."

Grant leaned back, shaking his head. "Wow! Since I've never been a part of a pack, I guess I never thought about what happens to the family of a deposed pack leader. How horrible for her — and for the kids."

"Joe, our former pack leader, recognized her fighting spirit when she applied for membership. She started out in security, but it didn't take long for her to work her way into the top leadership. She's a rock when it comes to dealing with emergencies, and fierce when defending the pack."

Grant nodded. "I remember seeing her standing between the two renegade wolves, and Diego and Saoirse when we were here last June."

"That's what she does. She puts her body between any threat and the pack. She's loyal to a fault. We're lucky to have her. And when Diego was declared leader by Joe before he passed, she took over the job of principal for the school."

"So everyone wears more than one hat?"

"Yup. I'm the fourth . . . I mean, the third, now, which means I'll be in charge of making sure that all of the guards maintain battle-readiness skills. I'm also one of the English teachers. And when someone needs to be driven to or picked up from the airport, I usually volunteer. I like to drive, and I don't get to do it very often."

"And John's other job, besides being second, and head of security, was to work with Diya on maintaining pack safety, right? "

"Yes. Diya is the leader of the guards, so Monique will now be working with her in John's place. You probably saw her on the way in through the gate. I think she's on days this week. She's the woman with the short gray hair."

Grant nodded. "I have met her before. I wonder if being back-up for all of you who are higher in the hierarchy, and being an assistant to Mrs. — I mean, Saoirse — will be enough responsibilities for me to earn my keep. Maybe I can help the gardeners or something."

"Have a green thumb, do you?"

"Yeah. I've helped my mom keep the grounds around our family place landscaped since I was a teenager. It's a relaxing therapy for me, and I enjoy the results."

"Then it's Manuel you need to talk to. He's the one who

runs the gardening division."

"So, where is the gym?"

They both got up, and Grant put his dishes onto the conveyor belt that moved them into the kitchen.

Nathan added his coffee cup and waved towards the back door. "Let's go out this way. It's closer to the gym. Plus, there are a lot of unique flower arrangements out back."

After his tour of the gym, Grant mentioned he needed a good work-out. What he really wanted was a chance to think. Doing physical activity that was mindless and repetitive had always allowed him to work through any issues he had.

Nathan said he was going outside to wash the cars. "They're not mine, but I still like to fondle them and make them look pretty." With a grin, he walked out into the sunshine.

Grant's wolf seemed to be asleep until he started to lift weights. Then it stretched itself inside of him, enjoying the feel of their muscles being challenged.

She has three children. Her husband was a pack leader who was killed in a challenge.

So? That doesn't change the fact that she is our mate.

No, but she might be harder to reach as a human because she's protecting her kids.

From us? We don't want to hurt them. We will protect them as hers — and ours.

I know. But I have to find out more about her. She's tightly wound. Something is bothering her. I don't think it involves me. But I need time to figure out how to approach her.

But not too much time.

You wolves are so impatient.

And you humans take too long to do everything.

Grant smiled as he continued to lift weights. As always, he was enjoying the feel of his body growing stronger.

As it will need to be, to win our mate.

Yes.

CHAPTER FOUR

After he was done lifting, Grant jumped into the pool to do some laps. That worked up his appetite. He went up to his room to change before heading down for the dining room for lunch. As he entered the room, he looked around for the tall woman he wanted to see, but she wasn't there. Instead, he heard, "Yoo-hoo! Grant! Over here!" He smiled when he saw the source of the noise was Saoirse, waving frantically at him to get his attention. He waved back, then got himself some food from the buffet before heading over to her table.

She was sitting with a woman who looked familiar. A young child sat next to her, in the process of covering every surface around them with what she was supposed to be eating. The woman looked exasperated.

He chose the cleanest looking chair and sat down.

"Hi, Grant," Saoirse said. "Do you remember Jerene? She's Joe and Janine's youngest. Jerene, this is Grant Knutsen, the Canadian hunter who has agreed to fill in for your brother while he's off finding himself."

Jerene smiled, and Grant instantly saw the family resemblance. The woman had her mother's dimples and her light brown skin. The light-colored hair she must have gotten from her father. She also, surprisingly, had her daddy's green eyes.

"Hey there, Grant. You probably don't remember me. You and your brothers used to play with John when your family came to visit. I was the pesky little sister you all ignored. Even your sister treated me like an annoyance. But I remember you. All of you boys were so good-looking, I wasn't sure which

26

one of you I wanted to marry. Maybe all three?"

Saoirse joined her in laughing when Grant gaped in surprise at her words.

"Jerene," Saoirse chided, "he probably hasn't read any of those *multiple-men, one-woman, reverse-harem* romances that you like so much."

"No?" Jerene winked at him. "Some of my favorites have three or four brothers who agree to share a woman because she's so hot that even having part of her is better than none of her. What do you think, Grant? Would you and your brothers be able to share one woman?"

Grant snorted, shaking his head. "Are you kidding? We wouldn't even share our toys when we were kids. The urge to possess your woman, or your mate in our case, is so strong that the fighting would never stop." He mimicked different voices arguing. "*Whose night is it with her? Which part of her did you get last time? Isn't it your turn to bring the condoms? Aren't you done yet? Quit hogging the best parts!*"

He grinned. "It would be a never-ending battle, until the woman either eloped with the one she liked the best, or we'd all fight trying to win her for ourselves, and she'd be stuck with what was left of the final winner."

Jerene and Saoirse both laughed out loud.

"See?" Saoirse said to Jerene. "He should write them! At least they'd be more realistic."

He shook his head, solemnly. "I know what brotherly dynamics are like, at least in my family."

Jerene had to break up a fight between her kids, who must have sensed no one was paying them any attention, so they'd begun hitting each other, half-heartedly.

Grant nodded towards them. "See what I mean?"

Saoirse smiled. "I was third of ten. I know exactly what you mean. Diego and I don't have any kids yet. But I've had lots of experience with sibling rivalry, and that's what I've been trying to tell Jerene about those books she likes so much."

"Hey, it's escapism, okay?" Jerene said. "I mean, you can see the allure. If one huge, sexy alpha male is good, then two or three of them would be wonderful, right?"

"My two brothers are alphas," Grant commented. "They couldn't even share a room. I had to live with one of them to keep family peace."

"Aren't you an alpha, too?" Saoirse asked.

Grant shook his head. "Nope. Not interested. Even though I'm the oldest brother, I'm definitely the beta male of the family. Actually, my sister Griselda is probably more alpha than both of my brothers put together. And not just because she's the oldest. She's got Mom's iron will and slow temper. She doesn't often get angry, but when she does . . . look out!"

"I'm kind of alpha myself," Saoirse remarked. "I'm the oldest girl, so I got stuck taking care of the rest when both of our parents were working. Plus, I've got the red hair that signals I'm bossy as hell, and I've got the temper to prove it."

Grant nodded with a smile. "Then Diego is a lucky man. I'd rather have a strong woman, so I don't have to carry all of the weight of life myself."

"Speaking of strong women . . ." Saoirse left the rest unsaid with a tilt of her head.

Monique appeared with her kids in the dining room. They all got their food, then sat at a table on the other side of the room.

Under the guise of eating, Grant watched them closely to study their family dynamics.

Monique was joking around with the two girls, both of whom resembled her, though with lighter skin. One had her hair cut short, like her mom, and the other had an afro, but both had brown hair. The boy had black hair like his mother, but it was straight. He needed a haircut to tame the messy cowlicks sticking up in odd places on his head. He wasn't participating in the family discussion, preferring to read a book.

And when he was done with his food, he went back up for seconds, filling his plate even higher the second time.

"He's gonna have a growth spurt soon, I'll bet," Saoirse remarked.

"He reminds me of me when I was that age." Grant smiled.

"Oh? Why?"

"I was always a husky kid. It only got worse when I was a pre-teen."

"You?" Jerene recoiled in pretend shock. "You look like *Ah-nold*. And I don't mean my husband."

"Now, yes. But it took a lot of work for me to get this fit, and it's not easy to stay that way. I will always have to work harder than the next guy to look half as good."

One of Jerene's kids chose that moment to overturn her bowl, and the food spilled all over her and her brother.

With a heavy sigh, Jerene stood and picked up the offender, taking the other one by the hand. "Now it's shower time for you guys. Then maybe I can get you down for a nap, missy, while your brother does his homework—so Mommy can have some reading time, to daydream about sexy brothers." She smirked and winked at Grant. Then she dragged her kids out of the dining room.

"So, do you intend to stare at her all afternoon? Or do you want to come up to see my lab and talk about my research?"

Grant felt the heat of his blush when he realized she'd accurately guessed what he'd been doing. He turned to Saoirse, apologetically, trying to change the subject. "I'm sorry. I actually did intend to seek you out today, to do just that."

"You'll have to tread carefully with her," she said, inclining her head in Monique's direction. "She's been widowed for five years and has been working overtime to be both mother and father to her kids. Plus, she's now the second for the pack. Plus, she's the principal for the school. Her son will be starting at the academy in August. But her two younger ones are still being mostly home-schooled, at least for the summer."

His attention snapped back to her, surprised. "There isn't a school for the younger kids of pack members? I guess I just assumed they'd go to the local school, in town."

Saoirse shook her head. "No. We keep to ourselves around here. Oh, we go into town for some supplies. But Janine has everyone's grocery needs delivered to the gate. The kids go on field trips into town sometimes, but for the most part, we try to be self-sufficient. No need for any outsiders to develop an interest in finding out how we live out here."

"No elementary teachers living in the compound?"

"There is one, and she was running all-ages classes for a while, with a volunteer who used to be an aide at a middle school. But she had a baby last year, so she's been on maternity leave, learning to be a mom. I don't think the aide is qualified to teach by himself. The kids are all on summer break right now. Hopefully, she will resume classes in the fall. But either way, when the school year starts again, Monique's workload will go up again."

"Sounds like she needs a partner, to help her with all of her work," he said casually. When she stared at him, he realized, to his horror, he had actually spoken that aloud. He could feel his skin heating up under her gaze.

"Your wolf wants her for a mate, right?"

He nodded in confusion, trying to stop blushing.

"I know about these things, you know," she continued. "I may not be a shifter, but I've had to learn an awful lot about you guys, very quickly. I went from not believing in werewolves to being married to the pack leader in less than a year. He said his wolf told him I was *the one* the first time he met me."

"How long did it take for him to tell you that?"

"Five months. But that included the time I didn't know *what* he was."

"Then I'll have to hope that John measures his vacation time in months, not weeks."

"I don't think that will be a problem," she answered cryptically.

Grant didn't want to pry, so he left that unanswered. "I'm done eating, so we can go see your lab if you're ready. I want to hear all about what you've tried, and what you've found out about our body chemistry."

"Then let's go there now."

They both got up, put their dishes on the conveyor belt, and headed out in the direction of the main staircase that led up to the second floor, and the classrooms.

CHAPTER FIVE

The rest of that week passed quickly. Grant developed a routine of getting up at seven, then eating breakfast before he worked out in the weight room. He'd spar with any security person who was in the gym, getting the measure of the others who were also responsible for protecting the pack. Then he'd swim for a cardio work-out. That usually took him to lunchtime when he'd eat in the main dining room again. Despite his best intentions, he was unable to interact much with Monique, whose children were often eating with her. When they weren't, she was usually in conference with Diego, or working through her meal, with her laptop and papers spread out in front of her.

Grant had gone running a couple of times at night, but after that first night, Monique was never out there when he was. So he was pleased and excited when he got to the clearing on Friday night, to find that Monique was there, already naked, and just beginning her change. Grant tore off his shirt, meaning to shift along with her. He startled when he felt a hand on his arm and turned to see Nathan shaking his head.

"On busy run nights, we don't go out in the same groups as other top security members," Nathan said. "You can go out with the next group. Diya is already out with the first one."

"Why?" Grant tried hard not to sound distracted, but he couldn't take his eyes off the object of his desires, who was now shaking off the last of the tremors of shifting and stood in her wolf form. She was the glorious ebony creature he'd been dreaming of for months. His wolf snarled in his mind, anxious to mate.

"To help keep the peace. You never know when there's going to be a disagreement between any two or more members, and there needs to be a top security member near each group. There are a lot of lesser security people, so there can be at least one or two of them with each grouping. But they all have to defer to us, as pack leadership."

"Okay," Grant said out loud, while his wolf objected.

How can I mate with her if we're not together?

We're new here still. We need to follow established rules.

You humans make everything take too long!

We can shift soon. You'll feel better when you're running on your four legs.

Five, if you count the one that needs to be satisfied.

Grant smiled inwardly, recognizing his wolf also felt the heavy ache in his loins from unsatisfied lust. Being near Monique was torture. Seeing her naked was agony. Being unable to spend any time alone with her, to present his intentions, frustrating. It wasn't only his wolf who was impatient about how long it appeared to be taking to move things along.

Soon another group of shifters had entered the clearing, where everyone left their clothing and shoes in neat piles so they could shift to their wolves. Grant removed the rest of his clothing and shifted along with them. He howled at the night sky with the glorious release that he always felt when the animal trapped within was allowed to rule the body that genetics and nature forced them to share. They took off into the deep woods, running along the trail that humans jogged on during daylight hours. But they soon spread out, since wolves didn't have to run single-file, or even on paths.

For a while, thinking became unnecessary, as the sheer joy of loping along, feeling a part of the natural surroundings, mollified even the most persistent of stresses, reducing them to a distant memory. His group hunted small game and shared what they caught. They drank from streams of cool, clear water that ran through the woods, and howled at the moon, rising almost full in the night sky.

Suddenly Grant stopped running and cocked his head, listening for . . . something.

She has trouble!

With that, his wolf took off, running away from the group they were with. It didn't take long to distinguish the sounds of wolves fighting. He raced closer, to find a small clearing where he could see, in the rising moonlight, that two male wolves were fighting over a female. Monique was patrolling the spectators, to keep everyone from interfering in a normal part of pack interactions. Grant assessed the situation, then walked in front of the wolves on his side of the clearing to let them know he was there.

The female wolf was young, and she was trembling. It was obvious, from her occasional loud whimpers, which one of the fighting males she preferred. One wolf was younger and thinner, and that was the one she cried out for. The other was older and stockier and obviously had more fighting experience. But the intensity that the younger wolf brought to the fight was working in his favor. Despite his human side wanting to help the female, Grant's wolf kept him patrolling to ensure there was no interference.

The younger wolf made a feint that the older wolf fell for. The thinner wolf twisted in mid-air, to land on top of the older wolf, crushing all the air out of him, leaving him temporarily dazed. Monique appeared over the older wolf and put both of her front paws on his chest to keep him down, as the two lovers resumed their interrupted mating.

The young female immediately resumed her presentation stance. The young male mounted her, his front paws on her back, eager to complete the mating ritual. Grant saw that Monique was watching the lovers and the spectators, so she apparently didn't see or feel the muscles bulging under the older wolf's skin. But Grant noticed.

With a howl, the wolf leapt up, throwing Monique off balance, and hurled himself towards the couple, clearly intending to knock the other male off and interrupt the mating. Grant launched himself at the same time and collided with the other male in mid-air. They grappled with one another as they fell to the side. Over his opponent's snapping jaws, Grant watched as the young lovers completed their mating, tying them to one another for the rest of their lives.

Grant pushed the other male off of him and stood his ground. He tried to express with his eyes that he was sorry for interfering and understood what the other male felt, but that this was the way things had to be.

The other male watched the mated couple for a moment, then turned to glare at Grant. He howled with frustration, then took off into the woods.

Grant looked around and saw Monique staring at him. He met her gaze, pleased when she nodded briefly to thank him for his help. Then she and the other wolves in their group also ran off, leaving Grant to head back to the group he'd left behind. It took him a while to find them, but wolves could find their way around even in total darkness.

The rest of the night passed without further incident. When Grant returned to the clearing to shift back to human form and gather his clothing, he was disappointed to see that Monique's belongings were already gone. As he walked back up to the mansion, carrying his clothing, still as naked as most of the others from his group were, he wondered what Monique thought of him. *At least she seemed glad that I helped out.*

We are still no closer to claiming her. And watching the two younglings tonight has made things worse. I will act soon if you don't!

Grant let out a long sigh, heavy with unsatisfied desire and longing. He made his way up to his room, and spent a long time in the shower, imagining Monique in there with him, first as a human, then as a wolf. He found both images so hot that he was spent and exhausted by the time he was done. As he made his way to his bed, he realized that his fingers were pruney, reflecting how long he'd taken in the water. *But at least I can sleep now.*

Soon, his wolf whispered, *it must be soon.*

CHAPTER SIX

The next morning, Grant was sitting alone, reading the news on his phone, finishing his last cup of coffee, when he suddenly became aware that he was being watched. He looked up sharply and met the eyes of the observer, who moved forward quickly.

"Is it all right if I sit here?" Monique asked, waiting until he nodded before she sat down.

"Of course it is." He gave her a friendly smile.

Now! Tell her now!

He ignored the voice in his head and simply watched as she stirred cream into her coffee.

Finally, she looked into his eyes. "How did you know there was trouble last night?"

Grant was taken aback by her directness, which pulled him out of his fantasies.

"Um . . . I'm not sure. One minute I was running along, enjoying the night. The next minute my wolf alerted me that there was trouble, and we ran towards it."

She continued to stare, then looked away. "I probably could have handled things myself, but I'm glad you were there," she said grudgingly. "I didn't notice that he was getting ready to spring. You did. How?"

Grant took a deep breath to calm himself before he spoke. "I think it's because I understand what made him act like that. The drive to mate is so intense that it takes over all thinking and turns a male into a creature of pure instinct. Rationally, it was obvious that the female had made her choice. By all rights, she deserved to be able to choose her mate. But the other male is a loner wolf, and the urge is all-consuming. I knew what he would be feeling, so I watched *him*, not the couple."

Because if I watched them, I'd have jumped over and mated with you, whether you agreed or not!

Grant almost didn't hear what his wolf was saying, over the pounding of blood in his ears. He'd never spoken alone to the object of all his fantasies, yet now that she was here, he had to let her take the lead. *Shh! She's thinking over what to say next.*

Monique tilted her head, watching him closely, while she obviously considered his words. "That's a very feminist way to think, saying that she deserved to choose her mate. Many males would say it was her lot to accept the winner, whether she liked him or not."

Grant flashed a quick smile. "My mother is a very alpha female. So is my sister. I'm the product of loving both of them very much. The idea that someone would try to force my sister to accept someone she didn't want as a lifetime mate makes me angry. Of course, knowing her, she'd kill him herself, then order her chosen male to get back over to finish mating with her. But that female last night was young. She was terrified. My job is to protect the pack, and she's pack. It's that simple."

"I wasn't much older than her when I mated with my Tim," Monique said, looking off into the distance. "Mom hated him. She wanted me to concentrate on my studies and graduate with my master's degree before I got involved with anyone. But she wasn't aware of what I'd discovered about myself. As far as I know, I'm the only shifter in the family. When I met Tim, we were both in grad school. I had skipped a year of school, so he was older than me. But we both knew it was right for us. She forbade me to see him, and I had never lied to her before, but I moved in with him on campus, without telling her. By the time I was twenty-two, I was pregnant. We ran off to get married in Vegas, then returned home to tell her what had happened. My grandmother forced her to accept us. She was very religious, and to her, marriage was a sacred pact between a couple and God. And a new life was a cause for celebration, no matter how you felt about the daddy."

Grant felt awkward but knew he should say something. He cleared his throat. "You must have loved each other very much. I'm sorry for your loss."

Monique shook her head as if to remove unpleasant memories before she looked back down at her hands wrapped around her cup. She took a long drink from her coffee, then put it down and leaned forward. "I . . . uh . . . don't know why I felt I had to tell you all of that."

"Your story is safe with me."

She stared at him for a moment. "You're not mated," she stated with a hint of hesitation.

He shook his head slowly, "No."

"Why?"

He shrugged. "I've never lived in a pack before. I've never met any female shifters besides my mom and my sister."

"Many of us choose non-shifters as mates. Diego did."

"Yes. But as I understand it, Diego's wolf and he both agreed from the start that she was *the one*. Maybe I've never met the one for me."

He took a deep breath before leaning forward to close the distance between them. He spoke in a low voice. "Or maybe I've met her, but I haven't told her yet."

Alarm sparked in Monique's large, soft, brown eyes. Then she looked away as if to hide her thoughts.

The silence between them grew, and Grant wondered what Monique was thinking. Was she conferring with her wolf, or perhaps considering what he was hinting at with his words?

Finally, she looked up and met his gaze again. And when

she spoke, it was almost a whisper. "Maybe she's not ready to hear it yet."

"Will she let me know when she is?"

Almost imperceptibly, Monique nodded. Then she got up, moved quickly to put her empty cup onto the conveyor belt, and exited the dining room.

Grant was trying to process what had just happened when Saoirse approached his table.

She smiled. "That looked intense. You need to think about something else. Let's go up to my lab and start writing down some of your ideas and see where we should direct my research next to look for some answers."

In a daze, Grant got rid of his dirty dishes, pocketed his phone, and followed Saoirse up the stairs to the academic hallway. They continued down the hall until they reached the science classroom, which Saoirse opened with a key. She walked into the room, and Grant followed her in, still trying to convince his wolf that the conversation with Monique had ended well.

CHAPTER SEVEN

"I think we can forget about anything in the blood. Don't you agree?" Grant rubbed the back of his neck.

After a couple of weeks of testing everything they could think of — including some ideas suggested by senior students — Grant was ready to call it quits on that line of research.

Saoirse leaned back from staring into her microscope and rubbed her eyes, nodding. "Yeah. I'd done some stuff with the students during the school year, but having another researcher here and free afternoons to work with, has helped. We've just about exhausted anything that blood could possibly teach us. I guess I have to admit defeat."

Grant shook his head. "No, just that blood is a blind alley. Maybe it's in the genes."

"Then we'll never find it. I don't have the kind of equipment that can do genetic investigation."

"You know, I just had a crazy idea." Grant leaned back and folding his arms over his chest, a habit he'd developed as a kid, to protect himself from attack whenever his brothers didn't like something he was proposing.

"Which is?"

"Why don't we send some test samples to one of those companies that promise to tell you where your genes show your ancestors were from? I mean, if it's a genetic thing, then maybe it's geographically-based."

"You mean like Tay-Sachs is in people from Eastern Europe? And Sickle Cell Anemia is for people whose ancestors lived in mosquito-borne malaria areas?"

He nodded, uncrossing his arms and leaning forward. "What if it's based on some obscure area that all of our ancestors might have been from? I mean, you'd still need to get the gene from both parents, probably, which would explain why shifters can have non-shifter children, and vice-versa."

"So it's some kind of recessive gene that only presents itself when the genetic dice are thrown the right way, and you get it from both parents?"

"Doesn't that sound plausible?"

Saoirse was smiling. "Not only plausible, but totally possible. Plus, we wouldn't be hindered by the lack of a world-class laboratory. We could just pay the organization to do the research for us, and they'd never know why."

Grant was already searching on the internet using his laptop. "How much do they charge? Under a hundred, per test, I'll bet. We can send them, maybe, ten or fifteen samples, to start with. We'll include some non-shifters, along with some shifters, so we can study the results for any differences. We can have the results sent back to a post office box in town. We could put it in my name, since I'm the stranger around here, and not someone anyone in town could identify as being with the academy."

Saoirse snorted with amusement. "Why? Are you thinking that there'd be spies trying to figure out why so many people from this area want their genetic background researched? Come on! These companies don't care why you're curious, as long as they get your money."

"Here's one of the websites. They promise quick and accurate results. You only need to swab the inside of your cheek and send them a saliva sample. And these guys give an analysis that includes the mtDNA Haplogroup and the Y-DNA Haplogroup, so you can see which side of your family, mother or father, gave you which DNA."

Saoirse leaned over his shoulder to read the screen. "And

the company is affiliated with an internationally-famous PhD in genetics. Wow! They have my vote, to be sure!"

"The only real negative is that some people are worried that once the results are known, they'll be owned by the company. Or that the government would be able to access them. Insurance companies might also be interested to read about the genetics of people applying for coverage, so they could deny anyone with something they don't want to cover. But I'm not much for conspiracy theories. Plus, we're kind of remote up here. The other thing is that it can take weeks for you to get results. But we aren't in any hurry, are we?"

Saoirse's eyes sparkled as she moved back to her own computer and pulled up the same website. "Nope. It doesn't matter how long it takes if it gives us the answers we're looking for. If we're right, it will give our parents some peace of mind. They could test their kid's DNA simply and anonymously and find out, with almost certainty, if a wolf is growing inside their child's mind and body."

"How do we get started?"

"I'll talk to Diego tonight, and we can order sets for the two of us. Then we can ask others to volunteer."

"I'll do one, for sure, I'll bet the rest of the security team would be willing."

"We can get Jerene and her husband to do one each, since he's a non-shifter. Then we can send in their children's samples also, to see what that might tell us. After all, it's only swabs from the inside of your cheeks that you send in. No need to draw blood or do anything that might hurt small kids."

"I think we may have something here." Grant stood up and stretched his back muscles, tired from sitting for so long, hunched over a microscope.

"I can't wait to get started! Having you join me in the research was a wonderful idea."

"Yeah, but now you don't need me anymore. At least not until we have some DNA test results to analyze. I'll have to find some other way to fill my time and make myself useful around here."

"You could help me plan my year of classes," Saoirse suggested with an air of nonchalance.

"Why? You don't anticipate a huge influx of extra students in biology classes, do you?"

She gave him an enigmatic look. "No. But it might be a good idea if there were two of us who can teach biology, chemistry, and physics. You never know when I might need a sub, and you'd already be familiar with the curriculum and the lab."

"Are you feeling all right?"

She flashed him a quick smile. "Of course! Never felt better!" She glanced down at her watch. "Gosh! Look at the time. I had no idea it was so late. Dinner will be served very soon. I think I'll head up to the penthouse and see if my husband is up there yet. That way, I can tell him about our plans. Maybe you can sit with us for dinner tonight?"

"Okay. I've never been asked to sit at the lead table before. Do I have to dress up or anything like that?"

She laughed, shaking her head. "Of course not! But be ready to explain to everyone what your idea is, and how we can implement it."

They both closed their laptops and carried them out of the lab.

As she locked the door, Saoirse said, "Oh, and be down for dinner by five-thirty. Diego is an early riser, so he likes to eat dinner at an *old people's time*. I used to hate when he made me eat at five, so I've gradually bumped him back to five-thirty. My plan is to eventually get him to wait until at least six."

"That explains why I haven't seen you two at most meals, then. I'm most definitely not an early riser. Seven in the morning is early enough for me to wake up."

"Oh Lord, I wish I could sleep that late! My husband is up at the ass-crack of dawn, rising before the birds have even taken a pee, as me da used to say. For Diego, a long lie in bed is if he doesn't wake up until six. Personally, I'm with you. But marriage involves compromise, and I'm still working on changing both Diego's, and my own system, so we meet in the middle. Luckily, we have a lifetime together to work on it."

As they walked down the hall, Grant's wolf started growling at him again.

When will we start our lifetime together with our mate?

Soon, I hope. But at least we now know that she's aware of our intentions.

If her wolf thinks as I do, we won't wait forever for you humans to work things out.

Just give me a little more time. I need to figure out how to make myself indispensable to her.

Do it quickly.

I'll try.

Don't try. Just do.

CHAPTER EIGHT

Grant looked around as he and Nathan headed to the library for the first time. He'd asked Nathan if there was one and had been pleasantly surprised to find out it was in a small wing near the academy area.

"Of course, it doesn't get much use during the summer, except for the few students who live here year-round," Nathan said. "They have to do their summer reading lists, but most of them will put it off until the last week before school starts, then they'll complain that there aren't enough copies of the books they need."

Grant grinned, nodding at the truth of Nathan's words. "I remember being a huge procrastinator when I was in school. I guess students never change, huh?"

Nathan sniffed. "Not me. I always read all of the books from the list at least twice, so I'd be better able to discuss them when the school year started."

Grant raised his eyebrows but held back the laugh that wanted to erupt.

Nathan shrugged, looking sheepish as he continued. "Destined to be an English major. Obvious even back then what I'd pick for my career, I guess. So why are you looking for a library? Don't you read stuff online, like most people?"

Grant shook his head. "Nope. I prefer to hold actual books."

"Excellent!"

"I've just finished the last of the new ones I had with me, so I need something else. I don't watch videos much. I'd rather read."

"I'll walk you over there," Nathan offered, "since I'm going that way. I'm heading to my classroom for the first time this summer, to take stock of what's there, and what I might need to procure for the new students."

Once they were at the door marked, *Library*, Nathan walked off towards the stairs, and Grant pushed the door open and inhaled deeply.

He spotted a tiny elderly woman, perched on a high stool behind a desk, peering at him through her cats-eye glasses.

"I love the smell of books," he said by way of explanation. "I'm Grant Knutsen. The replacement for John Johnson."

Her face crinkled in smile lines. "Ah, that's why I've never seen you before. I'm Dolores Moretta, the librarian."

"Do I need a library card of any kind?"

"No. Just let me know what you're taking, and I keep records on my laptop. I don't worry about getting the books back. I do, after all, know where you live. Is there anything in particular I can find for you?"

"Just point me in the direction of sci-fi, and I'll be able to find something to amuse myself with."

She waved towards the stacks to her right. "They're over there. If there's something you'd like to read that we don't have, feel free to leave me a recommendation. I don't have a large budget, except for required schoolbooks, but I do have some discretionary funds for special requests."

"Thanks," he said, already on his way to his favorite genre.

He'd been pouring over the titles, pleased with the variety and scope of the books, when he rounded one stack and saw a small group of tables and chairs. One boy was sitting on a chair he'd pulled over to the window. Grant recognized him and approached, holding a couple of books that he was trying to decide between.

"Hello," he said conversationally. "You're Monique's son,

aren't you? James, is it?"

The boy looked up, obviously annoyed at having his reading interrupted. "Yeah."

"I'm Grant Knutsen, the guy who's here as a sub for John Johnson."

James studied him through thick glasses. "I know who you are, Mr. Knutsen."

Grant pulled another chair closer and sat down, smiling at the boy. "Please, call me Grant."

The boy's eyebrows rose. "You're the second man in a week to tell me that I can call him by his first name."

"Who's the other one?"

James shrugged. "Some guy named Dan who's volunteering in the library, to help out old lady Moretta."

Grant smiled at the boy's slang for the librarian. "You're starting at the academy soon, aren't you?"

James nodded.

"Then that means you're what, thirteen or fourteen?"

"Fourteen in November."

"Then you're almost a man. You know, you don't just go to sleep one night, as a seventeen-year-old boy, and wake up the next day as an eighteen-year-old man. You need to practice being a man, so it feels more natural when it happens. So maybe the other guy is thinking the same way I am. That it's okay for you to start getting used to calling some adults by their first names."

"Maybe."

Grant leaned forward. "So what are you reading? Something from the required reading list for incoming students?"

James sneered. "Um, no. I already read all of them, twice, back in June. I'm almost done working my way through the *Percy Jackson* books again."

"Sci-fi? My favorite genre, too. Have you read all of the *Harry Potter* books?"

"Yeah, years ago, when I was lots younger."

"How about the *Artemis Fowl* books?"

"Read them all last year — twice."

"Hmm . . . Have you read Tolkien's books?"

"I read them over Christmas break. I even read *The Hobbit* and *Silmarillion*.

"Have you ever read the *Dragonriders of Pern* books?"

James leaned forward. "No. Are they any good?"

"Only if you like the idea of being your age, watching a bunch of dragon eggs hatching. Then, if one of the baby dragonets chooses you, you'll have him or her talking in your mind for the rest of your lives. And when your dragon grows up, you'll be able to ride on its back, over long distances, even through time, having adventures."

"What did you say that was called?"

Grant got up. "Let me go and see if the first book in the series is here."

James rose also. "I'll come with you. That way, if I like it, I'll know where the other books are."

After Grant found the first book for James, they returned to their seats near the window and resumed chatting about books.

"It will take you a long time to finish that series, since there are a lot of books in the main series. Then there are off-shoot series that continue telling stories about living in that world. There are even some written by the original author's son."

"Kind of like the Percy Jackson books, right? I've read all of the original series, then the next five also. I'm reading the third series now. I've also read the Nordic gods series, and the Egyptian gods books, though they weren't as good as the Greek gods books."

Grant nodded. "I thought the same thing when I read them."

"But they're kids' books. Why would an adult read kids'

books?"

"Um, because they tell good stories? Because I've always loved Greek Mythology? Or maybe just because I'm a voracious reader, and when I discover a book that I like, I want to read everything else that author has written."

James nodded, his face animated. "Me, too. I love Greek Mythology. And sci-fi. Mom thinks I'm silly, reading so much. She says I should be doing other things, like running, or working out, or hanging out with other kids my age. But there aren't that many that live here year-round."

"Don't you have some sisters?"

"Yeah, two of them. But they're almost babies. Selma is ten, and Selena is eight. They don't like any of the games I do, like chess or Scrabble. Besides, I'm not very good at sports. I don't care enough about them to learn any of the stupid rules." He stopped, looking at Grant defensively.

Grant smiled. "I was the same way when I was your age. I have an older sister, and she's always been the track star of our family. And I have two younger brothers, and both are very competitive in all kinds of games—even board games. But I was always sneaking away to find a quiet place to read. I was lucky there were some trees near my house that had low-enough branches, so I was able to hide up in them for hours, with no one able to find me and interrupt my reading."

"Wow! I never thought of hiding up in a tree to read. Wouldn't that hurt your butt after a while?"

"Yeah, eventually. But it was worth it, to not have anyone bothering me while I was reading."

James sat back, looking out the window for a while.

"You know, when you're done with the *Pern* books, you might like the *Dune* series. Then there's the *Foundation* books by Asimov. I can think of a lot of books that you'd like. So let me know when you need recommendations. And if you ever want to talk about what you're reading with anyone, I'd be glad to accommodate you. There's nothing I like more than yakking with another book lover about books we've both read."

"Cool! Thanks, Mr.—I mean, Grant. I'd really enjoy that, too. I've never had anyone who wanted to talk to me about books I like, except Dan. And he hasn't read most of the ones I have. I figure he just doesn't like sci-fi. My mom doesn't either. She only reads non-fiction, so she thinks I'm wasting my time reading fiction."

"Oh? Doesn't she know about the study that found that readers have more empathy for their fellow human beings? It's because when we're reading, we're imagining *being* the characters we most admire. So we learn, over and over again, to think of what it's like to be someone else. That's what empathy is—being able to feel what the other person is feeling."

"Even fiction?"

"Yes, especially fiction."

"Maybe I'll look online for that study, so I can show it to Mom. It might get her off my back about working out or running."

"Have you ever listened to any books on tape? That might help you not be bored, you know, if you do decide to do some running. Treadmills are especially boring. But listening to a book being read to you makes the time pass quickly. I should know. That's how I force my lazy butt to run, even though I hate sweating in public."

James grinned. "I hate that too! And I always figure that the skinny people will be judging me, since I'm so fat."

Grant rolled his eyes. "What I could tell you about that! Some of us just have a huskier body shape. I have to work twice as hard as my brothers to look half as good as they do. But then, alphas are always in better shape than betas."

James looked at him in surprise. "You're an alpha, too, aren't you?"

Grant chuckled. "Um, no. What makes you think that?"

"You're so big. I mean, not just tall. You're wide. You look like a bodybuilder. I thought all men who looked like you were alphas."

Grant shook his head. "Nope. It's not a matter of body shape or size. Alpha-hood is deep inside of a man. It's where he knows he's a leader, and others recognize it and follow him. I don't want to be a leader. I'm happy to follow and let someone else make the hard decisions."

James was silent for a minute. When he spoke again, his face was serious, and his voice was quiet. "My dad was an alpha."

"I know," Grant replied gently. "And I know what happened. I'm sorry for your loss. Life can be so unfair, sometimes."

A shadow passed over the boy's face. He looked down at his hands, clearly trying to think of how to end their conversation. Grant took the hint.

"Well, I found myself a couple of new books to read, so I'm going to head out now. It was nice talking with you, James. And like I said, any time you want to talk about books, come and find me."

"Thanks, Grant. I'll remember that."

Grant stopped to let the librarian input the titles he'd chosen into her laptop, then he headed out the door.

Once he was back in his apartment, he tried to explain why he felt encouraged to his wolf, who did not share his enthusiasm.

Maybe the way to get to what's bothering Monique is to help her son find a better way to deal with his teenage angst.

This is not telling her that we are her mate. That we belong with her and her pups.

No, but this may help her see me as someone who can help her deal with her recalcitrant teenager.

I will not wait much longer. She must belong to us.

Grant sighed.

Yes, she will. But when she's ready.

He had to smile at his wolf's impatient growling in reply.

CHAPTER NINE

Saoirse was in the classroom part of her lab when her cell phone rang. She quickly answered when she saw Freddie's name on the screen.

"Hey, Freddie! Long time no chat! I figured you must be so busy with your new bestie that you didn't have any time left over for little ol' me!"

"Ha, ha, sweetie. As if! I never know when it's a good time to call you. Last time you were . . . ahem . . . busy with your husband, remember? And the time before that, you were working in your lab with that new guy who took John's place."

Saoirse chuckled. "You're right."

"Is now a good time?"

"Yeah, I'm in my lab, but not working on anything. I'm waiting for Monique to get here with the class lists so I can see how many kids I'll have in each class and who they are. Then I can begin to finalize my plans for the fall. But I can surely take a break for my oldest and bestest bestie! So how have you been?"

Freddie sighed. "Okay, I guess."

"That doesn't sound encouraging. I thought when you had John there full-time, you'd be in seventh heaven. You two hit it off so well while we were working on the wedding and all. He's been morose ever since then, so I wasn't surprised at all when he said he was taking a leave of absence. I was just surprised that it took him so long to do it. And I'm one of the only people he told where he went. I take it that Jorge is still in Mexico, so you two have all the privacy you need?"

"Yeah, but that's part of the problem. He wants to spend all of his time just with me."

"Didn't he get a job? I thought he said he planned on doing something to help pay the rent."

"Yes, he got a job as a bouncer at one of the clubs near here. We actually went there for your bachelorette party."

"Honey, we went to so many clubs that night that it's all a blur to me. But if he's working, and you're still working, you can't be getting sick of each other already?"

"No, that's not the problem."

Monique knocked quietly on the door, then pushed her head in. Saoirse nodded at her and waved for her to come in, but she continued talking. Monique came in and sat on the other high stool behind the teacher's desk and waited quietly. Saoirse was aware that with her enhanced wolfen hearing, Monique could hear what Freddie was saying as well as her part of the conversation. But Monique had met Freddie a few times and was a close friend of John's. She was one of the few who knew where John had gone — partly for security reasons. Plus, she was the soul of discretion, so Saoirse continued talking.

"Come on, sweetie, you can tell me. What's bothering you?"

Freddie sighed again, loudly. "It's just that — that I'm his first one, you know? The first man he's ever been with. So I figure that he needs some time to explore other options. I keep telling him that I'm okay with him being with other guys. I told him that's why I keep taking him to clubs — so he can meet other men and have quickie affairs with anyone that he wants to be with. But he tells me that he only wants to be with me. It's so weird. I mean, I can barely remember the first man I was with, and there's been a whole lot of them since then. Some I've forgotten, some I still remember with fondness. But to only have one man and be happy about being only with him? It's totally unnatural!"

Saoirse raised her eyebrows and mouthed at Monique, "Mated?"

Monique shrugged, before nodding back.

"How are things between you, though? Are you still happy that he moved there? Are you enjoying being with him?"

"Are you kidding? Have you met the man? Ever seen him in a bathing suit? Or nude?"

Saoirse giggled since she *had* seen John nude many times when he was shifting into his wolf. She didn't want to lie, so she showed Monique that she was crossing her fingers. Monique smiled.

"Um, no? Bathing suit, yes. But if you're happy with the relationship you have with him, then what's the problem?"

"You know I always hold back, right? I've been hurt a few times by falling in love and having that person cheat on me when I least expected it. That really hurts. But I'm falling so hard and so fast for this big guy that it scares me. And the fact that he doesn't seem to want any other man is unnerving. What if we agree to be exclusive, and in a few years, he gets the itch to try others on for size? I don't know if my heart could handle it."

"Listen, honey, John's from a family of loyal, trustworthy people. I don't know about his oldest sister, because she lives in Portland, and I've only met her a couple of times. But his parents were married for over sixty years before his dad passed on. His younger sister is married with a couple of kids. They're not the kind of people who cheat on those they love."

"But none of them are gay. You know how it is with you *cis folks*? The man is always pursuing getting laid, because sex is all he's thinking about, and you women are supposed to be the ones to turn it down and keep him under control?"

Saoirse giggled. "I've never been very good at that."

"But most females are, right?"

"I guess."

"Well, with gay men, there's no female holding anyone back. When men pursue each other, there's no one to say *no*."

"There's no worry about getting pregnant, so I guess that's part of the reason. But you do have to worry about STDs."

"Yeah, but that's the only concern. And condoms mostly take care of that worry. But you see what I mean? Other gay men find John as hot as I do. It's only a matter of time before he wants to see if any of them can satisfy him better than I can. I don't know how to act around him. The only arguments we've had have been when I try to suggest that he sleep around. He says he doesn't want to, and acts hurt, accusing me of getting bored with him."

"Are you?"

"Are you kidding me? He's so the man of my dreams that he scares me. Hot, responsive, and totally committed to wanting to be sure that I'm satisfied. And the more I teach him, the better he gets. I could so easily fall in love with him for keeps. Maybe I already have. But his lack of experience makes me feel like I'm taking advantage of his innocence. Sooner or later, he's going to want variety. What do I do?"

"I think you should stop second-guessing yourself and just go with your feelings. I mean, the people who live up here are kind of different. I went from being the new teacher to falling head-over-heels in love with the man who hired me. We were married within six months of my taking the job. Sudden, yes. But I've never been surer of anything in my life."

Freddie was quiet for a while before he spoke in almost a whisper. "Then, you think it's safe for me to let myself fall in love with him?"

Saoirse smiled, watching Monique nodding.

"I think you can trust him not to hurt you, Freddie. And you know I've loved you for so long that if he ever did, I'd have to kick his ass all the way back here to Maine. I think you need to stop worrying and just go with your feelings. Weird as it sounds, some people really *do* fall in love with their first lover, and it can be a love that lasts."

Monique was nodding again, with a far-away look in her eyes.

Freddie sighed once more. "I know it's ridiculous for me to be worrying about this, but it's scary to be falling so hard for someone I know so little about. He gets cagey when I ask him questions, sometimes. I get the feeling that he's hiding something about himself. But I have no idea what it could be."

Saoirse took a deep breath. "Just trust him, Freddie. If he says he loves you, believe him. And if he doesn't want other men, believe him. I don't think he'll disappoint you."

"Okay, girl. It's getting close to when I have to get ready for work. Thanks for listening to me."

"Any time, you know that. Well, maybe not when I'm having sex with my man. But any time other than that!"

Freddie chuckled. "Ditto."

"It's good to hear that I can still make you laugh. I don't like to hear you sounding so unsure of yourself. You're *Freddie the magnificent*, remember? Men want you *and* want to be you. Remember that."

"Thanks, Sam. You're the only one I trust so much. I love you."

"Love you too, sweetie. Talk to you again, soon. I'll call you next time, okay?"

"Deal. Bye, love."

Saoirse hung up and met Monique's gaze.

"I married my first."

Saoirse couldn't hold back her surprise. "Tim was your first?"

"Yes. I was way into my studies when I was in high school, trying to earn scholarships to college. Plus, so many of my friends got pregnant too early that I knew I didn't want to do that. I met Tim when we were in grad school. He was surprised I was still a virgin at twenty-one. But we both knew instantly that we were mated."

"Your wolves told you?"

"Yes. But we knew, too, even without listening to them. I know I wasn't his first, but he hadn't had much experience with women. We learned everything there was to know from each other. And I could have been happy being with only him for the rest of my life. It never would have occurred to me to wonder what anyone else was like."

Saoirse shook her head. "See, I just don't understand that. I mean, I used to fall in love multiple times a day, when I first moved out to go to college. There were just so many cute men to choose from. How could I pick just one? Then once my classes got really intense, I didn't have time for anyone. Feast to famine. Once I started working on my masters, it was weird, because I didn't want to sleep with any men in my department, in case things ended poorly, and they'd be the ones giving me a recommendation.

"It was even worse once I graduated and was working full-time in a lab. I didn't have time to meet many guys. I'd been on kind of a long drought when I came here. And since Diego was the principal of the school, and the one who hired me, I thought he was off limits. But things moved along very quickly, and once I found out it was reciprocal, there seemed no reason to stall. Little did I know that he and his wolf had already decided that I was their mate, and I'd have no choice in the matter."

Monique smirked. "You didn't fight very hard against him."

"Of course I didn't! You've seen him, right?"

"Not my type."

"I know. You said you like them tall, skinny, and blond.

Like Nathan, but not *him* because he's your bestie."

"Yeah." Monique sighed, looking off into the distance.

Saoirse took a deep breath, deciding to take a chance. "So . . . What about Grant?"

Monique jerked her head back and stared at her, mouth agape.

Now that she'd started, Saoirse quickly blurted out the rest. "I mean, it's obvious that he wants you to be his mate. He's always watching you. I know he's kind of a body-builder-shaped guy, not skinny. But he's tall, and definitely blond. I mean, I'm whiter than white, what with my red hair and all. But in a *white-off*, he might win, depending on how white his ass turns out to be."

Despite her dark skin, it was obvious Monique was blushing. "I've never seen his ass. What I mean is, I have, but only from a distance, and right before a shift. And he certainly is a very *white*, white man."

"And he obviously wants you. What's stopping you? Or doesn't your wolf want to be his mate?"

Monique shook her head slowly. "Actually, she's been bugging me about presenting ourselves to him since he moved here."

"Then what's stopping you?"

"You don't know what it's like to have kids. The girls aren't causing me much grief, yet, but James is totally out of control. He never talks to me, so I have no idea what he's thinking. But he over-eats, seemingly on purpose. He never wants to do any exercise of any kind. He's always got his nose in a book, wasting all his time on that science fiction crap. And he doesn't have any friends and says he doesn't need any. I honestly don't know what to do with him anymore."

Saoirse kept her voice gentle, hoping to soothe her friend. "Maybe having a man around would be a calming influence on him. You've been mother and father to your kids for a long time. Maybe it's time to let someone else help you out."

Monique looked desperate. "But what if it isn't? What if that's the final straw that makes James explode? What if he runs away from home or something? What will I do then? Tell him I'm sorry, but now that I've mated, there's no going back to the way things used to be? Tell him he's got no choice but to accept that I have another mate to replace his late father? It might work out, but it also might be a huge disaster! I just don't know!"

Monique hid her face in her hands for a minute. She looked up slowly, her shoulders still shaking with unshed sobs. "My children are all I have left of Tim. I can't risk losing any of them—not for anyone. Grant and our wolves just have to wait until I get things sorted out with James."

Saoirse spoke slowly. "You're right, in that I don't have any kids of my own. Yet. But I did practically raise the other seven who came after me. And no matter what people say, it's harder to raise boys than girls. I mean, once you stop worrying about your daughter's virginity, then girls practically raise themselves. And when they're having emotional problems, they'll tell you about them—sometimes way more than you want to hear."

She gave an exaggerated shudder before continuing. "But boys? They have it rougher, trying to grow into men. Our society expects so much of them and teaches them so very little about how to become men. The old rules said they were expected to be tough and never express feelings of any kind. Except anger. They were allowed to be angry but were never to appear vulnerable, or to express self-doubt. No one can live like that for long. It's no wonder they crack so spectacularly, grabbing guns to kill each other, or starting fights for no reason. Or they do too much drinking and drugging to anesthetize themselves against the feelings that all humans have, but that they're not allowed to acknowledge they feel. Yes, boys are a lot harder to raise than girls."

"The rules haven't changed much, have they?"

"Nope. Only now they're also supposed to be nurturing to babies and small children and to allow those feelings when they've been taught their whole lives that men don't cry. How can you care for tiny people if you can't cry? It can't be done. I can't tell you how many times I saw my dad cry, and I never thought any less of him for it. In fact, it was his way to show how deeply he loved his family. And I respected him for being able to be honest about what he felt. To me, that's a strong man."

"Tim was a good man. He was a great father, also. I was so unprepared to have to take everything onto myself. I've been doing the best I can for five years. It terrifies me that maybe that's not good enough for my son."

"Maybe Grant can help. After all, he's a man. Maybe James will respond differently to him."

"Maybe. Or maybe he'll resent some other man being with his mom, and he'll act out even more. There's no way to predict. I could ask him about it, but how? He never talks to me. Even when I ask him direct questions, he acts like he didn't hear me and sticks his nose back into a book."

"I wish I could help. But there is *something* I can do." Saoirse got up and walked over to Monique and wrapped her arms around her troubled friend. "Sometimes, a hug helps. Draw on some of my strength. I'm not using it right now. And know that you're doing your best. Your kids love you. Yes, even James. Remember that saying about it taking a village to raise kids? Maybe you need to let other villagers help you with him."

Monique's shoulders shook for a while as her dry sobs escaped her lips. Saoirse held on until, eventually, Monique quieted down and returned the embrace.

"Thanks, Sam. There're very few people I trust enough to

talk about this with them. Thanks for being here for me."

Their gazes met, and Saoirse smiled. "Hey, I'm not the only one who cares a lot about you. You just have to be strong enough to ask for help, instead of trying to do everything by yourself. You're a school principal, you're the second in command of the pack, and you're raising three kids by yourself. You may be one of the strongest women I've ever met, but we all need friends to lean on when things get rough."

"I know. But it's not how I was raised. It's hard for me. I'll definitely think about what you said. Maybe I can share some of my worries with Grant. Or maybe with some other man, like Nathan."

"Or Diego. He *is* your pack leader, after all. If it affects anyone in the pack, he feels responsible. He'd be glad to at least listen, and maybe give some advice. Maybe he could have a chat with James."

"Maybe. Anyway, I came here to give you these," she handed a stack of papers to Saoirse. "It's the most current enrollment lists that I have. I hope this is what you need to plan your classes."

"Yeah, this is what I wanted. Thanks."

"And thanks for listening. I feel a little better now. I'd better be getting back to my office to see if any new fires need to be put out."

"Okay, Monique. But remember, I'm available any time to talk if you need me."

Monique grinned. "As long as you're not having sex with my pack leader?"

Saoirse flushed as she burst out laughing. "I knew you were hearing every word! Yes, as long as we're not doing the nasty. But any other time."

"Thanks. See you later."

"Bye, Monique."

Saoirse sat back in her chair and stared at nothing as she

pondered her friends' confidences. *I don't know who to worry about more — Freddie, or Monique. I'll have to talk with Diego about both of them later. Maybe he'll be able to think of a way to help them. At least he'll be able to share my worries about them.* Shared worries weigh less, *as Ma always says.*

Resolutely, she returned to working on preparing for her classes, which would be starting in the very near future.

CHAPTER TEN

Grant looked around the library entrance, once again inhaling deeply. The librarian was at her familiar perch, and she smiled when she saw him.

"A man who loves books that much is a deep thinker. Welcome back, son. The books missed you."

He smiled back at her. "Thanks. I'm returning the ones I'm finished with and looking for more." He put the two books on the counter, before asking, casually, "That new guy who's helping you with shelving books. What do you think of him?"

"You mean Dan? He's only here a few times a week. He picks up the heavy boxes that I'm not able to move anymore. He told me that his real interest is working with kids. He says he used to be an aide at a few parochial schools. He's been helping out with the little ones, entertaining them during the summer, when they're not in school. He's okay, I guess. Why do you ask?"

Grant shrugged. "Just wondering. I ran into Monique's son, James, here last time, and he mentioned that he and Dan spoke a few times."

"James is my favorite student! He's always offering to help me out around here. He spends almost as much time here as I do. He's a very deep thinker, that boy. I wish we had more like him around."

"Is he here now?"

She nodded. "Yes. He's around somewhere. Head back to the sci-fi section. That's where he usually sits."

"That's where I'm going anyway. See you in a bit."

Grant enjoyed the shadows cast by the sun bouncing off the bookshelves as he made his way to the same group of tables and chairs where he'd found James sitting at the last time. As he got closer, he could hear quiet voices. One speaker was James, and the other was a lower, male voice. On instinct, he approached them quietly, getting closer so that he could see them without them seeing him. He watched their interaction through the gaps between the tops of the books and the next level of shelving.

James had pulled a chair over to the windows again, and had a book on his lap. He was looking up at the man who was standing next to his chair. James was talking animatedly about what he was reading. But it was the man's stance that made Grant's spine tingle with warning.

The man had one arm over the back of James's chair and was watching him steadily. His hips were pushed forward, his groin against the side of the large armchair, and he appeared to be slowly moving himself back and forth. James was oblivious to any impropriety, but Grant had warning alarms going off all over inside of his head. He decided to interrupt their meeting. He strode forward casually as if he'd just gotten there.

"Hi, James. I'm here for more books. I can see that you are, also." He turned to face the man, who had immediately straightened up when Grant appeared.

The man's face was flushed, and he appeared furtive and guilty at the same time.

"And you must be Dan, the guy who is helping the librarian out by moving boxes of books around for her. I'm Grant Knutsen, fourth in security." He put a special emphasis on the word *security*. Grant held out his hand, and reluctantly, the other man took it for a brief handshake.

"I'm Dan Hadsburg."

This is the one we fought! When the young couple was mating. He tried to interfere.

Grant forced himself to act as if he had no idea who the other man was. "I'm still new here, learning who everyone is and what their jobs are. What do you do when you're not helping in the library?"

Dan mumbled. "I have a degree in early education. I've worked at a few schools, but it seems there's no need for me here since there's only a high school. I've been helping out with the little kids during the summer. Not sure what I'll do when school starts."

"That explains why I haven't seen you before. I'm usually in the academic wing, helping Saoirse with her research, or outside helping the gardeners. I am surprised I haven't seen you in the gym at all, or at the pool."

"I . . . uh . . . I'm kind of a loner. I do things like go to the gym or run at night when there's less people around."

"I see."

Grant turned to James. "I see you're reading the third book in the *Pern* series already. How are you liking them?"

James's voice reflected his excitement. "They're great books! And I have so many favorite parts and characters. I especially like the part about having another being able to talk to you in your mind. That's so cool!"

As James talked about his favorite parts of the series, Grant kept a steady eye on Dan, who was shifting from one foot to the other.

When Dan looked up to see Grant watching him, he suddenly checked his watch. "Will you look at the time? I have to be somewhere else now. I'll see you later, James." He nodded at Grant and turned to walk out of the area.

The minute he wasn't visible anymore, Grant felt himself relax. His wolf agreed.

We need to watch that one. Something is not right with him.

Grant nodded, even though his wolf already knew he agreed. Then he gave full attention to James, and they spent some time discussing the Pern books.

Diego was in his office, dealing with real estate tax documents, wishing he had a lawyer sitting next to him. When the phone rang, he picked it up quickly, since he'd been waiting for a call back from the pack lawyer, Jennifer. When he saw John as the caller, it was such a welcome distraction, he didn't bother to disguise his joy.

"Hi, John. It's so good to hear from you! How are things in Boston? And when are you coming home?"

"Hey, Diego. I wish this was a social call, but unfortunately, it's not. There's something you have to know."

"What? You sound really intense. What is it, old friend?"

"Remember when I told you I would check out the new guy that petitioned to join the pack a few months ago? He said that he'd been a teacher's aide in some parochial schools. You mentioned he might be useful with helping Suzy, since her baby is almost old enough for her to resume her school for the elementary kids. I asked a friend of mine from college, who's in the state police department, to check him out for us—on the Q.T., of course. She says it took her a while because he hadn't been at public schools, who keep better records. Turns out he was at a couple of Catholic schools and was asked to leave each time. But they don't pass information along to each other, let alone to anyone else. Luckily, my friend is a practicing Roman Catholic, and she was able to convince the principals that our new member might have access to young children, so we needed to know about him."

Diego had an uneasy feeling in his stomach. "And what did she find out?"

"He's a pedophile, all right. He doesn't like the really little ones. His preferred age is pre-teens. He really likes middle school-aged kids. He doesn't care what sex they are. He got in trouble at one school for molesting a couple of girls, but at the other school, it was the boys in a scout troop that he was abusing while helping out as a volunteer."

Diego uttered a long stream of profanities in Spanish, mad at himself for missing any sign the man had such tendencies.

John waited until Diego finished his growling before asking, "Do you want me to come back and help you evict him?"

"Not unless you're already planning on coming back home. Your mom misses you, you know."

"Yeah, I know. I miss all of you, too. But I'm still looking for answers as to where I belong. I'm still not sure."

"I'm sure that Grant will be able to help us out. He's a pretty big guy, and this Dan person is kind of puny."

"Maybe. But remember, some guys are like Nathan. He looks thin, but he's wiry and all muscle. You need to get that guy out of the compound before the kids arrive. That's what, in a couple of weeks?"

"Yes. They'll start arriving on the fifteenth of August, and classes start on the twentieth."

"That's why I kept calling her and bugging her. But once she had answers for me, I promised her dinner, if she ever gets to Boston. Knowing her, she'll take me up on that."

"Okay, John. Thanks for the info. I'll call an emergency meeting with the board tonight, and we'll deal with removing this guy. But otherwise, how are you?"

"If you're trying to be delicate about asking me if Freddie and I are cool, it's okay. We are. It's still a new thing for both of us, though, to be living with someone we're involved with. I'm working as a bouncer at a club near here, which has been okay, but I'm thinking of dusting off my accounting degree to see if I can find something that pays an actual salary."

"Let me know if there's anything we can do to help you out. We owe you big time for this one."

"Hey, my heart is with the academy, you know that. It's been my life for so many years that it will always be a part of me. Besides, my wolf is angry enough to want me to run home and personally kick this guy's ass. Wolves don't understand how grown men could want to hurt children. It offends their sense of right and wrong."

"And he's a shifter, too. I wonder how his wolf manages to live in his head."

"Who knows? Anyway, I've got to get ready for my job at the club soon. Give my love to Saoirse. I call Mom every Sunday, and sometimes I get to talk to Jerene, too. But Monique, Nathan, Grant, let them all know I think about them, and hope things are going well for them."

"Will do, buddy. Good to hear from you. Take care."

After ending the call, Diego sent out a group text to the board for an emergency meeting to be held after dinner, mandatory attendance.

When Diego shared his news with the board, there were shocked looks on almost all of the faces around the table. All except for Grant, who merely nodded grimly.

"I suspected something like that," Grant said. "The guy's been hanging around in the library, and he told James to call him by his first name. I met him earlier today, and my wolf didn't like him at all. He told me that Dan's the guy who was trying to interrupt the mating between the two young wolves a few weeks ago." He turned to Monique. "Remember?"

Monique's expression displayed her shock at the mention of her son's name. "He's been talking to James? Why didn't I know about this? Why didn't you tell me?"

"I didn't know who he was until today. James told me a week ago, in the library, when we were talking about books. He'd mentioned Dan was volunteering at the library, helping out the librarian. And Dolores seemed to think he was an okay guy. It wasn't until I saw him lurking over James today and interrupted their chat to introduce myself that I actually met him. My wolf recognized him and warned me that something isn't right with him."

Monique sputtered her outrage. "He's been talking with *my* son, and I didn't know about it? What if he's tried something with James?"

Grant tried to soothe her. "James didn't appear to even realize there was anything weird about him. He just thinks he's a nice man who likes books."

"Well, I'm going to give that *nice man* a piece of my mind — at the end of my fist!" She stood, ready to follow through.

Diego spoke firmly. "No, you won't. Sit down, Monique."

"But he's my son!"

"And we're going to have a whole lot of other people's sons and daughters arriving here very soon. This needs to be handled quietly. I'll call Dan into my office tomorrow and tell him that we've decided things aren't working out for him to join the pack. I don't like to send someone out who knows how we operate here, but there's no choice now. Nathan, you will need to be here, to accompany him back to his place, and to wait while he packs. Then you will escort him to the gate and be sure he goes through it."

"Why not me?" Grant asked.

Diego shook his head. "No. Your wolf fought his once already. He might see your presence as an invitation to fight again."

Monique sputtered. "Why—"

"No," Diego said, shaking his head again. "Not you. You have too much of a personal stake in getting him removed. Nathan will be impartial."

"I could be here and accompany both of them." Saoirse flashed an evil grin. "No one expects little ol' me to be a fighter. But I can punch out a man twice my size before he even knows what hit him."

"Um, no? I'm not letting my wife get involved with

someone who could pose a threat. I'll ask Diya to be present at the gate, so she can also make sure there's no trouble. I'll ask her to tell as few guards as possible about why we're evicting him, but we do want to be sure he doesn't get back in. Grant, you provide back-up for Nathan. Try to stay out of sight, but keep them in view. That way we'll know for sure that he's gone. That will be a huge relief" — he stared directly into Monique's eyes — "for *all* of us."

He looked around at everyone. "Are we all agreed?"

Heads nodded. Eventually, slowly, Monique nodded also.

"Fine. This meeting is adjourned."

"Monique, wait!" Grant chased after her, as she almost ran down the hall.

"No," she said over her shoulder. "I don't have anything to say to you."

He moved quicker and caught up to her, then reached out and grabbed onto her shoulders and forced her to face him. "I'm not the enemy here, Monique. The first time I saw James in the library, I told him he could call me by my first name. He told me that another man had told him the same thing. That's the first time I heard about this Dan guy. Dolores seemed to think he was an okay worker, so since I hadn't met him, I wasn't worried. But when I saw him talking to James today, I got a bad feeling, so I introduced myself. That's when my wolf warned me. I was planning on telling you the next time I saw you."

Emotions raged across Monique's face as she struggled with what to say. Finally, despair seemed to win out over anger. "So what should I do? Forbid him to go outside? Keep him locked up, like he's in jail? I thought the library was a safe enough place for him."

"And it will be once this guy's been removed. And I'll keep

tabs on James. I'm trying to use our mutual love of sci-fi books to form a bond of trust between us. I'm hoping that maybe he'll open up to me if he won't talk to you."

"Why? You're not family. You're a stranger. What are you to him? Nothing."

Grant used one hand under her chin to raise her head slightly, so she was looking into his eyes. "I want to be so much more to him. I want to be your mate. I want to help you raise your kids. Why won't you let me love you?"

His wolf pushed him over the edge, and he let out a low growl as he lowered his head quickly to claim her lips. That first taste was heaven! He was a drowning man, and she was the air he needed to survive. At first, she was unresponsive, but he deepened the kiss, leaning closer to her, and tracing a line with his fingers, from her face to her ear, then into the hair on the back of her head.

With a moan, she capitulated and returned his passion in equal measure. He licked at her lips, and she opened her mouth to allow their tongues to duel. Their breathing became synced, breathing in and out in unison. Her hands traced a path from his waist up his back to rub his shoulders, attempting to encompass their width. Then her hands moved lower, massaging his glutes, as their kissing became frenzied.

Grant had never felt so hard in his life. She pressed her mons against him and rotated her hips, making things so much worse for him—and oh, so good! His hands moved of their own volition, and he began working to remove her clothing, determined to strip her naked, and claim her as his for the rest of their lives, right there and then!

Suddenly Monique's phone buzzed audibly from her back pocket. The noise pulled them both back into reality, though she recovered quicker, pushing him back.

"No!" she growled. "Not here! Not now. Not like this—in a public place."

"Then where? I'll follow you anywhere. You own me."

She shook her head, pulling her cell phone out to look at the message. "It's time for me to read to my kids for their bedtimes. Then I need to have a chat with James. It isn't a good time for this, Grant. I'm sorry."

He struggled to bring himself back from the brink, leaning forward to rest his forehead against hers. "Not nearly as sorry as I am," he said in a husky voice, rough from passion.

"Soon, I promise." She pushed him away again, then turned and almost ran down the hallway.

Grant stood and watched her go, then leaned back against the wall, weakly, feeling the need to regain his strength to be able to move. He took some deep breaths to gain control over his breathing. Eventually, he was able to make his limbs obey his commands again, and he forced himself to walk back to his apartment.

Once there, he pulled out a bottle of single malt Scotch, which he had been drinking sparingly for years. It was used only for those occasions when a shot or two was called for.

And this is just such an occasion.

She was almost ours! Why did you stop?

She pushed me away.

We're bigger and stronger than her.

I will not force myself on her. It has to be her choice, too.

The sounds of his wolf raging in his head were eventually drowned out by the fuzzy insulation of a few shots of the potent alcohol. And when Grant finally collapsed on his bed, naked, he was too dispirited even to satisfy his longings himself.

CHAPTER ELEVEN

M onique's thoughts were morose as she headed to her office for an appointment with the parents of a prospective student. She knew why her mood was so dark.

When she'd gotten back to her apartment, she'd sent her nanny back home and read a couple of chapters of their latest favorite book to her girls. Then she'd kissed them both and told them goodnight. And had steeled herself for an encounter with her son.

James had his door locked, as usual. She knocked on it until he opened it to let her in, then she went to perch on the window ledge where he usually sat to read. He returned to his bed, where the book he was reading was placed face down.

"James, I want you to stay in the apartment tomorrow," she began.

"Aw, Mom! What am I? A baby? I'm going to be a freshman in the academy. I'm thirteen, Mom. I don't need a babysitter!"

"There's something happening tomorrow morning that I want you to stay clear of. There's a man who has been living here who will be getting escorted out of the compound."

He looked at her expectantly.

"He's . . . uh . . . not the kind of person we want living here when the students all arrive."

"Why not?"

Monique had never talked about sex with her son, mostly because he never wanted to talk to her, or to listen. This was the most words they'd shared in over a year. She tried to think of something to say that would warn him off, but also not scare him.

"He's . . . um . . . not working out in the job he applied for. So he's going to be asked to leave, and Nathan will see to it that he does."

"Why, Mom? Is he some kind of pedophile?"

She blinked, looking at him in shock. "What do you know about that?"

James sighed heavily. "Like I said, Mom, I'm not a baby. I know there are bad men in the world who like to molest kids. I chose clowns for my last research paper because I used to be afraid of them. While I was researching, I read all about Gacy. I know what he did to all of those boys."

"We don't know that much about this man. But we do know that he was asked to leave a couple of schools, for incidents that they won't tell us much about."

"How about if I just stay inside for the morning? He'll be gone by lunchtime, right? So I can go outside in the afternoon?"

Monique shook her head. "I don't feel comfortable with that. I'll be in meetings all day with parents who want to send their kids here. I won't be able to check on you."

He jumped up to pace in front of her. "Why do you keep treating me like a baby? I'm thirteen, Mom! Some guys have jobs by my age. And I'm lots smarter than anyone gives me credit for. I have street smarts, too. I read a lot, and you learn things from books."

She walked over to pick up the book lying on his bed. "Yeah, I'm sure you learn lots from them," she said sarcastically. "Things like how to ride dragons around, how to live on other planets. Really useful stuff."

"You just don't understand! Why don't you talk to Grant? He told me that studies show that readers have more empathy. We understand people more. He's the one who told me about this book series. And it's really good, too. You're just insulting it because you don't know how much you can learn from sci-fi books. Things like all about human nature and stuff."

Monique's arm twitched, tempted to slap her son for being disrespectful. But that wasn't the answer here. He was certainly too big for her to spank, and she refused to discipline him the way she'd always hated being treated by her own mother. So she got up and walked towards the door. "I'm sure. If Grant says it, it must be true. But you hear me, James Timothy Martin, you are not to leave your room tomorrow. I'll ask Mrs. Landon to have your meals brought up to you."

"Just like in prison," he spat out.

"Don't think of it that way. Think of it as room service in a hotel. I'll see you all later tomorrow afternoon. I probably won't be done until close to dinnertime, but when I get back here, I hope we can both be more civil to each other."

With that, she turned and walked out of the room. The instant she closed the door behind her, she heard him lock it. Monique leaned against the wall next to his door and sighed, rubbing her temples. Her head was aching, as it did every time she tried to talk to her son. *Timothy, why did you leave me? I really need you now, because our son is out of control! I don't know if I can handle this anymore.*

We are stronger than you think, her wolf assured her.

I sure hope so.

She made her way to her room and swallowed a couple of pain pills for her headache before taking a long shower, trying to relax. It took a long time for her thoughts to stop racing like squirrels on crack running inside her head. Then, just as she was beginning to drift off to sleep, she remembered how it felt to be in Grant's arms.

Instantly, she felt herself respond to the memory as if it was happening right then. She squirmed in her bed, wanting more of the man. At the same time, a part of her brain screamed at her that she was being unfaithful to the memory of her late husband, whom she'd promised to love forever.

Until death do you part, her wolf reminded her. *He's been gone for years. We hunger for the touch of that man and his wolf. They are our mates now.*

Groaning in frustration at her inability to fall asleep, Monique dragged herself out of bed and got a sleeping pill. She peered closely at the bottle as she swallowed one with some water. *Only two more left. It's been a rough year. I need to ask Rachel for more.*

No, we need to do a good, long run. It's been too long since you let me lead.

Not when I've got so much to worry about.

She ignored the snort of disapproval from her wolf and returned to her bed. It took a few minutes for the pill to take effect. During that time, she tossed and turned, remembering Grant's touch, his smell, and the taste of his mouth.

Impatiently, she pulled her nightgown up and touched herself. It didn't take long before she moaned with the pleasure of her quickie orgasm. Miraculously, she didn't have time to lie in bed feeling guilty over that. As her pulse gradually slowed back to normal, the pill helped her slide into a fitful, dreamless sleep.

As she unlocked the door to her office the next morning, she tried to rearrange her face into a smile that would appear welcoming to the eager parents. But all she could think of was what a shit-show her life had become. When she looked in the mirror on the back of her door, she realized she needed to apply some serious makeup to erase the bags under her eyes and look presentable to strangers. Once she was satisfied that at least she wouldn't frighten the parents away, she sat at her desk and began to review their files so she'd be ready for their questions.

When she returned to her apartment later that afternoon, Monique was exhausted, even though she was finished earlier than she'd thought she would be. She'd put on a good show all day, and all the parents she'd interviewed wanted to send their students to the academy. They'd begun the paperwork and promised to send it back to her in plenty of time for them to enroll their children before the school year started.

As she opened the door, her daughters, who were sitting in front of the TV screen and playing video games, both jumped up to give her hugs and kisses.

Monique looked at the nanny. "Where's James?"

Mrs. Landon shrugged. "Where he always is. In his room. The last time he opened his door was when I knocked and told him lunch was here. He reached out to grab the tray, then locked his door again."

Monique was irritated that James would be so rude to the woman who had been watching her kids for years. She quickly strode to his room and knocked loudly on the door. When there was no response, her anger rose even higher.

"James! You open this door right now! I want to talk to you, now!"

Still no response. Monique cursed under her breath, mindful of the girls who had resumed their gaming but were none-the-less listening to her. She walked over to the kitchen and grabbed the ring of keys to the individual rooms and quickly returned to her son's door. She made one last attempt to reason with him.

"James, you need to open this door right now. If you don't, and I have to use the key to unlock it, you'll be in big trouble, young man!"

Wearily she waited for the response that never came. With a sigh, she inserted the key and unlocked the door, then pushed it open. She moved into the room, dreading having to hit her child, yet positive that was the only way to discipline an unruly teenager. Her own mother used to tell her that as she delivered repeated blows with a hairbrush.

"James?" Her heart sank as she looked around and saw no sign of her son. "Where are you?"

The empty lunch tray was on the bed, but he was nowhere to be seen, not in the closet, and not in the bathroom that he shared with his sisters. Monique's heart started to pound with a feeling bordering on panic. It wasn't possible he'd gone along with that Dan person when he was evicted, was it? And why would he do that? She hadn't mentioned his name on purpose.

She hurried out of his room, back to question Mrs. Landon and her daughters. None of them had seen James since he took his lunch tray. But when the girls started to whimper with fear, Monique realized that her anxiety was affecting them. She tried to force herself to sound calmer. Mrs. Landon agreed to stay with the girls until she returned. Then she moved out into the hall and sent out a group text to the security board members: *James not in his room. Window was open. Has anyone seen him?*

When she got down to the foyer, Grant, Nathan, and Diego were already there, waiting for her.

Nathan spoke first. "He wasn't with Dan when he left the compound. I watched him leave alone, a bit before eleven."

"Did you check to see if James took his book with him?" Grant asked.

Monique gave him a scornful look. "What book? They're all over his room."

"The one he's been reading now. The third *Pern* book," he answered evenly, obviously modulating his voice in an attempt to thwart her incipient panic.

"I don't know! Why? Does it matter?"

"I think I know where he could be," he answered. "There are a few trees near the forest, out back, that have low-enough branches that he'd be able to climb onto."

With that, they all started moving quickly towards the back of the mansion.

She poked at him. "A tree? Why would he be up in a tree?"

He looked apologetic. "I told him that's where I used to spend hours reading my books, safely hidden from my pesky brothers."

Monique's voice went shrill with fear for her son. "Why the hell would you tell him to go hide in a tree? With everything that's been going on around here? What were you thinking?"

"Let's just see if we can find him," Diego broke into their argument. "Nothing else really matters right now."

He pushed open the door, and they all raced onto the back stairs.

"We'll split up," Diego said. "Find trees that have low branches that could give a child a leg up and see if he's in any of them."

They fanned out, heading towards the line of trees that signaled the beginning of the forest. As they moved, they all called out for James.

"James! If you can hear my voice, answer me!" Monique was almost screaming as she craned her neck to peer up into trees, looking for any sign of her disobedient son. The search went on for the next fifteen minutes—the longest fifteen minutes of her life. Her fear threatened to overwhelm her anger, and she fought hard not to burst into tears.

"Found him!" Grant's voice came from a distance.

Monique raced over, but by the time she got to where they were, Nathan and Diego were already there. Grant was reaching up and helping James climb down from one of the tallest oak trees in the area.

When James reached the ground, he looked around in surprise at the assembled adults. "What are you all doing out here?"

Monique ran up to him and slapped him hard across the face. His glasses flew off his face, and he gave her a stony look.

"I told you not to leave the apartment today! What the hell were you doing out here?"

She pulled her hand back to hit him again, and he looked resigned to another slap.

Grant grabbed her wrist. "No," he said to her, his voice firm but calm.

"Don't you tell me how to treat my son!" she screeched.

Diego walked in between Grant and Monique both to neutralize her anger, and to assert his authority over her son.

"James, you scared the hell out of your mother. You disobeyed her, and you will be punished. You will report to me tomorrow morning at eight. By then, I will have decided on pack justice. But until then, you are confined to your room. Do you understand me, young man?"

James nodded sullenly. Nathan handed him the glasses that he'd picked up, and James put them back on. They sat crooked on his face, and he glared at his mother, who'd bent them. Nathan took his arm and moved with him, accompanying him back to the mansion.

Diego turned to Monique. "I know he's your son, but don't even think of telling me it's none of my business. Everything that happens here is my business. I know how upset you are. But I can't allow you to beat your son in public like this."

Tears of anger and frustration ran down Monique's face. "You don't know what it's like."

"No, but I do." Saoirse joined them and moved over to take Monique's hand.

"Sorry I'm late, but I was in the middle of something. I got here as quickly as I could. Come with me, Monique. You need to rage and scream a bit before you have to face your kids again. You can do that in my place, and no one will hear you." Saoirse turned to face him and Grant.

Diego knew his gratitude for her arrival had replaced the harshness of his pack leader demeanor. Grant looked conflicted, as if he wanted to go with them, but knew that he'd be unwelcome.

"Gentlemen, you should go eat your dinner. Diego, I'll see you later." Saoirse pulled Monique's hand, almost dragging her back to the mansion.

The women disappeared through the door while Diego and Grant watched them.

Diego spoke first. "It's for the best. Her panic has been replaced with relief, but she's also still seething with anger. She needs time to realize that it should not be directed at you."

Grant shook his head. "I thought that by making friends with James, I could show her what a good father I could be. She's refusing me because of her trouble with him. But if she'd let me help her, I think together we could present a united front that he'd be unable to resist. See, I think there's something bothering him, but I don't know what it is."

"Teenagers are moody on the best of days. And this was definitely not one of the best days—for anyone." Diego reached out and patted Grant's arm. "Let's go have some dinner. I have a feeling my wife is going to be too occupied to come down to dine with me tonight. I'll ask Janine to send a couple of trays up to them."

"Okay."

They walked together towards the back stairs.

CHAPTER TWELVE

The next few days passed uneventfully for James. Diego's punishment had been that he had to replace Dan in the library. He was ordered to do everything that Mrs. Moretta asked him to do. He was to report to her at nine in the morning, five days a week, take only a quick half-hour lunch break, then return to work until four in the afternoon.

"And since this is the time of year when she's getting boxes of books delivered for the start of the school year, you're going to be a busy man."

James, who was at first thrilled at his punishment being in his favorite place, soon learned how seriously out of shape he was. After his first few days, he was exhausted and sore from picking up and moving boxes around. He barely had the energy to drag himself to dinner, then he'd go back up to his room intending to read. But he would fall asleep within the first few pages.

Grant visited the library on the fifth day of James's punishment, stopping to talk with the librarian on the way in. "Good afternoon, Delores. How's the new kid working out for you?"

She grinned. "I don't know what he did to deserve this, but he's working his butt off for me."

"Didn't you hear about it?"

She shook her head. "Heavens, no. I don't listen to gossip. I'm too old to care about that sort of rubbish. I judge people by how they act around me. That's all I have time for. I've always liked James because he reads so much. He spends more time here than any other kid. Of course, now, he's not enjoying it as much as he used to."

Grant leaned on the counter. "Has he ever mentioned being troubled by anything?"

Her bright blue eyes met his, and she stared for a moment before she shook her head. "No, he's never said anything," she answered slowly. "But something eats at him. It's just a feeling I have, but I'm sure of it. There's something he thinks about a lot but never talks about. I don't think it's just the usual angst. There's something more to it. Why do you ask?"

"Um, because he's a nice kid."

"And you want to mate with his mother. You figure that if you can get close to her son, maybe she'll trust you enough with her kids to accept your proposal."

He stared at her, open-mouthed. "I thought you don't listen to gossip."

She grinned. "I don't. But when a grown man befriends a young man like James, there are only two possible reasons. I understand that Dan was nice to him for the worst of those two reasons. I could kick myself for not realizing it. But my sciatica doesn't let me walk around much, so I never really saw the two of them together."

"I thought as much. No one blames you."

"But you? I know you're not that kind of man. You're a booklover and a deep thinker. Like James. That commonality will stand you in good stead as you help her raise her son to be a man. But first you have to convince her to accept your help. Having a relationship with her son is a very good start."

"So, where is he?"

"He's in the back, emptying boxes of books that are needed for the English classes and putting them on carts, based on the enrollment lists for each class. You just go through that door there," she waved her hand to the side, pointing to the sign for the restrooms. "Go past the restrooms, and there's a door marked *Private*. Go on back there, and you'll see how hard he's working."

Grant followed her directions and pushed the door open, only to be assailed by the heavy smell of a teenaged boy's sweat.

Wow! No wonder Mom always complained about the smell of our rooms. Did I smell this bad when my hormones were turning on?

His wolf snorted at him. *You humans are funny. You cover up your natural smells, then wonder why others don't know how to relate to you. Let them smell your emotions, and they'll know.*

He grinned when he saw James, pushing a cart heavy with books, come around the corner. "So, how goes it, being a working man?"

James looked at him, pushing his still-crooked glasses up his sweaty nose, and blowing at an errant strand of hair that fell into his eyes. "It sucks. If I got paid, it would be marginally better. But it's still hard work."

"I think there may be a failure of your deodorant, also." Grant kept his voice casual.

"I don't wear deodorant."

"Then I think you should start. All of this hard work is making you sweat a lot, and we don't want poor old Mrs. Moretta passing out if she happens to come back here."

James sniffed at an armpit. "I guess. I didn't think about that."

"It's a natural process, of course. Your hormones are turning on and starting to provide the testosterone that's going to be playing havoc with your body for a while. Most of us learn to control ourselves by around age twenty, or so. But you have a few years of a rocky ride in front of you."

"Worse than the total fuck-up that my life already is?" Once the words left his lips, James appeared horrified that he'd sworn in front of a grown-up.

"It's okay," Grant assured him. "Men swear in front of each

other. And there are women you can swear around too. Like my older sister, who is totally more alpha than most men. But some women, like your mother, get pissy about hearing that kind of language—especially from their children."

"You're not making me feel any better," James observed. "Maybe I should just kill myself now, to end this misery."

Grant stared intently until James finally shrugged and grinned weakly.

"J.K. I'm just pissed about how sore I feel. My back hurts, my arms are aching, and my stomach is growling, but it's hours until dinner. And I've been too tired to even do any reading. I go back to my room after dinner, take a shower, settle down with a book, and before I've read more than a page, I'm asleep. My life sucks right now."

Grant took a deep breath. "Why don't you start meeting me in the gym on Saturday mornings?"

James snorted. "Why? So I can hurt myself more? Is there going to be no end to my punishment?"

Grant smiled. "I can teach you some techniques that will save you from back pain. You need to learn to lift with your legs, not with your back. And strengthening your abs will also help protect your back. We can start doing some weight training, too, to build up your arm muscles. Now that your hormones are turning on, you'll find your muscles will get more definition. And working out will also help with that helpless, frustrated feeling that you get when you feel like you'll explode if you don't punch something . . . and break it."

James gaped at him. "You know that feeling? I thought I was just going nuts."

"No, you're not nuts. You're just reaching a new phase. That feeling has been responsible for many a fight in the streets, in schools, and in bars. Men feel they're being disrespected, and they retaliate. Then a friend of the loser wants revenge, and they hurt you even harder. Then the whole thing escalates, and before you know it, you have a war going on."

James sat on a stack of boxes and pulled his t-shirt up to wipe his sweaty face. "I don't think I want to grow up anymore. Which way is it to Neverland?"

Grant grinned. "Turn east at the North Star, or something like that, right? Believe me, James. You're not the first boy to ever think like that. And you won't be the last. The only other time your body changed this much before was when you went from being an infant to a toddler. But then you had no self-awareness, so you didn't care that you were still pooping on yourself and falling down hundreds of times a day as you learned to walk. Now you're aware of every excruciating detail. And just wait until you start noticing girls."

"Start? You can't avoid them. They're everywhere."

Grant nodded. "Yup. And they're going through their own private female version of hell while you go through yours. You're in for a rough couple of years, I'm not gonna lie. But when you get done, you'll be a strong, confident man. I promise."

"Like you?"

"Yes. Like me. But first, we have to get your body strong enough to do the job you're going to be doing here for the foreseeable future. So why don't you eat breakfast with your mom, then tell her you're going to meet me in the gym at, say, nine. That way, your mom and your sisters will be done and probably even out of the pool by then. And you and I can get to work, turning you into a fat-burning, muscular machine."

"I don't think that's possible. I'm too fat and out-of-shape."

"I'm going to ask my mom to send me a picture of myself at your age. You'd be surprised how much you can accomplish if you're consistent. We can start with every Saturday morning doing weight training. Maybe we can add some jogging on Tuesday and Thursday mornings also. I'll run on the treadmill next to you, showing you how to keep a steady pace.

We can start with just, say, fifteen minutes a morning."

James made a face and groaned. "More exercise? Great! Just what I need."

"Yes, it actually *is* just what you need."

"Okay," James got up. "But now I've got three more cases of books I have to open, count, and unload. Then I've got to get everything onto the carts, so on Monday, I can move them up to the classrooms they need to go into. So I'd better get back to work."

"See you tomorrow morning, James." Grant walked out of the backroom and smiled at Delores on the way out the door. "Thanks. See you later."

When he got to his room, he found a spare deodorant in his closet and tossed it into his gym bag. Then he picked up his book and read until it was time to go down for dinner.

CHAPTER THIRTEEN

Grant didn't see Monique or any of her children at dinner Friday night. He also didn't get a chance to talk to Monique on Saturday morning, although he did catch a glimpse of her when he entered the gym. As he was headed over to where James sat reading a book, waiting for him, he caught her looking into the gym. She and her daughters were still in their swimsuits and were obviously heading to the locker room to change.

Grant had to fight himself to not chase after them and beg her, in her sexy, revealing spandex, to mate with him. Sighing inwardly, he approached the boy and spent the next couple of hours teaching him how to lift safely and protect his back by using his legs and his abs.

As luck would have it, there were a few security guards in the sparring room, and James wanted to watch them. Grant agreed, but it didn't take long before the others were challenging him to join the sparring session. As he fought, he became aware that James was studying him, watching his every move. Since this was the first time Grant had seen James interested in anything other than a book, he tried to put on a good show for the boy. But when it looked like he was going to lose a round, James's eyes got very big, and he gasped a few times. Grant put renewed energy into his moves and won the round as he had the others.

Afterward, when they were heading towards the showers in the locker room, Grant asked, "Why did you keep watching if it bothered you to see me fighting?"

James jerked his head up and stared into Grant's eyes for a split second, then looked away. "I don't like violence. I don't like to see someone I know getting beaten."

"But I won. I wasn't beaten," Grant dryly observed.

"It's still kind of scary to watch."

"Would you like me to teach you some moves, so you will feel more confidence?"

"No!" James responded quickly.

After that, it felt as if James had slammed a door shut between them, and Grant didn't know how to pry it open. So they entered the locker room and took their showers in silence.

As they were getting dressed, Grant tossed the spare deodorant at James. "Here, I had an extra one in my closet."

James appeared somewhat embarrassed, but he caught it and used it, then stashed it in the backpack he'd used to bring a change of clothing.

"Thanks," he said awkwardly. He was silent for a few moments before taking a deep breath. "Mom's still mad at you for stopping her from hitting me, I think."

Grant's eyebrows rose at the shared confidence. *This is his way of thanking me for helping. I have a feeling he's also obliquely acknowledging that there is something between his mom and me.*

"I hope she gets over it. Your punishment was meted out by the pack leader, and since you're becoming a man, that's the right thing to do."

"She doesn't see it that way. She still thinks of me as a baby."

Grant shrugged. "When you remember your child as a helpless infant, and unsteady toddler, it's kind of hard to adjust to them being an adult in their own right. Or so I've heard," he added. "I don't have any children. I've never been married."

"An alpha like you never got married?" James appeared curious.

Grant smiled, shaking his head. "I told you, James. I'm not an alpha."

"But the way you fight . . . the way you look . . ."

"Alpha means leader. I may look fierce, and I do fight to win. But I'm not interested in leading anyone to do anything. I'm happy with being told by someone else what to do. The only exception is when someone I care about is endangered. Then I don't need to be ordered to do what is natural for any man—or any wolf."

James looked thoughtful. "So, learning to fight doesn't make you an alpha? You won't get challenged or be made to fight, just because you know how?"

"No, it's just the opposite. When you look weak, others who have no confidence will pick on you, because they figure they can beat you, and make themselves look better. When you look like you will take anyone apart who challenges you, those kinds of guys will leave you alone. And on the off chance they don't, you'll know you can take them. Learning how to fight, odd as it seems, may save you from having to use the skills you learn."

James appeared to be pondering his words.

"Think about it. The offer is always open. I learned to fight from my father. And actually, from my mother as well. He was big and strong, but I think in a real battle, she'd be the fiercer one. There's something about mother wolves that makes them impossible to beat since they'll never back down when their pups are in danger."

"I think I better get moving," James said. "I always have lunch with Mom and my sisters, and I'm late already. I don't want to get into any more trouble than I'm already in."

"Okay," Grant replied. "You did well today. Thanks for letting me have a chance to pass on what I know."

James gave him a crooked grin. "Yeah. Bye." Then he was gone.

Grant's wolf raged in his head, and he argued his side.

She's mad at me. Things are not going well.

She's our mate. She knows it. Why do you make us wait to claim her?

It's not as easy for humans as it is for wolves.

Then maybe you need to let me lead for a change.

No! Be patient.

His wolf snorted, then growled softly. Then he refused to speak again.

With a heavy sigh, Grant took his bag up to his apartment before heading down to lunch. Monique and her children were finishing up their desserts when he got there. Despite his best efforts, Monique refused to meet his gaze. So he sat by himself and brooded his way through what should have been a delicious pasta lunch but ended up tasting like sawdust.

At the pack meeting the next night, Grant once again tried to get Monique to speak to him, but she met his greeting with a stony glare. He finally sat down across from her on the stage, trying to be sneaky about watching her instead of focusing on Diego as he gave the pack his usual updates on the state of the pack's affairs.

The one thing that grabbed Grant's attention was when Diego announced that Suzie Wong was done with her maternity leave, and the grade school classes would commence on the same day the academy classes did. He asked that anyone who wanted to be an aide for her should talk to her or to Diego. There had been a baby boom a few years before, and there were more young children than usual who needed to be educated.

Good! This should take some of the responsibility off Monique.

When Diego had finished with pack business, he added a final comment. "There's just one more thing I need to tell you all about."

He turned and held out his hand to Saoirse. She got up to walk somewhat shyly over to him, clasping his hand once she was next to him. He turned to look at the suddenly expectant audience. "I'm thrilled to be able to announce that Saoirse and I are expecting a baby. Our little one will be born sometime in April."

There was an immediate reaction of jubilation that swept all around the auditorium. People cheered and clapped, and many were laughing and teasing each other.

"See? I told you!"

"Wonderful news!"

Saoirse's voice held a hint of wonder when she asked, "Why do they all care so much? Many of them don't even know me."

Diego kissed her before answering. "They know *of* you. They know you're the pack leader's wife. What's good for me is good for the pack. A happy leader is a good leader. And a leader who has a child will be twice as fierce in protecting the pack. It's good news for everyone, not just for us."

Grant scarcely heard what they were saying because his wolf was yelling so loudly in his mind. He shook his head to clear it, so he could walk over to shake Diego's hand and congratulate the couple.

Nathan spoke loudly over the intercom system. "Good news like this calls for an extended run to celebrate! Let's go howl at the moon, to share our joy with the cosmos."

Grant made his way off the stage, swept along with the crowd, out to the clearing where they usually start their runs. People all around him were stripping quickly, getting out of each other's way, then allowing their wolves to take over their bodies.

Grant still felt disoriented, but he peeled his clothing off and allowed his wolf to reclaim what they shared. Then he followed the crowd out into the woods, where howling could already be heard. Calls from the throats of those celebrating their pack leader's good news.

Grant knew he wasn't in control anymore. When they were in wolf form, he was just along for the ride, a second voice in the mind of the wolf in charge. At least the yelling in his head had stopped. What worried Grant, though, was that the silence seemed intentional. The wolf was trying not to let him know where he was going.

Suddenly there was a new smell in the air. Grant's wolf stopped to explore what it was and where it was coming from. It was an aroma Grant had never experienced, but his wolf seemed to know it, and only paused long enough to discern what direction he needed to go. Then he took off, purposeful in his pursuit.

Grant was enjoying the feel of the grass under his paws, and the sounds of the night were calming to his troubled soul. But he could feel an undercurrent of anxiety that was inexplicable. Finally, he got to a small clearing deep in the woods near a pool of water, and he trotted over to take a drink.

When he raised his head from the water, he sensed there was another wolf nearby. A jet-black wolf approached cautiously, moving to stand next to him, also taking a drink from the cool water. Then his eyes met the other wolf's, and he realized who she was.

Monique's wolf raised her snout in the air, then moved a little bit back before she presented herself to him, a ready and willing female. Grant tried yelling at his wolf to stop, but there was no reasoning with him. The smell of a female in heat was too overpowering. He found himself as single-minded as his wolf, wanting to take her now, to seal their pairing forever.

He moved over to place his front paws on her back, nipping gently at her ear. Then he thrust his hips forward and sealed their fates. Grant lost himself in the feelings of the primal mating drive. His only thought was to shoot his sperm into this willing female who was his mate. He had to try to get her pregnant. Nothing else mattered.

They spent the rest of the night near the water, having sex, then resting up by cuddling together. They licked each other's faces and nipped at each other, sharing love bites. When they both heard a rabbit nearby, Grant quickly hunted it down and brought it back to share with his love. Then they both drank more water before having sex again. Finally, they both rested. He slept lightly, hyper-aware of the nearness of his mate.

When the smell of the night changed, the nearness of morning awoke them both. They got up, drank more water, then trotted along together, back to where they had left their clothing. Most of the other clothing had been claimed, leaving only a few who would be shifting around them. They both began their transition, but Monique finished before Grant. She grabbed her clothing and began to make her way out of the clearing.

Once Grant's vocal cords became human again, he called out. "Stop! You can't run away from *us* any longer."

Monique whirled on him. "What am I supposed to say? I wasn't in charge any more than you were. They took it upon themselves to do what I'm still not ready for."

Grant picked up his clothing and walked over to her. "But don't you see? Wolves are not known for having patience with their human halves. So they did what they had to do. Now it's up to us to figure out how to make it work for us. The deed is done. We are mated."

Monique stared at him. "So what does that mean? You planning on moving into my place now?"

Grant studied her face as a myriad of emotions raced across it. "Not until I'm invited to. But we need to tell your children about us. And we need to discuss, together, what our living options are. But we can't dance around any longer. We belong to each other. There's no going back anymore."

To his surprise, the strong, powerful woman he loved burst into tears. Grant moved closer and pulled her into his arms, holding her closely yet awkwardly, since they both were still holding onto their clothing. He waited until her sobs ended before he used one finger to tilt her head up, forcing her to meet his eyes. "Monique, I've loved you for a long time. I will never do anything to hurt you. I want to marry you and help you raise your children. I don't want to replace their father. I respect his place in your memories. But I want to create new memories with you. I want to spend the rest of my life honoring you as the goddess of my dreams."

Monique snorted softly. "Some goddess. My eyes are probably puffy, and there's snot in my nose. I've made you wait longer than any man could be expected to, and I've refused your every overture. How are you going to put up with me?"

Grant smiled. "With great pleasure."

They gazed into each other's eyes for a long moment. Then Monique sighed heavily.

"We'd best be getting into the house. We both need a shower. Then we'll have breakfast together with my kids, and we can tell them what happened. I just hope they won't object."

"We'll handle whatever they dish out, my love. Together."

She raised her head and nodded.

They held hands as they walked up the stairs, and separated once they were in the foyer, heading to their own apartments. They had to shower, change into clean clothing, then prepare to present themselves as a mated pair to the pack.

CHAPTER FOURTEEN

Grant got to the dining room first and grabbed a cup of coffee before searching for a table big enough for him and all of Monique's family. When he saw an empty table with six chairs, he headed over to it and put his coffee cup on it. Then he went back and filled some plates with pancakes, eggs, bacon, and fruit. He made his way back to the table and started eating, while keeping an eye on the entrance, watchfully waiting.

He was surprised and amused when Nathan stopped at his table. The man first looked around to be sure he wasn't being watched. Then he gave Grant a sneaky *thumbs-up* sign, grinned, and continued on his way, walking over to the food.

Monique arrived first, followed closely by her children. She searched around the room until she saw him. She nodded, then led her children over to fill their plates with food. Once they all had their trays full, she ushered them over to Grant's table. The kids looked at her questioningly for a split second. James was the first to put his tray down next to Grant. Monique sat across from him, with her girls on either side of her.

Monique began introductions after she had a quick gulp of her coffee. "Grant, these are my children. James, you already know. Selma is my older daughter, she's ten."

The girl on her mother's right smiled at him.

"And Selena is the baby. She's eight."

"Oh, Mom! I'm not a baby anymore!"

"Moms always feel that way about their youngest." Grant

smiled. "My youngest brother is twenty-five, and our mom still calls him her baby."

"Kids, this is Grant Knutsen. And we . . . uh . . . we have something to tell you."

Grant looked at her, and she nodded to him.

"Your mother and I were mated last night. Our wolves took it upon themselves to take the decision out of our hands because they thought we were taking too long."

James smirked with adolescent awareness.

The two girls looked expectantly at their mother.

"Does that mean we have to call him Daddy?" Selma asked.

"I don't remember having a daddy," Selena added. "I was only a baby when he was killed."

Grant spoke up. "I don't care what you call me. You can call me Grant if you want to. I hope to earn the right to be your father by proving that I'm willing to do the hard work of helping your mom raise you all."

Monique was watching James closely. He seemed preoccupied, stuffing his mouth with his pancakes.

"James, don't you have anything to say?"

He shrugged before swallowing. "What's there to say? If the deed is done, then it's done. I'm just glad you picked a good man. I like Grant. It's okay by me." Then he reapplied himself to polishing off the rest of his breakfast.

Monique sat back in her chair, shaking her head slowly. "That's it?"

Grant smiled at her, reaching across to take her hand in his. "Seems so, my love. As soon as we can, I want to marry you. I think Diego can do the honors, since his word is law within the pack. But I want it to be official, that we're now a family."

"When are you moving into our apartment?" James asked.

Grant searched Monique's face before answering. "We haven't worked out all of the details yet. This is new for all of us."

"Cool," James remarked as he got up. "Heading back for more pancakes. Anybody want anything?"

Monique stared after him, looking like she was in shock over her son's reaction. Or rather, his non-reaction.

Grant broke the silence. "Girls, can you each tell me a little about yourselves? I know James pretty well already. But what kinds of things are you interested in? Better in math, English, or science? What do you do for fun? Help me get to know you better."

Both girls started talking at once, and Grant laughed. He tried slowing them down or shushing them when they started yelling over each other. Monique chewed slowly on a piece of toast and simply watched as her family accepted him more easily than he believed possible, from what she had told him.

James returned with his second helping, which was as big as his first had been. Grant teased him about it and stole one of his pancakes. They joked together, and the girls, wanting the attention back on them, jumped back into the discussion.

Saoirse and Diego walked in the dining room, pausing to look around. When they saw Grant and his new family chatting amiably, they quickly moved to join them.

"Is it true? Are you mated?" Saoirse asked.

Grant nodded with a huge smile.

Saoirse pulled Monique out of her chair to give her a big hug. "Congratulations, girl! Couldn't have happened to a nicer woman!" She turned to Grant, waggling her finger at him. "And you'd better be a good husband to her. She's one of my best friends. I won't stand for anything other than abject adoration from her mate."

Grant grinned. "That's an order I will be glad to fulfill."

Diego moved over to shake hands with him, then clapped him on the shoulder. "I guess you're a permanent part of our pack now. Good to have you with us."

He turned and hugged Monique. "I'm happy for you, my dear," he said, before addressing them both. "So, when can I do the honors of officiating my first wedding?"

Saoirse punched him in the arm. "Honey! Wait until they ask you. I mean, really. Look at them. This is going to be a big adjustment. Let's let them get acquainted with each other as family. Then they'll let you know."

Diego shrugged. "Okay, then. I'll wait to be asked. By the way, you two, is your current apartment big enough, or are you going to want another one?"

Grant smiled. "Actually, I haven't even seen it yet. Let us get back to you on that."

After that, it was as if word had been suddenly telegraphed around the compound. People began to stop by to give them all their congratulations and best wishes for a wonderful future together. It went on for so long that Grant's cheeks started to hurt from smiling so much.

When he noticed everyone's plates were empty, he cleared his throat. "Why don't we all head upstairs, so I can see your apartment? That way we can figure out if we're going to stay there, or if we need to move."

They got up to put their plates on the conveyor belt, then they headed out together. More people called out good wishes as they moved through the foyer and up the stairs to the living quarters.

Grant had never been in the wing that Monique led him to, so he looked around with great interest. When they got to the apartment, she opened the door and turned to beckon him inside. Once they were all in, he quickly locked the door, then leaned back against it, wiping his forehead dramatically.

Using an exaggerated tone, he said, "Phew! Who knew it was so exhausting to accept good wishes from everyone? I'm worn out from smiling! How about the rest of you?"

James nodded. "Yeah, me too."

Selma giggled. "My cheeks hurt from smiling so much!"

Selena nodded solemnly. "Mine too."

"So, give me the tour?" Grant said to Monique.

She led him to the room that the girls shared, and he admired the color of their walls, the designs on their comforters, and their collections of stuffed animals and dolls. They walked through the bathroom the girls shared with James, into his room.

Grant looked around, laughing. "Whoa, dude! You need to do some tidying up in here."

James grumbled his protest. "You know how tired I've been, after working all day in the library."

"Yeah, but I'd be surprised if you hadn't lost some books under piles of dirty clothes and dirty dishes. This looks like my room used to look. I never liked cleaning either, but it's easier to find your stuff when you can see it."

James shrugged, then defiantly went over to his window seat, cracked open a book, and started reading. Grant shot him the evil eye, which was ignored.

Monique pulled his hand. "I've been having that argument with him for years. Let's go look at the rest of the place."

The next room they went into was the living room, which was where they lost the girls. The two turned on their video game set and picked up a couple of controllers and began to play.

"You'll have to teach me how to play that game," Grant remarked.

The girls simply nodded, too engrossed in beating each other.

Monique took his hand again, showing him the dining area, before leading him into the master bedroom.

Grant looked around with pleasure. He smiled at the muted color scheme of sea green and turquoise on the comforter that covered the king-sized bed. "Someone likes the same colors I do."

Monique smiled shyly. "I've always liked this combination. It's restful."

Grant admired the long balcony, set up with two chairs and a small table as well as a futon. He turned from the futon to Monique and waggled his eyebrows at her, and she blushed, then led him back in to show him the bathroom.

Grant sighed with pleasure. "A Jacuzzi! Just what the doctor ordered! I mean, don't get me wrong. I do like the showers around here, what with the multiple heads that make sure every part of you gets massaged and rinsed. But this is what I call luxury! I can't wait to try it out." He turned to pull Monique into his arms. "With my new mate." He lowered his head and pressed his lips to hers. When she responded, he deepened the kiss, licking at her lips until she opened her mouth to let him taste more of her. Their passion ignited, and they both began to explore with their hands.

Suddenly, there was giggling coming from the doorway, and they both jumped apart, guiltily.

Selma held out her hand. "Grant, your phone was ringing. I answered it. It's your mom. I figured you'd want to talk to her."

Grant cleared his throat. "Um, yeah. I do. Thanks."

He mouthed at Monique, "Later," before turning to take his phone from Selma's hand. He walked into the bedroom, and out onto the balcony, to share the good news with his mother.

CHAPTER FIFTEEN

Monique couldn't believe how quickly her life had changed. Grant had brought so few belongings with him from Canada he was able to fit it all in just two backpacks. So he was able to move completely into Monique's apartment a few hours later. Once he had unpacked and put his things into the master closet and a couple of bureau drawers, he said he felt like he had established his presence.

After that, he sat on the couch in the living room and let the girls teach him how to play the video games they were so enthralled with. Monique sat in the dining area at the table, ostensibly working on some paperwork for school. In reality, she was watching him interact with her girls, and marveling at how his easy manner had charmed them so quickly. They were already teasing him about his lack of abilities to master the games they both loved so much. In return, he commented on how skilled they were, and how much he appreciated their playing at lower levels, allowing him to be able to compete at all.

When she got up to stretch, she peeked into James's room and found that he had made a small attempt to clear away some of the clutter. Then he'd obviously been overcome with his unusual level of activity and was snoring softly on his bed.

She moved into the master bedroom and used the bathroom, then stood in front of the mirror and shook her head at her reflection. *Can this really be happening? A new mate has become a part of my life so easily? Tim, I promised to love you for the rest of my life. But you left me so alone. I will always love you as my first husband. But it seems there is a second husband for me.*

Yes, there is, her wolf responded, purring softly and contentedly. *And we will be very happy with him.*

There was a light knock on the door, interrupting her musing. "Come in."

Grant walked over to stand behind her, his arms enclosing her waist, his hands clasped on her belly. He leaned forward and nuzzled her neck, breathing in deeply and sighing softly. "I can't believe how lucky I am to call such a magnificent woman my mate," he said in a quiet voice. "I live for tonight, when I can demonstrate to you just how happy I am, and how much pleasure we can share."

As he kissed her neck, Monique stared with wide eyes at her reflection, glad that he wasn't looking up, so he didn't see the anxiety on her face.

Selma yelled from the living room. "Hey, Grant! It's your turn! Do you want to play, or not?"

Monique smiled at her daughter's bossy tone, a good imitation of her own. "I think your presence is requested elsewhere."

"Alas, you are right. But they'll be asleep way before we are, later." He walked over to the door, winked at her, then returned to the living room.

Monique gripped the side of the sink and did deep breathing exercises to calm herself. Then she went back out to shuffle papers around again.

Monday night's dinner was an abundance of pizza, with a salad bar next to it. Grant and James challenged each other, and a prodigious amount of pizza was consumed by them both.

Monique shook her head at them. "You're going to be sick, both of you! How can you eat so much, but look so good?"

"I work out." Grant grinned. "I have to work hard to look this good. But remember, I'm not even thirty, so my metabolism hasn't slowed down yet. When it does, I'll have to concede that James can eat more than me. Until then, he's gonna have to step up his game."

She was shocked. "You're not thirty yet?"

He shook his head. "Nope. I'll be twenty-nine in January. Why?"

"I'm thirty-five."

Grant winked at her. "I've always preferred older women. So experienced and wise, you know."

Monique tried not to let her expression change, but her anxiety level ramped up again.

When the dessert bar was rolled out into the dining area, Grant groaned loudly. James jumped up with a gleam in his eye.

"Now I've got you beaten, old man!"

"Probably right, son. But let me get a look at what's for dessert."

When they were both up admiring the desserts, Selena turned to her mother. "I really like him, Mom. He's a good choice."

Selma nodded. "Me, too. He's a good sport about losing to us when we're gaming. And he's a good influence on James, who even did some cleaning in his room. Did you see he brought some dishes down when we came down for dinner? I'll bet Mrs. Johnson didn't even know he had them still. She'll probably be wondering why dishes with leftovers from weeks ago are on the conveyor belt."

Monique smiled at her girls. "I'm glad you approve of him. I was planning on waiting a bit longer, to give you all time to get to know him before we . . . um . . . moved in together. But our wolves kind of took over last night, and, well, here we are."

Selma nodded, looking wise at such a young age. "Sometimes your wolves know better than you, right Mom?"

"Where did you hear that?"

"Mrs. Landon told us. She said that sometimes your inner wolves act like a conscience, getting you to act up to their expectations. I sure hope I have an inner wolf in me."

"Mrs. Landon doesn't have one, you know," Monique reminded her daughter.

"Yeah, I know. But she married a shifter, so her kids are weres also. And since Dad was a shifter, and so are you, there's a pretty good chance that we will be, too, right?"

"Maybe," she answered carefully. "But remember the Johnson's oldest daughter, Jennifer, isn't one, though their other two kids are. It's a toss of the dice every time you have a baby as to who the child will resemble and what traits they will get. You know I love all of you, so it won't matter to me one way or the other."

Grant and James returned with their plates loaded with brownies, cookies, and scoops of ice cream in individual cups.

Grant explained, "Only one of them is for me. I got ice cream for all my girls, also. And the brownies and cookies on my plate are for us to share."

"I rule!" James said as he attacked his plate of brownies.

"Yup, you do," Grant said with an exaggerated sigh. "I bow to your gluttony. But remember, James, you and I have a date with the treadmill early tomorrow morning."

"You do?" Monique asked.

Grant nodded. "Yes. Treadmills for some running on Tuesday and Thursday mornings, then weight training on Saturday mornings. That's what we agreed to, right, James?"

James grimaced. "I'll bet you cooked up this exercise thing with Diego, or with my mom, right? Is there no end to the punishment I have to endure for one little mistake?"

Grant grinned. "Don't think of working out as punishment. Think of it as what will allow you to continue to eat all of the food you want to without ending up looking like a butterball."

"Yeah, I guess," James responded, but his doubt was clear.

"James is a butterball," Selena sang, then giggled.

Selma grinned until Grant glared at them both. "Your brother is going through a tough time now, girls. Be kind. That way, when you get into your early teens, he'll be nice to you in return."

Monique echoed his sentiment, and they finished their desserts, eating in chiding harmony.

That night Grant retired to the master bathroom after dinner to enjoy a long soak in the Jacuzzi. Monique played some board games with her daughters, while James read in his room. Then she tidied up the living room while the girls got ready for bed.

She had started years ago reading to them each night before they fell asleep. Tonight was no exception. She was working her way through a multi-volume saga involving a strong young girl who was leading a group of rebels to fight against an evil tyrant who had stolen her kingdom. Monique knew she was stalling, but it wasn't really that unusual for her to read more than two chapters. By the end of the third chapter, Selena's steady breathing announced that she was asleep and not listening anymore.

"I guess I should stop there?" Monique said to her barely awake older daughter.

Selma nodded. "Yes, please, Mom. Selena will be mad if she misses out on any of the good parts."

"Okay, then. Good night, my sweet." Monique leaned over to kiss Selma, then Selena, before making her way to the door. She peeked in on James, but he was already snoring loudly. She swallowed hard, then made her way down to the master bedroom.

Grant was out on the balcony, enjoying the night air. He

had opened a bottle of wine, and came back into the room to hand her a glass as she walked in.

"Champagne, to celebrate our mating."

Monique managed to smile at him. "Okay. But I'll take it with me into the bathroom. I need to grab a shower."

"Make it a quick one, or I'll have to join you in there."

Monique strode into the bathroom and closed the door behind her. She got naked and took a long, hot shower, trying to use the pulsing water to relax her tense muscles. When she glanced down and saw that her fingers were beginning to resemble prunes, she knew that she couldn't stave off the inevitable any longer. She wrapped a towel around herself and took a deep breath.

As she opened the bathroom door, the light had been dimmed, and Grant was sitting naked on the bed, in a yoga position. "The champagne bottle is in a bucket of ice on the low dresser," he said.

"I don't usually drink much this late," Monique said.

Grant spoke gently as he gazed into her eyes. "I was thinking it might help you to relax."

"What do you mean?"

"You've been tense ever since it became clear that we would be spending the night together as humans, not as wolves. I don't know what's bothering you, but whatever it is, you can share it with me. We're mated now, remember. There's no need for secrets anymore."

"It's kind of hard to talk about," she began hesitantly.

Grant patted the pillow next to him. "Why don't you lie face down and let me give you a back rub. That way, I can tell you a story, to amuse your mind, while I massage your tense muscles and help you relax."

Monique poured herself more sparkling wine. She gulped half of it down before walking over to the bed and lying down on the mattress as he had directed.

Grant had another drink from his wine glass, then put it down on the nightstand. He moved so he was straddling her butt. His legs supported him, so he wasn't putting any weight on her. But the nearness of his naked body was simultaneously alarming and exciting. Her breathing sped up a little.

Grant began with her shoulders, his strong hands digging deep into the muscles.

"Wow! You're tied up in knots. I don't want to think that it's because of me, so I'll write it off to your being so responsible that you take everything onto yourself and don't let anyone help. That's going to stop. You have me to help now. Whatever burdens you are laboring under, I'll help you carry. Anything you need me to do, you only have to ask, and I'll do whatever it is, or die trying."

Hot tears squeezed out of her eyes, so she rubbed her face on the pillow, acting as if she was getting more comfortable. If Grant noticed, he said nothing about it.

"Why don't I entertain you and take your mind off your troubles by telling you a story? This story is about a man who never expected to meet a mate. He had been to this place many times as a child, and as an adult, and had never even so much as looked at any of the females there. Some he knew so well that he regarded them as relatives. So when his family was invited to do a favor for the family that ran the place, he expected only to be able to repay them for his many vacation days spent running through the woods."

He moved his hands down her back, deep massaging the muscles, almost to the point of pain. But as he gradually got her muscles to relax, her spine began to tingle from his ministrations. And his words captured her attention.

"The man was being introduced to the wife of the new leader when the rebellious ones were brought forward. He was totally astounded to see a gorgeous black wolf, with silky fur and a sassy tail, accompany them. She placed herself between the rebels and the rulers, so there could be no mistaking that any attempt to hurt them would have to go through her. The man was enthralled. A female who was so loyal and brave? Her soul spoke to his wolf, who growl softly in the man's head, *She is ours.*"

Grant continued working on Monique's backside, moving lower to massage her glutes, then further down to her upper thighs. His hands not only relaxed her every muscle, but they also excited her skin. Every cell in her body was becoming alert to his touch, even though he was obviously avoiding directly touching any of her sexual parts.

"But the man was not an alpha male. He was not able to announce to everyone there that she was his. He had no time alone with her to claim her. In fact, he never even got to see what she looked like as a human. So he returned to his home in Canada, unhappy and anxious to return. But he could think of no way to invite himself there. He cursed his own beta-male self, while his wolf berated him for not returning immediately to claim her as theirs. He was afraid to say anything to his family. His mother would understand, but his sister would only tease him. And his brothers would try to win her for themselves just because they knew he wanted her. His misery grew until he finally took the one step he could handle, and gave notice at his job, which he hadn't enjoyed for quite some time anyway."

Monique giggled as Grant massaged her toes, having worked his way down the entire length of her body and her legs. Then he began to work his way back up again.

"To the man's surprise, his mother called a meeting at his ancestral home, giving no indication as to why. He got there right after his brothers arrived, and their sister a few minutes later. His mother told them that the pack they had helped before needed someone to step in to be a substitute security person for an unspecified length of time. The man's heart leapt with joy, which he carefully kept concealed. He let everyone else answer first, giving their reasons as to why they didn't want to do this favor for their friends. Then he announced that he might be willing to do it, since he was in need of a change, and he'd be done with his job at the end of the week. As he had hoped, his siblings took no notice of his offer, and his mother confirmed his acceptance. He arrived the next weekend."

Grant was now back up to Monique's lower back, and he was leaning closer to her, his hot breath exciting every cell on her skin. She tingled with excitement, wherever he touched her, and even she could smell her own excitement as he mesmerized her with his voice and the story of his love.

"When he finally met the woman in her human form, his wolf recognized her immediately. He was ecstatic that she was so beautiful but found himself tongue-tied around her. And when she stripped down for their run that night, he was undone. Clothed, she was magnificent. Nude, she was a goddess! Her regal bearing dared anyone to compete with her perfection, which was impossible. He'd never had to shift with a hard-on before, but soon he'd discovered ways to do it without it being as obvious as he feared. His wolf nagged at him incessantly, demanding that he claim the woman as mate soon, or his wolf would do it himself. He pleaded that she had children, and responsibilities, and tried to explain that for humans, there are more things involved than just the mating drive. But his wolf ran out of patience eventually."

He leaned over, breathing into her ear as he slowly and gently rubbed the now pliant muscles of her shoulders.

"But that brought new fear to the man's heart. He'd never been a part of a pack before, and the only female shifters that he knew well were his mother, his sister, and a daughter of the pack family, who he'd always regarded as a kind of cousin. He'd never had sex as a wolf. What if he disappointed her? What if his wolf didn't thrill her wolf, and she decided that it wasn't a good idea for them to mate? What then?"

He gently nipped at her earlobe, then trailed his tongue along her neck, to nip at the other earlobe as well. Her hips began to twitch with excitement.

"But fortunately, his wolf knew what to do. And her wolf had also decided she was done waiting for their humans to get things done. The experience was absolutely wonderful! It was better than he could have imagined. It mated their souls, as well as their bodies. And now the man is hoping that he will be as able to please his human mate, as his wolf was able to please her wolf."

Monique spoke quietly, the sharing of her inner fears easier when she wasn't looking into his eyes. "I'm worried that I might disappoint you because I've only been with one man. Tim and I learned together how to please each other. But my experience stopped abruptly five years ago. There has been no other man for me. Until now."

Grant was quiet, not touching her. She feared that she'd ruined the moment.

Then he spoke gently but firmly. "There is no possible way that you could ever disappoint me. Just being able to touch you like this is an honor."

"Then, if it's all right with you, I'd like to turn around now, and have you pay some attention to the front of me."

He lifted a bit so she could roll onto her back. When she saw admiration and love in his eyes, her fear melted away, along with the towel that she resolutely tossed onto the floor.

He lay next to her, resting his head on his arm that was curled up and over her head. His other hand began to explore her body, touching lightly, making her jump and twitch. He leaned his head forward and kissed her lips. Then his tongue traveled down her neck to her left breast, where he began a swirling tongue massage that made her gasp with pleasure.

His lips attached to her areola, sucking while his tongue flicked repeatedly over the nipple, making her squirm with desire. Then he moved to the other breast and repeated his pattern.

"Please . . ." Monique whispered.

Grant raised his head to stare at her, his hand now exploring lower, tickling her navel before traveling further south. He rubbed some of her moisture forward, to bathe her nub in it. The friction he was creating became a pleasurable torture as she jerked her hips forward, trying to get his fingers into just the right position.

"Is this what you want, my love?" he asked as he moved his fingers ever so slightly. "Or is this?"

He found the right spot, and Monique raised her hips up off the bed as she came with a cry, shuddering and trembling. His fingers now entered her, as his thumb continued to tickle her clit. He brought her close to another climax, then pulled his thumb back.

She reached one hand down to touch him, gratified by how hard he was, obviously as excited as she was. She explored the length of him, from the wide head, down the silky shaft to the root of him. Her fingers touched his sac, massaging his balls.

With an unintelligible oath, Grant moved over her. "I won't last long this first time. I've fantasized about this moment for far too long," he said as he rotated his hips to coat himself with a combination of their love juices.

He pushed forward, and the tip of his cock entered her.

She gasped, the stretching sensation unfamiliar, yet pleasurable, and her hips began to move of their own accord. She rolled them, helping him to create room within her for the rest of his hardness.

With a groan, he pushed himself forward, not gently anymore, but forcefully. She moaned as she felt her inner muscles react to him, clenching and releasing, only to squeeze tightly around him again.

He pulled himself back, and their hips began to move in tandem as he pushed himself forward and pulled back again. Monique stopped thinking about what she was doing and lost herself in the sensations of pleasure that swept across her entire body. Her nipples were tight beads that reacted to the silky hair on his chest each time he slammed himself into her.

Once again, she adjusted her hips to get him into just the right position. Just a little bit more to the right, just . . . just . . . there!

She squeezed her eyes shut, watching starbursts on the inside of her eyelids as she came. She screamed as her inner muscles clamped around him like a fist, pushing him over the edge. With a growl worthy of his wolf, he pushed forward one last time, grabbed her hips tightly to hold her against him, and he came. She could feel every jerk, every spurt shooting out of him, as he twitched helplessly on top of her in spasms of ecstasy.

As their eyes met, she saw into his soul. His wolf watched her, also, and she knew hers was looking back at him. In that moment, they truly became one. That knowledge, along with his hips jerking madly, sent her off on another round of orgasms that took her breath away.

With a huge gasp, Grant collapsed on top of her, crushing out what little air she had. Her hands clutched at his shoulders, and she braced her elbows on the bed to push him up a little bit.

"I need . . . to . . . breathe,"

"Sorry. Body . . . not . . . working. Can't move just yet."

She breathed in tiny gasps until he rolled over to lie next to her again. He pulled her into his arms, and she rested her head on his shoulder while she idly fingered the long blond chest hair that had provided her such unexpectedly pleasurable sensations.

"I know we were mated before," he began, "But did you just feel what I did?"

She raised her head to look into his eyes. "You mean when our eyes met as we were joined? And my wolf was looking out of my eyes at your wolf, looking out of yours?"

He nodded.

She smiled. "More than anything, that's proof that we are meant to be together."

"You've felt that sensation before?"

"Yes. But we don't need to keep talking about my late husband. I have a new mate now. And along with that, I have a new life to look forward to."

"I don't want you to think that I'm threatened in any way, or jealous of him. I know he will always live in your heart as your first, and the father of your children."

"But he's gone. That door has closed. And a new future is in front of me. With you."

She giggled as his cock, still hard, began to bounce against her thigh.

"Already?"

He shrugged modestly. "I *did* tell you that I'm only twenty-eight, didn't I?"

"That doesn't make me a cradle-robber, does it?"

He shook his head. "Anything less than ten years is okay by me. Besides, we wolves live longer than non-shifters. I hope to be able to pleasure you long into the future, my queen."

He pulled at her hips. "Why don't you get on top of me, for this round? I want to watch your face as you come. And play with your gorgeous tits while they bounce in front of me as you ride me like a cowgirl."

She climbed onto him, leaning over to exchange a passionate kiss with him. While their tongues were dueling, she lowered herself slowly, allowing him to enter her only an inch at a time. She'd push down, then rotate her hips as if she was belly-dancing. Then she'd lower a bit more, then rotate. When he began to whimper with frustration, she reared herself up to grin at him.

"Is this what you want, mister?" she asked as she pushed herself back hard, taking the rest of his length into her in one quick movement.

As he watched her, the pupils of his eyes were so large that their clear, sky-blue irises were only a thin corona. He reached up to fondle her breasts, teasing the nipples into even harder nubs than they were already, and his hips joined hers in the carnal dance.

True to his word, he lasted much longer this time. Monique had already moaned and screamed her way through lots of smaller orgasms, and at least one multiple one, before he pulled her hips down with a grip so tight, she'd surely have his finger marks on her skin as a reminder of just who her mate was. And when he shot his heat into her, she felt as if it blasted right up into her head.

This time it was she who collapsed onto him. But he appeared to be content for her to stay there. They lay like that for a long time, as they both regained their normal breathing patterns.

Grant's hands idly traced patterns along her back, his strong hands returning repeatedly to her glutes.

"God, you're a magnificent woman." His voice was still raspy from his harsh growling when he came. "I can't believe my good fortune."

She smiled against his chest as his touches became lighter, tickling her skin. "The way you keep on with my ass makes me think that you've been wanting to cross the color line for a long time." She raised her head to look into his eyes, so he could see that she was teasing.

117

His gaze was earnest. "Up until now, I'd never had any opportunity to do that. I've been with very few women. All of them were darker than me, I admit. But then, there're very few people whiter than I am."

She grinned. "Yeah. I've gotta agree. Tim was a white man, but he had dark brown hair all over him. You're so white that even your body hair is almost white. You're pretty close to albino, mister."

"But look at the contrast between us, woman, and tell me it doesn't excite you the way it excites me."

"I think pretty much everything about you excites me right now."

"But the whole *yin-yang* thing of male-female, light-dark, blond-black. I'm head-over-heels in love with you. I feel like I've won the mating lottery."

"Me too," she replied with a contented sigh.

"So . . . uh . . . are you ready for another round?"

She snorted in surprise. "You're kidding, right?"

"Um, no?"

"We need to get some sleep. I have to be up early with my kids, then I have work to do. The school opens a week from tomorrow. I have a lot of work to get done before then."

He sighed heavily. "I guess you're right. And you know, I think I know why Saoirse wanted me to help her plan her lessons. I think she wants me to step in to sub for her when she has the baby. She wants me to meet her in the lab tomorrow to plan—Hey! Does that mean you'll be my boss, as well as my mate?"

"I guess so. I may have to call you into my office to apply some discipline if I think you're not behaving yourself."

She giggled when his cock twitched again.

"See what you do to me? I'm helpless in my lust."

"Later, big guy. This woman may look like a goddess to you, but even goddesses need sleep."

118

"Agreed."

She slipped off him and curled up within his arm, still wrapped around her, and rested her head on his shoulder. Soon she drifted off into the relaxed and restful sleep of the sexually contented.

CHAPTER SIXTEEN

The next morning, Monique woke up with new anxieties she shared with her mate as they got up and dressed for the day.

"What if they heard us last night?"

Grant snorted. "So what if they did? It won't be the first time in history that kids heard their parents having sex. It's never done anyone any harm, so far as I know. My siblings and I used to laugh about it whenever our parents would get extra loud. When we got older, we'd even tease them about it, telling them they needed to get a room further away from the rest of us, so we could get undisturbed rest. They'd laugh back with us, telling us we were all old enough to move out of the house so they could get back to having sex on the dining room table. We'd look at each other and go *Ew! We eat there! Gross!* And they would nod, smiling at each other."

"I grew up without a dad, so the only men ever around were Mom's boyfriends. And Gramma wouldn't allow them to stay the night with kids in the house."

Grant shrugged. "It actually made us feel secure. We knew that our parents loved each other, and that love created all of us. So it's all good."

"I don't know. I haven't had *the talk* with any of my kids. I would have with James, but he never talks to me or listens to me anymore. I think he knows about sex, but I'm not sure. And the girls aren't old enough yet."

"Yes, they are. In fact, they should be told *because* they're so young. Innocent kids are easier to take advantage of, since they don't get the gut feeling that something is wrong. They don't know what the wrong moves might indicate. If you want, I'll talk with James. But it needs to happen in an organic way. You don't just sit a kid down and have *the talk*, then never mention it again. It should be an on-going dialogue, not a one-time lecture."

Monique sighed. "We certainly have different ideas about child-raising."

Grant moved closer, enfolding her in his arms, then burying his face in her neck to inhale deeply. "That's not a bad thing. Of course, I'll always defer to you. But I want to help you raise them, so please allow me to give my input. Sex was not a forbidden topic in my house, and I think we all grew up very relaxed about it because of that."

She stared at him. "Relaxed, but not enough for you to pursue many women?"

He shrugged. "I told you, I'm not alpha. I'm beta. I don't present myself well in situations where being flashy or loud makes you sexy and gets you the girl. I just quietly go about my business, hoping some female will notice."

"Well, this one did! And I'm sure glad that no one else did. I want you all to myself."

He grinned as he pulled her closer. "Done, my queen. You own me . . . body and soul. Your every wish is my command."

She moaned as his lips touched hers and the light touch grew deeper and more passionate. His hands moved down her back to squeeze her butt, and she ground herself against him.

After a few minutes, she shoved him away. "Down, boy! I've got tons of work to do today, and kids waiting out there for me to go with them to breakfast."

"With *us* to breakfast," he corrected her gently. "And then I'll hit the gym with James before he heads to his job at the library and I go meet Saoirse in the lab."

She sighed heavily. "All God's *chilluns* be too busy for what I'd like to be doing with you again, right now."

He gave her a lopsided smile. "That's what honeymoons are for. That's why, as soon as we can make the arrangements, I want to marry you. Then we can spend at least a week, testing the limits of just how often I can get hard and how many times I can make you come before we both collapse from exhaustion."

She pointed to his pants, tenting in front of him. "You'd better do something about that before breakfast."

He grinned. "I've had lots of experience since I got here having to make it *go away* whenever I'm around you. I'll just think about something totally non-sexy, like math or science formulas. Does it every time."

She was still smiling as she opened the door and went out to make sure her kids were all awake and ready for their day.

If the girls heard anything the night before, they gave no indication. Monique observed them all at breakfast, noticing James seemed to have a new respect for Grant, which made her feel guilty he'd been deprived a father for the past five years. But when she watched them together, discussing the exercise program they were doing together, she realized that a relationship couldn't be forced. It surprised her Grant had known that instinctively and had created an opening with her son by empathizing with his adolescent angst.

"See?" Grant held his phone in front of James. "I told you I was a chubby kid. Mom sent me a couple shots from the family archives."

James was grinning so widely that Monique had to see the picture also. Her eyebrows rose as she looked back and forth from the image on the phone screen to the sexy man in front of her. "From that" —she waved at the phone—"came this?" She pointed to him.

He nodded solemnly, before winking at her. He turned to James. "See, dude? I told you, no matter how little you think of what you look like now, with a little bit of effort, you, too, can become the man of some hot woman's dreams. I did."

James laughed out loud. "My mom? A hot woman?"

Monique glared at him, but Grant winked at her again. "Of course, *you* don't think of your mom as sexy. That would be totally weird and gross. But to me, she's the woman of my dreams. And I plan to put a ring on it as soon as possible — if she'll have me." He gave her an imploring look.

It was her turn to laugh. "You look like a sad puppy, which is totally incongruous with the big, strong man you are."

He leaned forward and kissed her, a light brushing of his lips on hers. She was unprepared for how quickly it excited her body parts, and she was acutely aware that her children were watching them.

"Well?" His light blue eyes fixed on her dark brown ones.

"Of course, I'll marry you. Duh! Though since we're mated already, it's not really necessary."

"Yes, it is. It is, to me. I want you to have my last name, and I want to adopt your kids. They can keep their last name, to honor their father. But you are all under my protection now, and I want everyone to know it."

Selma gave him a speculative look. "So . . . Does this mean we will have to call you *Daddy* once you're married?"

Grant turned to her with a smile. "Not unless you want to. You can call me anything you choose. James already calls me by my first name. If you and Selena want to, you can use my name, also. Or make up any other name you want, and I'll answer to it. What you call me isn't as important as you knowing that you can depend on me to always be here for you. Your mom isn't raising you by herself anymore."

Selena, who had been sitting quietly, spoke up. "How about *Papa*? It's what the princess in the books Mom's reading to us calls the king."

Selma nodded. "Good idea. You don't really remember, but I do. I called our *real* dad Daddy. It wouldn't feel right using that name for anyone else. But Papa is good. Does that work for you?"

Grant gave Selma a quick nod. "It sounds like an excellent choice. What smart and thoughtful daughters I have now, in addition to my handsome, hard-working son."

James muttered something under his breath, but Monique clearly heard *hip boots*.

"James, you show some respect to Grant," she admonished.

Grant shook his head. "No, it's fine. He called me on it, and he's right. I don't need to *tell* you all how I feel, how full my heart is to suddenly have a whole family to love. Instead, I'll just show you by my actions how much you all mean to me. Deal?"

To Monique's surprise, Selena jumped up to wrap her arms around Grant. "I'm glad you're family now, Papa."

Grant hugged her tightly. He looked up when Selma tapped his shoulder. He opened one arm to let her into his bear hug. He held them both for a long moment.

Monique felt her eyes tear up, and when he looked up at her, she was surprised and gratified to see his eyes were shiny with unshed tears. *What a man! He's loving and not ashamed of being emotional. Yet he's big and strong and able to do what has to be done to protect us all. What an excellent choice he is!*

Her wolf, sounding sleepy, growled softly. *It is, as I knew it would be. We are one.*

Since they were all done with breakfast, everyone got up to clear away their things and get moving on their busy days. Monique and the girls walked towards the gym with Grant and James. The males went inside, and the females headed for the pool.

And as she did laps, she felt as if a giant weight had been

lifted off her shoulders. For the first time in years, she felt young and optimistic again.

CHAPTER SEVENTEEN

When James looked at his watch, he discovered it was already three o'clock. He had been working so hard he'd lost track of time. Now he'd have to jog to get out to the park, where Mrs. Landon would be with his sisters. The girls would be letting off steam after doing lessons with the woman who'd cared for them all for the past five years. But she had a new puppy and had to get back to her apartment to let him out. That meant that James had to be at the park to stay with his sisters, either until she returned, or their mom showed up.

He grabbed his latest book treasure, the first in another sci-fi series Grant had recommended, and he headed out of the back room. "Bye, Mrs. Moretta."

She grinned at him, waving. "Goodbye, James. See you tomorrow. I won't have you around here helping me much longer, will I?"

"Mr. Vargas says that once school starts, I've paid for the trouble I caused everyone. But I like spending time around books. Would it be okay if I still came to help you out a couple of days a week after school?"

"Of course, it would! You know these old bones are not up to lifting much anymore. It's been a big help to me, having you around. In fact, I'll talk to Diego about paying you for your hard work. But you just let me know if you get a lot of homework, and you can take off whenever you want to."

"Okay. And thanks, Mrs. Moretta."

"Thank *you*, James. See you soon."

As it turned out, Monique got done with her paperwork earlier than she had thought she would. That, along with her general sense of bodily satisfaction, made her smile. She leisurely strolled out to the park, enjoying the beautiful sunny day, maybe one of the last few she'd have time to enjoy now that school was going to start. She was in no particular hurry. She felt relaxed and happy, which was a totally unfamiliar sensation for her. *And I owe it all to you, my love!*

When she got closer to the playground area, she looked around for her girls but saw no sign of them. She called out for them. "Selma! Selena! Mrs. Landon? Where are you?"

There was no response. The tiniest glimmer of fear snuck into her heart. "James! Selma! Selena!" She called out even louder but still heard no answer.

She pulled out her phone and texted Grant. *I'm at the park. No sign of any of my kids, or Mrs. Landon. Please come!* To give herself something to do, she forwarded the message to Diego, Saoirse, and Nathan. Then she resumed calling out, trying to find someone . . . anyone.

Grant came running up no more than two minutes after her text. She was at the far end of the playground, beginning to enter the woods behind it.

He jogged up to her and studied her face. "No luck?"

She shook her head, trying to squelch the feeling of panic and fear that clutched at her stomach. Her heart was racing, and she was sweating, despite the breeze. "I can't find any of them anywhere! I've been calling until my throat hurts. Oh, Grant, where are my babies?"

He pulled her into his arms for a quick bear hug. He spoke into her hair. "We'll find them. I promise you that."

Monique pulled out of his embrace, looking around desperately. Mrs. Landon was walking toward the playground. Right behind her, at a run, were Diego and Nathan. In the distance, Saoirse was also trotting toward them.

"Here comes the cavalry," Grant pointed out.

"Mrs. Landon, where are my children? And why weren't you here?" Monique tried not to sound accusatory.

The older woman looked around. "They must still be playing *hide and seek*. That friend of James suggested it to the girls to pass the time until James got here. But after they went to hide, I was sitting with him on the bench, and he spilled his coke on my white blouse. Not only would it stain, but the bees are out something fierce these days, what with the cold weather coming soon. So I went to change, and while I was there, I let Toby out and then came back." She looked around. "Didn't James ever get here?"

"What friend of James?" Monique asked through clenched teeth. Terror was creeping slowly into her body as she tried to remember the last time James had mentioned having a friend.

"That man he used to talk to at the library. I think he said his name was Dan. He said that he hasn't been around much since he got a job in town, but that he wanted to tell James about a new book he'd like."

Monique went rigid, panic filling her like water flowing into a drum.

Grant turned to Diego and Nate. "He must have gotten back onto the grounds. You didn't tell everyone about him, so he must have waited until a guard was there who didn't know about him being expelled."

Diego nodded, walking a short distance away, already on his phone, talking to the lead security person at the main gate. "He's on the grounds. He's contacted Monique's children, and we can't find any of them. Make sure the gates are heavily guarded and begin an immediate perimeter search. We can't let him off the grounds with any of the children."

Monique barely bit back a scream. "He's got my kids!"

Grant squeezed her tightly, then let her go, and lifted her

face with one finger, searching her eyes. "Can you hold it together to continue searching for the kids? Maybe if we all call out, we can reach them."

She nodded, trying to focus on taking action to quell her panic.

They fanned out, everyone calling out the names of the kids.

Grant was partway into the woods when he heard a sound and quickly located the source of it. He saw flashes of color in a hollowed-out log near a boulder that almost blocked the entrance. He stuck his head inside and saw both girls looking back at him, quizzically.

"Are you playing hide and seek with us, too?" Selena asked.

He stood up. "I've found the girls!"

Monique was there before the girls were completely out of the log.

"What were you doing in there?" Monique demanded.

Selena explained. "Playing *hide and seek* with that friend of James. But he's a really bad seeker. We've been in that log forever, and he hasn't been anywhere near here."

Selma sniffed. "I told you, I don't think he's coming. I think he just wanted us to go away so he could talk with James. He was weird. I didn't like him."

Monique grabbed both girls, squeezing them so tight they struggled to get away.

"Mom! I can't breathe! You're hugging me too tight!" Selena freed herself.

Selma reacted to the panic emanating from her in waves. "What's wrong, Mom? Why are you so upset?"

Diego had reached them by that time. "That man was a bad man, girls. He was told to leave because we didn't want him in the pack anymore. Did he say anything that might tell us where he was planning on going?"

Selma shook her head. "No. He just said that he got a job in town. He said his phone died, so he couldn't call. And that he wanted to visit some friends and thought James might want to hear about a new book." She looked around at all the serious faces on the adults. "Mom, where's James?"

Monique almost passed out from fear, trying to answer. "He's . . . he's . . . we don't know."

She turned to Grant. "He's got my boy! What are we going to do?"

Grant's normally affable face had turned dark and sinister. When he spoke, his icy tone made a chill run down her back, despite how much she loved him. But his words comforted her.

"Don't worry, honey. Remember how you met me. I'm from a family of hunters. We learned how to track prey before we were old enough to walk. Even before our wolves presented themselves, we were all accomplished at *seek and locate*. I'm on this."

"But how?

"I can't explain how. But he's got *my son*. I will find him." With that, he loped off into the woods, disappearing out of sight in the dense trees.

Monique turned to see Selma gaping at them.

Selena was crying. "I want James! Mama, where's James?"

Saoirse had reached them and spoke soothingly. "Girls, there's nothing else we can do now. Let's go back to the mansion and have some hot chocolate. Grant is a hunter. I'm sure he'll find James and bring him back."

Monique stared at her friend and spoke with a strained voice. "I wish I was sure."

Diego had returned from his phone call. "He's the best at what he does. Let him work."

"So what do I do? Drink hot chocolate like nothing's wrong?"

Nathan took her arm gently, leading her away from the others. "No, you come with me. He's the tracker, but we can try to follow him. I think we'll be better at it if we shift, don't you?"

They walked into the woods, waiting until they were out of view of everyone else before they stripped quickly and allowed their wolves to take over. With their enhanced sense of smell and hearing, they would try to follow the hunter.

James had never been so tired in his life. Not only had he gotten up early to work out, but he'd worked a full day. Seven hours at the library, lifting heavy boxes of books and moving them around. Now he felt like he'd been walking forever, and the man who was dragging him along kept insisting he walk faster.

"I can't walk any faster. I'm out of breath. I need to stop and rest."

"Fine," Dan snarled. "But just for a minute. We don't want to chance anyone being out looking for us, do we?"

James felt a momentary spark of hope, but it was quickly tamped down by the man's next words.

"After all, if I don't get to take you with me, I'll have to come back and get one of your sisters. You don't want me to do that, do you?"

James shook his head. The man offered him a drink of water from a bottle he had in a fanny pack, and James took a few gulps to wet his parched throat.

"Enough!" the bottle was snatched from him, and the man finished it off.

"Now, let's get going. I want to be out of here and in town before it gets dark. And since you can't shift, it's going to be slow going."

As he trudged along, James thought about how he'd ended up in this horrible position.

James left the library and was getting closer to the playground area, looking forward to reading the next chapter in his book.

I hope Mrs. Landon has something to drink because I finished my water bottle a long time ago. Maybe she'll even have cookies. That would be most excellent.

But when he reached the playground, he looked around in surprise. There was no sign of the girls or Mrs. Landon anywhere. A sudden movement to his left made him turn and gape when he spotted Dan.

"Yeah, didn't expect to see me again, did you? Guess they told you I was expelled, huh?"

He nodded.

"But I had to come back. See, I forgot something that I wanted to bring with me."

"You're not supposed to be here . . ." James began, then he stopped in confusion when Dan neared him.

Dan grabbed James's upper arms and pull him close enough to smell the liquor on the guy's breath as he spoke into James's face.

"Don't you want to know what I forgot? It's you, boy. You're going to come with me when I leave."

James shook his head. "I can't. School starts next week. Besides, I can't leave my mom and my sisters."

Dan laughed. A nasty sound that made his words sound even worse. "They don't need you anymore. That albino shithead's probably poking your ma right now. She won't even notice you're gone. Soon, she'll be popping out new babies, and they'll forget all about you. The only one who really cares about you is me, boy. Your best bet is to come with me."

"Where?" James looked around, hoping to see someone, or find

some way of escaping.

"I figured on heading west, out to Cali. Maybe when we get there, we can get on the crew to help build that museum the Star Wars guy wants to put all his shit into. You'd like that, wouldn't you, boy? I know sci-fi's your thing."

"But I'm not old enough to work. I'm only thirteen."

Dan rubbed his hands up and down James's arms, making him squirm at the implied intimacy of the moves.

"But you've been working out, haven't you? You just keep on doing that, and your good genetics will help you bulk up in no time. Plus, you Black boys always look older. You look like you're at least sixteen. That's old enough to work on almost any job site I've ever been on."

"But I don't want to leave here." James tried to free his arms, but it was no good. The man held on too tight, making James's arms almost feel numb.

"Would you rather I take one of your sisters?"

James stopped breathing and stared open-mouthed at the man. "What?" he croaked.

Dan cackled. "Yep. I figure that albino asshole stopped me from getting a mate, so he owes me. Of course, she was too old for my liking, and I'm not that much into females. But any hole will do when you're desperate, am I right?"

James fought off a wave of nausea as Dan continued to blather.

"So the way I look at it, since I didn't get to fuck that hot little bitch, he owes me. Your mom was being okay about it, letting me fight for her until that albino prick showed up. Then when she was holding me down, I got ready to make one last play for the pussy, but that dickhead rammed into me and made me lose my chance. I ain't been laid in so long my dick hurts. That's gonna change soon, right, kid? You and me are gonna have some real fun, once we get out of here."

"But I'm . . . I'm not gay," James said in a small voice, trying not to let his horror and revulsion make him throw up.

"But you've only whacked off yourself, right? So you have no idea what it can be like to have someone else making you come.

You'll find out how good it feels. Then you'll realize you made the best decision ever, once we get out to Cali, where the air is warm all the time, and clothes can be optional." He leaned in closer, spitting bits of saliva onto James's face. "I can't wait to see you naked!"

James pushed and twisted at the same time, catching Dan off balance, and he freed himself. He moved slowly backward. "I'm not going with you. I don't want to. You'd better leave."

Dan gave a big sigh. "Okay. Have it your way. I'll just have to swing back and pick up one of your sisters, then. The older one is cute, but the younger one would probably be a better choice. The younger they are, the tighter they are. And that way, I can tell everyone she's my kid."

"You can't take my sister!" James was shaking in his anger.

"Then you have to come with me. That's the only thing that will stop me from taking one of them with me. I told them we were playing hide and seek. I know where they're hiding, so all's I gotta do is go grab her and leave. Then you'll never see me – or her – again."

Dan approached James and grabbed one of his arms again, squeezing tighter this time to ensure James couldn't get away again.

He leaned in close. "So what's it gonna be, boy? I take one of your baby sisters, or you come with me? Decide fast, kid. I want to leave before everyone realizes I'm here."

James thought about how much he loved his little sisters. He tried to fight off another wave of revulsion, but the nausea was too much for him. He turned slightly and puked onto the ground.

Dan danced back. "What the hell?"

"I don't know. Must have been something I ate," James lied.

"Let's get moving. I've got the feeling that security probably knows by now that I'm here. We're going to get out by the south gate. One of my friends works that one. He'll let me out. I sucked him off real good a couple times, so he owes me."

He yanked James's arm so roughly he almost pulled it out of the socket. He dragged him along, as James struggled to keep up with the taller man's longer legs.

They had been walking for so long James was almost

falling asleep on his feet. He'd gone far beyond tiredness, even way past exhaustion. It wasn't dark yet, but night was coming soon. He had no idea how he knew that, but he did.

"C'mon, boy. Keep up with me. We're almost to the southern gate," Dan grumbled.

"I'm so tired."

"When we get to town, you can sleep as long as you want to. But we have to keep moving. It'll be dark soon, and I can't see any better in the dark than you can. I can't shift because I won't be able to keep a hold of you. And I'm not letting you go now."

A low, deep voice suddenly spoke out in front of them. "Oh yes, you will."

Dan stopped so suddenly James almost fell forward. But he recognized that voice!

Grant moved out of the shadows of the trees to stand directly in front of Dan. "If you don't take your filthy hands off my son right now, I'll rip your arms off."

Dan let go but responded with a sneer. "You and what army, albino-man? You don't scare me. I know you're not an alpha. So I figure I got a good chance of beating you in a fair fight."

Grant's face grew dark, almost evil-looking. "I was hoping you'd say that. But then you're not the kind of man who fights fair, are you? Good. Neither am I. By the way, my wolf says you are disgusting. He can't understand how your own wolf can stand living in your head. He feels sorry for your wolf and wants to set him free from you. There's only one way to do that, right? James, move back and give us some room."

Grant had moved between Dan and James, turning his back on Dan to search James's face.

"He didn't hurt you, did he?"

James knew what he was asking. He shook his head. But looking past Grant, he could see that Dan was already beginning his shift. His bones were cracking, and dark brown fur was covering his body.

James tried to talk through parched lips tight with fear. "He's . . . he's . . . already —"

Grant nodded, a slow smirk crawling across his face. "I know. But I grew up in a family of shifters. We used to race all the time. I always win. Just move far enough back that you don't get hurt."

The air around Grant began to shimmer. While Dan was still rolling around on the ground, becoming a full wolf, Grant effortlessly shifted, quicker than James had ever seen before. One minute he was Grant, standing tall. The next, he was a very stocky wolf, with almost white fur, a huge muzzle, and enormous paws.

Grant's wolf turned to face his enemy, just in time to avoid snapping jaws that were aimed where his head had been. Then the fighting began in earnest.

James shrank back against a tree, watching with horrified fascination as the two wolves tore into each other. The level of violence indicated the fight was to the death. Grant's wolf had superior size and bulk, while Dan's wolf had sneakier tactics. At first, they appeared to be evenly matched. Dan's wolf even seemed to be winning for a short time. But the smaller, darker wolf was panting heavily. He appeared to be getting tired, while Grant's wolf was almost dancing around, energized by the fighting.

Suddenly a black she-wolf snarled as it leapt out of the trees and landed on Dan's back. The jaws clamped around the nape of Dan's neck, biting down so hard that when he twisted to throw her off, a huge clump of skin and fur went with her, still clenched in her jaws.

Dan howled, whether in anger or fear, James didn't know. He gaped, fear clutching at his stomach, as Dan tried to fight off both of his parents.

James nearly collapsed with relief. He knew his mom was fierce, and now he could see Grant was her equal. It didn't take long before the combined attacks of their wolves brought Dan's wolf down. They both clamped their jaws down hard. Grant ripped out his throat, and Monique tore open his belly, spilling his intestines onto the ground. The light in his eyes quickly went out.

James was shaking with fear and excitement, adrenaline rushing through him, making his blood pound so hard he almost felt like he was going to explode. He took deep breaths, trying not to pass out as he watched the two mated wolves howling out their triumph over their enemy's body.

Suddenly, he heard a tiny voice in his head. *It is over. I am glad we survived.*

James shook his head, trying to clear it. *Am I going crazy?* He froze in place as the two victors began to shimmer and shift back into their human forms.

The voice spoke again. *No, man-cub. I am your wolf.*

Once Grant was human, he waited for Monique to join him. A heartbeat later, she stood next to him. Together, they both turned to James. Tears began to stream down his face.

Both adults moved closer, but James shook his head, both hands out to keep them away. He began to cry, huge wracking sobs that shook his whole body. Monique tried to approach him, but Grant held out a hand to stop her.

"But he's never seen death before," Monique began.

"Maybe," Grant replied, nodding his head towards the trembling boy.

James fell to his knees, unable to hold himself upright. His tiredness combined with his emotional upheaval, causing his shoulders to shake as the sobs continued. His whole body trembled. Suddenly, he gasped as he looked up into his mother's worried face. He glanced at Grant, whose face reflected a combination of sympathy, understanding, and pride, almost like he knew what James was about to say.

"I saw it! I saw it all!" His words were raspy, coming from a throat raw with lack of water, and repressed, long-overdue grief.

Grant moved closer, taking Monique's hand. He knelt before James and pulled her down, also. Grant spoke in a gentle voice. "You watched, didn't you? You weren't supposed to, but you wanted to see what your dad was going to do. So you snuck out, and you watched."

James nodded, giant sobs once again wracking his tired body as he finally expressed feelings he'd ignored for so many years.

Monique's face reflected dawning horror. "But you were only eight years old! I forbade it! You were too young!"

"I had to! I had to see my daddy!"

"Oh, my God! James!" Her eyes looked so sad. "It was too brutal! It was hard for *me* to watch! Oh, James, why didn't you tell me?"

"Because I wasn't supposed to be there. I knew I'd be in trouble. So I never told anyone."

"James, my son!" There was a hitch in her voice. "You've had nightmares for years. I'd wake up to comfort you in your bed, and you'd be crying in your sleep. You never told me. I wouldn't have been angry."

It was hard for James to speak through the emotions he was processing, but he spat out words, gasping between syllables. "I know that now. But I was just a kid. I had never disobeyed you like that before. But I had to see it. Then I ran back to the house and snuck in through the open window. When you got there, I thought you'd know from my face. But you were too upset. And you moved us so quickly, I guess you never noticed."

"You should have told me. It's too much for you to hold inside."

Grant spoke in a voice tinged with pride. "He's a strong

one, Monique. Strong enough to keep a secret like that for all of these years, despite the pain it caused him."

His mother looked at him with new eyes, finally seeing him for the man he was becoming. His sobs had subsided a bit, and she held out her arms to him. With a small cry, he pressed forward, into the loving embrace they both needed so badly.

Tears also streamed down Monique's face.

"May I?" Grant asked.

James looked up and saw tears in Grant's eyes as well. Monique nodded.

Grant leaned forward and wrapped James and his mother in a bear hug, his arms enfolding them in a tight, comforting embrace. They remained like that long enough for James's sobs to turn into occasional gasps, then to subside.

James spoke again, but more calmly now, comforted within the cocoon of love created by the two adults. "You moved us so many times, trying to find a safe place for us to live. You always had so much to deal with, Mom. I didn't want to add to your already overloaded plate of worries."

Monique pulled back slightly and stared at him for a long moment. She took a deep breath. "I'm sorry I wasn't there for you when you needed me, James."

James shook his head. "No, Mom. That was never the issue. I didn't let you know what I saw because you had enough to do without having to hold my hand while I cried over something I should never have seen." He gave her a crooked smile. "Besides, any punishment you could have come up with would have been nothing compared to how I've felt all these years. Unable to share with anyone what I'd seen . . . what I felt, as I watched Daddy get killed."

"That's why you don't want to be alpha?" Grant asked in a gentle tone.

James nodded. "I want to be big and strong, like you. But I don't want to have to make the hard decisions. Or to be the one that everyone wants to challenge. I just want to live my life in peace. Or as much peace as a shifter can have."

Monique and Grant both stared agape for a heartbeat, then a slow smile spread across Grant's face.

"Really? When?"

"Just now. When you were both shifting back. This little voice in my head told me he was glad we had survived. I thought that I must be going crazy. Then the voice called me a man-cub and told me he was my wolf."

"But you're not old enough for him to present yet," Monique stated. "And I've never heard of anyone's wolf talking to them this early before the first time they experience the change."

"But he *did* talk to me, Mom."

Grant was still smiling. "So, not only are you strong enough to carry the weight of what you saw as a child, quietly locked inside of you for years. But you are also breaking some traditional rules by having your wolf talk to you long before it's old enough to force you to change? Are you sure you're not an alpha?"

"No!"

Grant chuckled. "Okay, okay. Like I told you, it's always a choice. But if you find that others are obeying you, or asking your advice, or electing you to be in charge of things, you may have to rethink your options."

"I want to be like you, Grant. I want to get big and strong and look scary enough for others to leave me alone. I want you to teach me to fight, so I can take care of myself and those I love. But I don't want to have to face down challengers who hate me because they want to be in charge. I want to live long enough to read all the good books in the world. And that's going to take a really long time."

A golden-brown wolf suddenly loped into the clearing. He nodded at each of them in turn, before trotting over to sniff at the corpse of the dead wolf. He lifted his nose into the air and howled out a message that informed the rest of the pack where they were. Then he shifted quickly to become Nathan.

All three of them got up from their knees, brushing the dirt off themselves.

"James, good to see you, young man," Nathan said before turning to Grant and Monique. With a look of extreme distaste on his face, he nodded his head in the direction of the corpse. "Anyone else hurt?"

They both shook their heads.

"I didn't really need her help," Grant said with a shrug. "But I also knew she needed to take part in killing the man who threatened *our* children."

Monique looked into his eyes, nodding solemnly. "Yes. I did need to do that."

"I'll get a team here to bury him out back, where the other reprobates' bones are. He'll fit right in with the rest of them."

"Where's Diego?" Grant asked.

"Back at the mansion. He's been coordinating the perimeter searches and communicating with everyone in security about the importance of not allowing someone who has been escorted out of here back on pack grounds."

"We'll head up there now, then," Grant said. "He needs to be filled in on some recent . . . uh . . . developments."

Grant gave a significant look and nod to both James and his mom. Then he put an arm around James's shoulders, while his mom wrapped her arm around his waist on the other side of him. Together, they headed towards the mansion.

As they walked, James suddenly realized he was the only one wearing clothing, yet it didn't bother him at all. Even seeing his mother naked was no big deal when he was still marveling over the idea of having a wolf sharing his body and his thoughts. The sound of a wolf howling had always been a comfort to him, but now he was happily anticipating the idea that someday he'd be joining the other wolves in howling at the moon.

I am not strong enough yet. But soon.

James smiled in response to the voice inside his head. And he was shocked to realize that for the first time in over five years, the smile wasn't *just* on his face. He felt as if a burden had been lifted from him, and the future looked much brighter than he could have imagined just a few hours ago.

CHAPTER EIGHTEEN

James was happy when Diego appeared suitably impressed that his wolf had spoken to him so long before being old enough to present himself physically. And the idea that James had willingly gone with a man who meant to harm him because he wanted to protect his sisters was enough for Diego to proclaim him a hero in front of the entire pack at the next Sunday night meeting.

James was so embarrassed that he tried to sneak away from the gathering, but Grant pulled him into a knot of young men who wanted to congratulate him on his bravery. He wasn't used to talking so much to strangers, so he inadvertently slipped up and mentioned that his wolf had already spoken to him, despite him not even being fourteen yet. This further raised him in the esteem of the other male teens living on the premises year-round. They all promised to make sure he felt welcome when the school year started. Some even offered to show him around the classrooms, to be sure that everyone else knew he was not to be teased — as freshmen typically were.

"After all, if your wolf has already spoken to you, it's awake. Now it's only a matter of time before it's strong enough to force your first change. Looking forward to running in the woods with you soon."

Since those words were spoken by a student whose facial hair made him look more like an adult than a seventeen-year-old soon-to-be senior, James began to have a very good feeling about what he had been dreading — being the *new kid on the block* in high school.

The fact that his mom was the principal didn't seem to even come into the equation anymore, now that the pack leader had proclaimed him a hero in front of everyone.

Grant was trying to get Monique to commit to a date for their wedding and honeymoon. They were in the dining room, enjoying their after-dinner coffee while keeping an eye on the girls at a nearby table. Selma and Selena had some friends over, and they were playing a new board game Selena had gotten for her birthday.

"Not too close to the start of the school year, because there's too much going on then," Monique observed.

"But I don't want to wait four months until winter vacation, either," Grant pointed out. "Even Thanksgiving is too far away. I want to declare in front of God and everyone that we belong to each other." He gave Monique a look infused with love.

James, who was also still sitting at the dining room table, looked up from the book he was reading. "How about the fall equinox? I mean, it's not as big of a holiday as the solstices are, but we still observe it at the school. It's the third week of September, which will mean that everyone has gotten into a routine at school. We have a long weekend off for it. You guys could get married by Diego on a Wednesday night, and have the next four days as your honeymoon."

Monique regarded James with an open mouth.

Grant smiled. "See? I told you he's usually listening, even when his nose is in a book."

Monique shook her head. "When did you get so smart, young man?"

James grinned. "I've always been smart, Mom. It's just that you aren't treating me like a baby anymore, so I know if I speak up, I'll be listened to."

Monique stared at him, tears brimming in her eyes. "I'm glad that you *are* talking to me again. It's been so hard, not knowing what you were thinking about or how you felt about anything. I love you, you know. I felt so hurt that you didn't seem to want to share yourself with me at all."

Grant patted her knee. "Now we know why he was so conflicted."

James nodded. "I was afraid that if I started talking, I wouldn't be able to stop, and I'd tell you things I didn't want you to know. You're like a dog with a bone when you think one of your kids is hiding something. You worry at it and won't stop until you get the truth. Since I didn't want to tell you what I had seen, I just stopped talking to you." He shrugged with a lopsided grin. "Sorry, Mom. It won't happen again."

"Is that a promise?" Monique asked.

James regarded her for a moment before replying. "Yes, Mom. I promise."

"So what do you think of his idea?" Grant redirected her attention back to him. "I'm sure Diego would be amenable to officiating his first wedding for us. Where should we head for our quick honeymoon?"

Monique smiled shyly. "I don't know. I never had a real honeymoon before. Tim and I were too poor to afford more than a night at a hotel."

Grant reached over, stroking her fingers before lifting her hand to kiss the back of it. "Let's go together to talk to Diego. We can ask if that date works for him and see if he has any ideas about where we could go celebrate our love."

Diego was pleased to learn that he'd be officiating the marriage for Grant and Monique sooner, rather than later. "After all, once you've mated on both levels, as humans and as wolves, no one can or should try to separate you. I know being legally married is not necessary, but trust me, it makes everything feel different. I can't explain it, but you'll know what I mean after it's done."

He began searching through the Rolodex next to his desk phone. "I know I have the number of that affiliate who let Saoirse and me use his vacation cabin for our honeymoon. Maybe he can do the same for you two."

Grant pointed at the ancient device he was thumbing his way through. "Why are you still using that old thing? Wouldn't it be easier to have all of the numbers you need in a computer database?"

Diego smiled. "I suppose. But this belonged to Joe and still has all the numbers he collected over his years as pack leader. Every time I use it, it's like he's here beside me, helping me learn to do the job he nominated me for. I hope to someday be as good a leader as he was. So I'm not ready to sever this small connection to him quite yet."

By the time Monique and Grant left his office, the date and time of their wedding had been chosen, and their honeymoon arranged. They'd leave on Thursday morning, right after their early ceremony in the small chapel. They'd stay at the same cabin he and Saoirse had used, driving back Sunday morning to be home in time for dinner.

That night, Grant opened a bottle of champagne to share with his wife, then filled the Jacuzzi while she read to her daughters. He invited her to join him in the warm, bubbly water after she came in to report the children were all asleep.

"I'm looking forward to having you all to myself for a few days," Grant said, leaning over to clink his glass with Monique's.

"And for a few nights," she added as she took a sip from the glass.

"I want to hear just how loudly I can make you scream, with no one close enough to hear you, while I pleasure you, endlessly." He leered at her, waggling his eyebrows.

She arched one brow. "And I want to see if it's possible for me to tire you out. To make you finally have to beg me to stop making you come."

"Is that a challenge, my dear?"

She nodded with a sly smile. "Yes, big guy. Are you up for it?"

He pointed to the head of his cock, sticking out of the water, aiming at its favorite target. "Oh, yes, I think I am."

"Mmm, that looks kind of yummy." She knelt in front of him, leaning over to lick at the drop of pre-come leaking from the tip. "Let's practice a bit to get ready for the contest."

With that, she took a deep breath, lowered her head into the water, and swallowed as much of him as she could fit into her mouth.

Grant let out a strangled moan, then leaned back. He carefully set his glass onto the ledge, out of danger, and surrendered himself over to the pleasure given to him by his mate, who was certainly worth the wait.

PART TWO: CHANGES

CHAPTER NINETEEN

"Early in October is the best time to plant new trees," Grant explained to James.

They were both dressed in jeans and t-shirts, having thrown off their sweatshirts while digging holes in the dirt. Grant had gotten permission to plant an orchard in part of the huge field behind the garage. The baby trees with their root balls were delivered on Friday afternoon, and he and James had been working since early in the morning on Saturday to dig the holes so they could plant them all before the weekend was over.

James stopped to pull up his shirt to wipe the sweat off his face.

Grant smiled over at him. "Felt cool out here before we started digging, didn't it?"

James grimaced. "Yeah. Now I'm sweating bullets! Can we take a break?"

Grant looked at his watch before nodding. He opened the cooler they had nearby and took out two water bottles, tossing one to James, who caught it in mid-air.

"Good reflexes, son." Grant walked over to where James had flopped down on the ground and sat down next to him. He opened his bottle of water and took a long drink.

James gave him a quick glance, and Grant noticed it, raising an eyebrow. "What?"

"Your voice is different when you say that," James said.

"Say what?"

"Son. When you call me *James*, it doesn't change, but when

you call me *son*, it does."

"How does it change?"

James shrugged. "I dunno. Kind of softer . . . less rough sounding. It's hard to explain."

Grant thought about that for a moment. "I wonder if it's because I'm so proud to be your dad? I've never been particularly interested in having a family, but now that I have children, I'm honored to be allowed to help shape your lives."

James gave him a quirky smile. "Yeah, that must be it."

They sat quietly for a few minutes, resting.

James took a deep breath. "If you're helping to shape us kiddies into grown-ups, can I ask you a question?"

"Anything, son," Grant replied before smiling. "Now I'm self-conscious about saying it. But it feels good in my mouth to say it. Maybe that's why it sounds different."

"Um . . . yeah." James took a deep breath. "I know I probably won't be shifting for a while, but does it really hurt bad?"

"Yes."

"Every time?"

"Yes."

"Then why do you do it, if it hurts so much?"

Grant leaned back against a rock, using it to support himself as he thought. "How would you feel if it was the opposite?"

"What do you mean?"

"If the wolf was the primary owner of your body, and you could only exist independently when the wolf *allowed* you to take over. I mean, wouldn't you want as much time as you could get, to own the body you've been forced by nature to share?"

James gave him a surprised look. "I guess so. I never thought about it like that."

"I've had a wolf awake and living inside of my head for almost fourteen years. It's nice to have the company sometimes. Other times, like when my wolf wants to take over and it's not convenient for me, it's a nuisance. But he never goes away. Oh, he pouts, he rages, sometimes he even gives me the silent treatment when he's really upset with me. But we both know that he's there and that he's going to want to have his turn ruling over our shared body. The trick is to figure out how much time he needs to be satisfied, so you can own the body the rest of the time."

James was silent for a moment. "Did you have trouble figuring things out at first?"

Grant shrugged. "Not as much as some. Remember, I come from a family of shifters—both parents and all three of my siblings. I had lots of people to watch and to ask whenever I felt overwhelmed. You do too, you know. Not just your mom and me, but your pack leader and many of the folks around here. We've all been through what you're going to be dealing with soon, and we're all happy to share with you what worked for us. And I, for one, am not ashamed to tell you stories about what didn't work."

James grinned. "Like?"

"Oh, like when I went away to college, and I didn't feel secure enough about where to let him run, so I didn't let him take over, even when he was raging around in my head."

"What happened?"

"Things like sleep issues. If he couldn't take over when I was awake, he made me suffer by not allowing me to get any real rest. And he'd talk loudly to me when I was in conversation with someone—like a cute girl. Or when I was trying to listen to a professor's lecture or the lab assistant's instructions. Made it really difficult for me to concentrate on anything I had to do."

"How did you deal with that?"

"I went home for the weekend and let him out. Once he had some good long runs in the forest, had caught a few rabbits, and done some howling at the moon, he was willing to let me have some peace and quiet in my own head. Or rather, in *our* head."

James was picking up small handfuls of dirt and letting them sift through his fingers. "Wow. There's a whole lot I'm going to be dealing with soon, in addition to just acne and hormones, right?"

Grant patted his knee. "Yes. But like I said, you've got a whole village around you, willing and able to help you out."

He looked at his watch again. "Break time's over, dude. We've still got some holes to dig, and the sun won't last much longer. Let's get as much done as we can before it gets too dark. We'll finish digging, then plant all of the trees tomorrow."

James rolled his eyes as they both got up. "Ya know, after this weekend, I'll be glad to get back to school on Monday. Less hard labor, more sitting on my butt in a classroom."

Grant grinned. "Yeah, but when we have fruit on the trees, hopefully by next summer, but certainly the one after that, you'll be glad we did all this work. Nothing like the taste of fresh fruit that you just picked off the tree."

"I like fruit even better when it's baked into a pie," James said with a sly grin.

"Yes, but when you get older, like me, you'll realize that you don't have to work as hard in the gym to work off the calories from an apple. Not like you do for the calories from a piece of apple pie, especially with ice cream, and maybe caramel sauce on top."

James's stomach growled. "See what you did?"

Grant picked up his shovel and nodded at James. "The sooner we get these holes dug, the sooner we can head inside, shower up, then get to dinner."

"Slave driver," James mumbled under his breath.

The boy's lips were twitching as he said that—obviously

he was aware that Grant could hear him.

A week later, on Saturday afternoon, James sat in the dining room with Grant, taking a break after having spread compost around the trees they'd planted.

Nathan walked in, picking up a bottle of water on his way to their table. "I'm heading into town to go to the hardware store. Is there anything you need me to get you for the orchard?" Nathan asked the erstwhile gardeners.

James spoke up eagerly. "Why don't I just go with you?"

Grant nodded in approval. "Good. James, you know what we need."

"Yup. Plus, I never get to go into town, so it will be like an adventure."

Nathan snorted. "Some adventure. The hardware store is not that exciting, you know."

James shrugged. "Yeah, but when you never get off the grounds, at least it will be a change of scenery, right?"

Nathan smiled. "I guess." He looked around dramatically, even though there were few people around at that time since it was between mealtimes. He winked at Grant before speaking in a loud whisper. "Maybe I'll even let you drive part of the time."

James stared at him. "Really?"

Nathan put his index finger to his lips. "Shh. We'll take one of the Suburbans, since it's a virtually indestructible tank. There are quite a few miles before we'll even see another car. No time like now for you to get some practice in, right?"

Grant put his fingers into his ears. "La-la-la! I didn't hear any of that, you know. What I don't know can't reach your mother's ears."

James smiled. *It's nice to be treated like an older guy sometimes. Kind of makes up for the whole smelly armpits, acne, and weirdness of my voice changing in the middle of a sentence.*

His wolf's raspy voice spoke sleepily in his head. *And soon, I will be strong enough to emerge.*

James tried not to let his fear filter through to his inner wolf.

The car jerked around a lot at first. James was totally embarrassed. "I'm never going to be able to do this." He grunted in frustration after he got the Suburban to move forward a little bit, though he had trouble steering it down the center of the two-lane road. When Nathan told him to slow down, he applied the brakes, and if not for the seat belts, they'd have both flown through the windshield.

"There are a lot of things that are hard to do at first, James," Nathan said calmly, "but after you've been doing them for a while, you'll chuckle warmly, remembering how hard they used to be for you."

"Since I've never driven before, I think I've had enough practice for today," James said, this time gently applying the brakes to bring the car to a complete stop. He moved the gear shift into park and turned to Nathan.

"Are you sure? We've still got quite a few miles to go before we get onto what passes for a main road around here and possibly encounter another vehicle."

James nodded. "Yeah, I'm sure. I'm so nervous I'm sweating, even though it's a chilly day. I'll feel much better if you take over again, now."

So they got out of the car, switched positions, then clicked their seatbelts back on.

"You did pretty well for your first time," Nathan said. "With a bit more practice, you'll be able to drive around on the grounds independently well before you need to go to a DMV to get your license."

James snorted. "I'm only fourteen. That's not for two years."

"Yes, but we don't drive much around here, so the more

practice you can get whenever I'm heading somewhere into town, the sooner you'll gain the confidence to not fear the wheel."

They were both quiet for a while, and James stared out the window, enjoying the colors of the few leaves that were still on the trees.

"You know what I'm really afraid of?" He was still looking out of the window.

"Your first change?" Nathan asked.

James jerked his attention back to find Nathan smiling at him. "How did you know?"

"That's a huge *duh*, James. I presume you've seen enough of us changing to hear the bones cracking, and the moans and groans we all make when they're moving around. It's a scary thing to be facing, not knowing what it will feel like for you. Plus, you also have no idea *when* it will happen, and that adds to your anxiety. You're a deep thinker, since you read so much. So while others might not obsess over it, you're probably finding it hard to think about anything else."

James sighed. "You got that right. I try to remind myself how happy everyone looks when they get done with a run, and how relaxed and centered they seem to be. I know the aftermath will be great. It's just the actual changing that, quite frankly, horrifies me."

"Your wolf is probably afraid of that also," Nathan remarked.

"He is?"

Nathan nodded. "Yep. He's never been through a change before, either. He's not strong enough yet to force it on you, but he will be soon, now he's awake in your head. But as much as it scares him, it's the only way he'll ever get to exist. So there's a whole lot more impetus for him to want it to happen—at least at first. But after you've been through it a few times, it won't be such a terrifying event for you."

"I guess." James couldn't keep his doubt from his tone.

Nathan smiled, still watching the road. "You know, I've got a few female friends who are mothers. They've all told me that the pain of childbirth is pretty intense. In fact, the ones who are shifters have said that in some ways, it hurts more than shifting. But the end result is so wonderful that the pain is kind of overlooked in their memory. They know they'll ultimately enjoy it, so they willingly do it again. If they didn't, we'd all be only children, right?"

James was silent for a while, staring out of the window. Suddenly he turned to Nathan. "What was your first time shifting like?"

"I don't like to talk about it."

"Why?"

"Because I don't even like to remember it, and I was there."

"Did it hurt that much?" James's fear bumped up a notch.

Nathan shrugged. "It's not so much that, as I had no idea what was happening to me. No one in my family, at least to my knowledge, is a shifter. I was totally unprepared for what was happening to me. I mean, I thought I was doing okay dealing with adolescence because whenever I was totally stressed, I'd hide out in books."

James nodded, smiling. "Like me. That's what I do."

"Yeah. I guess I was always destined to be an English major. I wasn't the biggest or most attractive guy around, so I mostly avoided girls so as not give them the opportunity to avoid me. Since I wasn't into sports much, I didn't have many guy friends either. I spent a lot of time by myself. But that had the unforeseen result of making it more obvious to me when a voice started talking to me in my head."

"I thought I was going crazy when I first heard him," James remarked.

"It was even worse for me, dude. Remember, I had never encountered a shifter, so I had no one to ask about it. I was convinced that I was developing schizophrenia. I'd done some research online when the voice started getting too insistent to ignore. I was terrified to tell anyone, since we were on the poor side as a family, and I knew therapy was too expensive for my parents to afford. I didn't want to be a bigger burden to them than I already was, with my huge, teenaged-boy appetite. And since I had no close friends that I trusted enough to share fears like that with, and I was afraid my brother would just make fun of me, I was alone in my terror."

"What did you do?"

"I managed to ignore the voice by pretending I didn't hear it all through the school year. I was fifteen, a sophomore in high school, and just trying to survive. The voice yelled at me, raged at me, then tried to punish me by giving me the silent treatment. That was my favorite part, of course, since I was able to concentrate on my schoolwork when it wasn't incessantly yakking at me. But my sleep was filled with dreams of running through the woods on four legs. Those visions made me even more afraid, since from what I'd read, people with multiple personalities only imagine they are other people, not other species."

Nathan stopped at a stop sign and looked all ways before turning left onto the main road, which would eventually take them into the nearest town.

"So?" James prodded him to continue.

Nathan gave him a quick grin. "Come the summer, right after I turned sixteen, I was overwhelmed with a desire to seek the coolness of the forest. We didn't have AC in my house, so I was tired of always sweating. By the middle of July, when the temperatures were the hottest, I'd work my part-time job in the morning, then go for long walks in any woods I could ride my bike to. Luckily, I grew up in upstate New York, and there are a few state parks around close to where I lived. I had read about what the Japanese called *shinrin yoku*, which literally means *forest bathing*. So I'd leave a note for my parents, telling them that I was going for a long walk in the woods to cool off. They thought I was crazy not to just go to the local lake on the off chance that I'd get to ogle some teenaged girls in bikinis like my older brother did. But I had other things on my mind."

When Nathan remained silent, James turned to him expectantly. "Then?"

"Then came the day that my wolf took matters into his own paws. I was just strolling along with a book in my hand, meaning to find a good place to sit and read. All of a sudden, my body stopped responding to the commands from my brain. I mean the *human* part of my brain, which was telling it to keep walking and not to drop a library book in the mud. I tried to stay upright but fell forward onto my hands and knees. Then the change started for real.

"I was in more agony than I'd ever felt in my life. Every bone in my body hurt as they cracked and broke, then made themselves into new shapes. And I could feel organs inside of me moving around to new places. It was totally weird to be aware of and feel things that are inside of us, which we never pay any attention to since they don't have any pain receptors. Even my hair hurt. My face ached as it elongated, and my ears moved up onto the top of my head. I looked down at my body in horror and saw that hair was growing all over me. And my arms and legs had moved and were growing skinnier. My feet and hands were becoming paws. I was sure I was in the last stages of dying, so I prayed harder than I'd ever prayed before. But in the middle of all that horrible pain, the voice that I'd tried so hard to ignore, was exulting! It was howling with the joy of release as it took over the body we'd been forced to share."

"Wow!"

"When it was finished, I planned to just lie there.

Remember, I was convinced I was dying. But the other one living in me, the voice in my head, was now in control of *our* body. It kicked and chewed its way out of the gym shorts and t-shirt I'd been wearing. The wolf got up and howled in pleasure, then started to run. I'd never been an athletic kind of guy. I preferred to read about exercise, rather than actually do it. But this was totally cool! I was running in the woods, on four paws, and flying like the wind. I was enjoying myself so much I forgot to be afraid anymore. And the good humor of *the other* was a big part of it. I'd felt judged and found wanting for so long by that voice that I really enjoyed just feeling, and not thinking at all.

"I ran all through the woods, ending up making huge circles because it really wasn't that big. When I heard human voices, I hid in some bushes and waited until they had passed by. I heard every movement of the other creatures in the forest. I smelled layers of things I never knew existed. And when I got thirsty, I sniffed out a pond and ran to the edge of it to drink. I stared at the image of myself in the water, then I plunged my face into it, ignoring the fact that I wasn't even concerned about how pure the water was. I drank by using my long tongue to lap it up. I heard some forest mice rustling around in the dry leaves, and without even considering what I was doing, I hunted them down. I caught one of them and ripped it apart, enjoying the feel of the warm flesh in my mouth. And when I finally got tired, I lay down in the cool shade under a large bush, and I fell asleep."

"You could fall asleep? With all of that going on?"

"Well, remember, my body had been through a lot in just a short amount of time. I'd done my first change and romped around in the woods. The wolf might have wanted to keep going, but the body was exhausted. When I woke up, it was dark. I knew I'd be in big trouble at home for worrying my folks about where I was. But the wolf wanted to stay in charge. I tried to negotiate, but it was as unwilling to listen to my human concerns, as I'd ignored its desire to have a bit of freedom. That's when I realized that I'd have to learn to compromise with *the other voice in my head*. I had a lot of time to think about things while the wolf just enjoyed being free and in charge.

"When the first fingers of dawn appeared in the east, I rallied all of my strength to remind the wolf that I had a job to get to, that I had to get home. I promised him that as soon as possible, I'd find a bigger forest, so he could run again. The wolf resisted at first, fearing that I was lying. But as I pointed out, with flawless logic, he could force me to change without my permission. After all, that's what he had just done. But I didn't want to risk us being hunted and shot for being a stray wolf, or a danger to the local community. So if he let me take over again, I'd find a safer place for us."

"And he let you?"

"Uh-huh. The second change was just as painful as the first one, but it helped that I wasn't terrified anymore. I knew it was going to hurt a lot, but only for a short time. Then I'd be in my human body again. Of course" — Nathan grinned — "I was naked. And my clothes had been destroyed. I couldn't let my mom see them, so I buried them and put a big rock over them. Then I remembered I had eaten a raw mouse, bones and all, and I was so grossed out that I threw up. I washed off my face, then rode my bike, still naked, back to my house. I had my house key, so I let myself in as quietly as possible.

"I was sharing a room with my older brother, and he woke up when I walked in. He sat up, telling me that I was in big trouble, asking me where I'd been. But he stared when his brain recognized that I was naked. He asked me if I'd *gotten some*. I knew what he meant, of course, and in a way, I *had* really lost my virginity. I'd had my first experience as a shifter. So I nodded and tried to look modest. Since he'd only gotten laid for the first time earlier in the summer, he whistled softly, calling me *the man*. Then I pulled on a pair of gym shorts to sleep in and fell into bed. He tried to get me to share details then, and over the next few days. I refused, and eventually, he stopped asking. But it was a while before I was able to make good on my promise to my wolf, since I got grounded for the rest of the summer."

"But you did get to let him run again?"

"Yeah. It was always hard to find safe places, and I'd always check them out first as a human. But gradually, I learned just how often I had to let him out to keep him happy. And he learned to trust me to make sure the places would be safe enough for him to do what wolves do naturally without having to worry about being shot as a poaching renegade."

"Wow," James sighed. "I guess I'm really lucky then, right? I live in a compound that has huge grounds all around for wolves to run and frolic in. Many of the adults around me, including my parents, are shifters, so there's no need to hide what I am from anyone. I guess I don't have that much to be afraid of, after all."

"Yep. And your parents won't disown you, either, like mine did."

James looked at him in shock. "They did?"

Nathan nodded. "I finally tried to share what I'd learned about myself with my mom and dad after I'd graduated from college. I figured it would be a good time. I had my first teaching job and was moving out of the house for good, and I wanted them to know my secret. Huge mistake, that. They couldn't accept what I was telling them. I mean, who could blame them, really? They were both convinced that I was lying to cover up that I was gay, and in our religious household, that was not something they could accept. I laughed out loud, telling them that being gay would be a whole lot easier to deal with than what I'd been dealt. They told me to leave and not to come back."

"So that's why you never leave to visit family?"

"Yup. My siblings stay in touch with me using the internet. My brother emails me now and then. My sisters send pictures of their kids. But my parents have forbidden them all to bring my name up in the house. I'm sad about that, but it's been over ten years, so I try not to cry over spilt milk. I have found a home here, and I enjoy being a teacher. And I don't have to hide who and what I am around here."

"And you have friends here, who depend on you."

"That's right. I'm now the third in command, to one of the larger packs on the east coast. And your mom is one of my best friends. I tried a few other packs before I found the academy, but since I can teach as well as live here, I'm very pleased with where I ended up. And having such a large forested area to run around in is like heaven to my wolf."

James looked around with interest as Nathan navigated the narrow streets of the small town that was closest to their compound.

"There's our destination," Nathan remarked, as he got into the turn lane for the parking lot of the hardware store.

James giggled, then tried to cover it up with a cough.

"What's so funny?" Nathan asked as he put the car into park.

"I was just thinking. We're heading into a store full of people who would freak out if they knew that a couple of werewolves were shopping right next to them."

Nathan grinned. "Keep that to yourself, mister. We don't want any trouble with the locals. Our compound has managed to co-exist with this tiny town for a very long time. We want to keep it that way."

"I know. It's just funny. That's all."

"Behave yourself, and I'll buy you some ice cream before we leave town."

"A banana split?"

Nathan made a big deal out of pulling out his wallet to check the amount of cash he had. He sighed heavily. "If I must."

They were both grinning as they got out of the car.

Chapter Twenty

Late fall brought a roar of cold, northern air, and it wasn't long before the snow appeared. Halloween meant the yearly werewolf movie marathon, with lots of popcorn tossed at the screen. People who knew—or actually were—werewolf shifters laughed at the Hollywood treatment of their kind. The Halloween Dance, held on October 31, was a resounding success. The adults were immensely grateful that it came and went with no trauma, unlike the previous year, when the old pack leader had died right after the dance after naming Diego as his successor.

Thanksgiving found the compound snowed in, and grumpy students had to cancel their plans to fly home for that holiday. But right after the finals were finished in mid-December, there was a temporary thaw in the weather. The students, who'd been denied the opportunity to alleviate their homesickness earlier, were quick to head for the airport to fly home to spend their three-week December holiday break with family. The weather was problematic in early January, so some students weren't there for the first few days back, but eventually, everyone returned, and the second semester proceeded.

Saoirse asked Grant to start sitting in on her classes, to see how she ran things and to help with the labs. "After all," she said, "you're the one who will be subbing for me during my maternity leave." She grinned at him. *And before then, if I get as uncomfortable as other women have told me I will.*

"That's not going to be until April sometime, right?"

Saoirse rubbed her belly protectively. "Yes. I just started my third trimester. But from what other women have told me, this is when it starts getting really rough. I'll get bigger and bigger with each passing day, and more and more uncomfortable. Supposedly, I'll get to the point where I won't care if they go in with a saw and pliers and drag the baby out because I'll be so anxious to have it out of my body."

Grant snorted. "I've never heard it put quite that way before. But, yeah, I guess having all your innards squished down to accommodate a large, full-term baby must be really hard to deal with."

Saoirse rolled her eyes. "That's what I've heard. So I might be calling on you to take some days even before the baby is born. Or at least to take over the labs, while I sit with my feet up and brood over how awful I feel, and how I'll never let my husband touch me again."

Grant raised his eyebrows at her.

"Of course, I won't really mean that. Other moms tell me that amnesia kicks in once you start bathing in nursing hormones. I'll forget the pain and only remember how wonderful it is to hold a new baby in my arms. Watching Diego hold our baby will remind me of how much I love him. And that will obliterate any lingering ill-feelings I might harbor about how unfair it is that women have to do all of the childbearing. And soon, I'll want another one."

Grant's eyes bugged as he gaped at her.

"Not right away, of course. But once the baby gets big enough to walk and talk, I'll be ready for another one. Or so I've been told."

"You do come from a big family, don't you?"

"Um, yeah. But I don't want ten kids. Luckily, neither does Diego. But the poor man never felt loved by either of his parents or his siblings, so I owe it to him to at least pop out a few kids for him to get to enjoy playing with them. So he can enjoy true familial camaraderie."

"I'm a big fan of having siblings. My sister and my two brothers have always been my best friends. Until now, of course. Now my wife is my best friend."

Saoirse smiled. "And when your kids grow into adults, they can be the best friends that you raised them to be."

"I never thought of it that way. But, yeah."

Saoirse and Grant got back to inputting all the data they'd received from the cheek swabs they'd sent to the genetics lab into their laptops. She was hopeful that when enough of the results were returned, they'd be able to discover a link. A method to predict which of the children who attended their school would, at some point, have a wolf presenting itself to the community.

February was taken up with students worrying about having someone to give a Valentine's Day card to. The turn-about dance, traditionally held on the Friday after Valentine's Day, was a stress-inducing event for everyone who wasn't already part of a dating pair of teenagers. Of course, all students were welcome to attend without a date, but everyone knew that the best way to go was as part of a couple.

James attended alone, standing with the other unaccompanied boys on one side of the decorated gym. He watched the couples in the middle dancing, while the girls standing on the other side of the gym watched him hopefully. He knew they wanted him to ask them to dance, but he had no idea how to dance, or even talk to one of them without his voice cracking or blushing so much they'd notice it even on his brown skin.

As soon as he could, he retreated to his room and delved gratefully into a novel with more mature themes. Grant had introduced him to a new author, and James was enjoying learning about how to *grok.*

The beginning of March presented the exact same weather as the previous few months. There was snow, the ground was frozen, and no one wanted to run outside in their human forms. The gym was the most popular place, and usually crowded. Anyone wanting to stay in shape had to seek a time when there wasn't a long wait for whatever equipment they wanted to use.

But at night, when the moon rose, the call of the forest became too loud to be ignored. Those who were able shifted to their wolfs and enjoyed the freedom found in answering the call of nature.

James began to get jealous, anxious for when his wolf would appear. But the adults around him told him that it did no good to fret. When the wolf was strong enough, there'd be no doubt about it. So he tried to practice patience.

For an adolescent boy, that was hard enough. But then the mating hormones, which were particularly intense during early spring, began to flow through every cell in his body. He was glad he had Grant and Nathan to teach him how to fight, which used up some of that energy that he wasn't able to run off yet—at least not on four paws.

PART THREE: THE IMPOSSIBLE IS POSSIBLE

CHAPTER TWENTY-ONE

Nathan's wolf sniffed at the air as he rounded a corner near the perimeter of the grounds. He'd been running at a steady pace since he'd shifted. He'd had a stressful day with the students, who were acting up in typical early spring fashion. Then his brother had sent him an email with pictures of his newest child, a son, to join his older daughter. He'd also mentioned that their father was very ill but still refused to even discuss the idea of allowing Nathan to come to see him, even if he was dying.

My life is a shit-show. It's not fair! He's my dad, too. He might not care about me, but I still love him.

Earlier, others had invited him to run with them, but he had declined. He needed to be alone, to brood over his troubles, and try to quiet his mind.

His wolf had comforted him in its own way. *Run! Once we cover enough ground, you will forget human things and just enjoy being me.*

So he did. By the time he got to the perimeter, which every security person was supposed to check regularly while running, he was awash in endorphins, easing his stressed mind. But then he saw something move on the other side of the electrified fence, and was instantly alert to the possibility of danger to the pack. He approached the fence cautiously, sniffing deeply, wondering at the new aroma that was so enticing that it intrigued him. He stared at the spot where he'd glimpsed movement. He stood still and waited, his exhalations making steam in the cold night air.

The cloud that had blocked the light of the full moon moved, and he suddenly could make out eyes looking back at him from the dark of the tree line. He growled softly to scare away any smaller animals.

The eyes are almost level with mine. What is this creature looking back at me? And is it the source of the aroma that makes me want to inhale more deeply?

There was a low growl, and a thin, black she-wolf stepped out into the full light of the moon. She and Nathan stared at each other, and the night stood still around them. Her eyes were not dull, like those of a natural wolf. They reflected the intelligence of a shifter.

Our mate!

The excited tone of his wolf, and his words, made his throat tighten. His heartbeat, which had slowed down after he stopped running, suddenly began to pound loudly in his ears. *Only one way to find out.* He inclined his head in the direction of the nearest gate and began to trot slowly in that direction. He looked back to see the wolf was still sitting, watching him. He returned to her, inclining his head once more before resuming his slow trot toward the entryway to the grounds.

If she's a shifter . . .

Of course, she's a shifter. She's our mate!

If she's a shifter, and she wants to join our run, she'll follow us.

He resisted the urge to glance back for a while. His ears pricked up when he heard the unmistakable sounds of twigs snapping under paws as she loped along slightly behind him, on her side of the fencing.

When he got to the gate, the woman on the tower obviously saw them approaching.

"Halt!" she called out.

Both he and the she-wolf stopped and sat down. When the guard aimed her rifle at the wolf on the outside of the grounds, Nathan growled loudly.

She kept her weapon trained on the other wolf. "That's

you, right, Nathan?"

He nodded, knowing she could see him out of the corner of her eye.

"Do you want me to let her in?"

He nodded again.

"Has this been cleared with anyone higher up?"

He snarled, shaking his head.

She considered that for a moment. "Well, you *are* third in command. Will you be responsible for her conduct?"

He bobbed his head up and down vigorously as the female wolf turned to watch him.

"Both of you approach the gate, and I'll open it." She lowered her rifle to work the electronics to turn off the current in the gate and let it swing open.

The female wolf only hesitated a heartbeat, and Nathan watched her closely. She whined softly, looking from the gate to the security guard, then back to the gate.

Nathan moved in front of the entrance and stood in the open space. His green gaze sought the female's dark brown one. Once she looked into his eyes again, she nodded and made up her mind. She trotted over to the open gate and joined him on the compound grounds.

"Move, both of you," said the guard. "I need to swing it closed again in the next fifteen seconds."

Nathan began to move back in the direction they'd come from, thinking there might have been something on this side of the fence she'd wanted.

She is our mate. She knows it, as we do.

Now that she was nearer to him, the tantalizing aroma filled his nostrils with every breath. She matched his stride, staying by his side as they moved further from the fence, and into the forest.

She's probably thirsty.

Nathan took them on a direct path to the closest pond. Most of it was still frozen, but many wolf paws had cracked through the ice on the one side, allowing some of the ice to melt in what little sun they'd been having. He stopped, and so did the female, just behind him. He bent his head and drank from the water, then looked over at her invitingly. She moved closer and lowered her head to drink also. The liquid part was so narrow that their flanks touched as they both drank.

Nathan felt as if an electric shock had stunned him. His breathing sped up again, and he could feel the head of his cock begin to push its way out of the sheath that protected it.

He gazed at the female and saw she was beginning to pant, and her eyes were glazing over as instinct made her react to their nearness. The aroma got stronger and stronger, and he felt as if he would explode out of his own skin.

The female turned away from him and presented herself to him as a ready and eager mate.

What happens now? Nathan was suddenly aware that he was not in the driver's seat, and his wolf needed to direct their actions.

We claim her, his wolf said, moving over to mount the female, his front paws on her shoulders as he nipped at her ear. Nathan felt his haunches jerk forward, and his cock rising rampant out of the sheath. Then it connected with the softer fur that surrounded the female's slick channel.

The smell is her. Her message to us. Her invitation!

His wolf made no reply because it was too busy laying claim to the female that enticed them both.

Nathan had only had sex as a human before. He'd never mated with a female wolf, fearing he'd be trapped in a relationship that he didn't want. But the feel of the she-wolf's fur under his paws combined with the strong pheromones she was emitting meant that his senses were totally consumed in the moment. He joined his wolf in enjoying the tight squeeze of her inner muscles on his cock. It didn't take long before he came, howling out his release. She whimpered under his weight, quivering with her own enjoyment of their union.

Nathan's legs shook too much to hold him up anymore, and all of his weight landed on the black wolf's back. Her legs collapsed, and with a mutual *whoosh,* the air was driven out of both of them. He felt trapped within her body for a few minutes, then his cock softened enough for him to slide out.

I have to shift back now! I must tell her that we're now mated!

No! The mating has only begun. We have all night to enjoy each other.

No amount of arguing convinced the wolf otherwise, so Nathan resigned himself to enjoying the rest of the night as an observer. An extremely intimately involved observer, who felt every twitch, every intake of breath, every orgasm that the two wolves shared during their long night together. They rested, then hunted together and shared what they caught. They drank water again and had sex . . . repeatedly. Finally, when the first fingers of rosy light were starting to light up the sky, they lay close together in contented harmony.

Seizing the initiative when his wolf's defenses were relaxing into sleep, Nathan quickly forced the change. But when he turned to the female, to invite her to join him in expressing her humanity, he heard the snoring that indicated she was already fast asleep.

No matter. It will be full morning soon enough. Then I will get to see just how beautiful my mate is. As a wolf, you're ravishing enough. I can't wait to see what your human looks like!

That thought was his last conscious one, as he succumbed to the extreme tiredness his body felt after such a long, arduous night.

CHAPTER TWENTY-TWO

Nathan woke up with a start, immediately aware that the chilly morning air was way too cold for two naked humans with no blanket to share. In fact, he'd been dreaming of being trapped in a refrigerator. Not only was he shaking, but so was the female his arms were draped around. Memories flooded his brain, and he looked curiously at the sleeping woman, whose back was plastered against the front of him since they'd spooned while they slept.

What should I call her? I have no idea what her name is!

He cleared his throat, audibly.

"Um, honey? Sweetheart? We need to move into the mansion. I don't know if you've noticed, but it's freezing out here. Our body heat melted the snow, but we're both wet and shaking."

He sat up, and she rolled onto her back, giving him his first look at her face.

God! She's gorgeous!

Her skin was almost the same dark tan as the color of his fur when he was a wolf. Her hair was a mass of long, black curls. Her lips were full, and her lashes long and thick. They began to flutter as she struggled to open her eyes. Her eyes blinked open, then closed again, as the morning sun shone directly into them.

Nathan moved slightly so that his body was blocking the sun that had blinded her.

She opened her eyes again, and he was lost in the depths of their dark brown color as she regarded him intensely for a quick moment.

She sat up quickly. "What the hell? What are we doing out here in the cold?"

Her voice was low and sexy, despite her irritation, and the chattering of her teeth. Nathan fought the urge to lean over and kiss her, and instead, responded to her question.

"We fell asleep out here. I wanted us to change and go into my apartment last night, but you were so tired after our long night together that you fell asleep. I didn't want to disturb you, so I wrapped myself around you, to generate as much body heat as possible." He gave her a sheepish grin. "To tell the truth, I didn't even feel the cold after I shifted. And you didn't shift but fell asleep right away. So I guess that's why you didn't feel the cold until now."

"And why, exactly, are we naked out here in the woods, lying in the snow? I mean, what the hell kind of party was it, anyway?"

"Party?" he asked.

"Yeah. I assume I met you at some party in . . . what did you call it? A mansion? So where's everyone else? Didn't anyone think to check on us, after we decided to frolic *au naturel* in the snow?"

He smiled, shaking his head. "I was running alone when I saw you on the other side of the fence. Don't you remember?"

She shook her head. "Nope."

He gasped in surprise. "You don't?"

"No, and I'm freezing my ass off out here. Let's get somewhere warm, preferably where my clothes are, and then we can chat. Maybe over some hot coffee, hopefully."

He got up and reached out his hands to help her. She took hold with both of hers and stood. Nathan felt the electrical shock of her touch all the way to his groin. He looked into her eyes, which were now dark and stormy, and he wanted to lose himself in their depths.

She was quite a bit shorter than he was. The top of her head barely reached his shoulders. Her nipples were dark pebbles on the round globes of her shapely breasts. They were standing close enough that his hardening cock bouncing off her thigh could not be missed.

"Down, boy! I'm not into morning-after sex. Especially not when I'm in danger of losing all feeling in my fingers and toes. Let's get into that mansion of yours, and we can talk about whatever comes up." She gave his cock a sideways smirk.

He began to walk toward the clearing to find his clothes. They kept up a good pace, which slightly warmed them both. But it was still undeniably cold. He was relieved when they made it to the clearing without her falling too far behind. He pulled his sweatshirt from the bottom of his pile of folded clothing and offered it to her.

"Here, put this on. At least it will warm the top half of you."

She grabbed the sweatshirt and pulled it on. The sleeves were way too long, and she was short enough that the shirt reached half-way down her legs. She shivered, wrapping her arms around herself, her hands covered by the long sleeves.

Nathan pulled his pants on, picked up the rest of his things, including his shoes, and led the way to the mansion.

When they got out of the trees, she gasped at her first sight of the building. "When you called it a mansion, you weren't kidding!" She looked at him speculatively. "Just how rich are you, dude?"

He shook his head without stopping. "I don't own this. It's an academy—a school. I live in an apartment in it. We'll go up the back stairway to avoid running into a crowd. Lots of people get up early around here, even on a Saturday."

She followed closely behind him as they made their way around the side of the building nearest to them. He opened a small door that led to a stairway. He gestured for her to enter before him, but she shook her head.

"No, my momma didn't raise no fool. I want you to lead, so I can keep my eye on you. This is turning out to be a totally weird morning, and I want to at least pretend I'm in control."

He shrugged before leading her up the two flights to get to the third floor. He opened the stairway exit and walked across the hall to the door of his apartment. He dug the key out of his pants pocket, unlocked it, then walked in, looking back expectantly. "Aren't you going to come in? I'll order up some breakfast and some coffee, and we can talk more."

She peeked through the doorway, then nodded. "Okay. We can eat and talk. That way, if you're gonna kill me, at least I'll go with a full stomach."

He sputtered angrily, starting to reply, but she shook her head at him, grinning.

"Calm down, dude! Can't you take a joke? Anyway, then I gotta call an Uber and get the hell out of here. My manager will be crazy angry with me since I gave him the slip again last night. And the longer it takes for me to get back there, the more trouble I'll be in."

Since he didn't understand any of that, Nathan picked up his phone and texted the kitchen to bring up a tray of food for two people, along with lots of coffee. He looked up to see her walking around, checking out his place. "Do you want cream for your coffee?"

"Yeah, but no sugar. Not good for my girlish figure." She walked into the bathroom and closed the door.

Once he had ordered, he tossed the rest of his clothing onto his bed. Then he opened a dresser drawer and pulled out a pair of gym shorts and a t-shirt and put them onto the bed, also.

The door opened.

"My turn," he said, waving at the bed. "I put some shorts and a t-shirt on the bed for you to change into. Then you can go sit down in the living room, and we can talk."

"Okay, boss."

He inhaled deeply as she passed him, which was a mistake since he felt himself getting hard again. He stood for a while, leaning on the shelves above his toilet, willing himself to settle down enough to take care of business. When he was done, he looked at himself in the mirror. *You mated, and she's waiting out there. Time to discover who I'm going to spend the rest of my life with.*

She is perfect for us, his wolf commented, sounding half asleep.

Nathan made a face at himself. *I hope so.*

He opened the door and walked into the now-empty bedroom. He continued into the living room in time to hear a discreet knock on the hallway door. He walked over and opened it, bent down, picked up the tray, and kicked it closed behind him. He carried the tray over to the dining room table.

The woman rose from her perch on the couch and followed him, inhaling deeply. "I smell bacon! And coffee. The room service is great around here."

He smiled. "It's just because it's so early still. The ones who get up at the ass-crack of dawn have already eaten, and the late sleepers aren't up yet."

He gestured at a chair, to find she was already sitting on it. He took the top off the tray and exposed two plates with scrambled eggs, bacon, and hash browns. There were multiple pieces of buttered toast on another dish, with a selection of jelly next to them. There was a small pitcher of orange juice and a very large thermos, which Nathan picked up to pour steaming coffee into the two mugs. He pushed one over to the woman, amused that she was already eating from the plate she'd pulled off the tray to her side of the table.

He sat down and applied himself to the food, watching as she poured cream into her coffee, and took a long drink.

"Aah, nothing like good, strong coffee to make the

morning less harsh."

He nodded. "I'm surprised you're so hungry, though. We ate a couple of rabbits last night. But I guess that *was* hours ago."

She raised an eyebrow, her fork half-way to her mouth. "Rabbits?"

"You don't remember that either?"

She shook her head.

He was beginning to have a bad feeling in the pit of his stomach. "Do you remember that we mated?"

She put the food into her mouth, chewing as she spoke. "Well, duh! I figured that we *did the nasty*, though I have no idea why we did it outside in the snow when you have this totally huge place with that big bed in it, all warm and cozy, up here."

She grinned at the dismayed look on his face. "Honestly, dude, I wish I remembered. I mean, you're totally hot — totally my kind of man. Tall, thin, blond, with an ass that I'd never get tired of squeezing while you pump yourself into me."

He felt himself hardening slightly. He managed to wrestle control of himself while she obviously considered what to say next.

She shrugged. "But I do this all the time. I go to a party. I get high. I do some drankin', some druggin', and all that shit reacts with the maintenance drugs I take all the time. Before you know it, I'm entertaining everyone there, but I'm not in charge. It's like some other person is in the driver's seat. Then the next morning, I don't remember anything at all. I've been told that's a sign of alcoholism, but I don't care. I just wish I could remember all of the good sex I'm told I had, but hey, at least I get laid, right?"

Nathan stared at her in alarm. *She doesn't remember anything?*

He could feel his wolf waking up to pay attention.

"So . . . You don't remember meeting me at the fence?

Don't remember following me to the gate, so you could be let onto the grounds? Don't remember running through the woods with me? Or that we mated? Nothing?"

She shook her head. "I'm sorry. It's a total blank. But like I said, judging by how hot you are, I'm sure we had an excellent time. And any time I'm back in this state again, I'll be sure to look you up. Deal?"

Nathan took a deep breath, trying to quiet his rapid heartbeat. Trying to get his panic under control. "But we mated!"

"Yeah, I get that. You keep saying that like it's a big deal or something."

"Wolves mate for life."

She choked on the coffee she had been drinking, and put the cup down, coughing hard.

"What did you say?" she gasped out around her coughing fit.

"We mated as wolves. Once we also mate as humans, we'll be life-mates."

"Wolves?"

He nodded. "Of course. We're both shifters. You must have been running somewhere near here and heard the howling of the others in the pack. When I saw you, you were on the other side of the fence. But I knew when I looked into your eyes, that you were *the one* I've been waiting for."

She pushed the plate away, and her gaze darted around the room nervously. "Um, I don't see a phone around anywhere. I need to call for that Uber, so I can get back to my manager's place. He's probably going nuts, wondering where the hell I am." She swallowed hard. "In fact, I'll bet he's got the police, the firemen, and the National Guard out looking for me. So . . . I'd better be going soon."

He got up, and she twitched, watching him closely as he walked over to pick up his phone. He returned to the table and sat back down.

"Here's the phone, but I can't let you call for an Uber from here. I'll drive you into town, so you can do it from there."

"Why not?" Her voice was filled with rising panic.

"We're a private compound out here. We don't let strangers onto the grounds."

"You let me last night."

"That's different. You're my mate."

She got up and started pacing. "You keep saying that. What the hell does it even mean? You got me at a bad moment when the *other gal* was in charge of my body. We had sex, and now you're acting like it's some huge commitment? We fucked, dude, nothing more. In fact, I don't even know your name!"

"I'm Nathaniel Taylor. Everyone calls me Nathan. I teach English at this school. And you are?"

She turned and barked, clearly irritated. "Right! Like you don't know!"

He shook his head. "No, I don't."

"Everyone knows who I am. That's why you wanted to fuck me, isn't it?"

His eyes narrowed. "Um, no. I told you, we're—"

"Mated, yeah. So you keep saying. And I'm telling you that's horseshit!"

"So who, exactly, are you then?"

"I'm Nisha," she said, looking at him expectantly.

"Is that supposed to mean something to me?"

She gaped, her eyes wide open. "Nisha. You know, *I had a dream, and that dream was you.*" She sang the words and seemed astounded when he didn't react to them at all. "You really don't know who I am?"

Nathan shook his head, confused. "No, I don't have any idea who you are, other than my mate."

"Everyone in the world knows who Nisha is. I'm only the most popular singer on the planet. I've had more songs on the top of the charts than anyone ever has, and I've sold-out every place I've ever performed at! That Nisha."

Nathan shrugged. "I don't listen to pop music." He might have sounded unpleasant, but he was having a hard time controlling his escalating panic.

"What do you listen to?"

"Mostly blues, some jazz. Maybe some classical."

"Classic rock?"

"No, classical, like Bach or Beethoven. Maybe some Tchaikovsky."

She sank onto the couch, obviously in shock and pondering how to respond. A moment later, she announced, "Well, I'm Nisha. I write and sing songs. I'm famous. And you'd better get me back to my manager soon, before he tears the state apart looking for me."

He looked at her closely. "You think you're in danger, don't you?"

She jumped up again. "Well, duh! I wake up next to this totally hot guy, sleeping naked with him out in the snow. And then he walks me to this mansion that's close enough to where we were sleeping that there's no fucking reason we shoulda been cold all night. Then he keeps calling me his *mate*, like that's supposed to mean something to me. And he makes hints about some delusion that we were wolves when we met. I mean, how crazy is that?"

Nathan's wolf snarled in his mind, and he felt like doing the same.

He stared at her quizzically. "You don't remember shifting? You don't remember being a wolf?"

"And you ask me why I'm scared of you? You're fucking delusional, sweetie! Everyone knows there's no such thing as werewolves. *Now* I'm wondering just what kind of place this really is. Is it some kind of asylum? A place where rich folks can send their troubled relatives, so they can't hurt anyone?

What am I gonna find if I walk out that door? Bars on the windows? Guys in white lab coats, who are pussyfooting around, bringing meds to the occupants of this place? Should I place an order for my daily meds too?" Her voice ended on a shriek, and she stared at him with wide-open, frightened eyes.

Nathan picked up his phone and texted his pack leader. *Please come! Serious trouble with a female.*

"Who did you text? I thought you said you won't contact Uber until we're off the grounds. Now your story is changing?"

He shook his head. "No. I texted the pa — um, the boss. The guy who runs this place. He needs to know what's going on."

She eyed him suspiciously. "You're not gonna try to hold me here, are you? Because my manager will sue your ass and this place until you're all begging for spare change on street corners."

"No. You're free to go. But only after the boss helps me to figure out how it can be done safely."

"Safely?"

"I told you, we're a private place. I'm not sure he'll want you to know where you are. Why don't you have some more coffee while we wait for him to get here?"

The woman continued to pace around the room. She paused at the window, which overlooked a big clearing, with woods beyond the manicured lawn.

There was a loud knock on the door, and Nathan got up so quickly the woman jumped with alarm. She shrank back against the wall close to the window. He didn't like that she was scared, but he was at a loss for what to do. He strode over to the door and opened it, waving both Diego and a very pregnant Saoirse inside.

Diego spoke pleasantly. "Good morning, Nathan. I heard you let a guest onto the grounds last night?"

"That would be me," the woman said, emboldened enough to approach them.

"You're Nisha!" Saoirse cried with delight. "I recognize you from the videos that play almost non-stop in the gay bars my bestie used to drag me to all the time. You're a huge star! What are *you* doing here?"

"Um, that's a long story," Nathan began but was promptly dismissed.

Saoirse grabbed Nisha's hand, leading her over to the sofa to perch on it, their knees close together, as they chatted.

"My real name is Tonisha Gaines," the woman began, "but everyone just calls me by my stage name."

"Which would *you* rather we call you?" Saoirse asked.

"Nisha is fine," she answered, "since it's what everyone except my family calls me."

"Well, that handsome guy over there is Diego Vargas. He's the big boss around here. And I'm his wife, Saoirse McColl Vargas. So he's the one who *done the deed*." Saoirse smiled as she rubbed her large belly full of baby.

"Pleased to meet you, Ms. Gaines," Diego said with a formal bow. "Now, Nathan, can you join me in the next room a minute?" He turned to the females. "Honey, you'll be fine without us for a few minutes, won't you?"

Saoirse nodded. "Of course, we will. You guys just run along and talk your man-talk."

She turned to Nisha. "So what are you doing here in Maine? I heard that you live in L.A."

Nisha waited until Grant and Diego walked into the other room before she replied. But they still heard her words.

"My manager wanted to get me away from the party scene out in La La land since I wasn't getting any new songs written. See, I always write better when I have some peace and quiet. And I sure don't get that back in L.A., where everyone wants me to be at their parties all the time. So he rented this big place outside of some small town, where the owner had set up a studio in what used to be the barn. And I've been doing some writing, since it's so *natural* around here."

Satisfied the woman was safely occupied, talking with Saoirse, Diego closed the door and turned expectantly to Nathan. "Well? What's the problem?"

"I'm glad you brought Saoirse," Nathan began. "Nisha was terrified and ready to try to bolt out of the door."

"Explain."

Nathan sighed. "I saw this wolf staring at me from the other side of the fence last night."

Diego nodded. "So I've been told. You had Maggie let her in. Then what?"

"We ran around a little bit, then stopped for some water. Then she . . . um . . . presented herself to me." His face felt like it was on fire. "We mated. My wolf had been yelling in my head, telling me that what I smelled was my mate. I guess it was her pheromones."

Diego nodded. "Undoubtedly. Especially if she had already reached the same conclusion as your wolf. So what's the problem?"

Nathan exploded. "She doesn't remember anything! She says werewolves don't exist, and when I told her we mated as wolves, she got up off the chair, looking scared, and asked me if this was some kind of asylum. She said I was talking crazy and demanded that I call an Uber to get her back to her manager, who would be tearing the state apart looking for her. She accused me of wanted to keep her here against her will. She doesn't seem to even realize that she's a shifter!"

Nathan walked over to stare out the window before turning to Diego, certain his desperation was in his voice and on his face. "What am I going to do? She says that even though she doesn't remember having sex with me, it must have been fun. And she'll look me up the next time she's in the state. She wants to leave and not see me again."

Diego walked over to put his hands on each of Nathan's

shoulders, looking serious. "She remembers nothing?"

Nathan shook his head.

"I've never heard of anything like this."

"Me neither."

"I'll have to consult with Dr. Sullivan. He's been an expert on lycanthropes longer than anyone else I know. He may want to examine her and talk with her."

"That's all very well and good, but what are we going to *do* about her?"

"You mean, how are we going to get her off the grounds without her seeing where we are?"

Nathan nodded. "Yes. I'd like to also add . . . How can I get her to realize that we belong together?" His insides were in turmoil with his intense emotional pain. "She refuses to even admit that anything special happened between us. I've found my mate, and she doesn't want any part of me."

Diego walked over to look out of the window for a moment, then turned back to Nathan. "Well, unfortunately, she's right. We can't keep her here, no matter how much you want to do so. At least not long enough to convince her that you're a mated pair. We have to get her back to where she's staying. Then we'll see if Dr. Sullivan has ever heard of anyone like this. Maybe he can figure out a way to examine her to find out what's going on."

Nathan despaired at what he knew he must do. "So I should drive her into town, then call for an Uber for her?"

"Take one of the *burner* cars," Diego replied. "In fact, take the sedan. It will be harder for her to notice Rachel in the back seat. Once she's fastened into her seatbelt, Rachel will give her a shot of something to knock her out for the ride. Not a lot, but enough for her to sleep through it, so she'll have no idea how to get back here."

"Her wolf will know," Nathan pointed out.

"But if she denies even knowing there's a wolf inside of

her, she probably isn't aware of what the wolf knows."

Nathan swore softly.

"I know this is hard on you," Diego began, "but we don't know what we're dealing with. We need more information. Hopefully, Dr. Sullivan will be able to get that for us."

"And what if he can't? What am I supposed to do? My wolf craves her, now that he and her wolf mated. Do you have any idea how miserable he's going to make me?"

"He heard her talking, didn't he? He knows she's totally in denial about what she is."

"She says that whenever she drinks and takes drugs at parties, that another *person* takes over her body and runs things. She figures that means she's an alcoholic. But she has no idea who and what is taking over her body. She claims that she wakes up with no idea what happened. The shift is so painful. How can she not feel the after-effects?"

Diego shrugged. "Maybe she thinks she's just recovering from a really bad hangover."

"She says that she takes maintenance drugs, and they react with whatever she's partying with."

Diego scrutinized him closely. "Are you sure you want to pursue someone who regularly does drugs at parties with strangers, and wakes up not knowing what she did? Or with whom?"

Nathan gasped. "How can you ask that? You don't get to choose when your wolf tells you it's your mate. You, of all people, should realize that."

Diego sighed. "Yes, you're right. My wolf chose a non-shifter, which meant that I had to let her in on the big secret of this place. And I will never get to mate with her as a wolf."

"I guess I never thought of that. Your wolf is okay with that?"

Diego nodded. "He's the one who pressed me to mate with her as soon as possible. And he knew she wasn't a shifter."

He walked over to the bedroom door. "And you're right. When the wolf chooses, we have no say. So let's get her back to her life, and let Dr. Sullivan do what he can for us."

"Us?" Nathan choked.

Diego nodded, his hand on the doorknob. "Yes, us. You are pack. Anything that involves pack involves me. I'll call Dr. Sullivan right after I set things up with Rachel. Now let's get back out there and see what my wife has managed to find out."

Diego opened the door, and Nathan followed him back into the living room. They looked around, but both women were gone.

"Where are they?" Nathan's panic, which had calmed while talking with Diego, ramped up again.

Diego pointed at a note left on the sofa the women had been seated on. He walked over to pick it up and read aloud.

Gone to see if any of my clothing will fit Nisha. Come join us when you're done.

Diego smiled. "You see? She's making your woman feel more comfortable. Maybe we'll be able to figure out a way for you to do that also."

Nathan shook his head slowly. "I doubt it. She thinks I'm a certifiable crazy person."

"Maybe we can get Dr. Sullivan to introduce her to the other being living inside of her. Then she'll realize that you're both crazy in the same way."

As they walked down the hall, Diego spoke with Rachel on his phone. "Yes, that's right. Be out of sight in the back, passenger seat of the gray *burner* sedan. And bring that injector that you showed me. The one that has multiple doses of something to make her sleep on the ride. We don't want her too drugged, but she mustn't wake up until she's out of sight of the grounds." He hung up and smiled grimly at Nathan. "She's not happy about it, but she'll do it."

"Neither am I, but I don't see any other way to get her

safely into town."

"And using one of the *burner* cars means we can give it to George, who will strip it for parts and scrap the body. It's registered to a pack member who died a few years ago, but he'd brought it with him from another state. So there's no way to trace it to us. On the off chance your woman remembers anything about it, it won't matter. It won't exist anymore."

It didn't take long to reach the door to the penthouse. Saoirse had left it ajar, and Nathan followed Diego into the apartment.

"Oh, hey there, you two." Saoirse smiled brightly at them. "We found some crop pants of mine that look like long pants on her. And a t-shirt that I got from one of the bars Freddie used to drag me to. So are you ready to give her a lift into town, Nathan?"

"Are you gonna come with me?" Nisha asked Saoirse, while studiously avoiding looking at Nathan.

Saoirse looked at Diego, who nodded imperceptibly.

"I guess I can ride along as a chaperone for you two youngsters."

"I have some phone calls to make," Diego said, "so I'll just say goodbye to you now, Ms. Gaines."

She flashed him a million-watt celebrity smile. "Don't be silly. No one calls me that. Nisha is fine."

He bowed. "Okay, Nisha. It was nice meeting you."

She waved at him. "Maybe I'll see you again sometime."

When she finally glanced at Nathan, he tried to keep his face blank, to mask his pain.

Saoirse broke the awkward moment, gesturing to the door. "Lead on, Nathan. Let's get this celebrity back to her life before her manager tears the state apart looking for her."

With a sad heart and leaden lump in his stomach, Nathan led the way to the back stairway, to avoid any crowds of teenagers who might recognize the singer.

Luck was with them, and they made it out of the side door and quickly walked across the back lawn, past the newly planted orchard, to the garage that held the car they needed.

Nathan opened the front door, waving for Nisha to get into the passenger seat.

"Oh no!" she exclaimed. "Saoirse should sit in front. She's the preggo who needs the extra room."

"Um, no?" Saoirse said and grinned. "Believe me, it's roomier in the back. Besides, you'll want to enjoy the view."

Nisha gave Nathan an intense look. "Yes, you're right. I will."

Nisha slid into the front seat, while Saoirse got in the back and Nathan behind the wheel. As Nisha was fastening her seatbelt, Rachel quickly leaned forward and jabbed her upper arm with a hypodermic needle.

"What the—" Nisha sputtered, then she slumped over, her head hanging in front of her.

"I wish we didn't have to do it this way," Saoirse said as she opened her door to get out of the car.

Suddenly the car filled with bone-cracking noises.

"Oh, my God! Rachel! She's starting to shift!" Nathan pointed at Nisha, shimmering in the front seat.

"What the hell?" Rachel leaned forward and jabbed Nisha with the hypo again.

"Give her more!" Nathan reached out to hold Nisha still.

"I've already given her enough to stun a horse," Rachel pointed out.

The noises subsided, and Nisha collapsed back on her seat.

Saoirse walked around the car and opened the front passenger door, then she used the seat adjuster to recline the seat. Nisha was now snoring with her mouth open.

"I'd better ride with you into town," Rachel said. "Just in case she starts waking up and tries to shift again. And might I add, that's the weirdest thing I've ever seen! Shifting when you are drugged is a new one on me."

Nathan shook his head. "She's just full of surprises."

"Just get her onto a park bench in town, and call her an Uber," Saoirse said.

"I plan to stay with her until it gets there," Nathan said. "If she starts to wake up, I'll get up and watch her from a distance. But I won't leave a helpless woman by herself on a park bench. Especially not a famous one, who everyone will want to take selfies with, even if she's unconscious."

Saoirse gave him a smile before speaking in a soft tone. "You're a good man, Nathan."

He tried unsuccessfully to smile back at her. It ended up being a grimace. "At least *someone* thinks so."

She nodded decisively. "Text Diego when you get back. He might have some news for you by then."

Saoirse backed away and watched as the car pulled out of the garage. She rubbed her belly as a baby's body part pushed hard against her belly button. "Yes, little one. You're going to be born into a very interesting family." She was smiling as she headed back towards the mansion.

Chapter Twenty-three

Nathan drove around town for a while until he found what appeared to be the smallest, least-used park. He pulled into one of the few parking spaces around the back of it and spotted a bench close by. He turned off the car and sat quietly for a moment, his fingers gripping the wheel, looking straight ahead, taking deep breaths, trying to clear his mind.

Rachel spoke softly from behind him. "You mated with her, didn't you?"

He nodded. "But she doesn't remember. She has no idea she has a wolf living inside of her. She thinks I'm a dangerously crazy man. Or that I'm delusional."

Rachel shook her head. "That's the damnedest thing I've ever heard. It's not like our wolves are exactly quiet in our heads. How could she not hear hers?"

Nathan sighed. "I don't know. But she did say that she'd look me up if she ever comes to Maine again."

Rachel leaned forward to pat his shoulder. "Aw, honey. I'm so sorry."

Nathan sat up straighter, undoing his seat belt. "Well, better get her out there before she starts waking up again."

"I'll keep an eye on her from here, in case her wolf tries to break through again."

"I sure hope it doesn't. I don't want to have to explain to anyone why we're drugging Nisha, the famous pop star, in a park."

Rachel snapped her fingers. "*That's* who she is! I wondered why she looked so familiar."

Nathan grimaced again and got out, walked around the car to the passenger door and opened it. He met Rachel's eyes and felt undone by the compassion he saw there. He spoke around the lump in his throat, trying to keep things light. "I appear to be about the only person on the planet who doesn't know who she is. Just my luck, I guess."

Nisha was starting to stir as Nathan unlocked her seatbelt and lifted her out of the car. He carried her over to the nearby bench, then carefully set her down on it. Her head lolled back, and he gently turned it to a more comfortable position. He didn't want her to get a crick in her neck.

He sat next to her and used a disposable phone to call for an Uber.

"Yes, she's in the Bayland Park. Just come into the park and walk to the back of it. You'll see her waiting on the bench for you." He listened, then responded. "No, I don't know where she's going to want you to drive her to. Trust me, you'll get paid. Her manager will be only too happy to pay you when you deliver her."

He noticed her eyes starting to flicker, and she groaned.

"How will you know which woman needs a ride? Listen, dude, you'll be looking for Nisha. That's right, *that* Nisha. And if you're extra nice to her, she'll probably pose for a selfie with you. Now hustle your butt over here. She's getting impatient."

He disconnected the call, wiped his prints off the phone with his shirt, and put it on the bench next to Nisha. He sat for a moment, memorizing her face.

You're so beautiful! I don't deserve a woman like you.

His wolf snarled his disagreement.

Nathan ignored his wolf's difference of opinion and leaned over to kiss the luscious, full lips of the woman of his dreams. "Goodbye, my love," he whispered. "Remember me."

He touched his lips to hers again. At first, her lips were unmoving, but as he deepened the kiss, she began to respond.

She moaned softly, and her tongue darted out to lick at his lips.

Feeling as if he was a drowning man and her lips gave him what he needed to survive, Nathan became oblivious to his surroundings. He didn't even realize that she had opened her eyes until he heard the sharp intake of her breath and opened his. Her dark brown eyes opened wide, staring at him from between long, black lashes for a long moment.

He was shocked by what he saw. *Both of them are looking at me right now! How can this be, when she isn't even aware she's sharing her body?*

The silence of the moment was broken by the sudden blaring of a car horn. Nathan recognized it as the *burner* sedan's horn. He wrenched his gaze away from his love, to see that a man had entered the empty park at the gate and was carrying a large, hand-written sign that said, *Uber*.

He jumped up from the bench and quickly made his way back to the car, which Rachel had already started. He opened the door to the passenger side and got in. She put it into reverse and backed out of the space, then drove so quickly out of the lot that the tires squealed in protest.

"You can drive back to the compound if you want," she said. "But I didn't think it was a good idea for you to let that driver get a good look at you."

He managed to nod, his thoughts still with the beautiful woman he loved, but could not claim.

In silence, Rachel drove them to George's Place, a small garage on the outskirts of town. She drove around to the back, where the junkyard part of the business was set up. A gray-haired man, wearing coveralls that announced him to be George, walked out from the auto-bay area, wiping the grease from his hands onto a rag. They got out of the sedan, and Rachel handed George the keys. In return, he gave her a different set of keys and pointed to a small SUV, which was parked near the exit sign.

"Untraceable?" Nathan asked, inclining his head toward the SUV.

George nodded. "Of course. Rebuilt and unregistered. Like always."

As Rachel and Nathan began to walk to the SUV, she handed the keys to him.

"Hey!"

Nathan turned to see George had already opened the door of the sedan, but he called out to them over the roof. "Tell that darned son of mine that if his grades aren't any better this semester, I'll send his ungrateful ass to military school."

Nathan nodded before getting into the driver's seat of the SUV, shaking his head, and smiling.

Rachel got into the passenger side and buckled her seat belt. Noticing Nathan's grin, she asked, "What's so funny?"

"He says that every time he sees any of us. But the thing is, his son is a good student. I think it's just some kind of family joke. Whenever I pass it on to the boy, he always smiles. I think it's his dad's way of sending his love or something."

"Some people just have an odd way of showing how they feel, I guess," she answered.

Nathan headed the SUV onto the deserted highway that would eventually lead them home. "Yeah. I guess," he grumbled. He spent the rest of the drive brooding over parents who reject their children, and a woman who rejected her mate. Even though her wolf had chosen that mate.

Rachel looked in the side door pocket and found an old issue of a magazine. At least she would have something to amuse herself with as he sulked, and the SUV devoured the miles back to the academy.

CHAPTER TWENTY-FOUR

Since Nisha hadn't paid attention to where the house they were renting was located, she'd have to call her manager and give the phone to the Uber driver. Predictably, Richard exploded as soon as he heard her voice.

She interrupted his rant. "Save it for later, dude. Right now, you gotta tell this Uber driver where to go, or you'll never get to yell at me in person again, since I have no fucking idea what to tell him."

Nisha handed the phone over to the driver, who took it and got directions. As the Uber car got under way, she sat back, closed her eyes, and tried to quiet her racing heartbeat. *Damn it! I don't know why I'm so nervous. He's yelled at me for this kind of thing lots of times. It's not like he's my parent. And we haven't been lovers for a long time. Besides, I'm a grown woman! I should be able to do what I want, when I want, without him having anything to say about it.* She took some deep breaths, trying to calm herself. *How long has it been since I took any of my maintenance meds? I'll bet that's it. I need to get into my room, take my meds, then get some sleep. I don't think I got much sleep last night. At least, I don't think I did. But I sure think I need some now.*

As the car pulled up to the main door, it was thrown open by a very angry-looking man with a bald head and a long, gray mustache . . . Richard. He stomped his way to the car, followed by a younger, taller man with long dreadlocks.

Richard opened the back door and glared at her.

The Uber driver cleared his throat. "Uh, it was an honor to drive you home, Miss Nisha."

She gave the guy a small smile.

Richard didn't even glance at the driver. "Pay the driver, Jamar," he growled and held out a hand to help Nisha out of the car.

"I'm fine," she insisted, but he clamped onto her wrist and all but pulled her up and out of the car.

He shook her slightly. "What the fuck is wrong with you?" he barked.

She gave him a haughty look just as a huge blast of arctic winter air made her tremble with the cold and the lack of a jacket. "I'm going inside . . . where it's warm."

She started to walk away, then turned to glare at his hand, which was still on her wrist. His gaze met hers for a long moment, then he finally let go of her. She stalked into the house through the open front door. He growled again and followed her inside, slamming the door as he entered, then looked around. She had gone into the living room off the foyer and was pouring herself a shot of whiskey.

"Didn't you get enough of that last night?"

She looked up before defiantly throwing the shot down the back of her throat. Then she started to head over to the door.

"Where the hell do you think you're going?"

"Out to the barn. I'm going to my room. I need to take my meds, then get some sleep."

"Too busy partying to sleep last night? How many men was it this time? Or did you lose count?"

She whirled around, glaring at him. "That's none of your fucking business! I'm an adult, way past eighteen. And you're not my father. You also haven't been my lover for a very long time. So what I choose to do with my off-time is not your concern."

"It is when I'm watching you trying to kill yourself."

"Well, I've already aged past the infamous twenty-seven, so you don't have to worry about that. There isn't a twenty-nine club, so far as I know.

"Anything you do is my business when it stops you from doing what I brought you out here to do."

"I'm working on some new music."

"Not that I've heard. Noodling around with the piano, strumming a few chords on a guitar? None of that is producing the next album that you promised you'd write and record once you got into a remote place with peace and quiet. Do you have any idea how much it's costing me to have us out here? Almost two weeks, and still no new songs. Why don't you try *not* partying at night, and see if that helps?"

"I can't help it if the session musicians you hired like to party. And I work better with guys I'm familiar with."

"Meaning you have to fuck all of them first before you can record anything with them?"

"You're totally out of line, Richard! I haven't had sex with any of them. If I had, you'd have sent their asses packing by now, right? Isn't that how you operate?"

His eyes widened in surprise.

"Yeah, didn't think I knew about that, did you? Every time I have sex with anyone, you find out who he was, and you send someone around to *talk* to him. Then I never see him again. I used to wonder why I was the queen of one-night stands when that's not what I really want to be. But one of them called me last year to explain that, as much as he'd really enjoyed being with me, it had been made clear to him that, for his own health, he shouldn't see me again."

Richard's eyes narrowed. "It's for your own good. They all just want to fuck the famous Nisha. They don't really care about the real you. I'm protecting you."

"Oh, is that what you call it? And why? Because you really care about the real me? Bullshit! It's just part of how you try to keep me in line. I always knew you were a control freak, but I never realized just how far you're willing to take it."

"You don't need any other man besides me. I control your career. And you need a strong hand to keep you focused on the important things. Like putting out more music soon, before your fans find someone new to love."

"And heavens! The money train might dry up then, right? Yeah, you care about me, all right. You care about the money that rolls in when I sell out concerts and my CDs fly off the shelves. I'm your money-maker, that's all."

He started to walk over to her, his face a mask of what he obviously expected to be seen as affection. "Aw, honey, that's not true. After all we've been through together, how can you think that?"

"Because I've actually read my contract. I know what you expect from me. But I'm not going to be writing any music right this minute 'cause I've got a splitting headache. I need to go take my meds and get some sleep. If you want to bitch at me some more, you'll have to wait until later." She turned and walked into the hall.

"What phone did you use to call the Uber?" he called out.

She paused, answering without turning around. "Some disposable phone. The kind you buy cards for to load on minutes. You know . . . the kind you keep giving to me."

"That's because you keep losing your clothing as well as your phone and your keys every time you go out partying at night."

"I think I'm rich enough to lose a few pairs of jeans without any worries." She sneered at him.

"Let me have the phone."

"Why? So you can check it for prints?"

He strode quickly over and grabbed her wrist, twisting it until she yelped. "Yes. And to see if there's anything on it that will tell me where you were last night."

She fumbled with her free hand in the pocket of the pants she was wearing. She pulled out the phone and handed it to him. "Fine, but I want it back when you're done with it."

"Why?"

"Duh! Because I don't have my old one. This one will do until I lose it, too."

He nodded. "You'll get it back when I'm done with it."

"Good. Now let me go."

His eyes narrowed as he yanked on her wrist, pulling her closer until he was staring deeply into her eyes. "I should just put you over my knee."

"Just try it. I'll make sure you regret it."

Richard let go of Nisha so abruptly that she staggered. She turned without another word and strode down the hall to the door at the opposite end, heading for the barn, which was clearly visible behind the house.

The front door opened then, and Jamar walked through it. Richard thrust the phone at him.

"Here. Check it out. Anything you can learn, do it. You talked to the Uber driver, right?"

"Yeah. All he saw was a tall, skinny white guy with dark blond hair. There was a gray sedan in the parking lot near them, and someone was in the driver's seat, but the windows were all dark tinted, so he never got a look at the person. Oh, and it had out-of-state plates, but he didn't get a good enough look at them to tell what state."

Richard glared. "Did he see anything else?"

Jamar looked uncomfortable. "Um, yeah, boss. He said the blond guy was kissing Nisha when he first walked into the park."

Richard let out a string of swear words in Italian, Spanish, and English, using his favorites from each language.

Jamar backed away slowly. "I'll see what I can learn from the phone."

"You do that." He turned and walked back into the living room. "I'll make some calls myself."

"Do you want the phone when I'm done with it?"

"No. She wants it back." He poured himself a shot of whiskey and turned to Jamar with an evil grin. "Give it to her in pieces."

The first thing Nisha did when she unlocked the door to her room was to find her pill bottles. She eagerly twisted off the lids and swallowed them quickly, using the bottle of water she had left on the table nearby.

Sleep first, or shower first?

She lifted an arm and sniffed her armpit.

Phew! Shower first. Gotta wash off all the dirt and grass from sleeping in the forest.

While she was in the shower, she ran her hands all over her body, paying particular attention to the area between her legs. *Nope. Not sore at all. He must have been a considerate lover. And I'll bet I really enjoyed myself. I wish I could remember it. He's my kind of man, for sure! Tall, blond, strong, wiry, with a very nice-sized cock . . . from what I saw of it. And he has such a nice, tight ass. The kind I never get tired of squeezing. And those green eyes of his? I could happily get lost in them.*

She toweled off, then wrapped her hair up in another towel. She pulled on a robe, walked over to her bed, drinking the rest of the water from the bottle before she lay down. *I'm so thirsty. Must be dehydrated. What's that joke? How can I be so thirsty after all I drank last night? But I'm sure a good time was had by all. I just wish I could see that gorgeous man again. I didn't even get his number. Of course, there'd be no point in giving him mine. I keep losing phones. And Richard would never tell me if he called.*

A voice spoke in her head. *We must see him again, He's our mate.*

"Oh no you don't!" she said aloud through gritted teeth.

She got up and paced around the room. "You can't be talking to me again. I took my meds. I know they don't work that quickly, but they're supposed to keep you quiet. If you won't get out of my head, at least shut up, already!" She climbed on the exercycle near the bed and began to pedal furiously. *Meds work quicker if my heart is beating faster, so they get through my system.* "Must . . . shut . . . you . . . up!" She kept up the frenetic pace for a while, then looked at the clock. "I've been at it for ten minutes. Wonder if that's long enough?"

She cocked her head from side to side, then decided it was. She walked over to the bathroom and glared at herself in the mirror over the sink. "There's only room for one in my head. And that's me. So you, in there? You shut up!" She stuck her tongue out at her reflection, walked back over to the bed, and threw herself down onto it, then quickly pulled up the quilt. She lay on her back, taking deep, cleansing breaths, counting them, and she was asleep before she got to ten.

CHAPTER TWENTY-FIVE

Nathan was surprised to get a text from Saoirse's phone until he read it. Then he put aside the papers he'd been grading and locked up his classroom. He strode quickly through the halls, climbing the stairs two at a time until he got to the penthouse. When he knocked, Diego let him in, while holding his cell phone to his ear. He beckoned for Nathan to follow him and went into the small office, where Saoirse was already sitting, rubbing her belly absent-mindedly.

Diego sat behind his desk. "I'm going to put you on speakerphone now, Dr. Sullivan. Nathan has arrived. So you were saying that you were able to find out who Nisha's doctor is?"

Nathan perched on the edge of the chair next to Saoirse. She smiled at him, patting his knee, obviously sensing his anxiousness to hear what the doctor had to say.

"Yes, I made some professional inquiries as to who the first doctor of choice would be if someone lived in L.A. and had unlimited funds. I was given a few names. I called the top five, using various excuses as to why I wanted to consult with them. The last one I called was the right choice. I used the excuse that I had a question about the last paper he published, discussing what combinations of medications worked best for patients with severe schizophrenia. We discussed how difficult it is to treat patients who have multiple voices speaking in their heads. And how unusual it is for any patient to have just one voice speaking to them. He referred to a female patient who has been treated for her condition since she was in high school. I figured he must be referring to Nisha, so I kept asking leading questions."

The doctor paused, and Diego prompted, "What did you find out?"

"He was cagey at first, but then he relented and asked me where my practice is. I had identified myself to him when I called as a colleague from Maine. I told him my practice is in Bangor, and he asked if that was anywhere near Bingham. I assured him it was a short drive away, and that's when he asked if I could see his patient for him, as a professional courtesy.

"He mentioned that she's a famous pop star, and her manager had called, demanding her meds be changed since they obviously weren't working anymore. He was way too busy to fly across the country just to adjust her meds. He said he'd contact the manager and have him make an appointment for her to see me within the next twenty-four hours. True to his word, my office got a call later that day, and I saw her for the first time today."

"We won't ask you to break any privacy regulations about what you can tell us," Diego began. "But since her wolf mated with Nathan, we would like to know if there's any hope you can give him."

The doctor's voice rose in anger. "I'm not worried about any damn regulations. They've been drugging this poor woman almost into insensibility for far too many years. She comes from a wealthy family. Both of her parents are politically connected CEO's, and she's their only child. They've been sending her to specialists since she was fifteen."

"Probably when her wolf began to speak in her head," Diego pointed out.

"Yes. But the antipsychotic blends they've been giving her are way too much for a woman of her weight. If she wasn't a were, she'd probably be damn near a vegetable by now! They've been trying to correct a brain chemistry anomaly that she doesn't have. I presume it's kept her wolf relatively quiet in her head, but at least it hasn't seemed to dull her creative urges. I understand from my wife that her songs are trivial fluffy things, hinting around at enjoying life, but ultimately ending with her alone."

Saoirse leaned forward. "She's telling the story of her life, over and over again, without mentioning the whole *other-being-in-her-head* part. But she sings about how you need to *enjoy life while you can*. That vibe is what makes her such a huge hit in the gay bars."

Nathan licked his dry lips, clearing his throat. "What happened when you saw her, Dr. Sullivan?"

"I did some blood work under the guise of needing to figure out how to readjust her meds. I had her doctor fax me her file beforehand, so I already knew what a potent concoction of pharmaceuticals she's been taking on a daily basis. I've already started to replace what she's been taking, with my own proprietary blend of vitamins, minerals, and herbs. That will start to repair the damage that has been done to her body chemistry. I will have to gradually wean her off the heavy dosages she's been taking, but within a couple of weeks, she'll be completely off the meds she never should have been taking. In the meantime, I'll try to suggest to her that since she's been so unsuccessful in eliminating the voice she hears in her head, that instead, she might try to make peace with it."

"Isn't that a risk?" Nathan asked.

"Yes. There's always the possibility that she will contact her other doctor and tell him that I'm advising her to listen to the voice, rather than ignore it. But I'm hoping that she will realize the truth of what I'm saying. She's been over-medicated for half of her life, and the voice hasn't gone away. Maybe she'll be willing to try things a new way."

"I hope so," Nathan commented, his despondency echoing in his words.

"Nathan, I realize this doesn't begin to address your problem. But as a psychologist, my first priority has to be my patient. She's been misdiagnosed and over-medicated for a very long time. I have to try to repair the damage. Hopefully, that will result in her becoming aware of the other being she carries inside of her and coming to terms with it. Worst-case scenario is she calls me a quack and goes back to her heavy meds. Best case is she accepts who and what she is, and you may have a chance at reconnecting with your mate. It's the best I can offer to you, I'm afraid."

Diego spoke up. "Will you keep us apprised of your progress with her, Dr. Sullivan?"

"Of course, I will. You've given me a real challenge, and I'm hoping I'm up to it. I've never encountered anyone who has been medicated to the point she doesn't hear her wolf speaking. And I'm fascinated by the fact that her wolf has discovered that whenever Nisha drinks and drugs heavily, she is no longer in control, so the wolf can take over. I wonder how long this has been going on. I can't imagine how she isn't sore all over her body the next day."

Nathan spoke up. "She thinks she's an alcoholic. Maybe she just writes the bodily pain off as part of her hangover."

"That's possible. Anyway, I will let you know if anything new develops."

"Good luck, Dr. Sullivan," Diego said, and the line went dead.

Diego looked at Nathan. "It's not much, but it's all we can do for her. Now we just have to wait and see."

"That's not going to make my wolf happy. Which means he's not going to allow me to be happy. Not that I could be, knowing that the female I mated with has rejected me."

Saoirse shook her head. "No, Nathan. She didn't reject you. She rejected the idea of you and her mating as wolves and it being a lifetime commitment. She told me repeatedly that she thinks you're really hot and was upset that she couldn't re-member anything about what you two did the night before."

"Give Dr. Sullivan a chance to work his magic," Diego said. "There's a reason he isn't charged the usual affiliate price to be a pack member. He's identified and helped quite a few of our kind to accept their duality and find peace with them-selves. Hopefully, he can do this for Nisha, also."

"I hope so. I feel like I'm only half alive, since the other half of me is hurting so badly. I want to seek her out and make her realize what she means to me. But of course, I can't."

With that, Nathan got up, nodding to Saoirse to excuse himself. He walked out of the office and left the penthouse.

Saoirse got up and walked over to Diego, who turned to face her. He put his arms around her and rested his face against her almost full-term belly. She pulled off his hair band, strok-ing the silky strands.

"Is that how mopey you would have been if I'd have re-jected you?"

His gaze was serious as he stared into her eyes. "No. I doubt I'd have had the time to mope. I'd have been killed in the first challenge."

Her eyes grew wide, and she witnessed both of her loves peering at her through Diego's eyes. "Then I'm really glad I didn't let you scare me off with your talk of lifetime commit-ment and all."

He smiled, then rested his face against her belly again, just in time to feel a small body part push against him.

"What's that?" He rubbed his cheek against the spot. "You don't want me snuggling your mommy so closely? Too bad, little one. She was mine before she was yours. And long after you grow up and move out of our house, she will still be mine. I'm glad to share her with you, for now. But she is now, and will always be, mine."

Diego stood and took Saoirse into his arms, tilting her head up to kiss her passionately. She leaned back, her mind in a dreamy fog, her lips puffy from his kissing. "Um, Diego?"

"Yes, my love?"

"I've read that you can get things moving along nicely with labor by doing what got you into this in the first place."

His lips quirked up on the edges, and his eyes sparkled. "Is that a fact?"

"Well, it's what I've read. And you don't have any pressing appointments right now, do you?"

He shook his head, taking her hand and leading her out of the office. He quickly pulled her down the hall to the master bedroom.

Part Four: More Impossible is Possible

CHAPTER TWENTY-SIX

A week later, Saoirse morosely marked an X on the calendar. She sighed loudly, mumbling to herself as she perched uncomfortably on a dining room chair, sipping decaf iced tea.

"My due date isn't for another week and a half. Sheesh! I'm way past done with being pregnant. I can't eat because my stomach is too crowded with baby. I can't sleep because I'm so uncomfortable. But I'm exhausted all the time because I'm carrying around all this extra weight. And Diego must be tired of hearing me bitch all the time. How can women do this more than once?"

A tiny body part poked visibly at her belly, and she rubbed where the baby had announced its presence.

"Oh, yeah, that's why. Because I'm going to get Diego's baby out of it. Just don't take your time about things, you hear me, little one? I'd have no problem at all if you decide to make an early appearance." She looked at her laptop, bleakly.

How on Earth am I supposed to be able to concentrate on all this data Grant and I have been collecting? He's taken over my classes, so I know he's busy. Plus he's still a newlywed, so he and Monique are still getting to know one another. I told him I'd do it when I had the time. But I can't seem to think straight. Jerene told me it's baby brain, *due to the delivery being so close and all. But somehow we've got to track down whether any of these coincidences are important. We've got data from a lot of shifters and non-shifters. But it's tedious, trying to find the similarities present in the genetics of shifters versus non-shifters.*

Her cell phone buzzed from another room, and she got up to look for it. It was at the other end of the penthouse in the bedroom. She hurried over to it and picked it up without even looking to see who the call was from. Slightly out of breath, she gasped, "Hello?"

"You're not having sex with your man right now, are you?"

"Freddie! Bestie! No. I wish. It's supposed to help bring on labor, which, believe me, can't come soon enough for this gal. I'm panting because I just had to practically jog from my dining room to my bedroom to grab the phone. Just getting dressed exhausts me these days. So, how the hell are you, sweetie?"

"Um . . . Not good. That's why I'm calling you. I don't know who else to talk to."

"This sounds serious enough for me to have to sit down. Just a minute while I waddle over to the bed. Okay, now what's bumming you out so badly?"

"I'm freaking out, big-time. I have to see you, Sam. We need to talk in person."

"I'd love to, honey, but I'm not allowed to fly in my advanced stage of preggo-ness. You'd have to fly out here to see me."

"As a matter of fact, that's what I did. I don't know where the hell you live, but I looked up where I booked that ticket for you when you traveled out to have your job interview. So I flew overnight out here to Augusta."

"You're in Maine? Great! I can't wait to see you!"

"I'm staying in the same hotel I booked you into, the one right near the airport. Can you give me directions out to your place?"

"Um, not really since I never drive here. And I can't drive myself, either, since I'm too big to fit behind the wheel of any vehicle. But I can ask someone to give me a ride. We can talk in your hotel room, then maybe grab something to eat. Sound good to you?"

"I guess it will be okay. But I'm not going to be able to eat. I can't sleep either. I'm really not doing well at all, Sam. I need to talk to you."

"Does this involve John?"

"Not saying. Just come as soon as you can. I'm in room number two-thirty, at the end of the hall. I'll be waiting for you."

"Okay. As soon as I hang up, I'll get a fire lit under someone. Augusta is a couple of hours away from here. But I'm on my way."

Since it was a weekday, school was in session. That meant that Nathan was teaching, as was Grant. Jerene was also teaching, and Monique had to be in the building since she was the principal. Saoirse called Diego.

"How wonderful to hear from you, my sweet," he began.

"What are you doing right now?"

"Going through paperwork dealing with renewals of affiliates. Why?"

"It's not urgent is it?"

"No. Why? You're not going into labor?"

"I wish, but no. Freddie just called me. He's got to talk to me about something so important that he flew out to Augusta overnight. He says we've got to talk in person."

"Sounds like it involves John."

"That's what I asked him, and he was cagey about it. Which means, of course it does. I wonder if he's found out and is freaking out."

"This paperwork can wait. Besides, I could use a change of scenery. Plus, once I leave you at the hotel, there are a few people I can visit in town to touch base with. That way, I'll actually get some business done, also."

"So you're offering?"

"Yes. Meet me in the garage. We'll take the BMW."

"Joe's car?"

"Janine says it's the pack leader's car, so it's mine now. I don't get to drive it very often, since I don't get off the grounds much. So it will be a real treat for me. And I'll know I can trust your driver."

"Okay. I'll grab a jacket and meet you in the garage. Love you!"

It was a rainy day, so Saoirse grabbed Diego's jacket as well as her own, but they were tossed into the back seat. The drive was enjoyable, since the rain had melted most of the snow, and signs of spring were everywhere.

"So if this *is* about John, what am I allowed to say to Freddie?"

Diego glanced at her for a second, shrugged, then looked back at the road. "Well, if John has shared what he is with Freddie, then the cat, or rather *the wolf* is out of the proverbial bag already."

"That's what I was figuring. I have no idea where John is. I don't even know if they had a fight, or if Freddie just took off while John was at work. I won't know anything until I've talked with him."

"But if John has discovered him missing, he'll be moving heaven and earth to find him. Maybe after I drop you at the hotel, and see you safely up into Freddie's room, I'll text John just to let him know where Freddie is."

"I was hoping you'd say that. Unless you want me to text him now?"

Diego shook his head. "Don't you remember? There aren't any cell towers out here. We have our own on the grounds. But coverage is unreliable on these roads. Best to wait until we're in town so we can be sure he'll get the text."

"Okay."

"Just so you know, I plan to put a white noise device in the bathroom when I get there. The hotel room should be small enough that it will mask what you talk about, in case anyone is trying to listen in on your conversation. You two shouldn't be able to hear it, since neither of you has wolfen hearing. But it will confuse any electronic devices."

"Do you really think that's necessary?"

Diego shrugged. "Probably not. But being pack leader has taught me that you can never be too cautious. I'll leave it plugged in, and before we leave his place, I'll visit the bathroom again and remove it. He doesn't have to know it's in there. But it will give me peace of mind."

She stared out of the window for a while, and without even realizing it, started to drift off. Before long, she was snoring softly as the car devoured the miles.

Diego glanced over at his sleeping wife and smiled.

Get some rest, my love. You've been tossing and turning all night, trying to get comfortable. I'm glad the movement of the car has lulled you to sleep. I'll just continue to enjoy having such a primo driving experience. Just another thing to thank you for, Joe.

When they got to the hotel, Diego parked the car close to the entrance, then tapped Saoirse on the shoulder. "Honey? We're here."

She shook her head, glancing around at her surroundings. "We're at the hotel already?"

"Yes. You must have needed the rest."

She stretched, arching her back, and Diego watched her every move.

She turned to him, smiling. "What?"

"Do I need a reason to admire my wife, whom I adore so much?"

"I guess not." She smirked. "But I'll sure be glad when I don't feel like a whale anymore."

He shook his head. "You don't look like a whale, *mi querida.*

Just seeing how my child fills you makes me want to make love to you over and over again."

"Down, boy! I've got a bestie to calm down. And you've got some business to attend to, right?"

He nodded. "Alas, you're right. Let's get out and go find Freddie's room."

"I appreciate your walking me to the room. It's kind of weird, but I know you're just being protective. And that's what I appreciate."

He got out and moved quickly over to help her out of her opened door. As he pulled her up, he embraced her, whispering in her ear. "You are my world. I lost you once. I don't intend for that to ever happen again."

She grinned. "Twice, if you count when I went to my parents' house."

His distress at the memory must have shown on his face because she pulled his head closer for a tender kiss. "Remember what I told you? I can't promise to never leave you again, but I'll always come back to you. You're stuck with me, *señor*."

They walked into the hotel, ignoring the front desk and heading straight to the elevator to take it up to the second floor. Saoirse was panting heavily by the time they reached Freddie's room, so Diego rapped his knuckles on the door. Almost immediately, it was thrown open, and they saw relief wash over Freddie's haggard face.

"Sam! I'm so glad you came!" He grabbed Saoirse and pulled her tightly for a big hug. "Ooh, I didn't know a pregnant belly felt so hard," he said, pulling back and patting it gently.

"It also makes it hard for me to hug anyone face-to-face, these days."

"Diego, I'm glad to see you also. Thanks for bringing her to see me so quickly."

Diego nodded. "I'd like to use your bathroom if that's

okay. Then I'm off to take care of some business in town. I'll text you when I'm done to see if you're ready to get something to eat. My treat." He smiled at Freddie. "It's not every day Saoirse gets to see her best friend."

They all entered the room, and Diego slipped into the small bathroom. Once he emerged, he tried not to be too obvious about checking to ensure that no one else was in the bedroom. Once he was satisfied, he nodded and winked at Saoirse, who had sat down on one of the chairs by the window, facing Freddie, who was seated across the table from her.

"See you all soon." Diego left, pulling the door closed behind him.

Saoirse turned to Freddie. "So what's up, darlin'?"

Freddie got up and started pacing around the room.

"It's not a big room," she pointed out, "so it won't take you long to wear out the carpeting. You're exhausting me just watching you. Sit down and talk to me."

"Do you want any water or anything?"

"Yeah, I guess a glass of ice water would be nice."

He poured some water into a glass filled with ice, then put it on the table between them, and sat down again.

"I've been so anxious for you to be here. But now I don't know how to start."

"Just tell me what's got you so freaked out that you left John, flew overnight from Boston to here, and called me, begging me to come and talk to you. What gives?"

Freddie blurted out, "I think John's delusional. He's got some kind of psychotic problem going on. You told me it was okay to fall in love with him, and I did. I fell hard. Now I'm totally freaked out that the man I love so much has mental problems! What am I going to do about this?"

"What kind of delusion, Freddie? What, exactly, did John

tell you?"

Freddie gripped the arms of the chair tightly, speaking in a strained voice. "It was Saturday night. I had worked another extra-long shift and got home tired. He made us an excellent dinner, and we made love afterward. Then we were lying in bed, snuggling and talking, and he started proposing some long-range plans. He's been applying at some places to get a real job while he's working as a bouncer at some bars. He talked about us getting married. About us looking for a house out of the city. But I'm still so afraid of losing him, and I guess I was tired enough to sound as insecure as I feel. I told him, once again, how I'm okay with his having sex with other men just so he's sure that he's going to be happy with me for the long term." Freddie stopped to take a long drink from his glass.

"Wine?" Saoirse pointed at his glass.

He nodded. "For my nerves. Sorry, does it bother you if I'm drinking in front of you?"

"No. It won't be long before I'll be able to have alcohol again, in moderation, of course. But go on, then what happened?"

"He got angry with me. He jumped up out of bed and started pacing around the room. Honestly, Sam, he was like a caged animal. He said that I need to understand something about him that should end this argument once and for all. He glared at me, telling me that in his family, they mate for life. I just stared at him. I pointed out that was a weird way to talk about falling in love. I reminded him that I've been burned so many times that I can't totally trust any man with my heart anymore. I don't know how many more times I can live through it being broken." His eyes glistened, and he sniffed.

Saoirse got up and moved in front of him. She leaned over and hugged his shoulders as they shook slightly. "I love you, Freddie," she reminded him.

"I know. That's why I'm trusting you to listen."

She went back to her chair. "Go on."

He took a deep breath. "He yelled at me. He told me that he was going to let me know how impossible it is for him to ever want another man. He said that he was . . . he was . . . he said that *wolves* mate for life. I asked him what the hell that had to do with anything. He . . . he . . . told me he's a shifter. A werewolf. And that whenever he wants to, he can become a wolf. But that the two of them share a body and a mind, and the wolf would never allow him to have sex with anyone else now that they have both chosen me as their mate."

Freddie looked at her with trepidation, waiting for her reaction.

Saoirse took her time, considering how to reply. She tried to radiate peaceful calmness. "And that's why you think he's delusional?"

"Of course! Werewolves don't exist! There's no such thing as shifters! I'm a medical person. I've got a master's in cardiac nursing, for crying out loud! I've got a scientific background. There is no way a human body can remake itself to be a wolf. It's flat-out impossible."

Saoirse shook her head slowly. "No, it's not, Freddie."

He stared at her, open-mouthed. "What?"

"It's not impossible. I thought it was, too, until I watched it happen."

He gulped. "Um, honey? Are you feeling all right? Maybe the pregnancy hormones are affecting your hearing. Or I'm imagining things."

She grinned, then leaned over to pat his hand, gripping the armrest closest to her. "No, Freddie. I'm not delusional. I'm as sane as you are—and as John is. And for that matter, as Diego is. But you and I are late to this party. They've both known that werewolves exist since they were teenagers, and their wolves began to speak in their minds. Then, when their wolves were strong enough, they forced the first change on the person that fate had entwined their lives with."

Freddie's hand shook as he took another long drink, finishing what was in his glass. He got up and went to the mini fridge to get the bottle out and brought it back with him to refill his glass. Then he collapsed back into his chair, still staring at Saoirse.

She nodded. "Yes, Freddie. Werewolves exist. I had heard wolves howling on the grounds of the school for months before I made the connection. And I was already in love with Diego when I was forced to rethink all my scientific notions. I've watched him shift in front of me, Freddie. You should ask John to do it in front of you. That will convince you, more than anything anyone can say to you, that what he told you is the truth."

Freddie shook his head. "I don't believe what I'm hearing. I trust you more than any other person in the world, Sam. But I still don't believe you. I can't. This can't be real."

"And yet, it is. I've known for a little over a year now."

"And it doesn't terrify you?" He gasped suddenly. "My God! You're carrying his child! Is it going to be a human baby or a litter of wolf pups?"

Saoirse made a face. "Really? Come on, now. I told you, they are born with another being in their minds and their bodies, but that being doesn't have the strength to speak up until they get old enough. High school age, actually. That's why we run a high school, Freddie. So people who suspect their kids might have a wolf ready to force a change can send them to a place where they will be safely taught how to accept and embrace their inner wolves."

"You're talking about this like it's totally logical and rational. And not delusional. Not crazy. I'm hearing the words coming out of your mouth, and I don't know what to think."

"Not to change the subject too much, but does John know

where you are?"

He shook his head. "No! I laid awake almost all night on Saturday, crying into my pillow because the man I love is crazy. Then I had to work an extra-long shift on Sunday, so by the time I got home, John was at his bouncer job. I booked the flight and packed while he was at work. Then I pretended to be asleep when he got home. He was asleep when I got up early, and I watched him sleep for a while, just admiring how gorgeous he is, and thinking about how much I love him. Then, to save myself, I left him."

"Did you leave him a note or anything?"

Freddie shook his head. "No. I'm a coward. I didn't want him to know how much I was freaking out."

"Oh, I'm sure he was well aware you were. It's a huge burden to load onto anyone, so they don't often tell us non-shifters. They only share their secret when they've already mated with us. Or in my case, when Diego's wolf had already told him we were mates, and he knew I had feelings for him. Plus, I had an epiphany of my own. I'll tell you all about it sometime. But I had trouble believing it, too, honey. It's not cowardly to freak out. But what happens next is what's important."

His eyes opened wide as he stared at her. "Why?"

Saoirse took a deep breath. "I asked Diego to text John to let him know you're here."

"What?" he sputtered. "How could you? I don't want to see him! I'm afraid of him!"

She shook her head. "No, not of him. You're afraid of facing his reality. But if you really love him, you need to do that. And he'll be frantic with worry, wondering where you are, and if you're all right. He needs you, Freddie. He loves you, and he's mated with you. If you reject him, he'll be alone for the rest of his life."

"Gee, thanks. Not like that's a huge burden of guilt or

anything. I have to accept him, or I ruin his life? Thanks so much. Just the comfort I needed."

"You don't need me to comfort you. You need to accept what I'm telling you as the truth. John told you the truth. Now the question is, can you accept it? Can you accept loving him now that you know his truth?"

Freddie looked stunned. "I . . . I don't know. I came to you for advice, and now I'm afraid to listen to you. I don't know what to think. I don't even know what I feel, other than numb."

Saoirse's phone buzzed. She pulled it out and read the text.

"Diego's done with his business in town. He wants to know if we're ready to go to dinner."

Freddie shook his head. "I don't know if I can even face *your* man, let alone mine. I'll be imagining him as some kind of monster."

"Not a monster, honey. Diego is my husband. And John is a man who has a burden even bigger than being gay. Who has to keep what he is a secret from the rest of the world, for his own safety. You know something about feeling like that, right?"

"I guess."

"And John has been dealt a crappy hand in life. He's had to deal with a double burden since adolescence. Think of dealing with being different from everyone else, two times over. And weirdly enough, the *were* community isn't very accepting of gays living in their midst. Some of them think that one difference is quite enough to deal with. John's own father didn't even accept his gayness until he was on his deathbed."

"Well, at least he got to *be* at his dad's deathbed. I wasn't allowed to even be there."

"I know. I was the one who held you while you cried, remember?"

He nodded. "Yes," he murmured. "You've always been

there for me." He took a deep breath. "So I guess I owe it to you to trust you now, also. It's just . . . just that this is so huge to accept. So hard to believe. Like some kind of *Twilight Zone* thing."

"Or *Black Mirror*?"

"Yeah. Suddenly, reality is not what you think it is. Everything is changed."

Freddie jumped, startled by a knock on the door.

Diego's voice came from the hallway. "It's only me, folks."

Saoirse smiled. "I'll go let him in. I need to use the bathroom."

"What are we supposed to talk about?"

She made a face. "I won't be in there that long. You'll think of something."

She unlocked the door to let Diego enter, telling him, "I'm using the bathroom. I'll be right out."

Diego entered the room, smiling. Poor Freddie looked decidedly uncomfortable, so she dashed into the bathroom. She smiled to herself when she heard her husband clear his throat to break the silent tension.

"So, what kind of food would you like for dinner?" Diego asked.

"I don't know. Are there any good restaurants around here?"

"Of course there are. This is a big city. There are a couple of good Mexican places, and some good Italian Trattorias. If you want a steak, there's a great place right up the street."

Saoirse came out of the bathroom. "My vote is for the steak house. I can't eat Mexican because the hot peppers give me heartburn. Ditto with Italian red sauce. But a good steak would be most excellent." She turned to smile at Freddie. "That okay by you?"

He nodded. "I guess so. Let me use the bathroom also, then we can get going."

Diego arched an eyebrow at her, and she patted her purse, which she'd taken with her into the bathroom. He nodded, then they both turned to smile as Freddie opened the door.

"Have you got the key to the room?" Saoirse asked Freddie.

"Yes. In my pocket. Wait, let me put the bottle back into the fridge. For later."

When he returned, they all went out into the hall and made their way downstairs.

When Freddie saw the car that chirped in answer to Diego's fob, he whistled. "A Beemer? Wow, girlfriend! You're moving up in the world."

Saoirse giggled. "Just wait until you feel the seats. I didn't know leather could be so soft."

"Oh, I've had some experience with that," he said with a smirk, his usual personality asserting itself for a moment.

Diego waggled his eyebrows at Saoirse. "I can arrange for you to have some, ahem, experience with soft leather, also, my dear."

"Oh, really? Come on, baby. Get born soon. Mommy wants to get back to doing naughty things with your daddy."

The mood lightened, so they were all smiling as they got into the car and headed to the restaurant.

CHAPTER TWENTY-SEVEN

Almost two hours later, Saoirse moaned as she rubbed her belly.

"I didn't think I had room to eat that much food. But that steak was so good, and I do love me a wedge salad."

"Is anyone thinking dessert?" Their waiter had returned and was pouring more coffee into Diego and Freddie's cups. "I can bring the dessert cart, so you can see what we have to offer."

Diego got a text and glanced at his phone. He replied to it, before looking up and giving a quick shake of his head to Saoirse.

He turned to the waiter. "No, I think we're all good. Just the check, please."

"Coming right up, sir."

"So what's next?" Freddie asked. "You both head home, and I go back to brood in my hotel room?"

Saoirse had studiously avoided discussing Freddie's problem all through dinner. Instead, she kept the conversation about the upcoming birth of the baby, the antics of her students, and the kinds of anecdotes anyone working in the medical field has about seeing people at their best and their worst. So Freddie's oblique reference was the only acknowledgment of the elephant in the room.

"Maybe," Saoirse said, before rapidly changing the subject. "I've got to go to the bathroom again. Jeez, I'll be glad to have my body back to myself soon. This needing to pee every five minutes is really annoying. It's like when you drink beer, only

I don't get to have any fun beforehand." She sighed dramatically as she stood. "Life is so unfair."

The waiter returned with the check just as she got back to the table. Freddie excused himself to use the bathroom also. Diego had paid the bill and stood from the table when Freddie returned.

"No need to sit back down if we're all ready to leave."

When they reached the parking lot, Diego used the fob to make the BMW chirp. He was reaching to opened the door for her when suddenly the door opened on the car parked next to them, and John got out.

Saoirse reacted first. "John! So good to see you!" She pulled him close for a hug.

Diego shook his hand, murmuring, "Good flight?"

John smiled but kept his gaze locked on Freddie's face. "Bouncy. Small plane. Lots of turbulence. But I'm here in one piece, so there's that."

Freddie licked his lips before speaking. His voice broke, so he tried again. "Um, so what now? Obviously, I've been played — by all of you." He glared at Saoirse.

She shook her head. "Not played, honey. You need to talk this out."

John gestured at the rental car. "If you're willing to talk, you can ride with me. I promise I won't bite."

Freddie made a sound between a choking sob and a laugh. "Unless I ask you to?"

John nodded solemnly. "Yes."

"I think you should follow us back to the academy," Saoirse said. "That will give you a couple of hours to talk. And Freddie, you wanted to see where I live. This is a perfect opportunity for us to show you."

Freddie's voice sounded strained. "Plus, I'll be a captive audience, and I won't be able to get away on my own, right?"

John's face, which had the same haggard look as Freddie's,

now looked infinitely sad. "I swear to you, if at any time you want to leave, I will drive you back to your hotel."

Freddie shook his head.

"Or I'll get someone else to drive you back," John said, his shoulders slumping even more. "You are not my prisoner, Freddie. I just want a chance to talk to you—to better explain what I fucked up so badly, trying to talk to you about the other night. Deal?"

The hopeful look he gave Freddie tore at Saoirse's heart. It reminded her of Diego's expression when he had first tried to explain his nature to her.

Freddie stared at John for a moment, then sighed. "Okay. I guess so."

"Great!" Saoirse enthused, trying to lighten the mood. "Then let's all get to driving. The sun has already set, so you won't get to see how beautiful the surrounding land is, Freddie. But trust me, you're heading into God's country. You'll love it!"

"I hate wilderness. It's meant to be outside. I like to be inside." He shuddered. "It's too wild and untamed for me. I like city lights and noise."

"That's what compromises are for," John murmured. He clicked open the doors of the rental, and Freddie walked around to get into the passenger side, closing the door and putting on his seatbelt.

Diego opened the door for Saoirse, and she whispered, "Good luck" to John before she got into the car.

Diego nodded at John and walked around to get into the driver's seat.

John got into his car, and they set out for the long drive back to the academy.

"I hope they can work things out," Saoirse said.

"Me, too. There's no pain like being rejected by your mate. That's why I feel so much for Nathan."

"I hope he can get things settled, also. Boy, you shifters sure have it bad when you get around to choosing your one and only, don't you? It's not bad enough that you have to ascertain if the other person feels the same. But then, if your loved one of choice isn't a shifter, you have to break the big news and hope for a minimum of freaking out."

He turned to smile at her briefly, patting her thigh. "But it's so good when things work out, isn't it?"

She smiled back. "Oh, yeah. It's really good, *señor*. Better than I ever imagined."

His lips twitched as he turned back to watch the road. "Good. I hope you remember that while you're in labor and you don't suddenly decide that you hate me."

"Well, it's not like I'll be able to go anywhere. I won't be able to run away from you while I'm grunting and pushing our baby out. From what I've been told, the first few hours afterward are a haze of bonding with the baby and each other. So I think we'll be fine."

She yawned. "So, um, is it okay with you if I just rest my eyes for a minute?"

He nodded. "Go ahead, my love. I'll wake you up when we get home."

"Thanks."

John was silent as he followed Diego's car to the road that would lead them out of the city, and toward his ancestral home. Freddie was chewing on his lips, looking out of the passenger side window.

After they left the urban lights behind and been on the road for almost an hour, John broke the silence. "Is there anything you want to ask me?"

Freddie turned to him, taking a deep breath. "Did you really mean what you said about me being able to get a ride back to the hotel if I don't want to spend the night out at this place?"

John nodded. "I never lie. It's another think about *us*. Or maybe it's just how we were raised in my family. You are free to leave at any time. You're not my prisoner. You have to know you have a choice, Freddie. I . . ." his voice broke. He coughed to clear his throat and began again. "I love you. I want to spend the rest of my life with you. But you have to be able to accept me as I am. I want to show you everything."

Freddie looked at him with alarm. "What does that mean?"

"I want to shift in front of you, so you can watch. I won't be able to talk to you when I'm a wolf, because I'll have different vocal cords. But I hope you won't be so scared that you run out the door. Then I will shift back, so you can watch both parts."

Freddie leaned back, shaking his head. "This is so unreal. I feel like I'm in some kind of nightmare. I keep expecting to wake up to reality, but this is going on way too long to be a dream."

"I can't begin to imagine how you feel. Both of my parents were shifters, so I've always known it was possible that I might be one."

"Really? Do shifters always have shifter kids?"

He shook his head. "No. My oldest sister, Jennifer, is not a shifter. She was disappointed when no wolf presented itself to her, but she got over it. She's a lawyer and lives in Portland."

"Hmph. I don't remember if I met her at the wedding."

John's lips twitched. "She doesn't party much. She's the serious one in the family. She's not married. I'm not sure if it's because she just hasn't met the right person yet, or if she's afraid to have kids, for fear that they might inherit what she didn't."

"So it's not always passed on?"

"No. I'm a shifter, and so is my younger sister, Jerene. Her husband isn't a shifter, and she says the way she got him to accept her was to shift in front of him. Diego did that for Saoirse, also. That's why I want to do it in front of you. You have to see what it's all about. Only then will you be able to decide if you can handle being with me." He glanced briefly toward Freddie. "I hope you can."

Freddie looked troubled, visible even in the dim light in the car. "I honestly don't know. This is so surreal that I don't know how I'm going to react."

"Fair enough."

"So if two shifters can have a non-shifter kid, can non-shifters have shifter kids?"

John nodded. "Good question. And yes. In fact, that's part of why our school exists. Some non-shifters have it in their family, and they want their kids to be in a safe place during the crucial teen years when it usually manifests itself. If it doesn't, no harm done. The kids get a great education at our school. Since we're a private institution, we give lots of personal guidance that's hard to get in a huge, over-crowded public school. But if a wolf does appear, their kids have lots of help in learning how to co-exist with another being sharing their mind and body."

"Now that's just fucking weird! How do you know you're not just imagining the voice? I mean, ancient mankind used to think God was talking in their minds when they *heard* their own thoughts. The constant stream of thinking that we all do when conscious is bicameral, since our brains have two sides. Women are much better at integrating the two sides, but men also have to learn to control their thoughts. How do you know it's a wolf talking to you?"

"Sometimes the voice addresses you as *man-cub* when it

first starts talking. That's usually a give-away. And it speaks conversationally in your head."

"How does it know English? Or does it talk in *wolf* to you?"

"I speak English, and my wolf knows what I know. I suppose if I spoke another language, he would speak to me in that. He gets louder if I try to ignore him and tries to force me to listen any way he can."

"Is it talking to you now?"

"Yes," John murmured.

"What is it saying?"

"He hopes you will be able to accept us as we are. He loves you, also, since we're mated with you."

Freddie grunted. "Dude, I've done a lot of things I'm not proud of, but I draw the line at bestiality."

John shook his head. "No, it's not like that. Diego's wolf chose Saoirse, and they only have sex as humans. If you were a shifter, that would lend another dimension to our physical relationship. But my wolf is content to enjoy experiencing what I do when we make love. So no worries about that, please. You have enough to be freaked out about already."

"You got that right."

They drove in silence for a while, but it was a more companionable silence. Freddie seemed more relaxed, and John hoped he'd stay that way.

Freddie broke the silence this time. "Does it hurt?"

John nodded. "Yes."

"Every time?"

"Yes."

"Then why do you do it? Is it like in the movies, and a full moon forces the change?"

John was glad to hear more curiosity than fear in Freddie's voice. He'd happily answer any question his mate had.

"No. That movie stuff is crap. It has nothing to do with the moon, other than wolves like to howl at the moon. I do it because the wolf will make me miserable if I don't. He has no other way to exist. He's not able to jump out of my body into anyone else's. Unless I allow the shift, he can only occupy my mind. And for a creature that loves to run in the wild, to howl at the moon, to feel the grass under its paws—well, that's torture in the extreme. I'm not a monster, no matter what you might be thinking right now. I can't force the wolf in me to remain trapped forever. I have to let him out once in a while."

"Did you ever change while living with me?"

"Only a couple of times. I waited until you were working an overnight shift, then I'd drive to a forest preserve somewhere and let him out for a couple of hours. It's been hard on him, unable to take over, and not feeling safe in urban natural areas. But he loves you, too, so he's bided his time. That's why I talked to you about us looking for a place out of the city."

"I like the city."

"I know. Maybe we can find some kind of compromise? We can live in the city but be near someplace where I can let my wolf out to run without worrying about him being shot as a rabid animal."

Freddie looked shocked. "I never thought of that. You can't take that kind of chance, John. Not for me. Not for anyone."

John smiled at his vehemence. "I'm a careful man, Freddie. Look at how long it took me to act on my own urges. If I hadn't met you, I'd probably still be in the closet."

Freddie leaned back into the seat and closed his eyes, probably trying to absorb everything he'd heard.

"We're here," John announced when he reached the sign that said, *Northwest Maine Academy.* Just beyond was the gate and a brightly lit guardhouse. A woman with very short gray hair strode up to them.

"There's a high-security guardhouse here?" Freddie asked.

"Yes. The fence is reinforced steel and electrified. We take the safety of our pack and other people's children very seriously."

"Hey, John," the guard greeted. "Welcome home. Diego said it was you in the rental car. And he vouched for your guest, also." She inclined her head toward Freddie.

"Thanks, Diya. I wasn't sure if we'd be too late to see you on the way in."

She shrugged. "We've instituted a new rotation. Everyone, including me, takes a night shift once a week. Keeps us all on our toes."

"See you later." John drove through the huge gates.

Freddie turned to watch as Diya walked back into the guardhouse as the gates swung closed.

"Don't be worried," John said. "I promised that you can leave anytime you want to. I mean it. You're not a prisoner here. The security is to protect us from prying eyes, and to keep our students safe."

Freddie stared straight ahead, taking deep breaths.

John had been with his mate long enough to know he was using what he had learned in yoga lessons to calm himself.

"You know I'm anxious?"

John nodded. "I can smell it."

"Oh," Freddie said in a small voice.

They drove past streets that were lit, and some that were not. The drive to the mansion took a while from the gate.

"We're driving past where all of the pack members who aren't teachers live. They raise their families here. We're pretty self-sufficient. It's an entire community, centered around the school, which is about a third of the main mansion. The pack leadership all live in another third of the mansion in apartments, as do the teachers. The last third is the dorm for the students. The common areas on the first floor include the cafeteria and the foyer."

"Do you still have an apartment here?"

John shook his head. "No. When I moved to Boston, I gave

it up. But we do have guest apartments, so we'll be in one of those for tonight." He licked his lips. "For as long as you want to stay, that is."

Freddie stared at the mansion as John drove around to the back of the building.

"We're coming at it from the backside because this is where the garages are. We'll go up a back staircase."

John parked the rental car in an open spot in the huge garage, then spoke into the silence. "This is it, Freddie. Time to meet your destiny."

Freddie glared at him. "Or not. You said it's my decision."

"Yes, it is. So shall we get on with it?"

"Yes."

Diego and Saoirse were already out of their car, waiting. John turned to Freddie, who gave him a stiff nod, and they headed toward the other couple.

Saoirse waved as they approached. "Hey, you guys. You can either walk slowly with us while I waddle along as best as I can or go ahead on up to the mansion."

She threw her arms around Freddie. "Brave heart, honey. It will be exciting and scary and wonderful, all at the same time. But you've always been able to roll with the punches."

She released Freddie and turned toward him. "Take good care of my bestie, John. Remember, if you hurt him, you'll have me to answer to. And I've got a formidable right cross."

They all looked up when a voice called out, "John!"

His mother moved quickly out of the door, pulling a scarf off her gray afro as she got closer to them. She pulled him into a hug that almost took his breath away.

"My boy! I've missed you so much!" She gushed over him as she hugged him closely, patting him here and there as if her hands couldn't get enough of him.

"Mom," he said, grinning, "I haven't been gone that long."

"Yes, you have," she replied. "Long enough for me to miss

you. And you never call anymore. What's with not calling your mother?"

"Mom," he turned to Freddie. "You remember Freddie . . ."

She smiled. "Yes. Saoirse's best friend and *Man of Honor*. I remember. You two made such a cute couple, dancing at the wedding. How are you, Freddie?"

"Overwhelmed," he answered.

Janine nodded. "That's to be expected. Now, John, I'm giving you guest apartment number one. You'll be in the back, so you only need to go up the stairs to the second floor, and the door will be right in front of you."

"I know, Mom. I *have* lived here before."

She sniffed. "Don't be snotty with your mother." She turned to Freddie. "Honestly. Kids these days. No respect."

Freddie nodded uncertainly, clearly not sure if he needed to respond or not.

The group reached the back door of the mansion at the same time.

"Finally," Saoirse said with an overly dramatic tone. "I can't wait to not be lugging a bowling ball around under my ribs."

Janine eyed her critically. "Not much longer, my dear. In fact, I don't think you'll make it to your due date."

"I sure hope not!"

"Um, we're going to head upstairs now," John said. "See you all in the morning."

"Have a good night," his mother called as they made their way to the door.

"I sure hope so," Freddie muttered under his breath, just loudly enough for John to hear.

When they got up to the apartment, Freddie excused himself

to use the bathroom. He gripped the sink for a while, staring into his own eyes, trying to quell the incipient panic of having to go into the next room to face the totally bizarre. Finally, with a deep sigh, he made a face at himself and reluctantly opened the door.

John was sitting on an armchair, rotating a glass of red wine in front of his face, admiring the liquid.

"I opened a bottle of sparkling shiraz. I know you like sparkling wine, but this is a combination of my favorite, a rich, fruity red, and yours, what with the fuzziness and all. I poured you a glass. I hope you like it."

Freddie slowly walked over to pick up the glass, then perched on the edge of the second armchair with the table between them. He took a tentative sip. "This is really good," he said, then he put the glass down. "How is this going to happen?"

John sighed. "I had hoped that you'd want to relax a little first. Enjoy some of the wine. I grew up in the mansion, you know. I've been hoping for a chance to show it off to you."

"Why? I couldn't ever live out here in butt-fuck nowhere. You know that. I'm a city boy. I like the noises of civilization all around me. It helps me to sleep. Out here, where all I can hear is the occasional night critters, I feel all creeped out by the silence."

Suddenly, the sound of a wolf howling in the distance broke the silence, then an answering chorus joined in, followed by yipping and barking.

Freddie finished the rest of his wine in one gulp. When his widened eyes met John's, worry clearly punctuated the creases across his forehead.

"You're one of those?" he asked, trying to control his breathing. "I mean, it could be you out there, too?"

John nodded. "Yes. That's the whole point of this place. To give us a safe place to run freely."

John leaned forward, and Freddie couldn't stop his flinch as he shrank back into his chair. John reached for the bottle and poured more wine into both of their glasses, then leaned back.

"Freddie, none of us asked for this. I sure didn't, and I know you didn't. But the only way we can have a future together is if you accept me as I am."

"Then what are you waiting for? The suspense is killing me. Just do it and get it over with."

John got up and stretched his arms up, pulling his shirt over his head. Freddie sucked in a breath and caught the small smile that crossed John's face when he heard.

"Sorry," John said. "Not trying to seduce you right now. Though it helps me feel better, to have you react like that just from me being shirtless. I have to strip before a shift. Clothing gets in the way and usually ends up torn apart otherwise." He continued removing his clothes until he stood naked in the middle of the room.

Freddie, for his part, tried not to stare at the erection that was eye level while he sat in the chair. "Um," he cleared his throat. "Isn't that going to make it, ahem, *harder* for you to change?"

John shook his head. "Actually, no. A male is a male, no matter what species. Just means I'll be hard as a wolf, also. But it won't affect what I'm doing."

"How do you get started?"

"I just invite him to take over. Then he does. Like this."

Suddenly the room filled with the sounds of bones breaking. The air around John shimmered slightly as he fell to his hands and knees, writhing and grunting with pain. Freddie watched with horrified fascination as bones broke and reset themselves under the skin, which looked as if live things were crawling around underneath it. Dark brown hair started to cover John's torso, his face elongated into a muzzle, and his ears shifted to the top of this head. His arms and legs grew thinner and shorter, and his hands and feet were turning into huge paws. Almost as an afterthought, a tail grew out of the coccyx.

Freddie just stared, realizing his man was gone, and in his place stood a huge, dark brown wolf. The animal shook himself all over, like a wet dog. Then he sat down, watching Freddie expectantly.

Freddie quickly finished off his glass of wine, then poured more into his glass. He drank half of that, also. The silence grew, broken only by the panting of the wolf.

Freddie wrestled up the courage to speak. "Are you still in there, John?"

The wolf bobbed its head up and down.

"But you can't speak, since you don't have human vocal cords, right?"

The head nodded again.

"You won't hurt me?"

The wolf growled softly, shaking its head vehemently.

Freddie had flinched at the noise, but now felt emboldened. "Yeah, you're right. Stupid question, right? I mean, you could hurt me much more effectively as a man by breaking my heart. Instead, you've made yourself vulnerable to me in a way no man ever has before. You're sharing something so intimate that I feel like a voyeur."

Freddie slowly rose. "Um, is it all right if I touch you?"

The wolf panted and nodded.

Freddie reached out a hand, tentatively, then touched the wolf's head. "I feel like an idiot. I don't know what to do. I can't pet you like a dog. But your fur is much softer than I thought a wolf's would be." He ran his hand along the back of the wolf, marveling at the differing textures of the hair on its back, versus the softer hair between the ears. When he came around to face the wolf again, it was John's eyes staring back at him from the wolf's face.

"John, I . . ." Unexpectedly, Freddie burst into tears and moved back onto the chair. Sobs wracked his shoulders, and he felt himself lose control.

The wolf moved over to rub itself on his legs, but that just made him sob more loudly.

"I . . . don't . . . know . . ." he gulped. "I can't seem to stop myself. I'm sorry! I'm sorry!"

The wolf's eyes reflected alarm as it moved back to the center of the sitting area, and the air around it began to shimmer once again. The loud bone-cracking noises were back, and Freddie watched through his tears as the wolf whimpered as he remade himself into the man he loved so much. He felt so confused.

Freddie almost gasped when John, once again in human form, moved quickly over to kneel in front of him. John wrapped his arms around him and held on tight. As Freddie rode the crests of his emotional breakdown, John murmured words of love and assurance, caressing him with tenderness.

Gradually, Freddie's sobs abated, and his breathing regulated again. He snuggled into John's embrace but didn't return it. Finally, he gave John a gentle push. "I think I've had enough for one night," he said in a small voice. "Will you take me back to my hotel now?"

John's expression was so hurt that it almost started Freddie crying again. "Why?"

"I . . . uh . . . I just need to get back to something normal. Like a crappy hotel room near the airport."

John's eyes filled with tears, but he nodded. "If that's what you want."

"It is. But I want *you* to drive me back, and to stay the night with me. I don't want to be alone tonight. I'll have nightmares. I need you to hold me."

A quick spark of hope flashed across John's face as he rose

from his knees. He moved over to his discarded clothing and pulled it all back on again. "Ready when you are."

Freddie got up and walked to the door, hyper-aware that John was right behind him. He felt exhilarated and frightened by all he had heard and seen. He opened the door, and they headed for the staircase, moving in silence down to the first floor, then out to the garage. John pulled the keys out of his pocket, and the car chirped as the doors unlocked.

Silence continued to reign as they both got into the car and belted themselves in. Then John drove them to the gate, which opened automatically, then onto the road for the long, quiet drive back to civilization.

PART FIVE: ACCEPTANCE

CHAPTER TWENTY-EIGHT

Freddie woke slowly, keeping his breathing steady so as not to disturb the man spooned against his back. He shut his eyes tightly, remembering the previous night.

Once they reached the hotel room, John looked ready to cry, as if he expected the worst thing in his life to happen. Freddie went into the bathroom, then emerged wearing only his boxer shorts. John was standing by the window, holding the curtains open and watching the planes take off to parts unknown. He looked so lost.

Freddie walked over to the bed and pulled the covers back. "I don't want you to leave, John. I want you to hold me while I sleep. You need to chase the monsters away from my dreams."

John turned to look at him, and Freddie's stomach hurt at the idea he was the cause of so much pain in the man's eyes.

"I thought . . ." his voice broke, and he coughed. "I thought you just wanted to be done with me. To be back safe in a city once again. Away from all the monsters, including, and especially, me."

Freddie held out his arms. With a sob, John tore off his shirt and pants and joined him in the bed.

"Hold me," Freddie whispered.

Face-to-face, it was impossible not to notice that both their cocks, regardless of emotional upheaval, were instantly hard and throbbing, automatically sensing the nearness of their lover.

Freddie put a finger under John's chin and lifted it to gaze into his eyes, and he shook his head. "Not tonight, lover. Not in the mood. I just need to sleep. But not alone."

John nodded. "Don't know if it would be possible, anyway. Shifting twice so closely together took a lot out of me. I'm exhausted."

241

Freddie pulled John's face down for a long kiss, filled with tenderness.

"Turn out the light, will you?" He turned away from John and punched his pillow to make it more comfortable.

John clicked off the light, pulling the covers over them as he snuggled close and wrapped an arm around Freddie, holding him tight against his chest. He sighed deeply, then fell silent.

Freddie lay awake for a long time, aware that John was not asleep either, but loath to break the silence. He knew the decision about their future was his to make, and the weight of it suffocated him. He thought long and hard about what he wanted out of life. When, at last, he decided on what he would say in the morning, he finally relaxed.

Eventually, they both drifted off into the sleep of the exhausted.

Freddie opened his eyes to the bright light of the morning peeking through the curtains. It was time for him to tell John what he had decided. "John?"

Soft snoring answered him.

Freddie moved around a little to gently jostle John's sleeping body awake before he tried again. "John?"

A deep intake of breath sounded behind him, and the arm holding him moved slightly. "What time is it?" John's sleepy voice croaked.

"Time for you to wake up. It's now my turn to say we need to talk."

"Gotta go pee," John mumbled as he got out of bed.

He stopped at the coffeemaker before going into the bathroom. He came back with the pot from the coffeemaker filled with water, walking as if his entire body hurt. He emptied the small carafe into the machine as Freddie got up to take his turn in the bathroom.

When he got back, John was lying on his back, staring at the ceiling. There were two cups of coffee, one on each of the bedside tables.

Freddie sat on the bed next to John, crossing his legs, yoga-style, gazing at the reclining figure. He picked up the cup on his side, taking a few sips, then sighed. "This would be so much easier if you weren't so fucking gorgeous," Freddie murmured. "Makes it hard for me to think straight."

John sighed deeply, his face set in stone, as he continued to stare at the ceiling. "Allow me to make it easier for you. I won't even look at you. You tell me you can't handle the load of shit I've laid at your door, so we're through. I should get my ass out the door, and you'll send my stuff back to the mansion once you get back to Boston. Been nice knowing you. Yadda . . . yadda . . . yadda."

Freddie tilted his head and stared quizzically. "That's what you think I'm going to say? Why?"

John shrugged. "It's obvious. We're incompatible. You're a city boy, while I'm a country guy. You're a partier. I want to cocoon at home with the man I love. You like playing the field. I'm a one-man wolf-man. And that last part was the final straw. You might like hairy guys, but not when it's fur and they're not human anymore. You were petrified last night. I saw it in your eyes. You had a breakdown from the emotional strain. You're trying to figure out how to let me down easy. You may even still be afraid of me, which would be funny if it wasn't so sad. So I'm making it as easy as possible for you. I'll just leave." He got up and began to pull his clothes off the chair he'd dropped them on the night before.

"John, please put your clothes down and come back here to sit."

John looked at him in surprise, and Freddie patted the space next to him.

"Why?"

"Just do it."

John moved over and sat on the bed, facing him.

Freddie was shocked by the depth of sadness in the dull,

tear-filled eyes of his lover.

"I . . . um . . . I can't deny that I was majorly freaked out. It's not every day that a person with medical training finds out that some of the mythology surrounding us isn't just fiction. If you hadn't shifted in front of me, I'd have found a way to deny it was true. Now I can't get the image of you as a wolf out of my head."

John turned away, which gave Freddie the opportunity to admire his profile, that of a proud, handsome man.

"It's not something that I asked for. But it's a large part of who I am," John said softly.

"I know that now. I think part of why I broke down so hard last night was that I could hear the pain you were in while you were changing. No one would take that on by choice. Just like I never would have chosen to be gay if I had a choice. I didn't ask to be rejected by my family, unable to visit them, even when my dad was dying. We were just born this way."

John turned back to face him, and there was the slightest glimmer of hope in his eyes.

"But I listened when Sam told me that I could trust you not to hurt me. And I hoped she was right. So I let go and allowed myself to fall head-over-heels in love with you. Now I have to ask myself which is worse? Giving you up, and living with the pain, knowing it was my fault? Or continue living with a man who has shared his deepest inner secrets with me? Am I strong enough to stand by his side, to have his back, as I know he has mine?"

Freddie softened his voice as he stared into John's eyes. "Sometimes I wish I didn't remember all of the things I've done that I'm embarrassed about. Some I've even shared with you. I guess if you can forgive me for being a slut for such a long time, I can learn to live with your reality."

John's face reflected only love. "I don't care how many men you've had before me. As long as I'm the last man you have."

"And you don't think you'll ever get bored being with the first and only man you've ever had?"

John shook his head solemnly. "No."

Freddie leaned over to close the distance between them, his lips slightly parted as they gently pressed against John's. John leaned into the kiss, and Freddie enjoyed feeling as if his entire world had been reduced to that one contact point. Tongues joined in the caressing, and hands soon followed.

Freddie pulled John with him as he lowered himself to lie down. He wrapped his hand around John's cock, enjoying the velvety hardness. John returned the favor, stroking Freddie's cock with sure fingers, squeezing the head, and spreading some of the pre-come over the tip.

Freddie shuddered, licking John's lips, before trailing his tongue down to the soft skin around his ear, nipping gently, then sucking the lobe into his mouth. "I didn't bring any supplies. Sex was the furthest thing from my mind when I packed."

John moved against him, hardness against hardness, speaking breathily. "I didn't even pack. I just grabbed the first seat available. No luggage. Didn't think I'd need anything."

Freddie pushed John back. "Lie on your side."

The bed made some squeaking noises as Freddie maneuvered around, positioning himself to where he could lick at John's huge erection while settling his own quivering shaft within easy reach of his lover's mouth. He inhaled deeply, then lapped at the oozing pre-come before taking John to the back of his throat and swallowing.

John's moan was muffled by Freddie's cock as he showed how much he had learned about suppressing his gag reflexes. Freddie quivered when John swallowed him down to the root and buried his face in the dark nest of Freddie's tight curls.

The room filled with slurping noises and groans of pleasure as each expressed their love for the other. Freddie's emotions were magnified by how close he'd come to letting his doubts and fears overrule his heart, how close he had come to walking away from this man he loved with his whole being.

The speed and intensity of their movements increased, and Freddie knew he wouldn't last much longer. John's growl of release was just a split second before his own cry of pleasure. Neither relinquished his suction until their spasms had subsided. Freddie wanted to enjoy every last drop he could milk from his lover.

Finally they rolled onto their backs, keeping their bodies touching as much as possible as they relearned how to breathe again. Freddie recovered first, spinning himself around to snuggle into John's waiting arms.

"Can't ... move ... yet. Arms barely usable," John breathed out.

Freddie lifted his head, feeling a bit mischievous. "That's okay, lover. I know a good solution to our mutually depleted protein supplies."

As if to punctuate his point, John's stomach chose that moment to growl noisily.

Freddie smiled, patting it. "See? When was the last time you ate anything of substance?"

John frowned. "Yesterday's breakfast? I mean, I ate late, since I slept in. It took me until after I'd eaten to realize that your schedule didn't have you working during that day. After that, I couldn't think of anything but finding you, which I had absolutely no idea of how to do, since you didn't even leave a note. I was frantic until I got the text from Diego. Then I got moving, because to stop would have meant wallowing in despair. My wolf wouldn't let me do that until I'd found you."

Freddie tilted his head, smiling in wonder. "Really?"

John nodded. "He's been after me for a long time to tell you about him. He said we couldn't really be one until you accepted all of me."

Freddie bounced off the bed. "Then let's reward this wise wolf of yours and go get some breakfast. I'll bet there's somewhere close by that can supply me with a pound of bacon."

"And coffee," John agreed, pulling on his discarded clothing. "Lots and lots more coffee."

"And afterward, I want you to take me to the nearest hospital."

John shot him a worried look. "You're hurt?"

"No, silly. I want to see how big their cardiology department is. I've been at Boston General for about five years now. It's time for a change. And if we were to find a nice place here in Augusta, then your wolf would only have to convince you to make the drive back to your home grounds, where he could run free. I'd come along sometimes, so I could visit with my bestie and play with her new baby. Win-win for everyone, right?"

John moved so quickly that Freddie squeaked in surprise when he was grabbed and pulled into a tight embrace. John's lips demanded his, and they spent a long moment, lost in each other again.

Finally, John pulled back enough to lean his forehead against Freddie's to gaze into his eyes. "You would do all of that for me?"

Freddie shook his head, saying gently, "No, John. I would do it for *us. All three of us.*" Freddie startled a bit, as he looked into John's soft brown eyes, at the feeling of two beings looking back at him.

John growled softly to seal the deal.

Then they headed out to find a breakfast place.

CHAPTER TWENTY-NINE

Freddie had insisted on checking out of his hotel room right after breakfast before they set out to explore the hospitals and neighborhoods in Augusta. They had found a few areas with interesting apartments and a nice cosmopolitan feel to the local shops and bistros. Freddie was also pleased to find a sizeable cardiac care unit in the biggest hospital nearby. He chatted up one of the nurses and got some contact information for where to send his resume.

Afterward, he insisted John drive them back to the academy grounds, so he could tell Saoirse personally that they were staying together.

"That way," he said with a smirk, "we can mess up the sheets in your guest room like we messed up the hotel sheets."

"Only if we stop for some supplies first," John insisted.

He raised his eyebrows. "Ooh! Got some big plans for tonight?"

"You betcha."

"Are you going to shift and go running afterward?"

"No, I can do that anytime. You said you already have your return flight booked for tomorrow afternoon, right?"

"Yes, based on when I had to be at work. Even though I'm giving notice, I still have to show up for assigned shifts. That way I'll get a good recommendation from the big boss. She can be a real bitch if she's crossed. Don't want to risk that."

"How long will it take you to be able to move out here?"

"Not sure. Depends on if there's any interest from the local hospitals. I may have to fly out for an interview."

"I'm going to stick around here for a few days before I head back to join you in Boston. I'll visit with Mom and let Jerene's kids rub their sticky little hands all over my clothes. And I'll spend time in town, checking out apartments. I can send you pictures, or better yet, do a live video with you when I've narrowed it down to one or two."

Because it was late afternoon and still light, Freddie was truly awed by the beauty of the land they were driving through. The drive seemed to go much faster than it had before—perhaps because there was no tension, and he was deliriously happy.

When they walked through the main entrance to the mansion foyer, Saoirse called out through the doors of the dining room, waving for them to join her.

"Get over here and give me a hug, Freddie, you rascal, you!" She pushed herself up from the table with real effort, aided by Diego, and turned sideways to get a better angle for their embrace.

"Mind if we join you?" John asked, indicating several empty chairs at the main table.

"Of course not. We were hoping you'd be back. Go get some dinner, then come back and tell us all about your plans." Saoirse waved them toward the buffet.

Eating the delicious food was a pleasant surprise for Freddie. "Wow! Your mom cooks like this every night?"

"Yup. Has for years. Of course, as the pack leader's wife, she could have claimed any job. But she's always loved to cook, and even worked as a chef for a few years before she met my dad. She still enjoys being creative in the kitchen."

"Wait a minute," Freddie turned to stare at John. "Your mom was the pack leader's wife? So your dad was the pack leader? I didn't know I'd fallen for a celebrity."

"Ha, ha."

"But why didn't you inherit the leadership job when he passed on?"

"It's not hereditary. Besides, I didn't want it. By custom, the leader chooses his successor before or on his deathbed. He usually has someone's name written down somewhere, in case of accidents."

"So that's it? He — and I presume it's always a *he* — makes his choice known, and that's it?"

"These days it's not always a *he*. But yes, that's it. Unless someone is unhappy enough about the choice to mount a challenge."

"Or two, in some cases," Saoirse grumbled, rolling her eyes.

Diego narrowed his eyes sternly. "Now, honey —"

"What? I cheered loudly for you both times. Lucky I did since I'm sure my enthusiasm single-handedly energized you for your victories."

"Hold on a minute, here!" Freddie stared from Saoirse to Diego and back again. "So . . . You're the pack leader now? And my bestie is the pack leader's wife?"

"Yup." Saoirse gave him a huge grin.

"Do I have to bow or anything, your majesties?"

"No, smart-ass! Though maybe for you, I'll make an exception." She haughtily held out her hand. "Like if you want to kiss the ring or anything."

"Why would he want to do that?" Grant asked as he and Monique walked over to their table, carrying coffee cups and dessert plates.

Freddie smiled at Monique, who'd been at the bachelorette party he'd thrown for Saoirse.

Monique patted Grant's arm. "Freddie, this is my husband, Grant Knutsen."

Freddie nodded and accepted Grant's offered hand to

shake.

"He's just now realizing who the big boss is around here," Saoirse explained to Grant with a wink.

"He'll find that we don't stand much on ceremony," Diego pointed out. "The pack leader's main function is to protect the pack. That includes everyone living on the grounds as well as the students whose parents are entrusting us with them. And guests, of course." He nodded at Freddie.

"Speaking of the students . . ." Freddie changed the subject. "John told me that kids get sent here when their parents suspect but aren't sure if a wolf lives within their child. That seems rather inconvenient, especially in this time of modern medicine. Isn't there some way to find that out ahead of time?"

Saoirse shook her head. "No, not yet. My idea was that it might be something in the blood. But after over a year of testing everything that I could think of—aided, I might add, most ably by Grant—even I had to admit that was a blind alley."

Grant leaned forward. "Then I suggested we try genetic screening. You know, using one of those places that charge you lots of money to analyze a swab from inside your cheek. We had many volunteers, both shifters and non, and we sent them all in, in staggered batches."

"Yeah, but someone is falling down on her job, due to advanced *baby brain*," Saoirse said with a rueful expression.

Grant swiftly defended her. "Not really. It's a daunting job, trying to collate and coordinate all those results by hand. Even if it's all in a spreadsheet, it's still a shit-ton of data that needs to be checked and rechecked."

"Hmm," Freddie remarked. "Sounds like you need some kind of super-computer."

"Why, oh *Cheshire Cat*-faced one?" Saoirse quipped. "Do you know where we can find one?"

Freddie pretended to be checking his fingernails, blowing

airily on them. "Oh, I might. Like maybe this hospital I know of has just bought into a program that it isn't sure how to use yet. Various staff members have been asked to test it using lots of data to figure out the best way to input it, and what kind of commands will give the required results."

Grant's face lit up. "That would be magnificent! Much quicker and more accurate than trying to do it manually."

"But would it be secure?" Diego asked.

"Yeah, we can't risk any leaks of names or information that might give any clues as to locations of the owners of the DNA profiles," Saoirse added.

Freddie raised one eyebrow, offended. "Excuse me, Sam? Have you met me? My minor was in medical uses for computer technology, remember. I do know my way around medical computers. In fact, I can encode the data so tight they wouldn't be able to poke a toothpick into that sphincter."

John let out a bark of laughter, and Saoirse grinned, shaking her head. Diego's grin was more uncertain.

Until Saoirse poked his side. "Loosen up, sweetie."

Grant and Monique were both smiling as well.

"You do have a way with words," Monique pointed out. "Must be why you and our resident wordsmith are besties." She inclined her head toward Saoirse.

"Yes, and I know you all too well, you nasty boy." Saoirse nodded decisively. "And I'll be greatly relieved to have that huge project off my list of things I need to get done before the baby comes. Which better be soon. I'm really tired of being out of breath all the time."

Monique patted her hand. "It won't be long now, honey. The baby appears to have dropped, and I'll bet you're already dilated."

"That's what Rachel said. Two centimeters as of this morning."

Freddie had to chuckle when Diego and Grant looked

mystified.

He voiced what was surely going through their minds. "That is such a weird concept, Sam. I mean, how can you be walking all around with something opening your insides, yet the baby hasn't fallen out yet?"

She shrugged. "I dunno. Weird, right? Likely just another one of the miracles of life." She shot a sly glance at Diego. "Like finding out the man you love is also a wolf, on occasion."

Freddie smiled dreamily at John. "Yeah, kind of a miracle."

"Keep your head in the game, dude," Saoirse snapped. "When can I give you the flash drive with the data on it?"

John stood, grabbing Freddie's hand. "How about at breakfast in the morning? Freddie's got an afternoon flight back to Boston. Then I'll be sticking around for a few days. I want to check out some of the apartments available in Augusta."

Diego spoke up. "Oh, really? I can give you the name of an affiliate who owns some three-deckers in a hipster kind of neighborhood."

John nodded. "Thanks. That would be great."

"How wonderful that you'll be around for a while," Monique said. "Your mother will be really happy."

"Speaking of really happy," Saoirse smiled at Freddie and John. "You two love birds run along now. Go celebrate."

Saoirse smiled as she watched Freddie and John walk out of the room. She patted Diego's hand and sighed. "It's so nice to see someone you love so happy."

"Even better to *be* that someone, who is so happy," he replied.

"Amen to that," Grant said, as he and Monique rose and walked out hand in hand.

"So . . . We're left alone, my love," Diego murmured into

Saoirse's ear.

She frowned. "But we still don't have a happy ending for Nathan."

Diego shrugged. "It's been over a week since I spoke with Dr. Sullivan. I'll call him tomorrow, and you can listen in on the call."

"Should we call Nathan over for it as well?"

"Maybe check with Monique, first. She's his closest friend. She'll know if it's a good idea to keep him in the loop, or if that's just giving him false hope."

"Let's hope it's not false hope." She took his hands as he helped her rise from her chair. "I want all of my people to be happy."

"See how natural it is to call them *your people*?"

She grimaced, as an errant baby part poked particularly hard at her belly. "This little person of ours needs to get going on the whole birthing thing."

"Maybe we can help it along, somehow?" He gave her a sly smile.

She arched an eyebrow. "Are you willing?"

He shrugged. "Rachel assures me that if we're careful, it won't hurt the baby."

"But it will make baby's mama very happy."

"And baby's daddy, also."

They held hands and walked slowly out of the room to head upstairs to the penthouse.

CHAPTER THIRTY

Richard looked up from the paperwork he was poring over on his desk. Jamar knocked and poked his head around the door he opened.

"What is it?" Richard demanded. "I'm going over the contract for the concert Nisha's going to give at the county fairgrounds in the butt-fuck town close to here, called Sloggum. Sounds like a real dump, doesn't it? But it's the biggest place nearby that has a venue that will hold the kind of crowds she commands."

"Uh, about that boss," Jamar shifted uncomfortably from one foot to the other.

"What the fuck is it? Speak up, man. Don't just dance around in the doorway. What's the problem? She's writing and recording music, right?"

"Yeah."

"Good. That's why I brought her out to this God-forsaken wilderness. Once she's done producing a new album, we can go back to L.A., where it's civilized. And I can get good sushi at two in the morning."

"Uh, have you heard any of the new music she's recording?"

"No. I don't have time to spy on her. That's your job. Then you report to me. So?"

"It's fucking depressing stuff, boss. All her songs sound more like the blues than her usual bouncy, upbeat, dance sounds. I was in the recording room this morning with the tech guys when she was making a live recording. I swear, boss, she was *crying* while she sang!"

Richard put his pen down and glared. "Has someone been feeding her downers again? We had a fuck of a time getting her off them the last time."

Jamar shook his head. "No, boss. She's only been doing the drugs the new doctor's been giving her. And that's another thing. She's not drinking and partying with the guys anymore. In fact, when she's not recording or writing new songs in the studio, she takes her guitar with her and just goes and sits in her room. A few times, she told me she was going for a walk in the woods. Why? *To clear her head.* She's never done anything weird like that before."

"Naturally, you followed her?"

"Yeah. I kept a ways back, and I don't think she knew I was there. But for real, she just went walking. She sat on the grass by a pond and threw rocks into it. She sang little bits of some of her sad songs out loud. Especially one."

"Don't keep me in suspense."

"She calls it *Blue Over Green*. It's the one that made her cry. I swear, it's enough to make anyone cry. It's like her heart is breaking, and she's writing her pain in blood."

"You have the soul of a poet, Jamar. Try to lose it. It interferes with your job. So . . . You say she's been writing music, which is good. But it's downer music, which is not good?"

"That's right, boss."

Richard got up from the desk. "Sounds like I need to have a little chat with our star. Maybe she has a bit of a crush on the last guy she was with. Any luck in finding out who he is?"

"No. It's like he's a ghost or something. No one has any idea who he might be, no matter how many people I describe him to. He doesn't live in town. That much I'm sure of. The plates on the car he drove off in were from out-of-state. Maybe he is, too, and she knows it, so she's sad because she won't be seeing him again."

"Any chance they've been sneaking out to get together?"

Jamar looked offended. "She's watched twenty-four-seven. I take a twelve-hour shift, and Levon does the other twelve. I swear, she's never left the barn except to come in here to eat, or to go for her walks in the woods."

"She's given you both the slip before, to get away to party. That's how this whole problem started."

"Yeah, but we've been watching her like a hawk ever since. She doesn't go pee without one of us being aware of how long she spends on the toilet."

"Right." Richard strode angrily toward the door. "Where is she now?"

"In the studio. The session guys are learning her new songs. That's why I figured it was safe to come here to talk to you. She's surrounded and can't leave, or they'd get nothing done."

"Come with me. I'll get to the bottom of this. Maybe she needs to get back on those old drugs her L.A. doctor was feeding her."

They left the office and walked down the hall, heading out the back door. Outside, Richard led the way to the barn. He looked around with distaste at the budding trees and shrubs, swatting angrily at a bug that had the audacity to land on his arm, obviously unaware of who he was.

"She needs to get her ass in gear and produce another hit album," he grumbled. "I can't wait to get out of this fucking wilderness."

He pushed open the door that led into the converted barn. The first door on the left was the recording room, where the technicians worked their magic, blending the various tracks to produce new releases. The door ahead of them was the actual studio, and they could hear music coming from it, even with the big doors closed. Richard ignored the red letters over the entry that spelled out *Recording* and pushed his way into the studio.

True to Jamar's words, the song had a bluesy sound to it. The musicians all stopped when Richard strode in purposefully. Nisha was the last to see him and to stop playing and singing. She looked irritated when she saw what had distracted the others.

"What's your deal?" she demanded. "We're in the middle of recording."

"I can see that. But just *what* are you recording?"

She glared at Jamar, who shifted uncomfortably and glanced around, looking at anything other than her. "Why? Did your lap dog tell you he doesn't like my new music?"

"We need to talk." Richard turned to bark at the others. "Break time, everyone. Ten minutes. Then you can come back to see if we're done."

"If you try to interfere with my music, we are really and truly *done*," Nisha growled.

He turned on her. "Not according to your contract, honey. I own what you write, in return for providing you with the marketing services. Services, I might add, that you are really going to need if you insist on writing depressing shit that no one will want to hear."

Stunned silence greeted his words, followed by musicians making a hasty retreat from the room.

Even Jamar left, escaping the heat between him and Nisha.

Once they were alone in the room, Richard wasted no time. "Jamar says that you've been crying while you sing some of your new songs. That's not going to go down well with your pre-teen and tween fans who expect light, danceable songs from their Nisha. What the fuck is wrong with you?"

She looked at him with disdain. "I think you're selling my fans short. The ones who truly care about me will follow me on this new path I'm taking. I've been making the same kind of songs for too long. It's time for my music to evolve."

"Into what? Unmarketable crap that sounds like a bad Country song? Music that will have everyone reaching for a beer to cry into?"

"I've always written what I feel. I'm pouring myself into my music like I've always done. I can't help it that I'm in a different place now. My music is still flowing from that place deep inside of me, where my feelings live. It's just being re-modeled."

Richard advanced on her, and she didn't shrink back as she normally did. In fact, she drew herself up to appear taller, more in possession of herself. He stopped, taken aback by her uncharacteristic defiance.

"What's gotten into you lately?" He frowned. "Is it the new drugs that hick-town quack has been feeding you? You're not acting like yourself."

"I don't know. It's hard to explain, but I feel more like my-self than I've ever felt before. It's like I was walking around in a fog of pharmaceuticals all the time. Now I feel like I'm ex-periencing life on a whole different level of reality. And I like it. I'm going to keep following this path to see where it leads."

He narrowed his eyes. "Sounds to me like I'm talking to that *other voice* that lives in your head. Remember when your parents signed your first contract with me? You weren't eight-een yet, so you couldn't sign for yourself. They told me that you were being drugged to keep the *other voice* in your head silent. They warned me that you had to stay on your drugs, or your behavior would get erratic."

"And I've been on those drugs for half of my life. I'm thirty years old, and I've never experienced life as vividly as I am now. I'm sleeping better, and I'm enjoying little things, like a walk in the woods, or just feeling the sunshine on my skin. Did you know the earth smells differently as the spring pro-gresses? It's starting to smell green, like everything is coming back to life."

"Is that why your new song is called *Blue Green*? Because of the woods?"

"Partly. It's actually called *Blue Over Green*. I feel very comforted when I'm walking in the woods, with the blue sky above me and nature's greenery around me. I'm sure Jamar told you that I'm not meeting anyone out there. He thinks he's being quiet about it, but the man walks like an elephant. It's funny how loudly sounds travel when you're out in the peace and quiet among the trees."

Richard's mouth fell open. He shook his head, sputtering in his anger. "I'm calling that quack and demanding that he put you back onto your old drugs. I agreed he could substitute other ones, but only if they helped you. This is totally unnatural behavior, and I want it stopped."

"Excuse me? I'm way over eighteen now, dude. You have no right to insist on anything. According to HIPAA rules, my relationship with my doctor is my business, not yours."

His anger simmered near boiling. "Not when you're still under contract with me. Everything that happens to you is my business."

"Then maybe I need to find a new manager."

She appeared as shocked by her words as he was. They stared at each other for a long moment.

Richard recovered first. "Bitch, just try it. I'll sue your ass for everything you'll ever make in two lifetimes. You'll never get away from me. I'll get the best lawyers money can buy."

"Yeah, using the money that *my* music made for you. Where is *my* fortune?"

"In your bank account."

"The one you're a co-signer on? Suddenly that doesn't seem like a good idea anymore."

Richard stalked closer toward Nisha with his hand drawn back, his desire to hit her almost overwhelming.

Her chin tilted up in defiance, and she glared back at him.

He changed his mind, turned without a word, and headed for the door.

With his hand on the handle, he turned to face her, keeping tight control over his anger. "Fine. Write whatever crap you want to. You have a concert this Friday night, in four days, in the only shit-hole town close to here that has a big enough place to accommodate the crowds who will want to see Nisha for cheap. I expect you to give them the songs they've come to hear. If you want to play some of this new garbage you've been writing, you can work in a few songs. If the audience isn't receptive, I will expect you to go back to writing what they want to hear. You've been warned, girl. You will do what I say, or I'll take steps to ensure that you become more . . . shall we say . . . cooperative."

With that, he pushed through the doors, and they slammed behind him.

Nisha gnashed her teeth in anger and frustration.

He thinks he owns me. That he can force me to do what he wants me to. And I'm afraid he'll find some way to make me.

A small voice answered boldly in her head. *I am gaining strength with each passing day. Together, we are stronger than he can guess.*

She spoke aloud, in despair. "Oh, great. Nothing to worry about now. The *other voice* in my head says so. What a great comfort that is."

She jumped when the doors swung open again, but it was only the musicians returning from their break. She shook her head to clear it. "Okay, guys. Let's take it from the top again."

The drummer asked, "Um, shouldn't we practice some of your old songs, so we'll be able to play them at Friday night's concert?"

She appeared uncertain. "I guess so. But later. First, we need to be sure the new songs are perfect. I really believe in

261

them. I think my fans will be ready to follow me on this new path I'm on."

"If not, it's your career on the line, not ours."

She looked around sharply, trying to see who had spoken. But answering murmurs indicated many of the musicians agreed with the speaker. She ignored them all and strummed the first few notes of her favorite new song.

PART SIX: A NEW LIFE

CHAPTER THIRTY-ONE

Diego stopped by the principal's office to ask Monique how Nathan was doing.

"I think he needs to be included in the conference call," Monique said. "He's depressed and lethargic, and he hasn't been sleeping well, which is obvious from the bags under his eyes and his general listlessness. But he's been taking care of business, teaching every day, and holding things together. He's a strong man, but his wolf is hurting, and that pain is felt by both of them."

Diego nodded. "Thanks. I'll text him now to let him know I'm calling Dr. Sullivan and find out what time he can be in my office."

Nathan's reply said that he could be in the office by three-thirty. Diego went to the penthouse and found his wife napping on the couch in front of an open window. He stood there, admiring her for a few minutes before she opened her eyes and made a face at him.

"You know I hate it when you watch me sleep!"

He smiled. "But you're so beautiful that it takes my breath away, and I'm unable to move from the sight of the woman who completes me."

A smile twitched on her lips. "Well, okay then, I guess. What's up that you left your office?"

"I'm heading back there now, but I came to see if you wanted to come along. Nathan will meet us there, and we're going to call Dr. Sullivan for an update."

"Then help *the whale* up off the couch, and I'll waddle along with you. I want to hear this, too. I want Nathan to get his happy-ever-after. You and I have ours. Monique and Grant recently got theirs. Freddie and John are working on creating theirs. That leaves Nathan for me to worry over like a mother hen."

"It must be the mothering instinct made manifest. You weren't like this before you got pregnant."

She shrugged. "Well, I'm like this now. Just let me visit the bathroom, and I'll be ready."

Ten minutes later, they arrived at Diego's office to find Nathan sitting outside the door. He stood when they approached, and Diego saw the truth of what Monique had told him. Nathan's face looked haggard, and he'd lost a few pounds, which was very noticeable on his wiry frame. Nathan smiled at Saoirse when she beckoned for him to hug her, but his eyes were dull, and the smile didn't last long.

Saoirse fussed over him. "You're too skinny to be losing weight, Nathan. I think you need to have double desserts for a while. I'll speak to Janine about it."

He looked pained. "Please don't. Already she's been hovering over me at mealtimes, trying to get me to go up for seconds. I'm eating enough to stay alive, but I don't have much of an appetite these days."

"Let's go in and see what Dr. Sullivan has to say," Diego said. "Maybe that will brighten your mood."

Once they were all seated, Diego made the call. Before Dr. Sullivan got on the line, he punched the button for the speaker so they could all participate.

"Diego, always good to speak with you. Is your lovely wife there also?"

"Yes," Saoirse grunted, "But I'm hoping to avoid birth by explosion. If I get any bigger, I'm afraid that's what we'll be dealing with."

The doctor chuckled warmly. "My wife used to complain

like that, also."

"Did it help?"

"Not that I know of. But we have three children, so I guess she got over it. The last couple of weeks are the worst of it. Soon you'll hold the baby and forget how miserable you are now."

"I hope so."

"And is Nathan there as well?" Dr. Sullivan asked.

"Yes, I am. Is there any good news to report, to mollify my wolf?"

"I'm not sure. What I do know is that for the past few days, she's been completely off the nasty antipsychotic drugs she's been on for so much of her life." There was a slight growl to the doctor's tone. "She's responding well to the replacements I've given her. They're a blend of vitamins and minerals, along with extra protein her wolf needs to gain strength after being held back and ignored for so long. Her color is better, and her eyes are clear, not cloudy and dull anymore. I've been counseling her to stop thinking of the other voice in her head as an enemy or as a sign of psychosis. I've tried to get her to view it as another part of herself. I told her that she might find it has good advice at times."

Nathan heaved a sigh. "I'm glad that she's feeling better, doctor, but that doesn't make me feel any better."

"It should. For the first time in her life, she might be getting close to acknowledging her wolf. I think her wolf is building itself up to force a change while she's conscious and not drugged. But this will be a new experience for both of them."

"That gives me hope, but still leaves my wolf very sad at our loss of connection to our mate."

"Speaking of sadness, I should mention that her manager, or publicist, or whatever-the-hell that rude man who runs her career calls himself, called me earlier today. He demanded that I put her back onto her old drugs. Seems she's been acting *unnatural,* according to him. She hasn't been doing any drinking or drugging. When she's not writing or recording, she's either in her room alone or going for long walks in the woods near the place they're renting. He also says that the new music she's writing is crap."

"Some people might say that what she's famous for is crap," Saoirse commented in a wry tone. "Her fluffy pop songs are usually eminently forgettable until the next one comes out."

"That's what my wife told me. I'd never heard of her before. But her manager yelled at me that he wasn't going to allow her to continue to write sad songs. He said her fans expect a certain kind of music from her, and if she can't produce it without the drugs she used to take, then he wants her back on them."

"Sad songs?" Nathan leaned forward, his interest more intent.

"Yes. He says she has a concert Friday night—that's tomorrow night—in Sloggum. When I asked why there, he said the county fairgrounds there was the closest place to their rental property with a venue big enough to hold all of her fans. He says he's only allowing her to do a couple of her new songs, for fear her fans would turn on her and boo her off the stage. Imagine, saying he *allows* her to do anything! He acts like he's her father. I've never attempted to control any of my kids once they turned eighteen." The doctor huffed. "She's thirty years old, and he treats her like a child! I got so angry that I told him I couldn't discuss her any further with him because of HIPAA rules. He swore a lot then, only some of it in English. But I told him that unless *she* asks for her prescriptions to be changed back, I wasn't going to. And that it's really none of his business. Then I said goodbye and hung up the phone while he was still yelling."

"Good for you!" Saoirse cheered. "Serves that pushy

bastard right."

"Thanks for the update, Dr. Sullivan," Diego said.

He glanced at Nathan, whose face reflected new hope in place of the despondency he'd been wallowing in.

"I'm happy for the opportunity to help one of us to make peace with her wolf," Dr. Sullivan replied. "I thought I'd seen everything, but I've never before encountered anyone who'd been counseled and medicated so heavily into denying the wolf's existence. I sincerely hope this will work for this young woman. But you caught me as I was getting ready to leave the office. I'll have to text my wife that I'm going to be late, so she doesn't worry. Goodbye, all of you."

Silence reigned for a few seconds after the call disconnected.

Suddenly, Nathan stood and declared, "I'm going to that concert."

"Do you think you should?" Diego asked.

"Don't even try to stop me. I have to see her, even if it's from a distance."

"Then take someone else with you. I don't want you in town, possibly getting recognized by anyone around her, without any back-up. In fact, if you take Grant with you, there will be two tall blond men, so maybe that will help to confuse them."

"I'll see if he's willing to go," Nathan said.

Saoirse moaned loudly. "Um, Diego?" She was panting. "I think my water just broke on your office furniture. And I'm going into labor . . . like right now!"

Diego jumped up to help Saoirse stand up, while Nathan called Rachel to ask where they needed to take Saoirse.

"The clinic office," he relayed to Diego. "Rachel wants to know if you think you can walk that far, or should she send over a wheelchair?"

Saoirse gritted her teeth. "I'll try. But if I deliver the baby in the hallway, it's gonna be messy."

"Wheelchair," Nathan said urgently into the phone.

Diego supported his wife on one side while Nathan took the other to help her out the door.

They had made it only a few feet into the hall when Rachel's assistant came running toward them, pushing an empty wheelchair. They got Saoirse into it, then Diego pushed it as fast he dared to the clinic, where Rachel was already getting everything ready. Everything was set to help with the birth of the pack leader's first child.

Five hours later, Diego sat on the bed with his wife as she nursed their daughter. According to Rachel, the baby had been cooperative, and the birth was as easy as first-time natural childbirth could be. Saoirse had raged, screamed, sworn, and hollered at him for having put her into the position to endure so much pain.

Ultimately, they both cried tears of joy when the baby was placed on her mother's chest and began to root around.

"See?" Rachel pointed out, as she finished with the delivery of the placenta. "She's already determined to find the nipple and begin feeding. She's strong and healthy, and a credit to her strong-willed mother."

Diego was still teary-eyed when Rachel handed him the scissors. "It's traditional for the daddy to cut the cord."

His first attempt was clumsy due to the shaking of his hands. But he called upon inner strength and forced himself to stop trembling. He cut the cord and put the scissors down.

Rachel tied off the umbilicus on the baby, then set her back, face down, on her mother's chest. "I'll be right here, cleaning up and putting things away. You two bond with your new daughter. I'll need to clean her up and weigh and measure her soon. But take some time to introduce yourselves to her."

Saoirse looked up from the miracle on her chest and smiled

at him through her tears. "Honestly, someone would think it was you who went through childbirth, the way you're carrying on, *señor*," she chided him.

He wiped at his tears and took a deep, shaky breath. "*Now* I can tell you how worried I was. A thousand horrible images played themselves over and over again in my mind, all resulting in me losing both of you. I would be so alone, and the pain would be unbearable. And I would have to live with the knowledge that it was all my fault! But you're still with me, and we now have our daughter to love. I have waited my whole life for this moment. I'm so happy that my body is barely able to contain my joy. And my love for you will continue to grow with each breath I take for the rest of my life. *Eres toda mi vida. Y ella es hijita de mi corazón.*"

Rachel looked over at them and smiled softly. "You are my whole life, and she is the daughter of my heart." Tears shone in her eyes, also. "That's beautiful, Diego."

Diego didn't reply, and neither did Saoirse, since they were too busy staring lovingly into each other's eyes. Their daughter made some noises, and they both turned their attention fully to the new person who had just entered their lives.

Rachel called to Diego from across the room. "I hate to interrupt, Daddy, but could you bring the baby over here so I can get her vital statistics?"

He became panicked. "How do I pick her up?"

Saoirse rolled her eyes. "Like this, silly."

Deftly, she picked the baby up from her chest and flipped her over, holding her out to him. He held out his hands and mimicked the hold his wife used.

"Just be sure to support her neck and head, honey. And relax. It's a baby, not a Ming vase. She won't break. Babies are pretty durable."

Diego's gaze was transfixed as he pulled his daughter close to him. "She's worth more to me than a Ming vase — or anything else," he said in awe of the bundle in his arms. Then he looked up in surprise at Saoirse, then at Rachel. "Um, is she peeing on me?"

Rachel looked over, grinning. "Probably. She's not diapered yet. Babies do that sort of thing."

"How marvelous! She's so wonderful!"

Saoirse giggled. "You won't think so after changing a couple hundred diapers, honey."

Rachel winked at Saoirse. "But his attitude proves that he's going to be a great Daddy."

Saoirse nodded solemnly back at her. "He's already a great Daddy."

Diego slowly made his way over to the doctor, then reluctantly handed the baby to her.

Rachel took the baby from him with professional detachment. She wrote down the baby's weight, length, and APGAR scores, recording her important statistics that indicate how healthy a newborn is by measuring Activity, Pulse, Grimace, Appearance, and Respiration. She used a soft wet cloth to give the baby her first sponge bath, then she diapered her and wrapped her in a receiving blanket before handing the now outraged and squalling baby back to Diego.

"Take her back to Mama. She needs to be soothed."

Diego handed the baby to Saoirse and resumed his seat by her side, with one arm around her shoulders. He cooed loving words in two languages to the two females who were his world.

CHAPTER THIRTY-TWO

Nathan pulled a chair over to Grant and Monique's table and joined their family as they ate dinner.

"You heard that the baby is a girl?" he asked.

Monique nodded, smiling. "Everyone knows. Diego sent out a pack-wide text with a picture. No name yet, though."

"Give them time," Grant said. "They probably already know her name, but he might save it for the monthly meeting Sunday night, so it can be a formal announcement."

Nathan swallowed the food he was chewing and leaned forward. "Grant, can I ask you for a favor?"

"Sure, Nathan. You're my wife's best friend. Plus I've known you for years, and you've always gone out of your way to make me feel welcome. So whatever it is, I'll be happy to help you out. What do you need?"

Nathan spoke quickly, getting the words out in a rush. "Nisha's manager has her doing a concert tomorrow night. I checked online, and it's supposed to start at seven at night. It's in Sloggum, at the county fairgrounds. I need to be there. I need to see her, even if it's just from a distance. And Diego thinks I need someone to go with me as back-up. He suggested you, so if any of her security guys are looking for a tall man with blond hair, there will be two of us to confuse them."

At the mention of Nisha's name, Selma and Selena had both leaned forward.

"Can we come too? She's the best!" Selena squealed.

"I know all the words to all of her songs," Selma pointed out. "Plus, I'm older."

Selena shot her sister a murderous look.

Monique shook her head. "Certainly not! You're both too young to go to concerts yet. And besides, young lady," she addressed Selma directly, "her music has swear words in it sometimes. And she sings about things that are way too mature for you to be listening to."

"Aw, Mom, I'm not a baby anymore! I'm eleven!"

James patted the back of his mother's hand, where it rested on the table. "There, there, Mom. They grow up so quickly, don't they?"

"Don't you mean *we*, white man?" Selma said in a snotty tone.

"I was trying to be funny, girlie," he sniffed. "And who are you calling white man? I'm only half-white. I'm also half-Black. And might I add, I'm the best of both sides."

Nathan shook his head but smiled along with everyone else. Even though the girls were still upset that they wouldn't get to go to the concert, they were mollified when Grant promised to keep an eye out for age-appropriate concerts he could take his beloved daughters to in the very near future.

"You just be careful tomorrow night, my love," Monique warned Grant.

He blew her a kiss. "Of course, my sweet. It will seem like forever until I can be back home in your arms."

Selma stuck her finger into her mouth, making gagging noises, and James rolled his eyes.

"See what we have to put up with?" James asked Nathan in an aggrieved tone. "You'd think they were still on their honeymoon, the way they talk to each other. And they don't care that we can hear them — or see them!"

Grant had leaned over to kiss Monique, and they both turned to stick out their tongues at James.

Nathan sat back, relieved, yet anxious. *I got Grant to be my back-up, which is good. But will I ever be able to have my woman be so comfortable with me? Will she ever accept me as her mate? Or am I butting my head up against a brick wall?*

His wolf answered with steely resolve. *We will win her because her wolf chose us. Once she learns to listen to her wolf, they will become one. Then we can all become one. That is how it must be.*

Nisha was feeling her usual before-show jitters, made worse by the lack of an abundance of alcohol and drugs in her body. She had opened a bottle of champagne and only drank one glass. Now she was sitting at the vanity, in front of the mirror, breathing deeply to calm her nerves.

Reflected behind her was the interior of the trailer Richard had rented to hold her costumes and cosmetics. He'd told her that since this wasn't an important show, they were on a budget. She could do her own makeup and costume changes. When she'd argued that changing costumes herself would slow her down between sets, he said he'd arranged for a forty-five-minute video montage of some of her bigger shows to run while she ran to the trailer and got ready for the second half of the show. She had considered arguing further with him, but he hinted that uncooperative behavior might cause him to forbid her to do her new songs. So she accepted his terms.

She stared at herself in the mirror, studying how her appearance had transformed. She'd lost a few pounds, so her face appeared almost gaunt. But it was mostly her eyes that had changed. They had always sparkled, shiny from the drugs she did, and her excessive alcohol consumption. Now they looked more alert than they ever had, but they seemed dulled with sadness. She leaned closer to the mirror and was shocked to see another being's eyes staring back at her. She jumped back with a start. "What the hell? Who are you?"

I am your wolf. I have always been in you, but you never allowed me to speak before.

She gnashed her teeth, still speaking aloud. "Why now? I've got a concert to do! You need to go away. I'm in the driver's seat around here. This is my body and my mind. You need to go away."

I will be silent as you do your concert. But I am almost strong enough to convince you that we are one.

"Yeah, whatever. Some other time, okay? Now I've gotta finish doing my makeup and get out there to entertain the masses."

True to her word, the voice stopped speaking. Nisha hurriedly finished getting the heavy stage makeup onto her face and stood to look at herself in the full-length mirror hanging next to the door.

"I hope the pounds I've lost don't make my top fall down," she mused. "I think I've got some of that double-sided tape in my makeup bag." She rooted around in the bottom of the bag and triumphantly lifted out the roll. "I thought so. Mary gave it to me the last time I wore this suit. Even then, with bigger boobs, she was worried they'd make an appearance in a major costume malfunction. Richard woulda had her head on a pike if that happened. So I've just got to tape the whole thing around the boobage and voilà! No more danger of me flashing the audience."

There was a loud rap on the door.

"Almost showtime, sweetie."

Richard's unctuous voice made her skin crawl. *He's still acting like he owns me. Who the fuck does he think he is?*

There was an answering wordless growl in her mind that, for some reason, made her smile. *Ya know, I'm glad you agree. I think it's time I get a new manager.*

She took one last long, self-appraising look at her appearance, deciding it was good enough to represent the famous star, Nisha. She strode over to the door and exited the trailer. With Richard by her side, acting as if he cared about her safety, she made her way to the back entrance of the venue.

Once inside, she was surrounded by a phalanx of hired muscle, ushering her to the edge of the stage. She heard her name being announced, and the crowd wildly cheering as the band played the introductory notes that were her cue. Taking a deep breath, she strutted onto the stage in her four-inch heels and began to sing.

The seats had been first-come, first-served, with the gate opening at six. Despite finding a parking space on a street close to the venue, and jogging across the fairgrounds over to the bleachers by six-fifteen, Nathan and Grant found themselves standing amongst a crowd of adoring fans who had also gotten there too late for a seat in the stands. The section in front of the stage appeared to have another life as a football field. The area had been repurposed with lawn-chair seating, but that was only a euphemism. No one was seated. Everyone was on their feet, screaming, the minute the stage got dark and the musicians started to play the first notes.

Grant poked Nathan in the ribs, waving around at the crowd. He leaned over to holler in Nathan's ear. "Monique was wrong, and Selma was right. There are more pre-teen girls here than you can shake a stick at."

Nathan didn't reply. He was staring so hard at the stage, waiting for a glimpse of his beloved, that his eyeballs actually hurt from the effort.

Grant stared at him then shrugged. "I'm gonna go check out the surroundings, dude. This isn't my kind of music—or my kind of scene. I hate big crowds. I'll be back in a few. Just stay in one place."

Nathan acknowledged with a quick nod. He was transfixed by the object of his desires strutting onto the stage, half-naked, on heels, as she sang the first few notes of her opening song. The words were drowned out by the frantic screaming of her fans going up a few decibels as they saw her. But their excitement was nothing compared to his.

There she is! His heart beat faster, his breathing sped up, and he could feel his cock straining against the zipper of his jeans.

Take her! Take her now! She is ours! That exultant cry was the first time in a long time his wolf had expressed any emotion other than anger and bone-deep sadness. Nathan smiled despite himself.

I can't take her now! Not in front of all these people! We'd be arrested on the spot if we made it up to the stage. Which we wouldn't. There are security guys all over the front of the stage to keep errant fans from climbing up to claim their idol. To them, I'd be no different from all these screaming adolescents.

There was an answering growl that became a howl in his mind, but he had trouble hearing it over the loud amps that blasted Nisha's music all over a five-mile area. He tried to listen to the music, but to him, it was all just tuneful noise and earworms. Catchy lyrics about looking for love and the joy to be found in partying your life away. He marveled that every girl around him was singing every word along with their idol. *I'm about twenty years too old for this kind of music.*

Suddenly Grant was next to him again. He glanced over to see Grant pantomime that he should look around at the fringes of the area. Uniformed security guards were strolling up and down the aisles, keeping a close watch on the crowd. Nathan had removed his hat when he started to sweat. Grant pulled it out of his hand and jammed it back onto his head.

Then both turned to look at the stage when Nisha stopped singing and addressed the audience directly. "How are you all feeling tonight?"

The answering roar was deafening.

"I'm so glad to be here in Maine, making your dreams come true by singing just to you!"

The audience shrieking got so loud that Grant covered his

ears, rolling his eyes.

"But I'm gonna ask you to do one thing for me. For the first time in about two years, I've been writing some new music, and it's totally different from what I usually write. I want to do a couple of new songs for you. After that, I'll take a quick forty-five-minute break for a costume change while you enjoy watching some videos of me perform all around the world. Then I promise to come back out here and blow your socks off with more of your favorite hit songs. But are you willing to give a listen to where my muse is taking me right now?"

It didn't seem possible, but the sound level rose another few decibels as the audience proclaimed its undying love for their Nisha. They quieted down as she walked over to pick up a guitar and adjusted the mike she'd just been dancing with so she could sing without holding it.

The first few notes were quiet, then the sound technicians adjusted the volume, and everyone listened as Nisha sang. She sang about Gaia, Mother Earth, and how unhappy she was at being so abused by her children. She sang about the perils of thinking only of today and not planning for tomorrow. She sang about how she wanted to leave a beautiful place for her children, but she first had to find a man worthy of her. She ended with the chorus again, chanting love for the planet and for all the people who lived on it.

When she ended the song, there was polite applause, but nothing like the manic reactions that her old songs had produced.

She shrugged and smiled out at the audience. "What can you expect when I'm surrounded by the beauty of Maine while I'm writing music? Your state is fucking gorgeous!"

At that, she got more wild applause, but only from the kids in the audience. Their parents appeared split between those who nodded in agreement that the Earth was in peril, and those who shook their heads, probably wanting her to go back to singing fluffy songs.

She tuned her guitar again, saying, "If you're out there, mister, you know that this song is for you. I call it *Blue Over Green*."

The first few notes of the song wafted across the audience, and Nathan's entire body became as rigid as his cock. He stopped breathing. All he could do was stare at the woman he loved as she poured out her love for him in front of a crowd of thousands.

She sang about the green that surrounded them when he took her and made them one. She sang about the joy of smelling the green of spring, as they made love all night long. She sang of the color of his eyes, the green she saw in her every waking moment, and that haunted her dreams. She sang about how empty she was without him, and how she would live a life of loneliness because he was the only man she would ever love.

When the last notes were still echoing, the audience was shock still. Polite applause was just beginning when Nathan suddenly started for the exit closest to the backstage area, with Grant right behind him.

Grant nodded at the security guards who barely glanced their way. "My brother's really gotta pee."

He followed Nathan out to stand beyond the lit area, into the semi-darkness that surrounded the back of the bleachers.

"Where the hell are you going?" Grant muttered at Nathan.

"I don't know. I have to find her. I have to hold her. I have to claim her."

Nathan's eyes were glazed and unfocused. Grant could clearly see both Nathan *and* his wolf looking out of the eyes he'd never really noticed were so green.

Grant grabbed Nathan's shoulders and shook him. "I'll

show you where I think she's going. But you have to be very careful! Don't take off your hat. They're prowling around looking for a tall, blond man. And whatever you do, don't let anyone get close enough to see your eyes."

Nathan's eyes regained their focus, and Grant breathed a sigh of relief when his friend nodded his agreement.

Grant pulled Nathan along, heading for the rear of the stage area. When they were almost to the back, he pulled Nathan further into the shadows.

He pointed across the lot. "See that trailer? I took a peek in the window. There are costumes all over the place, and a big crate of makeup. I think that's what she's using as a dressing room. The video is gonna play for forty-five minutes. You have to act fast. And she has to go back on stage after that. Keep that in mind."

Nathan checked out the security guards as Grant made his way over to a random man who was walking toward the long row of porta-potties. When Grant got close to the man, he shoved him, pushing hard enough for the guy to fall against one of the potties, knocking over another man who was just exiting.

"Hey! Watch where you're going, asshole!" the guy yelled.

With that, a minor scuffle began. It drew the guards over, leaving the trailer unguarded long enough for Nathan to make a mad dash for it. He pulled open the luckily unlocked door and fell into it, then slammed the door closed, locking it behind him. He turned around to get his bearings.

Nisha was in the process of unzipping the back of her costume. Her head whipped around, and they stared at each other for a heartbeat. Then Nathan crossed the few feet between them and pulled her into his arms. She didn't resist. Instead, she tilted her head up to meet the punishing kiss his lips inflicted on her.

For a few minutes, the only sounds were their rapid breathing, the whimpers she made as their hands explored each other and their lips devoured each other. His wolf howled with triumph as he tore at her costume, the tape no match for his passion. He got the costume half-way down, and his lips moved down to encase her breasts, licking and rubbing, first one, then the other of the hard knots of her nipples. He pushed the rest of her costume to the floor, ecstatic to discover that she wore nothing under it.

"Oh, God, I need you!" she gasped.

She moaned as she tore at his pants, taking care not to damage him with the zipper. His cock sprang free, swollen and throbbing and ready for her. Nathan pushed her up against a wall, thrusting his hips forward, panting harshly into her ear.

"Do you want this as much as I do?"

"Yes! Oh, God, yes! Take me now!"

In seconds, he had his hands on her butt, lifting her off the floor. He rubbed himself against her, feeling her passion leaking onto him. With a moan, he pressed forward, stopping to stare into her eyes with the tip of him paused at her entrance.

"Once we do this, we are one," he said, his voice a hoarse whisper.

Nisha nodded at the man she'd thought to never see again, and the rightness of the moment flowed through her whole body. When he still didn't move, she pushed herself forward to take all of him into her body. She gasped as she felt herself being stretched open by him. As she stared into his eyes, she saw two beings looking back at her, and felt the other inside of her join to watch him in return. Then there was no more time for reflection.

Her passion skyrocketed as they ground against each other

like wild animals. He seemed determined to embed himself so deep within her body that he would never be separated from her again. She was determined to squeeze him so tightly he'd never be able to remove himself. They moved in perfect harmony toward the same goal. Their movements became quicker, more frantic, and she felt her climax reaching epic proportions.

Suddenly, he howled in a good human imitation of a wolf. She followed a split second later, writhing and screaming as she rode wave after wave of orgasms, pulling him along with her. She rejoiced at the connection she felt to this man who she knew, instinctively, was hers for a lifetime.

Nathan let her back down to the floor, panting. "Can't stand up anymore. Legs not working."

She pulled him over to the chair, pushing him back to sit down. She curled up onto his lap, almost purring in her happiness. His arms held her tight against his chest as her breathing gradually slowed down enough to have coherent thoughts again.

With that came reality.

"Oh, my God! How long has it been? It's only a forty-five-minute video. You've got to get out of here. He can't find you in here." She almost wept with her building panic.

Nathan shook his head. "I'm not afraid of him. No one can separate us, ever again. We are one."

"Yeah, but I've gotta finish my show. I've got to get into the next costume." She jumped off his lap and ran over to begin pulling on the new costume. She glanced at herself in the mirror. "My makeup. It's smeared. Shit! Shit! Shit! He's gonna be here knocking on the door soon. You've gotta get out of here!"

No sooner had the words left her mouth when a loud knocking pounded on the door.

"Nisha? Who are you talking to? It's time for you to get

your ass back out there." Richard's voice came through loud and clear.

Her eyes widened with terror, and she tried to keep the fear from her voice. "I'll be right out. I was . . . um . . . having some trouble with the zipper on this damn thing."

The door handle jiggled, but the lock held.

"Open the door. I'll help you get into it."

"No, I've got it now. I'll be out in a minute."

Nathan moved behind her to pull up the zipper, and he reached forward to help her adjust her breasts into the revealing costume.

He leaned his head forward and whispered, "I'll make him pay for hurting you."

She whirled around. "Great, great. But for now, just hide. I'll pull the door closed and locked behind me, but he'll send someone in here to look for you. I don't know how you'll get out, but you have to."

She took a deep breath, to steady her nerves, then made a face and picked up a perfume bottle. Nathan's lips twitched as she sprayed it around the room, missing herself entirely, trying to cover up the olfactory evidence of their passion.

She sat at the vanity to fix her makeup while watching Nathan in the mirror. He looked around and then walked over to the door that led to the bathroom. He pressed himself against the wall where the shower hose came out and pulled the door closed.

Nisha walked over to the door, took another deep breath, and opened it.

"Finally! Took you long enough," Richard groused. "Now, you better run your ass back on stage."

"Don't you mean *we*, dude? You need to introduce me."

"Yeah . . . right." He glanced around the area for a moment. "Hey you! Yeah, you! I want this trailer searched. If you find anyone in it, hold him until I get back."

"Yes, sir!" A male voice answered.

"That's not necessary," Nisha said.

Richard grabbed her arm roughly, pulling her along with him as he walked quickly toward the door leading to the stage.

Nathan leaned against the bathroom wall, listening to Nisha continue to argue until he couldn't hear her voice anymore. The door to the trailer opened, and he steeled himself for the fight of his life. When the bathroom door opened, he leapt out onto Grant, who was stocky enough to keep them both from falling over.

"Dude! Be careful," he groaned. "We gotta get out of here ASAP. If you break our bones, we'll be too slow to outrun that asshole's hired muscle."

They walked to the trailer door, and Grant signaled for Nathan to wait, then stuck his head out to look around. He nodded and walked through the door, waving for Nathan to follow.

"How?" Nathan whispered.

Grant smirked, pointing under the trailer at the guard's body. "He looked tired. He can use the rest."

They quickly left the fairgrounds and jogged back along the street, not stopping until they got to the car. They jumped in, belted up, and Grant drove to the outskirts of town before he pulled over under a tree.

"Now what?" Nathan asked.

"I don't have to ask. It was quite obvious that you mated in there. So did you make plans to meet her later?"

Nathan shook his head. "There wasn't time. But I know now that I need to kill him for how he treats her."

Grant held up his hands. "Hold on there, Romeo. That kind of talk is for teenagers who think only of *right now*. Use your brain, dude. You're old enough to know there's more than one way to hurt a man. Especially a money-grubbing little piece of shit like him. Take away his prized filly, and he'll have a fuck of a time replacing her, along with the income he's used to living on. And that won't get you thrown in jail. Where, I might add, you would never be able to enjoy your mate."

Nathan sighed deeply. "You're right." He looked around. "This is the main road out of town, right?"

Grant nodded. "Heading north-west it is. Back the way we came."

"I don't know where he's keeping her, but it has to be in the same direction. Otherwise, she couldn't have run close enough to hear our wolves howling. And Dr. Sullivan said that the rental place is near Bingham."

"Plan?"

"I'm shifting. I'll follow their cars. You drive to Bingham. I'll find you once I know where she is. Then we can figure out how to get her out of there."

"Probably not tonight, though."

"We'll see." Nathan got out of the car, slamming the door shut. He stripped quickly, throwing his clothing into the car's open window, before trotting into the woods to do his change, out of sight.

Grant shook his head. A few minutes later, Nathan's large, thin, tan-brown wolf with green eyes nodded, then loped into the woods to wait for the limo they'd seen beyond the trailer.

"I'll drive into Bingham, all right. But then I'm going to shift and see what I can find. Your emotions are too high, dude. You'll make mistakes. Plus, I'm the tracker." He looked up at the half-moon in the sky. "Bright enough for wolves to see everything. Dark enough for humans to have trouble seeing anything. A good night."

He started the car and headed toward the next town.

CHAPTER THIRTY-THREE

Nathan was crouched on his belly, hidden by shrubs and tall grasses, watching the grounds of the rental property Nisha was staying in. He had followed the limo, easily loping along the road in the shadows, unseen by anyone in the vehicle.

When the car turned onto the driveway of the property, Nathan quickly surveyed the area. He spotted several guards around the barn and chose his spot nearby to wait. The limo stopped near the barn doors, and one of the back doors opened. The manager jumped out, then pulled Nisha out by her arm.

"You're hurting me, Richard." She attempted to pull her arm free.

"That's not all I'm gonna do to you, you whore!"

"What I do, and who I do it with, is none of your business!"

He slapped her across the face. Nathan started to rise when he saw more heavily armed guards walking over, and these ones had viciously barking dogs with them. Luckily, he was downwind from them, so they wouldn't notice the scent of a wolf. He settled back down, seething with anger.

"I told you, I own your ass, bitch! You do what I tell you to, or I'll make you pay for it."

"I'm not your slave, in case you didn't notice. You can't *make* me do anything."

"Oh, can't I? I'm taking you back to L.A. tomorrow. That quack you've been seeing out here won't put you back on the drugs you need. I'm taking you back, and you're going to

287

your real doctor to get back on the right drugs."

"No, I'm not!"

His eyes narrowed. "We'll see about that. I'll get your parents involved if I have to, since they're the ones who first told me about your needing to be drugged. Then I'll get a judge involved. He'll agree with your parents and me once we get your doctor to testify. We'll get a court order to get you back on the drugs that keep you *normal*. Enough of this bullshit about the planet and blue green whatever."

Even from a distance, Nathan's wolf's vision could see the real fear reflected in Nisha's face.

"You can't do that to me! I'm an adult!" she blurted. "I'll get Dr. Sullivan to speak up for me."

The manager spat on the ground. "That small-town quack? Who gives a fuck what he thinks? Now you get into that barn and stay there. I'll deal with you in the morning. Right now, I gotta whole lotta plans to make. I've got plane tickets to get, and doctors and lawyers to line up. And your parents haven't heard from me in a long time. I think they need to know what their little girl has been up to."

"I'm a grown woman, you asshole!"

He slapped her again, sending her reeling against the door of the barn.

"Get in there," he grunted, "before I really lose my temper and do something you'll regret."

He opened the door and shoved her through, following behind and slamming it shut behind him. A few minutes later, he emerged, locking the door from the outside with a key.

"You!" He waved at a guard with a dog standing at attention nearby. "You stand out here all night. If she makes a peep, I want to know about it. If anything bigger than a bug tries to get in, shoot first. No questions asked. Understood?"

"Yes, sir!"

"And the rest of you? Surround the barn. There are a

couple other doors and some windows. No one passes, either in or out. Got it? Anyone or anything moves nearby, shoot it."

There was rapid bobbing of heads as the guards all acknowledged their assignments.

Nathan gnashed his teeth.

"Dude, you're going to ruin your dental work," Grant whispered, as his human form belly-crawled next to Nathan's wolf.

"Yeah, I heard it all, too. We can't go in there and get her without a whole lotta bloodshed. Most of it will be ours. Plus, I don't like to kill dogs. And we're *not* impervious to bullets that aren't silver, remember?"

Nathan's wolf growled softly.

"I know you want to rescue her. But we've gotta bide our time. I figure we wait here and watch. In the early morning, if the guards are all still there, I'll call nine-one-one and report someone being held by an active shooter. That'll bring out the cavalry. Which, realistically, is probably only a couple of cars. But that should be enough to get the scumbag up to explain himself. And since there's only one little woman in the barn, hopefully, he'll decide he doesn't need such high security. At least not while the police are still on the grounds questioning him. That's when you make your move."

Nathan's wolf narrowed eyes as he listened.

"I'll shift and run around a bit, give the dogs something to get excited about. Hopefully, they'll give chase with their masters. You go up as a wolf and shift behind the barn, in that little hay bale pile out back. Get in there and get her out. Get her to shift, and you can both run out. The car is just north of Bingham, at George's other garage. We'll meet up there and take her back to the academy. Then we'll get Diego to help figure out how to keep her safe. Sound like a plan?"

Nathan nodded his shaggy head up and down, then went back to watching the barn.

"It's gonna be a long night, I can feel it in my bones."

Grant joined Nathan in watching for any sign of a break in security.

As the first streaks of light from the sun turned the sky pink, Nathan remained vigilant in watching the barn. Grant commando-crawled back a bit to make his call. When he returned, he nodded at Nathan's wolf, and they resumed watching the barn. About ten minutes later, sirens could be heard, blaring as they neared the property.

"Not like they could make a sneaky entrance or anything, right? Probably more excitement than these small-town guys have ever had before. I'm heading back to the car to dump my clothes. Later."

Three squad cars squealed into the driveway with lights wildly twirling on top of the vehicles. When they stopped, the police all jumped out with their guns drawn. None of the guards moved.

"Where's the woman who's being held here against her will?" one officer yelled.

None of the guards spoke.

One of the police officers moved forward, flashing his badge around. "I'm the Chief of Police! I demand answers! Where is the woman being held against her will?"

A tall thin Black man walked out the front door of the main house with his hands held up. All the police officers turned their guns on him. There were many audible *clicks* as they all cocked their weapons in readiness.

"My boss, the man who rented this place, will be right down, officers. Please don't shoot anyone while he gets dressed."

"Are you being smart with me? Who the hell are you?" the chief said.

"My name is Jamar Smith, sir, and I'm the head of security

for Richard Madison. I heard your sirens and woke him up. He'll be right down."

"I'm here." Richard pushed past Jamar to glare around at the squad cars in his driveway, while he belted his robe. "What the fuck is going on here? Can't a man get any sleep in this God-forsaken wilderness?"

The Chief of Police strode forward to confront Richard. "We got a nine-one-one call that there's a woman on the grounds here being kept against her will by armed guards. Lo and behold, we pull up and find a barn surrounded by armed guards. Now I'm asking you, mister, where is the woman? And why the hell do you need so many machine guns and dogs, in a peaceful place like this?"

Richard obviously decided to try a civilized approach. His voice took on conciliatory tone, which, being faked, sounded totally insincere.

"We're from L.A., sir. We're used to needing high security. The only woman on the premises is the singer Nisha. You've heard of her, right? I'm her manager. She's sleeping in the barn, where she has a room next to the recording studio in there. We could wake her up, but she did a concert last night and got to bed pretty late. Why don't you come in, and Jamar can make some coffee. We can talk about who might have swatted you, placing a prank call like that. Then if you still want to talk to her, I'll go in and wake her up."

The Chief of Police looked around, his eyes narrowing. "Fine. But all these guards need to assemble where my officers can keep an eye on them. There won't be anyone sneaking around on the grounds with us around. And I still fail to see why you feel the need to have armed guards with machine guns out here in the country."

Jamar had already gone through the doorway, and Richard waved for the Chief of Police to precede him. Nathan caught the eye contact Richard made with some of the guards, a clear signal that he still expected them to make sure no one entered or exited the barn. Then he turned and entered the house, letting the door close behind him.

A tall, gray-haired man with mountain-man facial hair, now presented himself as the officer in charge.

"You guards stand down. I repeat, stand down. This isn't a combat situation. You need to lower those weapons and relax. We may be out here a while. I don't want anyone getting shot because someone's finger gets itchy."

A streak of white ran across the grounds behind the barn, and suddenly every dog was barking, straining its leash, trying to pull its master along with it.

"What's going on?" The lead officer made it sound like an order.

"I don't know," one of the guards trying to control his dog answered grimly. "They smelled something, and now they want to give chase."

"Then let them go!"

"We have to go with them. That's how they're trained."

"Then go."

"But we're supposed to stay here, guarding the barn."

"You've got three cars of police officers here. No one is getting into that barn without being seen."

The guard shrugged, then blew a whistle, and suddenly all the dogs dragged their guards along behind them as they gave chase to the big white wolf, who was long gone.

Nathan waited until the dogs and their guards disappeared into the wood, then he sprinted over to the barn, jumping over the hay bales. He quickly shifted, staying hidden from prying eyes. Then he slowly crept up to the nearest door. He was naked and had no tools, but he found a pitchfork in the hay. He used the tines on the crack of the door by the handle and worked at it until he broke the lock. With a small creak, the door opened. He kept the pitchfork with him in case any guards were in the barn. But no one was visible.

He whispered loudly, "Nisha? Honey, where are you?"

The wall next to him had windows that showed a room with musical instruments, along with mics and amps. *That's the studio. He said she has a room next to it.*

He moved quickly down the hall and pushed open the next door, but the room, as well as the bed, was empty. He went back into the hallway and peered into the studio. In the corner, he saw a flash of clothing.

"Nisha!" He ran across the room to her. She sat up and pointed at her ankle.

He looked down to see a manacle. One end was around her ankle, the other attached to a steel post, which was part of the support for the huge amps. The chain was just long enough for her to lie on the blanket on the floor near the post. He looked up into her face, and her tears tore at his heart.

"He's . . . he's going to drug me again."

He nodded. "I know, love. I heard his plans last night. Grant called the cops to report a woman being held against her will. Once the squad cars pulled up, he shifted to wolf and drew the attention of the canine guards. They're all off chasing a wolf that isn't a wolf anymore. He'll have gotten dressed again. He's going to meet us at the car once we get to Bingham."

She shook her head, pointing at the chain. "I can't go anywhere. He won't let me leave. That asshole's going to drug me, and never let me see you again!"

He shook his head. "That's not going to happen. Here's what you have to do, my darling Tonisha. You have to shift. Once you're a wolf, your paw will be much skinnier than your leg, so the manacle won't hold you anymore. And then we can run out the back door together as wolves. None of the guards will bother to shoot wolves."

She looked at him incredulously. "You really believe this stuff, don't you? Is that why you're naked? So you can pretend to be a wolf?"

"Honey, there isn't time to debate whether or not were-wolves exist. We do, and you're one of us. That voice you hear in your head all the time? That's your wolf. Right now, you need to invite her to take over. Let her shift your body to make it hers. Until now, she's only been able to do it when you were so drugged you didn't know what was going on. This is the first time she's going to do it with you aware of it. I warn you, though, it's going to hurt. But then we'll be able to get away from here, and you'll be safe back at the academy."

She shook her head, tears running down her face. "I love you, even though I don't remember your name. I feel like I belong with you. But I can't do what you're telling me to do. It's just not possible."

He leaned forward to tilt her head up and kissed her, a long, lingering kiss that promised so much more to come. She whimpered slightly when he backed away from her.

"Don't you feel that connection deep inside of you? It's our wolves, who mated and who want us to be together."

"I can't!" She looked around frantically. "He'll probably be in here any minute. You need to get out of here! You don't know what he's capable of. I don't want anything bad to happen to you."

"Here's how it needs to happen. I'm going to shift. Once I'm a wolf, I won't be able to talk to you anymore. But you watch me and see how it's done. Then you go into your head and invite her to take over. She will, because she wants us to be together as much as you and I do."

"What if I can't do it?"

"Then I'll stay here until he comes to get you, and I'll tear out his throat for how he's been treating you."

"Then they'll shoot you as a rabid wolf."

Nathan smiled at her.

"Or a man . . . or whatever."

"You were right the first time. My name's Nathan, by the way." He gave her a quick kiss and stepped back. "Now watch closely, my love. And welcome to our world."

Nisha gasped when the air around her lover started to shimmer and he fell to the ground with things moving around under his skin as his bones cracked and reset themselves. She watched in horror as his body became covered with hair and his face elongated into a snout, while his ears shifted up and a tail grew out of his spine. It only took a couple of minutes before Nathan the man was gone, and in his place stood a golden-brown wolf. He panted, watching her with his intent, green eyes.

"Oh my God!" She started hyperventilating. Then she looked into his eyes again, which somehow calmed her. "Green eyes. Wolves don't have green eyes. I finally believe you, my love. But I don't know how to do it. Run out of here and save yourself!"

The voice in her head howled in triumph. *You may not know how to do it. But I do!*

Suddenly Nisha started to scream with pain as every cell in her body felt like it was on fire. Her horror continued as her own bones began to move around under the skin like Nathan's had. She felt her body remaking itself—her own nose growing forward into a snout, her ears moving to the top of her head, and the tingle of a tail growing out of her spine. But the pain was unimaginable. She screamed until her vocal cords were no longer able to make that sound anymore. Then she realized she was howling. That frightened her so much that she quieted down.

At last! We are one! And we are free!

She looked down through the eyes of her wolf. Her paw was now much smaller than the manacle that had held her human leg. She bit and tore her way out of her clothing, and stood, looking around for her mate.

Nathan trotted over and rubbed his muzzle against hers before leading her to the door. Luckily, it opened outward, so all he had to do was push at it. She followed him closely as they moved quickly to the doorway he'd entered through, which he'd left slightly ajar. He pushed that one open also, and she breathed in the fresh air of freedom.

Together, they bounded quickly across the open land behind the barn and into the nearby relative safety of the woods she'd grown so fond of. Nathan led, and she kept close behind him. They loped along at a steady pace for a very long time. She marveled that she, who never enjoyed running when human, was now truly enjoying the feeling of running on four paws. With her heightened senses on full alert, and trusting her instinct—and her mate—to keep her safe, she felt exhilarated.

CHAPTER THIRTY-FOUR

Grant looked around, idly, whistling tunelessly as he waited, leaning against the car he'd driven to the concert. He had called Monique earlier to let her know what was going on and trusted her to keep Diego informed. But as she told him, Diego was busily learning how to be a father, so he might not be of much use for a little while.

Grant smiled to himself. *I can't wait to get you pregnant, my beautiful wife. I want to watch as your body swells from our love, and to welcome a new baby into the world that was created from you and me.*

He was interrupted from his reverie by the sudden appearance of two very tired-looking wolves, who stopped a short distance away at the edge of the woods. He looked all around, and satisfied that there was no one nearby, he spoke to them. "Go ahead and shift there. I'll get out Nathan's clothing and a shirt and shorts, so you'll be decent while we drive. Don't want to get a speeding ticket and have to explain why you crazy kids are nekkid in the back of my car." He was grinning as he pulled the clothes out of the car and put them on the hood. He heard the bone-crunching noises of the shifters changing, so he turned away and went back to leaning on the car, giving them time to finish their metamorphoses.

Nathan stood up, fully human again, while Nisha was still struggling with her change. When she was finally human, she fell forward, but he caught her and held her close.

He could feel wetness on his skin and used a finger to lift her chin and look into her eyes. "Tears, my love? I know it hurts, but you'll learn that the pain is bearable, since the results are so wonderful."

"I'm so tired," she sniffled. "I've never been so exhausted in my life."

Grant walked over, extending the clothing to them. "Dude, here are your clothes. And I had a t-shirt and shorts under the back seat. Never know when you'll need extra running clothing, right? And that's to be expected, Nisha. You've never shifted consciously before. It takes a lot out of you, especially the first few times. After that, you learn how to deal with it better."

Nathan made a face at him. "Remember, dude. We also just ran all the way from the barn to here, *after* her first change. So she has a bit more reason than usual to be so tired."

Grant held up his hands in defensive mode. "No argument from me. I was just trying to assure her that being tired is part of the whole process. So is being thirsty and hungry. There are water bottles in the back seat and some egga-muffins that I picked up just a little while ago. I was trying to figure out how long it would take you to get here. I think they're still warm."

Both Nathan and Nisha quickly pulled on the clothing. Nathan held Nisha's arm to walk her over to the car, and he opened the door. She slid onto the seat, and he followed her in. They both put on their seatbelts, and Grant started the car.

"Ready, folks?"

"Yes," Nathan replied, watching Nisha gratefully gulping from a water bottle.

"Next stop, werewolf academy." Grant grinned into the rear-view mirror.

Nathan stuck out his tongue at him before smiling back. He and Nisha tore into the food.

As she chewed, Nisha said, "This is better than any egg-thingies I've ever gotten from a fast food place."

"You're just starving, that's why you think so. It's okay. But I, for one, am looking forward to whatever will be on the menu for lunch at the academy. We can have it sent up to my apartment."

She grinned at him with a mouthful of food, which she hurriedly swallowed. "I remember the food there. Quick room service and excellent food."

Nathan nodded. "Yup. And we're together, finally."

She gave him a coy look as she swallowed the last of her food. "Am I worth the wait?"

"Oh yes, honey. You are." He gave her a long, passionate kiss, which she responded to with enthusiasm.

She pulled back and snuggled into his side. "All of a sudden, I think I need a nap."

"We've got a bit of a ride ahead of us. So you go right ahead."

Her only answer was a quiet snore.

"Holding your mate, who you finally won. Heading back to the safety of the pack home. Knowing there's a good driver taking you back. You go ahead and get some sleep, too, if you need to."

Nathan yawned widely. "Are you sure?"

"Yup. I took a cat nap while I was waiting for you."

"Thanks, Grant. I owe you so much after tonight."

"There's no *owe*, Nathan. We're pack, remember? That's what pack is for."

"Yeah."

Nathan settled down, his arms wrapped around his sleeping mate, and he closed his eyes.

Nathan woke up while Grant was parking the car. He looked around, realizing where he was, and gently shook the woman who was curled up under his arm. "Honey? We're home."

She stretched and yawned. "Home?"

"Yes. We're at the academy. Let's go up to my apartment. We can order up lunch, and afterward, we can soak in the Jacuzzi, while we talk about our future."

She gave him a shy look. "Our future? Do we have one?"

He got out of the car and helped her up. He pulled her close and wrapped his arms around her in a passionate embrace. Their lips met, and she moaned as they expressed things to each other that don't involve words.

"Ahem." Grant reminded them he was still there. "You two should *get a room*. I think you'd better use the back stairs, too. It's Saturday, and the students are all off school. Those who aren't doing homework, which is probably most of them, will be milling about, looking for something to use as an excuse for not doing it. If they see the famous Nisha, you'll have a hell of a time getting free."

Nathan reluctantly let go of his lady. "He's right. We need to get upstairs now."

Her lips were puffy, her eyes half-lidded, and she spoke in a husky voice. "Yes. We need to get up there now. You need to explain more of this mating thing to me. Will you always have this kind of effect on me?"

His lips turned up, and he lifted one eyebrow. "I certainly hope so. Let's go find out."

Grant preceded them to the back door, opened it and stuck his head through, looking around. "All clear, for now. But I can hear voices, so you want to get upstairs quickly,"

Nathan held Nisha's hand, pulling her along up the three flights to the door, which he opened with a key. He used another key to open the door directly in front of them and led the way into his place. He gestured around, as she followed him in. "Welcome home, my love. You're safe here."

Her face looked troubled. "Am I? Richard will be tearing the state apart, looking for me. How can you be so sure that he won't find me?"

"What's he going to be looking for? The famous Nisha, of course, but who else? A tall, blond man that no one can give a better description of? Grant sucker-punched the guard who was supposed to be searching your trailer, and he never saw what hit him. There's nothing to connect Grant to the minor skirmish he started at the porta-potties to distract the guards, so no one saw me enter your trailer. And no one saw either of us, or our car, at the studio property."

She shook her head, gazing at him in wonder and speaking in a whisper. "Is it possible, then? Am I really safe, and he can't find me and force me to take those drugs again? Or make me his prisoner again?"

Nathan's anger simmered. "I still want to rip his throat out for the two times I saw him hit you. I'll bet those weren't the only times he did that. And he chained you up like a rabid animal. He needs to be punished. But as Grant pointed out to me, a money-grubbing weasel like him will be hurt more by taking away his star. I'm sorry, honey, but he acted like your pimp, including punishing you when you wouldn't do what he wanted you to. Men like him are a sickness in the body of society."

She smiled at him, reflecting a combination of relief and love. "You're right. He's hit me many times before, always telling me it was for my own good. Basically, my parents sold me to him when I started making music. I think they were tired of dealing with my psychological problems and embarrassed that their daughter was diagnosed with schizophrenia. Besides, they didn't know anything about the music world, and he was highly recommended to them by one of Dad's clients. He became my manager when they signed the first contract. We had a brief affair, but he only likes his women when they're really young. Once I got out of my teens, he lost interest in *that* part of *owning* me. As long as I was producing music that sold well and made him lots of money, he didn't care what I did with my free time. The more drugs I did, the more drinking and partying, the more I would write songs about that lifestyle. It sells well to the young, who haven't yet figured out the emptiness of the whole thing."

There was a discreet knock on the outside door, which made Nisha jump.

Nathan gave her a reassuring kiss and went over to open the door.

One of the assistant chefs was carrying a tray of food that he held out to him.

"I didn't order anything yet," Nathan said.

"No. But Grant ordered this to be sent up to you. He said you might be . . . uh . . . indisposed, but that you and your mate would be hungry."

"We are, and thanks." Nathan took the tray, carried it to the dining room table, set it down, and returned to shut and lock the door. He grinned at Nisha, who had lifted the cover and was inhaling deeply. "What did he bring us for lunch?"

"Fried chicken and mashed potatoes with gravy. There is some kind of green bean salad, too, with what looks like cherry pie for dessert. There's even a small pot of coffee. I don't know if it's my newly-enhanced sense of smell, but I'm starving."

"Let's eat first. Then we can soak in the Jacuzzi and make some plans."

They sat and ate until the plates were all empty, then they both leaned back.

Nathan rubbed his belly. "Now *that's* good food. Not like fast food crap. Janine's cooking rocks."

Nisha opened her mouth to respond, but Nathan's phone suddenly buzzed.

"Shit! Where did I leave it? Oh yeah, it's charging." He headed over to the outlet next to the fridge and picked it up. It was a text to him and Grant from Diego.

Wife and baby sleeping. Need to debrief both of you. My office, ten minutes.

He turned to Nisha. "I have to go to see the pack leader. He wants to know what happened. Both Grant and I will be interviewed. He'll probably want to also talk to you at some point. But not right now."

Her face looked troubled. "Should I be worried?"

He shook his head. "No. What you could do is go fill the Jacuzzi. I'll be back as soon as I can."

"I don't have any clothing here," she pointed out. "So no worries that I'll go anywhere."

He looked at her appraisingly. "Saoirse is the woman you met before, who gave you something to wear. But she just had her baby yesterday, so she's sleeping now. I can ask Monique to drop by, if you like. Maybe she'll have something you can borrow."

She shook her head. "No. I'm fine in this shirt and shorts. I don't really want to talk to anyone right now. I'm kind of . . . overwhelmed, actually. I need some time to think about what happened and how I feel about it."

He moved over to pull her out of her chair, wrapping his arms around her, to hold her close. He spoke into her hair. "Please know that our future is together. We're truly a mated pair now. I hope that's not something you need to think about."

She stared up into his eyes. "No. But there's someone I need to apologize to, and the sooner the better."

His eyebrows rose, then he smiled as he realized she meant her wolf. He spoke gently, "I think you'll find that she's happy now."

"I don't even know *how* to talk to her. I've spent years ignoring her and telling her to be quiet. I need to try to make amends. So having a little bit of time alone will be a good thing. Go, talk to your boss-man. I'll be here waiting for you."

He nodded. "You have no idea how happy that makes me." He proved it to her with a long, passionate kiss, fondling her through the thin clothing. Reluctantly, he lifted his head and took a step backward. "I have to go now, or I won't be able to leave. It's not good politics to ignore an order from the pack leader. Especially when we need him to approve your petition to join the pack."

She looked thoughtful. "There's a lot I have to learn. So go, and come back quickly."

He turned and quickly strode to the door. "Just put the tray outside the door when you're done with the coffee."

He closed the door behind him, locking it to keep her safe.

Half an hour later, Diego leaned back in his chair and re-garded the two men seated on the other side of his desk. "So, you say that there's no way to trace either of you back to us?"

Grant shook his head. "Like I told you, no one saw the car we took to the concert, since we parked a couple of blocks away from the fairgrounds. No one got a good look at either of us at the concert either because we both had hats pulled down low. I even stuffed my hair up into the hat."

"And no one saw us at the property she was being held at," Nathan added. "Though their dogs got a brief smell of the white wolf that ran across the property before it took off into the woods."

Diego turned to regard Nathan intently. "And she's up-stairs now, in your apartment?"

"Yes."

"Please, go and accompany her back here. I need to inter-view her, as well."

"Why? We told you what happened."

"I need to speak to her. Alone."

Nathan's face turned apprehensive.

"Nothing to worry about, Nathan. I just need to confirm with her that what you have told me about your mating is true. If we are to possibly endanger the pack by giving her sanctuary here, then I need to first make sure that it's worth the risk."

Nathan opened his mouth to speak, but Diego waved his hand at him. "I know how you feel, Nathan, believe me. But a mating involves two people, and in this case, two wolves. I need to be sure in my own mind, that this is what *she* wants, also."

Nathan and Grant both got up.

"Grant? A word extra with you?"

Nathan stared at Diego for a quick moment, then turned and walked through the door.

Diego waited a few moments before turning to Grant. "Is it your opinion that they are truly mated?"

Grant nodded. "Oh, yeah. Signed, sealed, and delivered. They're one."

"She's accepted her wolf?"

"She ran up to the car as a wolf, so I'd say yes."

"But I have to be sure. Nathan is an important part of the pack, but I have to ensure that no one will regret this decision."

"I understand, boss. And may I add, this is why I don't want to ever be an alpha. I prefer to leave the big decisions in someone else's more capable hands."

Diego couldn't stop the huge yawn that slipped out.

"But even you need sleep, boss. I can see if Monique is interested in accompanying me to see your wife and baby, once they're awake, so Rachel gets a break and you can nap."

Diego nodded. "That's an excellent idea. And thank you."

Grant's lips twitched. "No problem. Someday soon, I hope

to need the same favor."

Diego smiled. "Fatherhood is glorious."

Grant turned and walked out of the door.

CHAPTER THIRTY-FIVE

Once she heard the door lock, Nisha poured more coffee into her cup and looked around. She carried her cup of coffee into the bedroom and opened the doors that led to the balcony, where she could sit and enjoy the sunlight. She sank into a chair. "Now, how do I start this conversation?"

It started out easy. She sat quietly, trying to figure out how to communicate with the being that she'd spent so many years trying to eradicate. She thought of a simple question. *How long have you been living inside of me?* When there was no immediate answer, she asked the next question on her mind. *What has it been like living inside of my head?*

Immediately, she was blind-sided by searing agony that made her feel like her head was going to explode. She felt too weak to even scream. All she could do was whimper as her wolf demonstrated what it had felt like being drugged into non-existence. Her eyeballs were on fire, and she gasped for air. She couldn't catch her breath and doubted she could live through the intense pain. When she tried to get up, to move away from it, her suffering dropped her to her knees. She ended up prostrate on the balcony floor, moaning as she experienced the effect the pharmaceuticals she'd taken for so many years had on her wolf.

And while tears ran down her face onto the concrete floor, she cried out in her mind. *I'm so sorry! I didn't know! Forgive me!*

When Nathan entered the apartment, he stood still for a moment, listening.

His wolf spoke urgently. *Something's wrong. She suffers.*

Alarmed, he called out, "Nisha? Where are you?" When there was no answer, he moved quickly through the apartment, into the bedroom, then into the bathroom. He came out of the bathroom, beginning to panic. He stopped to open his senses, listening again. He heard a faint whimper from the direction of the balcony, so he raced over to it, to find his beloved lying on the floor.

He fell to his knees, picking her up. "Nisha! Can you speak? What's wrong, love?" The lack of an answer or movement of any kind from his woman alarmed him. He leaned against the wall behind him, cradling her in his arms, and began to rock back and forth, hoping the rhythmic movement would soothe her. He used one hand to smooth back the hair that covered her face. He saw the tear stains on her cheeks and tried to reach her again.

"Tonisha, can you hear me? I'm here. I love you. How can I ease your suffering? My wolf and I would both gladly die for you. What do you need from us?"

Still she lay silent, barely breathing. Unwelcome thoughts intruded into his mind. He remembered Dr. Sullivan's opinion of her having taken such a high dosage of antipsychotic drugs for so long. The doctor had concluded that only her shifter status had kept her alive through it all. Nathan prayed it would do so now.

He leaned his face down and gently kissed her lips. He was in so much pain that when he spoke, all he could manage was a whisper. "If you leave me now, it will break me. I've waited for so long to find my mate. Please, Toni, don't leave me."

Tears ran unheeded down his cheeks, falling onto her face.

Nisha took in a deep, staggered breath, then opened her eyes to stare into Nathan's intense green ones, now swimming in tears.

She tried to speak, but her voice broke. She cleared her throat, starting again. "No one has called me Toni since my grandparents died."

He studied her face for a moment. "Did you love your grandparents?"

She managed a slight nod. "They didn't care about my problems. They always loved and supported me. Gramma died before Grampa. He was lost without her, but he told me that I became the light of his life. He tried to shield me from the disapproval of my parents." She stopped, suddenly aware of possibilities. "I wonder if he had a wolf living inside of him, also? Maybe that's why he was so accepting. I wish he'd just told me. It would have saved me so much grief." She quailed at the memory of her recent pain. "It would have spared *her* from so much pain."

Nathan continued to rock her gently as her breathing returned to normal. The comfort of his arms calmed the turmoil of her emotions, and those of her wolf.

"What happened?" he asked in a soft tone.

She fought back her inner anguish. "I asked her how it had felt, living inside of me all these years. She showed me — with a vengeance. I've never felt such pain before. Inescapable and inexorable. Bone-deep agony that made her want to die. That, combined with the unhappiness of knowing that the one who should be her best friend wanted her dead. Until recently, I was too afraid to even acknowledge her existence when she tried to speak to me. So she felt unwelcomed, ignored, and in pain. I don't know how she managed to survive all that I did to her." New tears swam in her eyes.

He stroked her hair, rubbing her scalp, attempting to ease her suffering of self-recrimination. And it helped.

"Does she know that you did what you did because that's what all the experts told you to do? That you had no idea she was a viable being, separate from you, yet forced to share a body with you?"

She took in another staggered breath, before letting it out. "I will spend the rest of my life explaining that to her and trying to atone for the pain I caused her. I was in so much agony when she showed me that I tried to throw myself off the balcony. I thought only death would end the pain. I now know that's what she often thought. And having experienced just a tiny moment of her years of suffering, I understand why. But she wouldn't let me do it. She told me that would kill her, without her ever having any real chance to live. And I realized that I owe her that much, at least. She deserves a chance to own our body and to enjoy it. I made that promise to her. I also promised her that I would stay away from any kind of drugs, from now on."

Nathan leaned forward and gave her a gentle lingering kiss, then drew back slightly and rubbed his nose against hers. He took a deep, shaky breath, his face reflecting concern. "Are you both happy that we have mated?"

She softened, feeling the genuine love she had for the man holding her so tenderly. A smile played around her lips as she nodded.

Nathan and his wolf both rejoiced.

Suddenly they were interrupted by the insistent sound of his phone alerting him to a text. He pulled it out of his back pocket and read it aloud to her.

Need to nap soon. Please bring Nisha here so I can make my decision.

Nathan looked steadily into her eyes. "Are you feeling up to going to the pack leader's office to answer a few questions?"

She looked troubled. "Is there a problem with his accepting me into the pack?"

"I don't think so. I think he's just trying to establish a precedent that females have an equal voice under his leadership. He won't take just *my* word that you want to join. He wants to hear it from you. I won't even be allowed to stay in the room while he talks with you."

She pushed herself out of his arms and gradually stood upright.

He stood, also, pulling her into a close embrace, burying his face in her hair, breathing deeply.

She leaned into the embrace, resting her face against his chest. She raised her head and smiled up at him. "Is it because I'm aware of my wolf now that my sense of smell has taken on new meaning? Your chest hair smells wonderful. It makes me feel warm . . . like a signal that I'm home, and I can relax."

He grinned. "Why do you think I was sniffing your hair? Humans are mammals too, but we don't rely much on smell. Wolves are more aware of scents. You smell like home to me also. Like I've now found what I was missing, and I'm complete."

She sniffed an armpit, then raised her head with a grimace. "I wish I had time to clean up and change, but if the pack leader is that tired, he won't care. Let's not keep him from his nap any longer."

Nathan held her hand and led her through the apartment to the door. "Let's also hope that being so tired, his interview won't last long. Then we can come back here for a nice, long soak in my Jacuzzi."

She gave him a hungry look. "Then we can take care of whatever pops up?"

Nathan snorted, patting her on the butt. "Yeah. That's what I was thinking. If you're feeling up for it." He gave her a solicitous look. "And then we can sleep as long as we need to.

That catnap in the car wasn't nearly enough. I feel tired to my bones."

"Then, can I let her take over and run?"

He turned to smile at her. "We can wake up in time for dinner. After that, we can run all night with the pack."

"Good. I owe her a lot of time to be in charge. Might as well start today."

They went into the hallway and headed for Diego's office.

Nisha knocked on the closed door, giving Nathan a quick smile when Diego told her to enter. She pushed the door open and went in. Diego was sitting behind his desk, looking at his phone.

He motioned for her to sit. "Have a seat, please. And really, have you ever seen a more beautiful baby?" He leaned forward, showing her the picture on his phone.

She smiled at him. "No, I haven't. I've never spent much time with babies. In fact, I've never had much of a life at all, since I've been too busy making lots of money for my manager."

Diego set his phone upside down on his desk. Leaning back in his chair, he stared appraisingly at her.

His intense scrutiny made her acutely aware of how long it had been since she'd bathed, and how she must look with her hair unkempt, wearing only a borrowed shirt and gym shorts.

He doesn't care about any of that. He only wants your honesty. Her wolf's words made her sit up straighter, raising her head proudly, to meet his gaze.

His lips twitched with amusement. "It takes some getting used to when *they* talk to you while you're supposed to be having a discussion with someone."

She nodded. "Yes. I'm only just beginning to learn what there is to know about sharing my body. But I want to catch up on what I should know." She paused, a cloud passing over her heart before she continued. "And I have much to atone to her for."

Diego spoke gently. "That's between you and your wolf. All I need to know is if you have truly accepted Nathan and his wolf as your mates."

"Oh, yes. I have. I mean, *we* have. He waited so long for me, even when I refused to accept what he had told me. And he risked his life for me. I know he loves me. I'm not sure that I know how to repay him for all that he's done for me." She felt embarrassed but took another deep breath. "My wolf says that all we need to do is love him. That will be enough. But then she also tells me that she's forgiven me already. I don't know how she could say that. I wouldn't be so quick to forgive after so many years of such intense pain."

Diego leaned forward. "Do you hate your parents for starting you on years of drug therapy?"

Nisha was appalled and shocked he would make such a suggestion. "What? No! How could I hate them? They thought they were doing the right thing. They did what they did out of love. Love and fear."

"Your wolf feels the same way, I'll bet. You did what you did out of fear. But it's over now. Dr. Sullivan will be glad to hear that you have come to terms with your wolf. He'll probably want to continue you on the vitamins that will strengthen both of you."

Understanding struck. "Oh, I see. Is he one of us, too?"

Diego nodded. "Yes. And he'd never met anyone in your situation before."

Nisha frowned. "I'd rather not have had to present him with such a challenge. I'm just glad it's over." She looked into his eyes, seeking reassurance. "It *is* over, isn't it? Nathan tells me Richard won't be able to find me here. I'd like to stay here as Nathan's mate, if that's all right with you."

"There's official paperwork for you to sign." Diego pushed

a paper across the desk. "It's your petition to join the pack." He smiled and spoke gently. "It's just a formality. As pack leader, I have the final word on any new members." He stood and extended his hand across the desk to her. "Tonisha Gaines, welcome to the Northwest Maine Pack."

Tears blurred her vision as she stood up, and her arm trembled as she shook his hand.

"Thank you, sir," she said with a shaky voice.

"We're not that formal around here." He smiled again. "Diego is fine. The rest of the Council calls me boss, but you don't have to. As our newest member, I give you permission to call me Diego." He stopped, surrendering to an immense yawn. "But now, if you'll excuse me, I haven't slept for two days. I can hear my bed calling me."

Nisha smiled with relief. "Nathan offered to start the Jacuzzi, then we plan to sleep away most of the afternoon, also." She gave him a shy look. "I'm looking forward to falling asleep, knowing that I'm finally in a safe place where Richard can't hurt me anymore."

"Please, try to restrain Nathan from enacting any kind of revenge on that cretin who abused you for so long."

"I will. I agree with what Grant told him, about how the best revenge on Richard is losing me as his cash cow. And as soon as I can figure out how, I will get his name removed from my bank account. I'm afraid otherwise he'll empty it to repay himself for losing any future money he planned to make off me."

"Let me talk to our pack lawyer. She's very good and may be able to do that discretely." He yawned again.

In the usual kinetic fashion, his yawn made Nisha yawn as well. She asked, "Are we done, then? I can leave?"

Diego nodded.

Nisha grabbed the paperwork and walked through the door to Nathan's waiting arms.

Chapter Thirty-Six

It was all over the news immediately. Headlines screamed in capital letters that everyone's favorite pop singer, Nisha, had disappeared. Richard was telling the media he suspected foul play. He begged her kidnappers to let her come back to him, explaining that all would be forgiven as he pleaded his case to the world.

"She's come under the influence of an evil man," he spouted with a straight face, looking into the cameras aimed at him, with an approximation of what he surely imagined would be a sad expression.

Nisha had giggled when she finally saw his news conference. "He doesn't know how to feel a real emotion. He thinks he looks sad. He just looks constipated."

But she hadn't watched any television her first night in the pack. Instead, she and Nathan had spent a long, relaxing soak in his Jacuzzi before retiring to his bed, making lush and lingering love, enhancing the deal that had been sealed when they'd made love in her trailer. They fell asleep, exhausted by their passion. When they awoke to the sound of the alarm Nathan had set, he ordered dinner to be sent up to them.

"I know I'll need to face everyone soon," Nisha said. "But not tonight . . . not yet. I want to run with the pack after dinner. Tomorrow morning is soon enough for me to let all of your teenaged students know that I'm living here now."

Sunday morning, after getting some sleep, Diego had some

concerns about Nisha staying in the pack house. He texted Nathan to bring Nisha to his office. He also asked that they eat their breakfast in Nathan's apartment, and promised to explain when he saw them.

When they were both seated across from him, he smiled. "You both look so much more relaxed than you did the last time I spoke to you. That is all the proof I need that your mating was successful, and you are one with your wolves in full agreement."

Nathan and Nisha smiled at each other, both nodding.

"However," he continued, "I've been giving a lot of thought as to how to keep your existence here a secret from the world. Our students already have to keep a very big secret from the outside world. To expect them to also keep silent when they know the answer to the questions being posed on headlines everywhere is asking too much of them. In other words, as much as I trust them and have full confidence that any electronic communications sent from here are untraceable, I don't think introducing you to them is a wise thing to do right now."

"Wow!" Nisha pursed her lips. "I didn't realize that my being here would create so much trouble for everyone." She looked at her hands folded in her lap before raising her gaze to meet Diego's. She spoke in a small voice, "Do you want me to leave?"

Nathan's protestations were immediate and intense, but Diego merely raised a hand and shook his head.

"No, Nisha, that's not necessary. You are pack now, but if you decide at any time in the future that you want to live elsewhere, you are welcome to do that. For now, you've asked for protection, and you will get that from us. As I'm sure you've noticed, we're pretty high-security around here."

She nodded. "Yeah, the electric fencing around the place is kind of daunting."

"It's meant to be. Not only do we have an entire community here, including families with young children, but we also have young people whose parents trust us with their lives. We're also protecting the secret of what so many of us are from a public that might over-react. Especially upon finding out their cherished ideas of normal and abnormal are, shall we say, not as they've been led to believe."

Diego leaned forward. "I think I've figured out a way you can continue to enjoy the safety we can provide for you. One that will avoid any of our teenagers having a nervous breakdown over being unable to let the rest of the world know where you are."

He leaned back in his chair, turning to Nathan. "Do you know where our librarian, Mrs. Moretta, lives?"

Nathan's eyes opened wide as he nodded. "The house attached to the old barn that was used for cars back in the day when they were much smaller?"

Diego nodded. "That's the place. She'd been complaining for a while that it's way too big for her and too much to clean since becoming a widow. Also, with her knees giving her grief, it was too far for her walk to the main house and the library. So a week ago, we helped her move into a small, vacant apartment near the library. She took what she wanted to out of the house, but it's still mostly furnished. If you two are interested in moving there, I think that might be the solution we need right now."

Nathan looked at Nisha and took one of her hands out of her lap, stroking her fingers. When Diego cleared his throat for attention, both turned back to listen to the rest of his proposition.

"See, I think the whole publicity thing will blow over soon. Having grown up as the son of a celebrity, I'm very well aware of how hard my mom had to work to keep herself in the public eye. When attention would turn away from her, she'd despair and come up with elaborate plans for how to get back into the limelight."

He smiled at Nisha. "But you don't want to be back in that glare of publicity anymore, do you?"

She shook her head. "No thanks. I've had enough of that to last ten lifetimes."

"Then, if you and Nathan move into the now-deserted house, it won't be that long of a walk for Nathan to get back up here for school. Yet you will be far enough away from the students that I think we can keep your presence here a secret. At least until the end of this semester. You won't be able to dine with the rest of us, but you are certainly welcome to set up delivery whenever you might want a break from doing your own cooking. You can also give Janine your grocery list, and she'll add it to what gets ordered, like she does for the many other families who live here."

Nathan was smiling from ear to ear.

Nisha still looked apprehensive, though. "So, if we lay low for a while, at least until the summer break, you think that will be long enough for the publicity to die down?"

"Yes. And hopefully, by the beginning of the fall term, your disappearance will have fallen off the news cycle. We won't introduce you to the whole pack in a meeting, but as people run into you, they can organically get to know you for the wonderful person you are. They will realize that since you are pack, your safety is paramount, and it will behoove all of us to be circumspect regarding public statements."

Nathan grinned. "Boss, you're talking like your wife. I guess it's not only the students who are gaining a larger vocabulary due to her extensive knowledge and everyday use of multi-syllabic words."

Diego pictured his Saoirse, a grin forcing the corners of his lips upward. "Yes, I've gained so much from my lady." He smiled at Nathan. "You are just beginning your journey as a mated pair. It's marvelous."

He shook himself, forcing himself to concentrate. "Must get mind back in the game." He turned to Nisha. "There are some pressing issues we need to resolve, and the sooner we get someone working on them, the better. Nisha, are you feeling up to talking with the pack attorney in Portland?"

"About?"

"I want her to examine your contract to see if you can break free from it. I also want her to see if she can access your bank account, which you said your manager has access to, in order to preserve at least some of your money."

Nisha shrugged. "Richard has probably already emptied the joint account. But he doesn't know about the other one. I've been making small withdrawals regularly for years and stashing it away in an account that's only in my name. I can give her access to that one, also, so she can take out whatever she's owed for her services."

"Excellent. Let's get her on *Skype* now, so you can talk with her."

Diego typed in the required passwords and got the program running.

In minutes, a female voice responded. "Hello, Diego. You hinted in your text last night that you had something interesting to talk with me about. This is earlier than I usually get up on a Sunday, but you got me so intrigued that I took my laptop into the kitchen and ate my breakfast near it, waiting for your call. What's up?"

"Jennifer, I have someone here who needs your help." He turned the laptop around. "Jennifer Johnson, meet Tonisha Gaines."

Nisha smiled at the image of the lawyer, whose mouth opened in a gasp. "Hello, Ms. Johnson," she said. "Sorry to wake you up so early. I've never had an attorney of my own before. My manager handled all the business details of my career. But I'm finally strong enough to be done with him and his abuse. I'd appreciate any advice and help you can give me."

Jennifer cleared her throat. "Wow, Diego, you weren't kidding! This is certainly worth waking up early for. Ms. Gaines, I'm very pleased to meet you. And I feel like I should hug myself because I now know the answer to the current *question of the day* that has everyone in a tizzy. But alas, I can't share this news with anyone for two very important reasons. One is that once you sign the contract that I'm sending you, I'll be bound by our professional relationship not to speak to anyone about you. And two, the fact that you've sought sanctuary in the compound where I grew up means you belong there in a way that I don't, even though the late Joe Johnson was my father."

Nathan leaned closer to Nisha to be visible on the screen. "Hello, Jennifer. Nice to see your smiling face this morning."

She grinned, nodding. "Ah, Nathan. You and Nisha? The plot thickens. So what do you need me to do, Ms. Gaines?"

"For one thing, I need you to call me Nisha, like everyone else does. Then I need you to access my bank accounts. One has my manager's name on it, also, so he's probably already emptied that one by now. I'm hoping he doesn't know about the other one, which I set up secretly and has only my name listed. Any fees you incur can be taken out of that one. And I need you to find out if I'm still under contract with him."

"You don't know?"

Nisha shrugged. "He's had me signing something every couple of years to renew our contract. I don't really remember when I signed the last one." She grimaced. "For the past fifteen years, I've done a lot of drugs, some of which were prescribed by the doctors he took me to, and others were purely recreational. I've lost entire days and nights, memory-wise. So details like when I last signed a contract are the kinds of things that my brain jettisoned along the way as unimportant."

Jennifer lifted a well-shaped eyebrow. "Unimportant? Indeed. Yes, Nisha, you really do need an attorney of your own. I've already sent a copy of the contract to Diego's computer. You can sign it electronically and return it to me. That way, I'm your lawyer as of the minute I receive it back. I'll be glad to take care of those *unimportant* details for you."

Diego indicated to Nisha that he had received the contract on the desktop computer and invited her to use his chair so she could view it. She sat in the chair and filled out the necessary details as Jennifer chatted with Diego.

"So why haven't you sent me any pictures of the baby yet, you bad boy?"

"I'm sorry, Jennifer. I'm truly overwhelmed with fatherhood, and lack of sleep is making me fall behind on many things. I'm texting you the first picture I took of our daughter."

"Ah, got it. She's beautiful, Diego! Who knew that *you* could produce such a gorgeous girl?"

"That part was Saoirse's doing, I'm sure."

"Of course it was. Producing the baby was all up to her, right? Is she asleep now?"

He nodded. "She's been sleeping whenever she can get the baby to sleep. Rachel says we'll soon need to get the baby off of *uterine time* and onto a regular schedule of being awake during the day and sleeping at night. But for now, she's still doing her own thing. And her poor parents are doing our best to accommodate her."

"I notice you haven't supplied a name. Are you announcing it tonight?"

"Yes. I'll be sure to send you more pictures and the name after that."

Jennifer sniffed. "You'd better, or I'll tell Mom to spit in your dinner."

Diego grinned. "Anything for you, oh most capable of legal eagles."

"Yeah, right. Hey, Nisha, I just got the contract back. Obviously, you've memorized your bank account numbers, which is really unusual, considering your other memory lapses."

"That's something that I knew I had to do. I couldn't risk having them written down anywhere when Richard regularly snooped in my things. If it wasn't him, it was one of his flunkies."

"He sounds like a real piece of work. I really enjoy taking down assholes like him. Ah, good, you gave his full name, also. Okay, I won't be able to get much done today, since law offices and banks are closed on Sundays. But I'll get on this first thing in the morning. And I'll be in touch with you, Nisha. Do you have a phone I can reach you at?"

"Um, no."

Nathan leaned over. "Use my number, Jennifer. She's with me now." The smile he gave to Nisha was so filled with genuine joy and love that she blushed.

"Or I can just *Skype* with Diego again, with you two in on the call. I'll let you love birds go back to whatever it is you do when no one's watching. Can you give me some time to talk with just Diego?"

Nathan got up, pulling Nisha to her feet. "Good talking to you, Jennifer. I know we'll be hearing from you soon. But we've got some packing to do. Let's get to it, my love."

Nisha lifted an eyebrow. "We, white man? I brought nothing with me. All of the stuff is yours."

"Ah, but I think I have a guitar buried somewhere in the back of one of my closets. If you help me pack, we should be able to locate it. Then you can claim it."

They both made their way to the door, stopping to wave at Jennifer before leaving the room.

Diego turned the laptop to face just him. "Do you think there will be problems?"

"Not on my end. Digging up information like this is easy, especially now that she's given me the names and bank account numbers that I need. But what about you? Isn't it endangering everyone, having her there? How will you keep the students off social media?"

"I thought about using the same procedures as when the challenge made the transfer of power problematic for a while. But then I came up with an easier solution. Nathan and Nisha are going to move to the now-empty Moretta house."

"Oh no! Mrs. Moretta?"

"She's fine. She moved into a small apartment in the main mansion last week to be closer to the library. The *commute* was getting to be too much for her. She's not getting any younger, you know."

Jennifer smiled. "I'm sure. She was old when I was attending the academy, and that was many years ago."

"So I figure that should keep Nisha out of sight until the end of the semester. Then, hopefully, enough time will have passed, and she won't be the subject of screaming headlines anymore. Then we can introduce her to the students as the new music teacher."

Jennifer smiled. "That's a great idea. You haven't had one of those since the old one moved out when I was a senior."

"That was before my time. Wasn't it because he wrote a song that became popular?"

"No, he wrote a whole musical that went onto the stage. That's why he had to move to New York. We got a good musical background from him. I can still hit some of the high notes from when I sang soprano. Like this . . ." She opened her mouth and hit a few notes on key, then a couple off-key.

Diego made a face. "I believe you. But please, my wife and baby are sleeping. Those high notes are enough to wake the dead."

Jennifer looked offended. "Fine. But tell Saoirse that I want to see the baby when I *Skype* with you again tomorrow. I'll text to let you know when I have something to report."

"Then goodbye for now, Jennifer. And thanks."

Once Diego ended the connection, he turned his chair to stare out of the window. "Did I do the right thing in letting her join the pack, Joe?"

His wolf growled softly. *It was the only way. She and her wolf are mated with Nathan and his.*

So they are, he answered his alter ego. *Speaking of mates, I wonder how my lovely wife and our gorgeous baby are doing? Let's go find out.*

He closed his laptop and left his office, striding purposefully down the hall.

CHAPTER THIRTY-SEVEN

Diego sensed an expectant air of excitement as the people gathered in the auditorium for the monthly Sunday night pack meeting. When Monique trotted onto the stage and howled for the meeting to begin, everyone quieted down, watching as she shifted, then pulled on shorts and a tank top before speaking into the microphone.

"This meeting is called to order. The pack leader, Diego Vargas, will now speak to his agenda."

Diego spent time discussing pack issues, including the resolution to problems that had been raised by various people during previous meetings. Most listened attentively, but he gained everyone's full attention when he paused.

"There are two special announcements for tonight. One is that John Johnson has returned to our pack. He's here tonight as a visitor but will be moving permanently into the area soon. He's looking for an apartment and a job in Augusta, but he will be here often to run with the pack. Since he won't be living on the premises, he won't be resuming his position in the pack leadership. This means that Monique Knutsen will remain as second, third is Nathan Taylor, and fourth is Grant Knutsen, with my wife and mate, Saoirse Vargas, as our fifth."

There was polite applause as everyone expressed their acceptance of the leadership roster.

Diego held up his hands for quiet. "And one more thing. My wife has presented me with our first child." He turned to the back of the stage, where Saoirse had been waiting, holding their baby. She walked up to join him, and Diego showed all he had learned recently by deftly taking the baby into his hands, holding her up for all to see. "It gives me great pride to present to the pack our daughter, Diésha" —he stressed the pronunciation, *Dee-AA-sha* —"Anne Vargas."

The applause was loud and boisterous as everyone welcomed the newest pack member. His daughter's eyes widened before she scrunched up her face, drew her tiny fists in tightly, and let out a healthy howl of disapproval.

Diego lowered her down and handed her back to Saoirse, who moved back to sit on a chair to rock and soothe her baby.

"That's it for now, people. As always, my wish is that everyone has a wonderful and productive week."

Nisha spent Monday arranging things in their new house while Nathan was at school, and learning what had been left by the previous occupant. She was moving furniture around when Nathan walked in, carrying a tray emitting glorious aromas.

"Honey, it's lunchtime. Take a break, and eat with me, while it's still hot."

"Speaking of hot . . ." she began as he removed the cover and set the plates laden with food onto the small kitchen table. "Did you know there's a hot tub out back?"

His eyebrows rose. "There is?"

"Yeah. It's right behind where the house attaches to the old barn. There's a door there, and I couldn't figure out what it was for until I opened it. Looks like the hot tub needs a good cleaning. Maybe it needs to be emptied first? I don't know much their upkeep, but I sure know I'd love to go out at night and be naked in a hot tub under the stars."

Nisha felt the heat of the blush spreading across her face from the naked lust sparkling in Nathan's eyes.

"We'll have to get it cleaned and into service." He smiled.

"I can't wait to be in it with you, my gorgeous mate. It will be a wonderful way to soak our tired muscles after a strenuous run in the woods."

They applied themselves to lunch, finishing quickly. Apparently, Nathan had the same thing in mind as she did. Nathan rose and pulled her up into his embrace. She gazed into his green eyes, lost in their color and in the passion that made his pupils almost take over the iris. His lips were gentle, at first, then their passion ignited. He moaned as she opened her mouth so their tongues could caress each other while their hands explored favorite places.

"We'll have to be quick," Nathan panted into her ear. "I have to be back in class soon."

"What's wrong with right here, right now?"

He pulled back and smiled. "Have I told you lately how much I love you?"

Nisha was breathing quickly, her eyes unfocused. "Not in the last few seconds. Why don't you show me instead?"

So he did.

Nathan made it back to class on time, but just barely. He hoped his students would have no idea why he couldn't stop smiling. But he soon got them engaged in discussing their reading, and even he forgot about his joy as his wolf slept on in contented bliss.

After school, Nathan was helping Nisha move furniture around to suit their own ideas of *feng shui* when his phone chirped that he had a text.

He read it, then took Nisha's hand. "We need to go to Diego's office. He says Jennifer has some news for us."

Her eyebrows rose, reflecting her worry. "I'm not sure I want to hear it. He's had control over me for so long that I'm afraid I'll never escape from his clutches."

Nathan pulled her close, whispering into her ear. "He'll never touch you again. If he even tries, my wolf and I will tear out and eat his entrails."

She gasped, pulling back to study his face, then a slow smile crept over her face. "Good. Then let's go hear what she found out."

Nathan knocked on Diego's office door and heard his *Come in.*

When they entered, Saoirse was sitting in front of the computer holding the baby for Jennifer to admire. The baby's eyes were wide open, looking around at her unfamiliar surroundings. Nathan led Nisha to the chairs in front of Diego's desk.

Jennifer gushed her praise. "She's beautiful, Saoirse! Such an alert baby, too. And what a chub. Are you feeding her cream?"

Saoirse grinned. "That must be it. She's a great nurser, and even snorts a little bit, like a piggy, as she feeds."

"I'm sure *that* part comes from her daddy."

Saoirse poked Diego. "She's got you there, honey."

Diego shook his head. "Such disrespect."

"I'm not a pack member, remember?" Jennifer interjected. "I don't have to tiptoe around you. To me, you're just Diego, the dude who made himself an integral part of my family's pack by being compassionate, honest, and loyal. But still, I remember running with you in the woods and beating your ass easily."

Diego sniffed. "That was when I first got here and wasn't in good shape. That will never happen again."

"Maybe I should take you up on that, next time I come to visit Mom."

Diego glanced over at him and Nisha and nodded. "Enough of this family banter, Jennifer. Nisha has arrived to hear what you found out today."

The baby chose that minute to take a deep breath before she let out a huge wail.

Saoirse smiled. "See, Jennifer? This is her dark side. This is the stuff of my nightmares. Just when I've just gotten to sleep, she lets me know it's feeding time again."

"Then go tend to your baby. I can't wait to hold her. I'll set something up with Mom and let you know when I will visit."

"Deal. See you soon." Saoirse got up and carried her crying baby, smiling at Nathan and Nisha as she passed them. "See what's in your future, you two?"

Nathan smiled. "I can't wait."

Nisha's eyebrows rose. "I can. Let me get used to being *me* first, totally sober. Then I can entertain the notion of being responsible for someone else."

The door shut as Saoirse left the room, and Diego turned the laptop to face Nisha, moving to stand behind them. "Okay, Jennifer. They're both here. What did you discover that might help our newest pack member?"

"Good afternoon, Nisha, Nathan. I have had a most interesting day, and it's all thanks to you, Nisha."

Nisha leaned forward. "Interesting? Do I have any money left?"

"Yeah, but let's talk about your contract. The first thing I did today was drive to my Augusta office, because I wanted to give my partner a head's up on what I was getting us into. I found out that your manager's lawyer died suddenly last year. Is that correct?"

Nisha nodded. "Yes. He dropped dead on the golf course. Richard made some crude jokes about how that was the way to go—wearing your golf shoes, cheating on your scores, like always. Richard didn't find out about it until he tried to contact him about some concert business. The office hadn't even bothered to let him know."

"I'm surprised by their inefficiency. You should have

signed a contract earlier this year. They didn't assign another lawyer to take his place?"

"Richard didn't like the first lawyer they assigned to him. He ranted on about how the guy was gay, and what were they thinking, sending him a fairy to do a man's work. The next replacement was a Hispanic woman, and she let him know immediately that he was to keep his hands to himself. So he threw her out. He's such a pig."

"Yes, he is, as I found out for myself. Right after I downloaded your most recent contract for my files, I got in contact with your bank. I was in the process of sending them our contract, to prove that I have the right to manage your finances when I got a call on my office phone. When I picked it up, an angry man was sputtering into the phone, demanding that I tell him where you are, or he'd make me sorry I was ever born."

Nisha started to tremble. Nathan moved his chair closer and put his arm around her shoulders, lending his strength to his mate.

Jennifer noticed the gesture and grinned, a look that lifted only her lips, because her eyes became cold, dark coals. "Oh, don't worry, Nisha. He had no idea who he was dealing with. He does now. See, I demanded to know his name, and when he identified himself, I told him he has no right to make any demands on me, or on you ever again. That shocked him into silence, but only for a moment. Then he started swearing loudly at me, so I hung up on him."

Nisha's eyes were big and round. "You did?"

"Yup. No one talks to me like that. Of course, he called right back, and when I saw that it was the same number, I didn't say hello. Instead, I immediately said that if he swore at me again, I'd hang up and block his calls. He tried to sound polite but demanded to know why I was looking into your contract. Obviously, someone in his lawyer's office has been assigned to react to inquiries, and he was contacted. I told him that you are my client now, and I wanted to find out when your contract would expire. Imagine my surprise, I told him, to find out that it had expired last year. That means you are a free agent, and that any music you've written lately is yours, and he has no claim over it."

"Really?"

"He choked and sputtered, trying to insist that you *had* signed a contract, but that the new lawyers were too incompetent to file it. He has a copy of it, he said, and he'd fax it to me. I told him not to bother. See, if a contract is signed but not properly filed, it's not valid. So whether or not you signed anything, and I'm sure you didn't, it's not legal." Jennifer leaned closer to her computer, an evil grin on her face. "That made him apoplectic. He started yelling again, swearing liberally, insisting that he still owns you and your music. He'll contact your parents. He'll contact your doctors. You're a sick woman, and you need to be back on your meds. He'll ruin me for even thinking that I can stop him. Then his final salvo was to insist that I tell him where you are, or he'd destroy me."

Nisha spoke in a small, frightened voice. "He'd do it, too. He has the power."

Jennifer shook her head. "Not legally. Not anymore. Honey, you're well over eighteen. They can contact all the doctors they want to. We have Dr. Sullivan on our side. I've already spoken to him about testifying to your state of mind if we need him. Your parents have no say over your life. And your manager isn't the first misogynistic, over-bearing asshole I've ever dealt with. I don't intimidate easily. I told him that I'm your lawyer now and that I'm blocking his number. He can have his lawyer contact my office if he has anything more to say. And I told him that from now on, any money going into your joint account will be divided up immediately. Only the percentage specified in your old contracts would be left there for him to access. The rest of it will be transferred to your solo account."

Nathan nodded his approval, patting Nisha's trembling hands clasped in her lap.

"Then I told him that he's been an abusive asshole to you for far too long. I told him that as an adult woman, you are free of his control. And I told him that since you've left the country, and he has no legal jurisdiction over your music anymore, that I expect to receive a file that has anything you've written and/or recorded since the last contract expired. If I don't have it within the week, I'll sue him to get it. Then while he was inhaling, getting ready to start yelling again, I hung up on him again."

"Wow!" Nathan whistled softly. "Remind me to never get on your bad side, Jen."

Jennifer smiled, and this time it included her entire face. "So actually, Nisha, getting the chance to tell off an arrogant pig like him was like Christmas and my birthday rolled into one. I'm regarding it as your first installment to me. No money needed."

Diego snorted with laughter. "Take her at her word, Nisha. She's really expensive."

Jennifer sniffed. "I give the pack a discount, Diego. You should see what I charge everyone else."

Nisha leaned forward, her voice sounding stronger. "My money?"

"You have a significant amount in your solo account. Do you want to add anyone else as a co-signer?"

Nisha nodded her head vigorously. "Nathan."

"I'll draw up the paperwork and get it to you. And you should probably talk with Arnold, the pack accountant. I'm sure he can recommend ways for you to invest your money to grow it into the kind of fortune that someone with your fame should have."

"Do you think he'll really send you the files with my new music on it?"

"I've already sent a registered letter to him, demanding that he do so immediately, or face court proceedings. And it's been registered with the court, so he knows that I mean it."

"I . . . I don't know how to thank you, Jennifer. I've been so afraid of him for so long that I wasn't sure there was anything anyone could do to keep me safe. But why did you tell him that I'm living out of the country?"

Jennifer's gaze sought out Diego. "Didn't you tell her about your internet?"

He shrugged. "I've been kind of busy, what with the new baby and the not sleeping and all. It never came up."

Jennifer made a face at him before turning to Nisha again. "Nathan can probably fill you in. But in a nutshell, years ago, the pack techies set up a complex arrangement with our contact up in Quebec, so that any internet signals go to a satellite, then to a server in Canada. So it always seems like the messages are coming from our neighbor up north."

"So if I go online, no one will be able to trace it back to here?"

"That's right. That's part of pack security. Relax, Nisha. You're being protected by impenetrable layers. No one will find you unless you want them to. And I'm glad to do my part to keep you safe. After all, you're pack."

Inexplicably, Nisha burst into tears. Nathan tried to pull her closer into his arms, but she shook her head, pushing him away.

She gulped, inhaling to steady her voice. "I'll be all right. Jennifer, Diego, you don't know what it means to me, to be able to think that I'm safe. For the first time since my parents signed me away to Richard when I was a teenager, I can finally make my own decisions. You don't know what a gift that is. I'll never be able to repay all of you. There's no price on peace of mind. I've never had it before, and I'm going to enjoy it for as long as I can."

Jennifer's voice was gentle. "That will be for as long as you want it, Nisha. Diego has welcomed you into the pack. And I'm glad to represent you. Together, we'll make sure that you never have your agency taken away from you again."

Diego added his support. "She's right, Nisha. You're pack now. We protect our own."

Nathan growled softly. "And both of us would die for you. We are one."

Jennifer smiled on screen. "I think that's all for today. I'll send the bank forms adding Nathan to your account. Whenever you sign them, get them back to me. And since you seem anxious to get the files, can I assume you've written new music? It's been a while since Nisha put out a new CD."

Nisha nodded, leaning forward excitedly. "You have to hear it! I wrote a song for Gaia, encouraging us all to help heal our mother. And I wrote a song for Nathan, called *Blue Over Green*. I'm especially proud of that one. In fact, I think I'll release them both for free, with an announcement to my fans that I'm in love and moving in a new direction with my music. If they prefer the old music, fine. But if they're willing to, I'd love to have them come along with me on my musical journey, as I find my way to new sounds."

"Then it's even more urgent that I get those files ASAP. I look forward to hearing them. But it's getting late, and I have a dinner date. Goodbye to all of you. I'll be in touch when there's anything I need to tell you." Jennifer grinned. "After all, I know where you live."

Once the connection had been broken, Nathan and Nisha rose from their chairs.

Diego reached over to hug Nisha. "Let me personally assure you that you are safe here. I've pledged my life to this pack. We are enhanced by your being here. And speaking of that, I want you to consider becoming a music teacher, some-time in the future. I'm sure some of our students have musical skills, whether they know it or not. We haven't had a music teacher to encourage them for many years."

Nisha nodded, her eyes bright with excitement. "Nathan, remember that converted barn you found me in?" She turned to Diego. "It was a barn converted into a music studio, com-plete with a recording room. We could work on the barn con-nected to our house, and once I start teaching here, the stu-dents would be able to record their music there."

Diego smiled before an enormous yawn surprised even him. "Great! There are students taking trade courses who would love to have a place to work on their skills, even over the summer. But for now, I think I'll go see if Diésha has fallen asleep. If so, I'll crawl in with my wife and try to catch up on my rest."

Nathan took Nisha's hand and walked to the door. To-gether they walked through on their way to the united life they were constructing.

CHAPTER THIRTY-EIGHT

Two months later . . .

The auditorium was once again crowded with pack members, waiting to hear Diego's regular updates. He was excited about the new information he was going to be sharing this night.

Monique's wolf howled from center stage, and the room quieted down. When she shifted into her human shape, a low murmur traveled around the room when several people noticed her lower abdomen had a noticeable bulge to it. She straightened up proudly, smiling as she pointedly pulled on a baggy shift before she spoke. "This meeting is called to order. The pack leader, Diego Vargas, will now speak to his agenda."

Diego strode to center stage and started his agenda with some of the changes that had occurred since the last meeting, and answered any questions posed to him. He included confirmation of the fact that Grant and Monique were indeed expecting a child to add to their happy family.

Finally, he looked around, smiling. "It gives me great joy to have two final announcements. The first is that John Johnson will be getting married next week. As many of you are aware, he's moved into an apartment in Augusta with the man of his dreams. Some of you met Freddie Landon, my wife's best friend since grade school, when he was the man of honor at our wedding. There will be a small ceremony in our chapel here on the grounds, followed by a special luncheon with many of his favorite foods, prepared by his mother. Anyone who wants to attend is welcome to help the happy couple begin their new life together."

He carefully observed the reactions of the pack. As he had expected, there were a few disgruntled members who were surprised by his announcement. But most seemed genuinely happy for someone who had been a fixture of their pack for so many years.

He gave the crowd a few moments to quiet down before turning to invite Saoirse to join him for his second announcement. She was swaying gently, rocking their daughter, who slept peacefully in the baby carrier she wore. She rose as gracefully as was possible and smiled as she stepped forward to join him, holding his hand as he spoke.

"And the final announcement is the culmination of a lot of hard work by many dedicated people. Students and staff, and indeed, many of you, helped in the research which has now born fruit. And though my wife is still coming to terms with our discovery, it gives me great pleasure to make this announcement. Our darling daughter, Diésha, will someday be joining her father in the woods, howling at the moon and running on her own four paws."

There was an immediate uproar. People jumped up in excitement. Lots of people shouted out questions. Some were hugging each other. Some were demanding answers. Diego held up his hands to ask for quiet. The gesture was noticed by enough people that, eventually, everyone quieted down, so he could speak again.

"As many of you are aware, when I hired Saoirse as our new biology teacher, she wanted the students to be involved with actual science. Once she learned she was living among a pack of werewolves, she became determined to help us discover what biological secret led us to our unique twinned fates. She and the students, with the help of Grant, our other resident biologist, learned that there is nothing in our blood that separates us from non-shifters. So they switched their attention to genetics. Many of us swabbed our cheeks and submitted samples to a company that promised to provide nationalities of ancestors. What we ended up with was a lot of data, making it difficult to process it all.

"Luckily, Freddie and John were at a point in their relationship where John had shared our secret with his man. Before Freddie moved out here to Maine, he had volunteered to help test a new computer program his hospital had recently purchased. He took all the genetic data we had received and inputted it into the program to see if it could find any similarities in the samples supplied. It did. All of us who have wolves living inside of us carry a specific gene set from both of our parents. If we receive what we call the *wolf-gene* from only one parent, we will not be shifters but will remain able to have children who are. Only receiving the gene from both parents produces a shifter."

Diego turned to smile at Saoirse, who nodded to encourage him to continue.

"Saoirse could probably explain this better than me, but it seems that our genetic marker traveled a long way in becoming what it is today. In ancient times, our ancestors lived in the Middle East. They practiced a minority religion that was banished, so they were expelled from the region. They traveled to India and thrived there for a while. Then they were driven out of there, also. They became wanderers, often referred to by others as *Gypsies*, since they were assumed to have originally come from Egypt, the only Middle Eastern country that was well-known at the time. They called themselves the *Romani* people. And yes, that's probably why the old movies that we enjoy making fun of so much feature Gypsies, who understand the nature of what we are better than anyone else. We have no way of looking into the past to discover *how* this phenomenon of nature occurred. We will probably never know. But now that we have identified the gene, we can predict, with certainty, which children will grow up to howl at the moon."

"But how will anyone find out about it? And why does that matter?" A tall man stood to shout the question to Diego.

Diego nodded. "Good questions. To the first one, I can attest that Dr. Sullivan will share this information with the unofficial group of psychotherapists and other medical professionals that he's a part of. This will be a way for them to determine, for sure, the shifter status of their patients. They are always on the look-out for those being sent to them for hearing voices in their heads."

A murmur of laughter traveled around the room. Many were nodding in acknowledgment, since that was how they ended up in the pack.

Nathan moved forward and tapped Diego on the arm. "I would like to answer the second question."

Diego nodded, passing the microphone to him.

Nathan faced the assembly. "The most terrifying moment of my young life was the day my wolf stopped merely speaking in my mind, and forced an unexpected and totally unwelcome change to my body. I thought I was going insane, since I had no idea what was happening to me. I thought I was dying. Those of you who always knew this was possible can't imagine the terror that I felt. I would give anything to have had an idea of what was going on in my body. To me, this is the most important thing that we can give to our children. They won't have to be as terrified as I was. They won't have to face telling their parents what they have discovered about themselves. And hopefully, they won't have to be outcast from their families when . . ." His voice broke. He looked down for a moment before taking a deep breath to compose himself. "My parents thought I was lying. They accused me of being gay, which in our religious household, meant that I was automatically an outcast. If I had known this was a *normal* occurrence, I would never have shared it with people who can't possibly understand. Then I would have been allowed to visit my father on his deathbed."

Nathan looked backstage for a quick moment, obviously seeking the quiet strength Diego saw radiating from his mate. Nisha smiled back at him, blowing him a kiss.

Nathan stood taller and turned back to the crowd. "I have found myself a home here in the Northwest Maine Pack. All of us have. Some have traveled longer than others. But once we arrived here, it was to find that we have a new family to belong to. This discovery of a genetic marker puts my mind at ease, knowing that when I have children, I will be able to help them accept themselves, whether they have been gifted with a wolf or not. And speaking for myself, and for my mate, I say that this answer has certainly been worth the wait."

There was silence for a heartbeat before the room exploded with applause. Diego took the microphone back to announce the end of the meeting. He invited anyone who wanted to help celebrate the good news to run with the pack in the woods.

And for those who hadn't been gifted by nature with a shared body? The howling that echoed through the night was an affirmation that even for the non-shifters, living as a part of the Northwest Maine Pack was a very good place to be.

"Well, this sucks." Saoirse McColl scanned the multiple internet links for appropriate jobs she could apply for.

"Can't apply to some of them because I know people who work there, who might sabotage my application by talking about me. Can't apply to others because I already know what it would be like to work there, and setting myself up for another failure is stupid. And the rest don't need my special skills, so they won't pay what I'm worth. What to do?"

She sighed and glanced around the empty room, discouraged. She was staying with her long-time best friend, so none of the furniture was hers, and she still felt like an intruder, even when the two other residents weren't home.

"Guess I'll have to keep sending out resumes and pestering HR departments for interviews. I need some kind of income-producing thing, and soon, or I'll be tossed out of this dump and have to live on the street."

"Why are you calling our home a dump?" Her longtime friend and roommate walked through the door, tearing off his nurse's uniform top as he strolled through the room into the kitchen.

"Oh, hey Freddie. Because I don't have any money to contribute to the bills, so I feel like a loser. I guess I'm taking my bad attitude out on everything around me."

"If you stay, I'm not any worse off than I was before you moved in." Freddie poured some chardonnay he pulled out of the fridge into a glass, then entered the living room and sat on the couch.

"But if I move out, you and Jorge can let one of your other friends move in . . . hopefully, someone who can help you pay the bills."

"When you moved in, you were helping."

"Yeah, but then I got fired again. Insubordinate, they called me. Just because I was following correct lab procedures, which made the tests take longer. So they said they had to let me go. I refused to cut corners, and I absolutely refused to fake data to produce the results their clients wanted. Hell, if even science is going to lie for corporations, then there's no one left to trust anymore. Right?"

Freddie took another sip from his glass, then shrugged. "I guess. You know I don't know anything about what you do at work. Or why you care so much. But that's a part of your charm, I guess."

"Your friends didn't appear to be nearly as taken with my charm as you are." She sighed. "Last night, when you had some people over, they seemed kind of uneasy that you have a female living with you. Almost like I'm some kind of different species."

He smiled. "Some of my friends are uneasy with anyone who is straight listening in on our conversations. Nothing personal."

"No, but some did tease you a lot about turning straight because you're allowing a woman to share your place."

"Then I explained that we've been friends since grade school and that ended, right?"

"Well, kind of. At least they stopped being actively rude to me."

"I seem to remember you saying you had to go meet some friends, and you left after about an hour."

"I lied. There are acquaintances that I used to work with, but you're the only friend I have in this city. My family is mostly all back in Chicago. You know us Irish . . . we tend to stay where we landed when we got here. And Chicago is a city of neighborhoods, where even in the middle of urban crowds you can choose to live among people who look like you."

"Yeah, you can even find places where people think like you. I liked Chi-town's Boystown for a while. But when I got the offer to move out here to Boston, I realized that you can find like-minded folks everywhere. You just have to be open to finding them."

Freddie stared at her, serious for a moment before smiling. "Maybe that's your answer, Sam. You need to be open to new people and hope the universal karma will toss in folks who think like you, and who will appreciate you, your way."

"And just how am I supposed to do that? It's not like heading into the local gay bar to find other gay folks. There aren't any science bars where geeky researchers hang out. Where am I supposed to go to find people who believe in doing the best job they can, and who don't let money issues dictate what to research? People who want to help people improve their lives through science, but who still want to be able to afford to pay the bills?

"Even when I was working full-time, I barely had enough to pay a third of the rent on this place. I was just lucky that you and Jorge were all right with me crashing on the air mattress in your spare room when I was desperate for a place to stay. And that you took pity on an old friend and let me mooch off your good nature."

He got up and pulled her out of her chair for a big hug.

"Honey, you know I'd do anything for you. We go way

back. Remember when you beat up Danny O'Toole when that snot called me a faggot in fourth grade?"

She nodded, smiling. "Yeah, he didn't expect a girl to be able to hit so hard. I guess he didn't know that I had six brothers who made me fight them frequently, just to keep themselves in shape. I guess they did teach me how to protect myself."

He laughed. "And others. Danny ran away crying, with blood gushing from his nose. I don't think he underestimated girls after that."

"At least not me, anyway." She smiled and sat back down. "I didn't even know what a faggot was back then. I was just pissed that he was insulting my best friend."

Freddie resumed his position on the couch. "And honey, I sure was glad we were besties, especially since other guys thought twice about messing with me after that."

"Well, it was never fair that they would gang up on you, either because you were Black, or because you were gay. They needed to know that you had a crew who would fight with you. Even if your crew only consisted of one girl with a redhead's temper."

Saoirse was lost in thought for a few minutes, reminiscing.

Then Freddie broke the silence. "No luck with the job search today, then? Is that why you're in such a pissy mood?"

She sighed. "Yeah. There are only a few labs around doing the kind of research I'm interested in doing. Most of them I've either worked for or know people who work there, who would advise their bosses not to hire me. I don't know what to do anymore."

Freddie tapped his phone and began to scroll through things quickly. He stopped after a few minutes and looked back up. "Why don't you think about something completely different?"

"Like what?"

"Well, here's an ad for a high school biology teacher."

She snorted. "I can't even get along with adults. What

makes you think I could get along with teenagers?"

"You're very good with troubled people. I can't think of any time in my life when I was more troubled than in high school. You talked me out of a whole lot of stupid mistakes, and you picked me up and helped me recover after the bad ones I did make. Maybe that's your calling?"

"I don't have any teaching certification."

He scanned the ad again. "It says teaching experience preferred but not required. It's a private school, up in northwestern Maine. See?"

He passed his phone over, and Saoirse read the ad.

"Hmm, it says you would have to live on the premises, but living quarters are provided. It also says that the school lab needs to be updated and remodeled, so the new teacher would be expected to help with that project. I would really love the chance to design a lab myself. I have so many ideas about what to put into it, and what not to."

"And you have a master's degree in biology, right? You're a researcher. If anything, you're probably over-qualified. But as long as the salary is decent, them supplying you with a place to live would enable you to not have to pay rent anywhere."

"Yeah . . ."

"Honey, what can it hurt to apply?"

"How will I be able to afford to get up there to interview?"

"You have a birthday coming up, right? I can pay for you to fly up there and rent a car to get to the place."

She smirked. "Just so you can get rid of me?"

He tossed a pillow at her, which she just barely avoided by ducking in time for it to fly by her head.

"No, silly bitch. So I can repay you for all of the times you held my hand when I needed a friend."

Saoirse shrugged. "I grew up in a big family, remember? Lots of people around all the time, many of whom needed a listening ear followed by hugs . . . or a slap upside the head. It's not any special kind of skill."

"No, but damn few people know how to do it as well as you. So apply, already."

She picked up her laptop and typed in the e-dress that was listed in the ad. "Okay, it's worth a shot, I guess. I wonder what kind of area it's in. Northwestern Maine is pretty rugged, right? No big city pollution up there. Worst-case scenario is I don't hear anything back from them."

"A better case is you get to fly to a state you've never been to and rent a new-ish car to drive into the countryside. You like that better than city driving anyway, right?"

"Uh-huh." She was distracted by filling out the application form.

"Let me get you a glass of that sparkling wine you like . . . I think there's an open bottle in the fridge, right?"

"Uh-huh."

"Good luck, girlfriend."

ABOUT THE AUTHOR

Mom taught me to read when I was five. Since then, I have always had characters intruding into my thoughts, showing scenes from their lives. When I ignore them, they start to yell louder. If I write their stories so they can live in readers' heads as well, they usually leave me alone . . .until the next voices appear. I like the noise.

Learn more about me and my books, read excerpts and reviews, at: www.fionamcgier.com

Or come visit me on Facebook: https://www.facebook.com/fiona.mcgier/